Ben Jonson, Francis Cunningham, William Gifford

The Works of Ben Tonson

With notes critical and explanatory and a biographical memoir (Volume VII)

Ben Jonson, Francis Cunningham, William Gifford

The Works of Ben Tonson
With notes critical and explanatory and a biographical memoir (Volume VII)

ISBN/EAN: 9783337015879

Printed in Europe, USA, Canada, Australia, Japan

Cover: Foto ©Raphael Reischuk / pixelio.de

More available books at **www.hansebooks.com**

THE WORKS OF

WITH NOTES CRITICAL AND EXPLANATORY
AND A BIOGRAPHICAL MEMOIR
BY W. GIFFORD ESQ.

WITH INTRODUCTION AND APPENDICES BY

LIEUT.-COL. F. CUNNINGHAM

IN NINE VOLUMES

VOL. VIII.

LONDON

BICKERS AND SON

HENRY SOTHERAN AND CO.

1875

CONTENTS OF VOLUME VIII.

	Page
TIME VINDICATED.	I
NEPTUNE'S TRIUMPH.	21
PAN'S ANNIVERSARY.	39
THE MASQUE OF OWLS.	51
THE FORTUNATE ISLES, AND THEIR UNION.	61
LOVE'S TRIUMPH THROUGH CALLIPOLIS.	83
CHLORIDIA : Rites to Chloris and her Nymphs.	93
AN EXPOSTULATION WITH INIGO JONES.	106
LOVE'S WELCOME AT WELBECK.	117
LOVE'S WELCOME AT BOLSOVER.	131

EPIGRAMS 141
Dedication to the Earl of Pembroke 143
1. To the Reader 145
   Pray thee take care, that tak'st my book in hand.
2. To my Book 145
   It will be looked for, Book, when some but see.
3. To my Bookseller 146
   Thou that mak'st gain thy end, and wisely well.
4. To King James 146
   How, best of Kings, dost thou a sceptre bear.
5. On the Union 148
   When was there contract better driven by fate.
6. To Alchemists 148
   If all you boast of your great art be true.
7. On the New Hot-house 148
   Where lately harboured many a famous whore.

Page

8. On a Robbery 148
   Ridway robbed Duncote of three hundred pounds.

9. To all to whom I write 149
   May none whose scatter'd names honour my book.

10. To my Lord Ignorant 149
    Thou call'st me poet, as a term of shame.

11. On Somebody that walks Somewhere . . . 149
    At court I met it, in clothes brave enough.

12. On Lieutenant Shift 150
    Shift, here in town, not meanest among squires.

13. To Dr. Empiric 151
    When men a dangerous disease did 'scape.

14. To William Camden 151
    Camden ! most reverend head, to whom I owe.

15. On Court-worm 152
    All men are worms : but this no man. In silk.

16. To Brainhardy 153
    Hardy, thy brain is valiant, 'tis confest.

17. To the Learned Critic 153
    May others fear, fly, and traduce thy name.

18. To my mere English Censurer 153
    To thee, my way in Epigrams seems new.

19. On Sir Cod the Perfumed 154
    That Cod can get no widow, yet a knight.

20. To the same 155
    The expense in odours is a most vain sin.

21. On Reformed Gamester 155
    Lord, how is Gamester changed ! his hair close cut.

22. On my First Daughter 155
    Here lies, to each her parent's ruth.

23. To John Donne 156
    Donne, the delight of Phœbus and each Muse.

24. To the Parliament 157
    There's reason good, that you good laws should make.

25. On Sir Voluptuous Beast 157
    While Beast instructs his fair and innocent wife.

26. On the same 157
    Than his chaste wife though Beast now know no more

27. On Sir John Roe 158
    In place of scutcheons, that should deck thy hearse

CONTENTS.

Page

28. On Don Surly 158
Don Surly, to aspire the glorious name.

29. To Sir Annual Tilter 159
Tilter, the most may admire thee, though not I.

30. To Person Guilty 160
Guilty, be wise; and though thou know'st the crimes.

31. On Banks the Usurer 160
Banks feels no lameness of his knotty gout.

32. On Sir John Roe 160
What two brave perils of the private sword.

33. To the same 161
I'll not offend thee with a vain tear more.

34. Of Death 162
He that fears death, or mourns it, in the just.

35. To King James 162
Who would not be thy subject, James, t' obey.

36. To the Ghost of Martial 163
Martial, thou gav'st far nobler Epigrams.

37. On Cheveril the Lawyer 163
No cause, no client fat, will Cheveril leese.

38. To Person Guilty 163
Guilty, because I bade you late be wise.

39. On Old Colt 164
For all night-sins, with others' wives unknown.

40. On Margaret Ratcliffe 164
Marble, weep, for thou dost cover.

41. On Gipsy 165
Gipsy, new bawd, is turned physician.

42. On Giles and Joan 165
Who says that Giles and Joan at discord be?

43. To Robert Earl of Salisbury . . . 166
What need hast thou of me, or of my Muse.

44. On Chuffe, Banks the Usurer's Kinsman . . 167
Chuffe, lately rich in name, in chattels, goods.

45. On my First Son 167
Farewell, thou child of my right hand, and joy.

46. To Sir Luckless Woo-all 168
Is this the sir, who, some waste wife to win.

47. To the same 169
Sir Luckless, troth, for luck's sake pass by one.

Page

48. On Mungril Esquire 169
    His bought arms Mung' not liked; for his first day.

49. To Playwright 169
    Playwright me reads, and still my verses damns.

50. To Sir Cod 170
    Leave, Cod, tobacco-like, burnt gums to take.

51. To King James 170
    That we thy loss might know, and thou our love.

52. To Censorious Courtling 171
    Courtling, I rather thou should'st utterly.

53. To Old-end Gatherer 172
    Long-gathering Old-end, I did fear thee wise.

54. On Cheveril 172
    Cheveril cries out my verses libels are.

55. To Francis Beaumont 172
    How I do love thee, Beaumont, and thy Muse.

56. On Poet-ape 173
    Poor Poet-ape, that would be thought our chief.

57. On Bawds and Usurers 174
    If, as their ends, their fruits were so, the same.

58. To Groom Idiot 174
    Idiot, last night I prayed thee but forbear.

59. On Spies 174
    Spies, you are lights in state, but of base stuff.

60. To William, Lord Mounteagle . . . 175
    Lo, what my country should have done, have raised.

61. To Fool, or Knave 176
    Thy praise or dispraise is to me alike.

62. To Fine Lady Would-be 176
    Fine Madam Would-be, wherefore should you fear.

63. To Robert, Earl of Salisbury . . . 176
    Who can consider thy right courses run.

64. To the same 177
    Not glad, like those that have new hopes, or suits.

65. To my Muse 178
    Away, and leave me, thou thing most abhorred.

66. To Sir Henry Cary 178
    That neither fame nor love might wanting be.

67. To Thomas, Earl of Suffolk . . . 180
    Since men have left to do praiseworthy things.

                                                    Page
68. On Playwright   181
     Playwright, convict of public wrongs to men.

69. To Pertinax Cob   181
     Cob, thou no soldier, thief, nor fencer art.

70. To William Roe   181
     When Nature bids us leave to live, 'tis late.

71. On Court Parrot   182
     To pluck down mine, Poll sets up new wits still.

72. To Courtling   182
     I grieve not, Courtling, thou art started up.

73. To Fine Grand   182
     *What is't, Fine Grand, makes thee my friendship
        fly.*

74. To Thomas, Lord Chancellor Egerton . .   183
     Whilst thy weigh'd judgments, Egerton, I hear.

75. On Lippe, the Teacher   184
     I cannot think there's that antipathy.

76. On Lucy, Countess of Bedford . . .   185
     This morning, timely rapt with holy fire.

77. To one that desired me not to name him . .   185
     Be safe, nor fear thyself so good a fame.

78. To Hornet   186
     Hornet, thou hast thy wife drest for the stall.

79. To Elizabeth, Countess of Rutland . .   186
     That poets are far rarer births than kings.

80. On Life and Death   187
     The ports of death are sins : of life good deeds.

81. To Prowle, the Plagiary   187
     Forbear to tempt me, Prowle, I will not show.

82. On cashiered Captain Surly . . .   187
     Surly's old whore in her new silks doth swim.

83. To a Friend   188
     To put out the word, whore, thou dost me woo.

84. To Lucy, Countess of Bedford . . .   188
     Madam, I told you late how I repented.

85. To Sir Henry Goodyere   188
     Goodyere, I'm glad, and grateful to report.

86. To the same   190
     *When I would know thee, Goodyere, my thought
        looks.*

Page

87. On Captain Hazard, the Cheater   .   .   .   190
     Touch'd with the sin of false play in his punk.

88. On English Monsieur   190
     Would you believe when you this Monsieur see.

89. To Edward Allen   191
     If Rome so great, and in her wisest age.

90. On Mill, my Lady's Woman   .   .   .   192
     When Mill first came to court, the unprofiting fool.

91. To Sir Horace Vere   193
     Which of thy names I take not only bears.

92. The New Cry   194
     Ere cherries ripe ! and strawberries ! be gone.

93. To Sir John Radcliffe   195
     How, like a column, Radcliffe, left alone.

94. To Lucy, Countess of Bedford, with Master
     Donne's Satires   197
     Lucy, you brightness of our sphere, who 'are.

95. To Sir Henry Savile   198
     If, my religion safe, I durst embrace.

96. To John Donne   200
     Who shall doubt, Donne, whêre I a poet be.

97. On the New Motion   200
     See you yon motion, not the old fa-ding.

98. To Sir Thomas Roe   201
     Thou hast begun well, Roe, which stand well to.

99. To the same   202
     That thou hast kept thy love, encreased thy will.

100. On Playwright   203
     Playwright, by chance hearing some toys I'd writ.

101. Inviting a Friend to Supper   .   .   .   203
     To night, grave sir, both my poor house and I.

102. To William, Earl of Pembroke   .   .   .   206
     I do but name thee, Pembroke, and I find.

103. To Mary, Lady Wroth   206
     How well, fair crown of your fair sex, might he.

104. To Susan, Countess of Montgomery   .   .   207
     *Were they, that named you, prophets ? Did they
     see.*

105. To Mary, Lady Wroth   208
     Madam, had all antiquity been lost.

Page

106. To Sir Edward Herbert 209
   If men get name for some one virtue; then.

107. To Captain Hungry 209
   Do what you come for, captain, with your news.

108. To True Soldiers 211
   Strength of my country, whilst I bring to view.

109. To Sir Henry Nevil 212
   Who now calls on thee, Nevil, is a muse.

110. To Clement Edmonds on his Cæsar's Commentaries, Observed and Translated . . 214
   Not Cæsar's deeds, nor all his honours won.

111. To the same. On the same 215
   Who, Edmonds, reads thy book, and doth not see.

112. To a weak Gamester in Poetry 215
   With thy small stock why art thou venturing still.

113. To Sir Thomas Overbury 216
   So Phœbus make me worthy of his bays.

114. To Mistress Philip Sidney 217
   I must believe some miracles still be.

115. On the Town's Honest Man 218
   You wonder who this is, and why I name.

116. To Sir William Jephson 219
   Jephson, thou man of men, to whose loved name.

117. On Groine 220
   Groine, come of age, his state sold out of hand.

118. On Gut 220
   Gut eats all day, and lechers all the night.

119. To Sir Ralph Shelton 220
   Not he that flies the Court for want of clothes.

120. An Epitaph on Salathiel Pavy, a Child of Queen Elizabeth's Chapel. 221
   Weep with me, all you that read.

121. To Benjamin Rudyerd 223
   Rudyerd, as lesser dames to great ones use.

122. To the same 224
   If I would wish for truth, and not for show.

123. To the same 224
   Writing thyself, or judging others writ.

124. Epitaph on Elizabeth, L. H. 225
   Would'st thou hear what man can say.

Page

125. To Sir William Uvedale 226
    Uvedale, thou piece of the first times, a man.

126. To his Lady, then mistress Cary 226
    Retired, with purpose your fair worth to praise.

127. To Esme, Lord Aubigny 227
    Is there a hope that man would thankful be.

128. To William Roe 227
    Roe, and my joy to name, thou'rt now to go.

129. To Mime 228
    That not a pair of friends each other see.

130. To Alphonso Ferrabosco, on his Book . . 229
    To urge my loved Alphonso, that bold fame.

131. To the same 230
    When we do give, Alphonso, to the light.

132. To Mr. Joshua Silvester 231
    If to admire were to commend, my praise.

133. On the Famous Voyage 232
    No more let Greece her bolder fables tell.

THE FOREST 241

1. Why I write not of Love 243
    Some act of Love's bound to rehearse.

2. To Penshurst 243
    Thou art not, Penshurst, built to envious show.

3. To Sir Robert Wroth 248
    How blest art thou canst love the country, Wroth.

4. To the World. A Farewell for a Gentlewoman, Virtuous and Noble 252
    False world, good night, since thou hast brought.

5. Song : To Celia 255
    Come, my Celia, let us prove.

6. To the same 255
    Kiss me sweet : the wary lover.

7. Song : That Women are but Men's Shadows . 256
    Follow a shadow, it still flies you.

8. Song : To Sickness 257
    Why, disease, dost thou molest.

9. Song : To Celia 258
    Drink to me only with thine eyes.

CONTENTS.

Page

10. Præludium. 260
    And must I sing? what subject shall I chuse?
11. Epode 263
    Not to know vice at all, and keep true state.
    The Phœnix Analysed (Note) . . . 261
    Now, after all, let no man.
    Ode ενθουσιαστικη (Note) 262
    Splendor! O more than mortal.
12. Epistle to Elizabeth, Countess of Rutland . . 267
    Whilst that for which all virtue now is sold.
13. Epistle to Katharine, Lady Aubigny . . . 273
    'Tis grown almost a danger to speak true.
14. Ode to Sir William Sidney, on his Birthday . . 277
    Now that the hearth is crowned with smiling fire.
15. To Heaven. 279
    Good and great God, can I not think of thee.

UNDERWOODS: Consisting of Divers Poems . . . 281

POEMS OF DEVOTION. 285

THE SINNER'S SACRIFICE.

1. To the Holy Trinity 287
   O holy, blessed, glorious Trinity.
2. An Hymn to God the Father 289
   Hear me, O God.
3. An Hymn on the Nativity of my Saviour . . 290
   I sing the birth was born to-night.

A CELEBRATION OF CHARIS: In ten Lyric Pieces . 291

1. His excuse for Loving 293
   Let it not your wonder move.
2. How he saw her 294
   I beheld her on a day.
3. What he Suffered 295
   After many scorns like these.
4. Her Triumph 296
   See the chariot at hand here of love.
5. His Discourse with Cupid 297
   Noblest Charis, you that are.
6. Claiming a Second Kiss by desert . . . 299
   Charis, guess, and do not miss.

Page

7. Begging another, on Colour of Mending the former   300
For Love's sake, kiss me once again.

8. Urging her of a Promise   301
Charis one day in discourse.

9. Her Man Described by her own Dictamen .   .   302
Of your trouble, Ben, to ease me.

10. Another Lady's Exception, Present at the Hearing   304
For his mind I do not care.

MISCELLANEOUS POEMS.

1. The Musical Strife : A Pastoral Dialogue   .   .   305
Come, with our voices let us war.

2. A Song   306
Oh do not wanton with those eyes.

3. In the person of Womankind. A Song Apologetic.   307
Men, if you love us, play no more.

4. Another. In Defence of their Inconstancy .   .   308
Hang up those dull and envious fools.

5. A Nymph's Passion   309
I love, and he loves me again.

6. The Hour-Glass   310
Consider this small dust, here in the glass.

7. My Picture left in Scotland   .   .   .   312
I now think Love is rather deaf than blind.

8. Against Jealousy   312
Wretched and foolish Jealousy.

9. The Dream   313
Or scorn, or pity, on me take.

10. An Epitaph on Master Vincent Corbet   .   .   314
I have my piety too, which, could.

11. On the Portrait of Shakspeare. To the Reader .   316
This figure that thou here seest put.

12. To the Memory of my Beloved, Master William
Shakspeare, and what he hath left us .   .   317
To draw no envy, Shakspeare, on thy name.

13. On the Honoured Poems of his Honoured Friend,
Sir John Beaumont, Baronet   .   .   322
This book will live; it hath a Genius; this.

Page

14. To Mr. John Fletcher, upon his "Faithful Shep-
    herdess " 324
    The wise and many-headed bench that sits.

15. Epitaph on the Countess of Pembroke . . . 324
    Underneath this sable herse.

16. A Vision, on the Muses of his Friend, Michael
    Drayton 326
    It hath been questioned, Michael, if I be.

17. Epitaph on Michael Drayton 330
    Do, pious marble, let thy readers know.

18. To my truly beloved Friend, Master Brown, on his
    Pastorals 331
    Some men, of books or friends not speaking right.

19. To his much and worthily esteemed friend, the
    Author (John Stephens) 332
    Who takes thy volume to his virtuous hand.

20. To my worthy and honoured Friend, Master George
    Chapman 332
    Whose work could this be, Chapman, to refine.

21. To my chosen friend, the learned Translator of
    Lucan, Thomas May, Esquire . . . 334
    When, Rome, I read thee in thy mighty pair.

22. To my dear Son and right learned friend, Master
    Joseph Rutter 336
    You look, my Joseph, I should something say.

23. Epigram. In Authorem (Nicholas Breton) . . 337
    Thou, that would'st find the habit of true passion.

24. To the worthy Author, on the Husband . . 338
    It fits not only him that makes a book.

25. To the Author (Thomas Wright) 338
    In picture, they which truly understand.

26. To the Author (T. Warre) 339
    Truth is the trial of itself.

27. To Edward Filmer, on his Musical Work, dedicated
    to the Queen 341
    What charming peals are these.

28. To Richard Brome, on his Comedy of the
    " Northern Lass " 342
    I had you for a servant once, Dick Brome.

Page

29. A Speech at a Tilting 343
    Two noble knights, whom true desire, and zeal.

30. An Epistle to Sir Edward Sackvile, now Earl of
    Dorset 345
    If, Sackvile, all that have the power to do.

31. An Epistle to Master John Selden . . . 351
    I know to whom I write; here, I am sure.

32. An Epistle to a Friend, (Master Colby,) to persuade
    him to the Wars 354
    *Wake, friend, from forth thy lethargy! the
    drum.*

33. An Epitaph on Master Philip Gray . . . 360
    Reader, stay!

34. Epistle to a Friend 361
    They are not, sir, worst owers that do pay.

35. An Elegy 361
    Can beauty, that did prompt me first to write.

36. An Elegy 362
    By those bright eyes, at whose immortal fires.

37. A Satirical Shrub 364
    A woman's friendship! God, whom I trust in.

38. A little Shrub growing by 365
    Ask not to know this Man. If fame should speak.

39. An Elegy 365
    Though beauty be the mark of praise.

40. An Elegy 367
    Fair friend, 'tis true your beauties move.

41. An Ode to Himself 368
    Where dost thou careless lie.

42. The Mind of the Frontispiece to a Book . . 370
    From death and dark oblivion, near the same.

43. An Ode to James, Earl of Desmond . . . 371
    Where art thou, Genius? I should use.

44. An Ode . . . .
    High-spirited friend.

45. An Ode 374
    Helen, did Homer never see.

46. A Sonnet to the Noble Lady, the Lady Mary
    Wroth 376
    I that have been a lover, and could shew it.

Page

47. A Fit of Rhyme against Rhyme 378
    Rhyme, the rack of finest wits.

48. An Epigram on William, Lord Burleigh, Lord High
    Treasurer of England . . . 380
    If thou wouldst know the virtues of mankind.

49. An Epigram to Thomas, Lord Elesmere, the last
    Term he sat Chancellor 381
    So, justest lord, may all your judgments be.

50. Another to the same 381
    The judge his favour timely then extends.

51. An Epigram to the Counsellor that Pleaded and
    Carried the Cause 382
    That I hereafter do not think the Bar.

52. An Epigram to the Small-pox 384
    Envious and foul disease, could there not be.

53. An Epitaph 385
    What beauty would have lovely styled.

54. A Song 385
    Come, let us here enjoy the shade.

55. An Epistle to a Friend 386
    Sir, I am thankful first to Heaven for you.

56. An Elegy 387
    'Tis true, I'm broke, vows, oaths, and all I had.

57. An Elegy 391
    To make the doubt clear that no woman's true.

58. An Elegy 393
    That love's a bitter sweet I ne'er conceive.

59. An Elegy 395
    Since you must go, and I must bid farewell.

60. An Elegy 396
    Let me be what I am! as Virgil cold.

61. An Execration upon Vulcan 399
    And why to me this? thou lame Lord of Fire.

62. A Speech according to Horace 409
    Why yet, my noble hearts, they cannot say.

63. An Epistle to Master Arthur Squib . . . 412
    What I am not, and what I fain would be.

64. An Epigram on Sir Edward Coke, when he was
    Lord Chief Justice of England . . . 414
    He that should search all glories of the gown.

Page

65. An Epistle answering to One that asked to be
    Sealed of the Tribe of Ben   .   .   .   416
    Men that are safe and sure in all they do.

66. The Dedication of the King's New Cellar to
    Bacchus   419
    Since, Bacchus, thou art father.

67. An Epigram on the Court Pucelle   .   .   .   420
    Does the Court Pucelle then so censure me.

68. An Epigram to the Honoured Countess of * * *   422
    The wisdom, Madam, of your private life.

69. On Lord Bacon's Birthday (22nd January).   .   424
    Hail, happy Genius of this ancient pile.

70. The Poet to the Painter. An Answer.   .   .   425
    Why, though I seem of a prodigious waist.

71. An Epigram. To William, Earl of Newcastle   .   427
    When first, my Lord, I saw you back your horse.

72. Epistle to Master Arthur Squib   429
    I am to dine, friend, where I must be weighed.

73. To Master John Burges   430
    Would God, my Burges, I could think.

74. Epistle to my Lady Covell   431
    You won not verses, Madam, you won me.

75. To Master John Burges   432
    Father John Burges.

76. Epigram to my Bookseller   433
    Thou, friend, wilt hear all censures ; unto thee.

77. An Epitaph on Henry, Lord La-ware .   .   .   434
    If, passenger, thou canst but read.

78. An Epigram to the Lord Keeper.   .   .   435
    That you have seen the pride, beheld the sport.

79. An Epigram to King Charles for an Hundred
    Pounds he sent me in my Sickness   .   .   436
    Great Charles, among the holy gifts of grace.

80. To King Charles and Queen Mary, for the loss of
    their Firstborn, 1629   437
    Who dares deny, that all first-fruits are due.

81. An Epigram to our Great and Good King Charles,
    on his Anniversary Day, 1629   .   .   .   438
    How happy were the subject, if he knew.

Page

82. An Epigram on the Prince's Birth, 1630 . . 440
And art thou born, brave babe? blest be thy birth.

83. An Epigram to the Queen then lying-in, 1630 . 441
Hail, Mary, full of grace! it once was said.

84. An Ode or Song, by all the Muses, in celebration
of her Majesty's birthday, 1630 . . . 442
Up, public joy, remember.

85. An Epigram to the Household, 1630 . . . 445
What can the cause be, when the King hath given.

86. An Epigram to a Friend and Son . . . 446
Son, and my friend, I had not called you so.

ADDITIONAL NOTES 447

TIME VINDICATED

TO HIMSELF AND TO HIS HONOURS;

IN THE PRESENTATION AT COURT ON

TWELFTH-NIGHT, 1623.

—— *Qui se mirantur, in illos*
Virus habe : nos hæc novimus esse nihil.

8   B

TIME VINDICATED, &c.] This Entertainment, which forms a kind of *retort courteous* to the scurrilous satires now dispersed with mischievous activity, appears only in the second folio. The light parts of it are composed with great gaiety and humour; and the singing and dancing must have been given with great effect among the rich and beautiful concomitants of scenery, &c., that surrounded them.

In the Dulwich College MS. this is called the *Prince's Masque;* its unusual splendour seems to have induced the Master of the Revels (sir John Astley) to enter into a more particular mention of it than is common with these costive gentlemen.

"Upon New-year's day at night, the *Alchemist* was acted by the King's players.

"Upon Sonday, being the 19th of January, (1623,) the *Princes Masque* appointed for Twelfe daye, was performed. The speeches and songs composed by Mr. Ben Johnson, and the scene made by Mr. Inigo Jones, which was three times changed during the tyme of the Masque, wherein the first that was discovered was a prospective of Whitehall, with the Banqueting House; the second was the Masquers in a cloud; and the third a forest. The French embassador was present.

"Antemasques were of tumblers and jugglers. The Prince did lead the measures with the French embassadors wife.

"The measures, braules, corrantos, and galliards being ended, the Masquers with the ladies did daunce two contrey daunces, where the French embassadors wife and Mademoysal St. Luke did daunce." *Malone's Hist. of the Eng. Stage.*

TIME VINDICATED.

The Court being seated, a Trumpet sounded, and
FAME *entered, followed by the* CURIOUS, *the* EYED,
the EARED, *and the* NOSED.[1]

Fame.

IVE ear, the worthy, hear what Fame
    proclaims.
    Ears. What, what? is't worth our
    ears?
    Eyes. Or eyes?
Nose. Or noses?
For we are curious, Fame; indeed, THE CURIOUS.
    Eyes. We come to spy.
    Ears. And hearken.
    Nose. And smell out.
    Fame. More than you understand, my hot in-
quisitors.
    Nose. We cannot tell.
    Eyes. It may be.
    Ears. However, go you on, let us alone.
    Eyes. We may spy out that, which you never meant.

---

[1] *The Eyed, &c.*] It appears, from the sequel, that the masks
of the performers were furnished with numerous eyes, ears, and
noses, respectively.

Nose. And nose the thing you scent not.   First,
   whence come you ?

Fame. I came from Saturn.

Ears. Saturn ! what is he ?

Nose. Some Protestant, I warrant you, a time-
   server,
As Fame herself is.

Fame. You are near the right.
Indeed, he's Time itself, and his name Chronos.

   Nose. How ! Saturn ! Chronos ! and the Time
      itself !
You are found : enough.   A notable old pagan !

   Ears. One of their gods, and eats up his own
      children.

   Nose. A fencer, and does travel with a scythe,
'Stead of a long sword.

   Eyes. Hath been oft call'd from it,
To be their lord of Misrule.[2]

   Ears. As Cincinnatus
Was from the plough, to be dictator.

   Eyes. Yes.
We need no interpreter : on, what of Time ?

   Fame. The Time hath sent me with my trump to
      summon
All sorts of persons worthy, to the view
Of some great spectacle he means to-night
To exhibit, and with all solemnity.

   Nose. O, we shall have his Saturnalia.

   Eyes. His days of feast and liberty again.

---

[2] *To be their* lord of Misrule.]   " In the feast of Christmass,
there was in the king's house, wheresoever he was lodged, a *lord of
misrule*, or master of merry disports ; and the like had ye in the
house of every noble man of honour, or good worship, were he
spiritual or temporal." *Stow.*   In the following verses the poet
alludes to that liberty which reigned amongst the Romans during
the Saturnalia, or feasts of Saturn.   These were appointed to remind them of the general equality between all men in the first age.
Whal.

Ears. Where men might do, and talk all that they
list.

Eyes. Slaves of their lords.

Nose. The servants of their masters.

Ears. And subjects of their sovereign.

Fame. Not so lavish.

Ears. It was a brave time that!

Eyes. This will be better :
I spy it coming, peace ! All the impostures,
The prodigies, diseases, and distempers,
The knaveries of the time, we shall see all now.

Ears. And hear the passages, and several humours
Of men, as they are sway'd by their affections :
Some grumbling, and some mutining, some scoffing,
Some pleased, some pining ; at all these we laughing.

Nose. I have it here, here, strong, the sweat of it,
And the confusion, which I love—I nose it ;
It tickles me.

Eyes. My four eyes itch for it.

Ears. And my ears tingle ; would it would come
forth :
This room will not receive it.

Nose. That's the fear.

Enter CHRONOMASTIX.

Chro. What, what, my friends, will not this room
receive ?

Eyes. That which the Time is presently to shew us.

Chro. The Time! Lo, I, the man that hate the
time,
That is, that love it not ; and (though in rhyme
I here do speak it) with this whip you see,
Do lash the time, and am myself lash free.

Fame. Who's this ?

Ears. 'Tis Chronomastix, the brave satyr.

Nose. The gentleman-like satyr, cares for nobody,
His forehead tipt with bays, do you not know him ?

Eyes. Yes, Fame must know him, all the town
    admires him.
Chro. If you would see Time quake and shake,
    but name us,
It is for that, we are both beloved and famous.
Eyes. We know, sir : but the Time's now come
    about.
Ears. And promiseth all liberty.
Nose. Nay, license.
Eyes. We shall do what we list.
Ears. Talk what we list.
Nose. And censure whom we list, and how we list.
Chro. Then I will look on Time, and love the same,
And drop my whip : who's this? my mistress, Fame !
The lady whom I honour, and adore !
What luck had I not to see her before !
Pardon me, madam, more than most accurst,
That did not spy your ladyship at first ;
T' have given the stoop, and to salute the skirts
Of her, to whom all ladies else are flirts.
It is for you, I revel so in rhyme,
Dear mistress, not for hope I have, the Time
Will grow the better by it : to serve Fame
Is all my end, and get myself a name.
Fame. Away, I know thee not, wretched impostor,
Creature of glory, mountebank of wit,
Self-loving braggart, Fame doth sound no trumpet
To such vain empty fools : 'tis Infamy
Thou serv'st, and follow'st, scorn of all the Muses !
Go revel with thine ignorant admirers,
Let worthy names alone.
Chro. O, you, the Curious,
Breathe you to see a passage so injurious,
Done with despight, and carried with such tumour
'Gainst me, that am so much the friend of rumour ?
I would say, Fame? whose muse hath rid in rapture
On a soft ambling verse, to every capture,

From the strong guard, to the weak child that reads
    me,
And wonder both of him that loves or dreads me ;
Who with the lash of my immortal pen
Have scourg'd all sorts of vices, and of men.
Am I rewarded thus ? have I, I say,
From Envy's self torn praise and bays away,
With which my glorious front, and word at large,
Triumphs in print at my admirers' charge ?
    Ears. Rare ! how he talks in verse, just as he
   . writes ! [3]
    Chro. When have I walk'd the streets, but happy he
That had the finger first to point at me,
Prentice, or journeyman !   The shop doth know it,
The unletter'd clerk, major and minor poet !
The sempster hath sat still as I pass'd by,

---

[3] *Rare ! how he talks in verse, just as he writes.*] From the particular description given us of Chronomastix, it appears that the
character was personal ; and there is reason for thinking that the
author intended was John Marston : who, besides his dramatic
writings, was the author of three books of satires, called *The Scourge
of Villainy.* WHAL.

Whalley writes very carelessly.   Had he ever looked into Marston, he could not have formed so strange a conjecture.   The *Scourge
of Villainy* was written nearly thirty years before this Masque appeared, to which, in fact, it has not the slightest reference.   Chronomastix is undoubtedly a generic name for the herd of libellists,
which infested those times ; but the lines noticed by Whalley bear
a particular reference to George Wither the puritan, the author of
Abuses stript and whipt, and other satirical poems on the *Times :* the
style and manner of which Jonson has imitated with equal spirit
and humour.   The allusion to his

> ———— " picture in the front
> With bays and wicked rhyme upon't,"

and which was in great request with " the godly," was probably not
a little grateful to the courtiers.

In some editions of *Abuses stript and whipt,* there is a print of a
Satyr with a scourge, such as Chronomastix enters with ; but Wither
had displayed his "glorious front and word at large " (*nec habeo,
nec careo, nec curo*) in the title-page of another poem not long before

And dropt her needle! fish-wives stay'd their cry!
The boy with buttons, and the basket-wench,
To vent their wares into my works do trench!
A pudding-wife that would despise the times,
Hath utter'd frequent penn'orths, through my rhymes,
And, with them, dived into the chambermaid,
And she unto her lady hath convey'd
The season'd morsels, who hath sent me pensions,
To cherish, and to heighten my inventions.
Well, Fame shall know it yet, I have my faction,
And friends about me, though it please detraction,
To do me this affront.   Come forth that love me,
And now, or never, spight of Fame, approve me.

Enter the Mutes *for the* ANTIMASQUE.

Fame. How now! what's here! Is hell broke loose?
Eyes. You'll see
That he has favourers, Fame, and great ones too;
That unctuous Bounty, is the boss of Billinsgate.[4]

the appearance of this Masque, in which he refers, with sufficient
confidence, to his former works:

> " Had I been now dispos'd to satyrize,
> Would I have *tamed* my numbers in this wise?
> No.   I have Furies that lye ty'd in chaines,
> Bold, English-mastive-like, adventrous straines,
> Who fearlesse dare on any monster flye
> That weares a body of mortality:
> And I had let them loose, if I had list,
> To play *againe*, the *sharp-fang'd Satyrist.*"

This man, whom nature meant for better things, and who did not
always write doggrel verses, once thought more modestly of himself; but popularity gave him assurance. In the introduction to
his *Abuses Whipt,* he tells his readers "not to looke for Spencer's
or Daniel's well-composed numbers, or the deep conceits of *the
now flourishing Jonson;* but to say—'tis honest plain matter, and
there's as much as he expects."

   [4] *That unctuous Bounty, is the* boss *of Billinsgate.*] Boss is an
head or reservoir of water. It frequently occurs in Stow, who also
mentions that of the text. "The *Bosses* of water at Belinsgate, by

Ears. Who feasts his muse with claret, wine and
    oysters.
Nose. Grows big with satyr.
Ears. Goes as long as an elephant.
Eyes. She labours, and lies in of his inventions.
Nose. Has a male poem in her belly now,
Big as a colt——
    Ears. That kicks at Time already.
Eyes. And is no sooner foal'd, but will neigh
    sulphur.
  Fame. The next.
Ears. A quondam justice, that of late
Hath been discarded out o' the pack of the peace,
For some lewd levity he holds *in capite ;*
But constantly loves him. In days of yore,
He us'd to give the charge out of his poems ;
He carries him about him in his pocket,
As Philip's son did Homer, in a casket,
And cries, *O happy man!* to the wrong party,
Meaning the poet, where he meant the subject.
  Fame. What are this pair ?
Eyes. The ragged rascals ?
Fame. Yes.
Eyes. Mere rogues :—you'd think them rogues, but
    they are friends ;
One is his printer in disguise, and keeps
His press in a hollow tree,[5] where to conceal him,

Powles Wharfe, and by St. Giles without Cripplegate, were made
about the year 1423." *Survey of London.* This word has escaped
Mr. Todd.

  [5] *His press in a hollow tree, &c.*] There is very little exaggeration in this lively satire ; it is sufficient to read the state-papers of
the day, to be able to appropriate it with sufficient accuracy. Nothing gave the great officers of the law such trouble, as ferreting
out the obscure holes in which the libels which overflowed the
country were produced. Almost every scurrilous writer had a
portable press, which was moved from one hiding place to another
with a secrecy and dispatch truly wonderful.

He works by glow-worm light, the moon's too open.
The other zealous rag is the compositor,
Who in an angle, where the ants inhabit,
(The emblems of his labours), will sit curl'd
Whole days and nights, and work his eyes out for him.

    Nose. Strange arguments of love ! there is a school-
        master
Is turning all his works too, into Latin,
To pure satyric Latin ; makes his boys
To learn him ; calls him the Times' Juvenal ;
Hangs all his school with his sharp sentences ;
And o'er the execution place hath painted
Time whipt, for terror to the infantry.

    Eyes. This man of war i' the rear, he is both trumpet
And champion to his muse.

    Ears. For the whole city.

    Nose. Has him by rote, recites him at the tables,
Where he doth govern ; swears him into name,
Upon his word, and sword, for the sole youth
Dares make profession of poetic truth,
Now militant amongst us: to th' incredulous,
That dagger is an article he uses,
To rivet his respect into their pates,
And make them faithful. Fame, you'll find you have
        wrong'd him.

    Fame. What a confederacy of folly's here ?

They all dance but FAME, *and make the first* ANTI-
MASQUE, *in which they adore, and carry forth*
CHRONOMASTIX.

After which, the CURIOUS *come up again to* FAME.

    Eyes. Now, Fame, how like you this ?

    Ears. This falls upon you
For your neglect.

    Nose. He scorns you, and defies you,
He has got a Fame on's own, as well as a faction.

Eyes. And these will deify him, to despite you.

Fame. I envy not the 'Αποθίωσις.
'Twill prove but deifying of a pompion.[6]

Nose. Well, what is that the Time will now exhibit?

Eyes. What gambols, what devices, what new sports?

Ears. You promised us, we should have any thing.

Nose. That Time would give us all we could imagine.

Fame. You might imagine so, I never promised it.

Eyes. Pox! then 'tis nothing. I had now a fancy
We might have talk'd o' the king.

Ears. Or state.

Nose. Or all the world.

Eyes. Censured the council ere they censure us.

Ears. We do it in Paul's.

Nose. Yes, and in all the taverns.

Fame. A comely license! They that censure those
They ought to reverence, meet they that old curse,
To beg their bread, and feel eternal winter!
There's difference 'twixt liberty and license.

Nose. Why if it be not that, let it be this then,
(For since you grant us freedom, we will hold it)
Let's have the giddy world turn'd the heels upward,
And sing a rare black Sanctus,[7] on his head,
Of all things out of order.

Eyes. No, the man

---

[6] *'Twill prove but deifying of a pompion.*] Alluding to the burlesque deification of Claudius, by Seneca.

[7] *And sing a rare* black *Sanctus.*] The black Sanctus was a profane parody of some hymn in the Mass book; and the tune to which it was set was probably loud and discordant, to assist the ridicule. As a satire on the monks, whom it lashes with some kind of coarse humour, it appears to have been very popular. It may be referred to the times of Hen. VIII., when to criminate the ancient possessors of the monasteries, was to render a most acceptable service to that hateful tyrant, and his rapacious court. Sir J.

In the moon dance a coranto, his bush
At's back a-fire; and his dog piping *Lachrymæ.*
  Ears. Or let's have all the people in an uproar,
None knowing why, or to what end; and in
The midst of all, start up an old mad woman
Preaching of patience.
  Nose. No, no, I'd have this.
  Eyes. What?
  Fame. Any thing.
  Nose. That could be monstrous—
Enough, I mean.   A Babel of wild humours.
  Ears. And all disputing of all things they know not.
  Eyes. And talking of all men they never heard of.
  Ears. And all together by the ears o' the sudden.
  Eyes. And when the matter is at hottest, then
All fall asleep.
  Fame. Agree among yourselves,
And what it is you'd have, I'll answer you.
  Eyes. O, that we shall never do.
  Ears. No, never agree.
  Nose. Not upon what?   Something that is un-
    lawful.
  Ears. Ay, or unreasonable.
  Eyes. Or, impossible.
  Nose. Let it be uncivil enough, you hit us right.
  Ears. And a great noise.
  Eyes. To little or no purpose.
  Nose. And if there be some mischief, 'twill be-
    come it.

Harrington, who printed it entire, calls it " the Monks Hymn to
Saunte Satan."   It occurs in Beaumont and Fletcher:

> " Let's sing him a *black Sanctus*, then let's all howl
> .   In our own beastly voices."   *Mad Lover.*

And is also introduced by Phil. Holland in his translation of Livy:
*Nata in vanos tumultus gens, truci cantu, clamoribusque variis, hor-
rendo cuncta impleverunt sono.* Lib. v. c. 37. " With an hideous
and dissonant kind of singing like a black Sanctus, they filled all
about with a fearful and horrible noise."

Eyes. But see there be no cause, as you will
    answer it.
Fame. These are mere monsters.
Nose. Ay, all the better.
Fame. You do abuse the time. These are fit
    freedoms
For lawless prentices, on a Shrove-tuesday,
When they compel the Time to serve their riot;
For drunken wakes, and strutting bear-baitings,
That savour only of their own abuses.
    Eyes. Why, if not those, then something to make
    sport.
    Ears. We only hunt for novelty, not truth.
    Fame. I'll fit you, though the Time faintly permit it.

The second ANTIMASQUE *of* TUMBLERS, *and* JUGGLERS,
brought in by the CAT AND FIDDLE, *who make sport
with the* CURIOUS, *and drive them away.*

    Fame. Why now they are kindly used like such
    spectators,
That know not what they would have. Commonly
The Curious are ill natured, and, like flies,
Seek Time's corrupted parts to blow upon:
But may the sound ones live with fame, and honour,
Free from the molestation of these insects,
Who being fled, Fame now pursues her errand.

Loud Music.

To which the whole Scene opens ; where SATURN *sitting
with* VENUS *is discovered above, and certain* VOTARIES
coming forth below, which are the CHORUS.

    Fame. For you, great king, to whom the Time
    doth owe
All his respects and reverence, behold
How Saturn, urged at request of Love,
Prepares the object to the place to-night.

Within yond' darkness, Venus hath found out
That Hecate, as she is queen of shades,
Keeps certain glories of the time obscured,
There for herself alone to gaze upon,
As she did once the fair Endymion.
These, Time hath promised at Love's suit to free,
As being fitter to adorn the Age,
By you restored on earth, most like his own ;
And fill this world of beauty here, your court :
To which his bounty, see, how men prepare
To fit their votes below, and thronging come
With longing passion to enjoy the effect !
Hark ! it is Love begins to Time. Expect. [*Music.*

Ven.   *Beside, that it is done for Love,*
       It is a work, great Time, will prove
       Thy honour, as men's hopes above.
Sat.   *If Love be pleased, so am I,*
       For Time could never yet deny
       What Love did ask, if Love knew why.
Vot.   *She knew, and hath exprest it now :*
       And so doth every public vow
       That heard her why, and waits thy how.
Sat.   *You shall not long expect ; with ease*
       The things come forth, are born to please :
       Look, have you seen such lights as these ?

    The MASQUERS are discovered, and that which
          obscured them vanisheth.

1 Vot. *These, these must sure some wonders be !*
Cho.   *O, what a glory 'tis to see*
       Men's wishes, Time, and Love agree.
                                   [A pause.

    SATURN and VENUS pass away, and the MASQUERS
                descend.

Cho.   *What grief, or envy had it been,*
       That these, and such had not been seen,

But still obscured in shade !
Who are the glories of the Time,
Of youth, and feature too, the prime,
And for the light were made.

1 Vot. *Their very number, how it takes !*
2 Vot. *What harmony their presence makes !*
1 Vot. *How they inflame the place !*
Cho. *Now they are nearer seen, and view'd,*
For whom could love have better sued,
Or Time have done the grace ?

Here to a loud Music, they march into their figure,
and dance their ENTRY, or first DANCE.

After which.

Ven. *The night could not these glories miss,*
Good Time, I hope, is ta'en with this.
Sat. *If Time were not, I'm sure Love is.*
Between us it shall be no strife :
For now 'tis Love gives Time his life.
Vot. *Let Time then so with Love conspire,*
As straight be sent into the court,
A little Cupid, arm'd with fire,
Attended by a jocund Sport,
To breed delight, and a desire
Of being delighted, in the nobler sort.
Sat. *The wish is crown'd, as soon as made.*
Vot. *And Cupid conquers, ere he doth invade.*
His victories of lightest trouble prove ;
For there is never labour where is Love.

Then follows the MAIN DANCE ;

Which done, CUPID with the SPORT, comes forward.

Cup. [to the Masquers.]
Take breath a while, young bloods, to bring
Your forces up, whilst we go sing

Fresh charges to the beauties here.
Sport. *Or, if they charge you, do not fear,*
Though they be better arm'd than you;
It is but standing the first view,
And then they yield.
Cup. *Or quit the field.*
Sport. *Nay, that they'll never do.*
They'll rather fall upon the place,
Than suffer such disgrace.
You are but men at best, they say,
And they from those ne'er ran away.   [Pause.
Cup. [to the King.]
You, sir, that are the lord of Time,
Receive it not as any crime
'Gainst majesty, that Love and Sport
To-night have enter'd in your court.
Sport. *Sir, doubt him more of some surprize*
Upon yourself; He hath his eyes.
You are the noblest object here,
And 'tis for you alone I fear:
For here are ladies, that would give
A brave reward, to make Love live
Well all his life, for such a draught;
And therefore, look to every shaft:
The wag's a deacon in his craft.   [Pause.
Cup. [to the Lords.]
My lords, the honours of the crown,
Put off your sourness, do not frown,
Bid cares depart, and business hence:
A little, for the Time, dispense.
Sport. *Trust nothing that the boy lets fall,*
My lords, he hath plots upon you all.
A pensioner unto your wives,
To keep you in uxorious gyves,
And so your sense to fascinate,
To make you quit all thought of state,
His amorous questions to debate.

> *But hear his logic, he will prove*
> *There is no business, but to be in love.*

Cup.   *The words of Sport, my lords, and coarse.*
      Your ladies yet, will not think worse   [Pause.
      Of Love for this : they shall command
      My bow, my quiver, and my hand.

Sport.   *What, here to stand*
         And kill the flies ?
      Alas, thy service they despise.
      One beauty here, hath in her eyes
      More shafts than from thy bow e'er flew,
        Or that poor quiver knew.
           These dames,
      They need not Love's, they've Nature's flames.

Cup.   *I see the Beauty that you so report.*

Sport. *Cupid, you must not point in court,*
      Where live so many of a sort.
      Of Harmony these learn'd their speech,
      The Graces did them footing teach,
      And, at the old Idalian brawls,
      They danced your mother down.   *She calls.*

Cup.   *Arm, arm them all.*

Sport. *Young bloods come on,*
      And charge ; let every man take one.

Cup.   *And try his fate.*

Sport. *These are fair wars ;*
      And will be carried without scars.

Cup.   *A joining, but of feet, and hands,*
      Is all the Time, and Love commands.

Sport. *Or if you do their gloves off-strip,*
      Or taste the nectar of the lip ;
      See, so you temper your desires,
      For kisses, that ye suck not fires.

The REVELS follow; which ended, the Chorus appear
again, and DIANA descends to HIPPOLITUS, the
whole scene being changed into a wood, out of
which he comes.

Cho.   *The courtly strife is done, it should appear,*
       Between the youths, and beauties of the year :
       We hope that now these lights will know their
                sphere,
       And strive hereafter to shine ever here :
       Like brightest planets, still to move
       In the eye of Time, and orbs of Love.

Dia. Hippolitus, Hippolitus!
Hip. Diana?
Dia. She.
       Be ready you, or Cephalus,
       To wait on me.
Hip. We ever be.
Dia. Your goddess hath been wrong'd to-night,
       By Love's report unto the Time.
Hip. The injury, itself will right,
       Which only Fame hath made a crime,
            For Time is wise,
       And hath his ears as perfect as his eyes.
Sat. Who's that descends? Diana?
Vot. Yes.
Ven. Belike her troop she hath begun to miss.
Sat. Let's meet, and question what her errand is.
Hip. She will prevent thee, Saturn, not t' excuse
            Herself unto thee, rather to complain
       That thou and Venus both should so abuse
            The name of Dian, as to entertain
       A thought, that she had purpose to defraud
            The Time, of any glories that were his :
       To do Time honour rather, and applaud
            His worth, hath been her study.
Dia.   And it is.

I call'd these youths forth in their blood, and
    prime,
  Out of the honour that I bore their parts,
To make them fitter so to serve the Time
  By labour, riding, and those ancient arts,
That first enabled men unto the wars,
And furnish'd heaven with so many stars :

Hip. As Perseus, Castor, Pollux, and the rest,
  Who were of hunters first, of men the best ;
  Whose shades do yet remain within yond'
    groves,
  Themselves there sporting with their nobler
    loves.

Dia. And so may these do, if the time give leave.

Sat. Chaste Dian's purpose we do now conceive,
  And yield thereto.

Ven.   And so doth Love.

Vot. All votes do in one circle move.

Grand Cho.   *Turn hunters then,*
               Again.
Hunting, it is the noblest exercise,
Makes men laborious, active, wise,
Brings health, and doth the spirits delight,
  It helps the hearing, and the sight :
It teacheth arts that never slip
  The memory, good horsemanship,
Search, sharpness, courage, and defence,
  And chaseth all ill habits thence.

      Turn hunters then,
        Again,
          But not of men.
          Follow his ample,
          And just example,
That hates all chase of malice, and of blood :
And studies only ways of good,

To keep soft peace in breath.
Man should not hunt mankind to death,
But strike the enemies of man ;
Kill vices if you can :
They are your wildest beasts,
And when they thickest fall, you make the gods
true feasts.

THUS IT ENDED.

NEPTUNE'S TRIUMPH

FOR THE

RETURN OF ALBION.

CELEBRATED IN A MASQUE AT THE COURT ON THE TWELFTH-NIGHT, 1624.

Omnis et ad reducem jam litat ara Deum.—MART.

NEPTUNE'S TRIUMPH, &c.] Charles (i. e. Albion) returned from his ill-fated expedition to Spain on the fifth of October, in the preceding year (1623). Before this Masque appeared, the Spanish match was completely broken off, and James, who had long set his heart upon it, and for several years honestly and sedulously laboured to effect it, wearied out at length by the interminable juggling of the court of Spain, was, by this time, reconciled to the disappointment. *Neptune's Triumph* appears to have been celebrated with uncommon magnificence. All hearts and hands were in it ; and the Spanish influence then received a check, from which it has not recovered to this day.

NEPTUNE'S TRIUMPH, ETC.

His Majesty *being set, and the loud music ceasing.
All that is discovered of a scene, are two erected
pillars, dedicated to Neptune, with this inscription
upon the one,*

NEP. RED.

On the other.

SEC. JOV.

The Poet *entering on the stage, to disperse the argument, is called to by the* Master-Cook.

Cook.

DO you hear, you creature of diligence
and business? what is the affair, that
you pluck for so, under your cloke?

Poet. Nothing, but what I colour
for, I assure you; and may encounter
with, I hope, if luck favour me, the gamesters'
goddess.

Cook. You are a votary of hers, it seems, by your
language. What went you upon, may a man ask you?

Poet. Certainties, indeed, sir, and very good ones;
the representation of a masque; you'll see't anon.

Cook. Sir, this is my room, and region too, the
Banquetting-house. And in matter of feast, the solemnity, nothing is to be presented here, but with my
acquaintance and allowance to it.

Poet. You are not his majesty's confectioner, are you ?

Cook. No, but one that has a good title to the room, his Master-cook. What are you, sir ?

Poet. The most unprofitable of his servants, I, sir, the Poet. A kind of a Christmas ingine : one that is used at least once a year, for a trifling instrument of wit, or so.

Cook. Were you ever a cook ?

Poet. A cook! no, surely.

Cook. Then you can be no good poet : for a good poet differs nothing at all from a master-cook. Either's art is the wisdom of the mind.

Poet. As how, sir ?

Cook. Expect. I am by my place, to know how to please the palates of the guests ; so you are to know the palates of the times ; study the several tastes, what every nation, the Spaniard, the Dutch, the French, the Walloun, the Neapolitan, the Britain, the Sicilian, can expect from you.

Poet. That were a heavy and hard task, to satisfy Expectation, who is so severe an exactress of duties ; ever a tyrannous mistress, and most times a pressing enemy.

Cook. She is a powerful great lady, sir, at all times, and must be satisfied : so must her sister, madam Curiosity, who hath as dainty a palate as she ; and these will expect.

Poet. But what if they expect more than they understand ?

Cook. That's all one, master Poet, you are bound to satisfy them. For there is a palate of the understanding, as well as of the senses. The taste is taken with good relishes, the sight with fair objects, the hearing with delicate sounds, the smelling with pure scents, the feeling with soft and plump bodies, but the understanding with all these ; for all which

you must begin at the kitchen. There the art of
Poetry was learn'd, and found out, or nowhere; and
the same day with the art of Cookery.

Poet. I should have given it rather to the cellar, if
my suffrage had been ask'd.

Cook. O, you are for the oracle of the bottle, I see;
hogshead Trismegistus; he is your Pegasus. Thence
flows the spring of your muses, from that hoof.

Seduced Poet, I do say to thee——
A boiler, range, and dresser were the fountains
Of all the knowledge in the universe,
And that's the kitchen. What! a master-cook!
Thou dost not know the man, nor canst thou know
     him,
Till thou hast serv'd some years in that deep school,
That's both the nurse and mother of the arts,
And heard'st him read, interpret, and demonstrate.
A master-cook![1] why, he's the man of men,
For a professor! he designs, he draws,
He paints, he carves, he builds, he fortifies,
Makes citadels of curious fowl and fish,
Some he dry-ditches, some motes round with broths;
Mounts marrow-bones; cuts fifty-angled custards;
Rears bulwark pies; and, for his outer works,
He raiseth ramparts of immortal crust;
And teacheth all the tactics at one dinner:[2]

[1] *A master-cook! &c.*] Cartwright has reduced this into practice
in his *Ordinary*, and furnished out a military dinner with great
pleasantry, at the expense of *Have-at-all*, who is desirous to grow
valiant, as lawyers do learned, by eating. This speech is also
closely imitated by the master-cook in Fletcher's tragedy of *Rollo
Duke of Normandy.*

[2] *And teacheth all the tactics at one dinner.*] This seems to be
taken from the poet Posidippus, who in Athenæus compares a good
cook to a good general:

Αγαθου στρατηγου διαφερειν ουδεν δοκει.

And Athenion in like manner (see Athenæus, l. 14. c. 23) attri-
butes to the art of cookery, and kitchen-philosophy, what the poets

What ranks, what files, to put the dishes in,
The whole art military ! then he knows
The influence of the stars, upon his meats ;
And all their seasons, tempers, qualities,
And so to fit his relishes, and sauces !
He has Nature in a pot, 'bove all the chemists,
Or bare-breech'd brethren of the Rosy-cross !
He is an architect, an inginer,
A soldier, a physician, a philosopher,
A general mathematician !
    Poet. It is granted.
    Cook. And that you may not doubt him for a Poet—
    Poet. This fury shews, if there were nothing else ;
And 'tis divine !
    Cook. Then, brother poet.
    Poet. Brother.
    Cook. I have a suit.
    Poet. What is it ?
    Cook. Your device.
    Poet. As you came in upon me, I was then

assign to the legislators of society, and the first founders of states and commonwealths. WHAL.

The Greek poet is truly excellent ; and the apparent seriousness with which his cook descants on the importance of his profession adds greatly to its genuine humour. The concluding lines are very amusing :

Καταρχομεθ' ἡμεις οἱ μαγειροι, θυομεν,
Σπονδας ποιουμεν, τω μαλιστα τους θεους
Ἡμιν ὑπακουειν, δια το ταυθ' εὑρηκεναι
Τα μαλιστα συντεινοντα προς το ζην καλως.

                " We slay the victims,
We pour the free libations, and to us
The gods themselves lend a propitious ear ;
And, for our special merits, scatter blessings
On all the human race, because from us
And from our art, mankind was first induced
To live the life of reason."

There is no translating the sly felicity of ζην καλως, which looks, at the same time, to good morals and good eating.

Offering the argument, and this it is.
    Cook. Silence!
    Poet. [reads.] *The mighty Neptune, mighty in his*
        styles,
And large command of waters, and of isles ;
Not as the " lord and sovereign of the seas,"
But " chief in the art of riding," late did please,
To send his Albion forth, the most his own,
Upon discovery, to themselves best known,
Through Celtiberia ; and, to assist his course,
Gave him his powerful Manager of Horse,
With divine Proteus,[3] *father of disguise,*
To wait upon them with his counsels wise,
In all extremes. His great commands being done,
And he desirous to review his son,
He doth dispatch a floating isle, from hence,
Unto the Hesperian shores, to waft him thence.
Where, what the arts were, us'd to make him stay,
And how the Syrens woo'd him by the way,
What monsters he encounter'd on the coast,
How near our general joy was to be lost,[4]
Is not our subject now ; though all these make
The present gladness greater, for their sake.
But what the triumphs are, the feast, the sport,
And proud solemnities of Neptune's court,
Now he is safe, and Fame's not heard in vain,
But we behold our happy pledge again.

[3] *With divine Proteus, &c.*] This, I believe, was sir Francis Cottington. He had been secretary to sir Charles Cornwallis, and was, at this time, private secretary to the prince ; he was well versed in political affairs, and particularly in those of Spain, where he had resided many years in a public capacity.

[4] *How near our general joy was to be lost.*] This alludes to the storm which took place on the Spanish coast, and in which the prince, together with a number of the Spanish nobility who came to take leave of him, was nearly wrecked. The other dangers which Charles is said to have encountered are probably exaggerated by the " poet."

That with him, loyal Hippius is return'd,[5]
Who for it, under so much envy, burn'd
With his own brightness, till her starv'd snakes saw
What Neptune did impose, to him was law.

   Cook. But why not this, till now?
   Poet. ——*It was not time,*
To mix this music with the vulgar's chime.
Stay, till the abortive, and extemporal din
Of balladry, were understood a sin,
Minerva cried; that, what tumultuous verse,
Or prose could make, or steal, they might rehearse,
And every songster had sung out his fit;
That all the country, and the city wit,
Of bells and bonfires, and good cheer was spent,
And Neptune's guard had drunk all that they meant;
That all the tales and stories now were old
Of the sea-monster Archy,[6] *or grown cold:*
The Muses then might venture, undeterr'd,
For they love, then, to sing, when they are heard.

   Cook. I like it well, 'tis handsome; and I have
Something would fit this. How do you present them?
In a fine island, say you?
   Poet. Yes, a Delos:
Such, as when fair Latona fell in travail,

---

   [5] *That with him loyal* Hippius *is return'd.*] By *Hippius* is meant
the duke of Buckingham, master of the horse to James I., who
accompanied the prince into Spain, to which this speech alludes.
WHAL.

   [6] *Of the sea-monster, Archy.*] Archibald Armstrong, the court
jester, who followed the prince into Spain. Charles seems to have
taken a strange fancy to this buffoon, who joined the surly savage-
ness of the bear to the mischievous tricks of the monkey. Howell,
who was at Madrid during the prince's visit, says, in one of his letters,
" Our cousin Archy hath more privilege here, than any, for he often
goes with his fool's coat where the Infanta is with her Meninos and
ladies of honour, and keeps a blowing and blustering among them,
and flurts out what he lists." In conclusion, he gives a specimen
of his ill-manners, which must have been offensive in the highest
degree. Book i. let. 18.

Great Neptune made emergent.

 Cook. I conceive you.
I would have had your isle brought floating in, now,
In a brave broth,[7] and of a sprightly green.
Just to the colour of the sea; and then,
Some twenty Syrens, singing in the kettle,
With an Arion mounted on the back
Of a grown conger, but in such a posture,
As all the world should take him for a dolphin:
O, 'twould have made such music! Have you nothing
But a bare island?

 Poet. Yes, we have a tree too,
Which we do call the tree of Harmony,
And is the same with what we read the sun
Brought forth in the Indian Musicana first,

---

[7] *In a brave broth——*
 With an Arion *mounted on the back*
 Of a grown conger, but in such a posture
 As all the world should take him for a dolphin.] This is humorously imitated by Fletcher:

  " For fish, I'll make a standing lake of white broth,
   And pikes come ploughing up the plumbs before them,
   Arion on a dolphin, playing Lachrymæ," &c.
            Rollo, A. ii. S. 2.

Mr. Weber has happily discovered the *pronomen* of this celebrated musician. He was called, it seems, *Bike* Arion, without the Mr.—"Bike," as he aptly observes, "which signifies a *hive of bees,* is not in the least applicable, *for which reason* I must leave it to the reader." This is kind: but Mr. Weber is unjust to the merits of his own text. Does he not know that bees will swarm to a brass kettle? How much rather, then, to the harp of Arion! Hence the name. The verse stands thus in his precious edition (vol. ii. p. 55):

  " Ride like *Bike* Arion on a trout to London."

Former editors, whom Mr. Weber treats with all the contempt which his superior attainments justify him in assuming, had supposed that *bike* (which destroys the metre) was merely an accidental repetition of *like,* and therefore dropt it; but as this was done without writing a page or two about it, Mr. Weber wonders at their presumption, and very judiciously reinstates it in the text.

And thus it grows : The goodly bole being got[8]
To certain cubits height, from every side
The boughs decline, which taking root afresh,
Spring up new boles, and these spring new, and newer,
Till the whole tree become a porticus,
Or arched arbor, able to receive
A numerous troop, such as our Albion,
And the companions of his journey are :
And this they sit in.
    Cook. Your prime Masquers ?
    Poet. Yes.
    Cook. But where's your Antimasque now, all this
        while ?
I hearken after them.
    Poet. Faith, we have none.
    Cook. None !
    Poet. None, I assure you, neither do I think them
A worthy part of presentation,
Being things so heterogene to all device,
Mere by-works, and at best outlandish nothings.
    Cook. O, you are all the heaven awry, sir !
For blood of poetry, running in your veins,
Make not yourself so ignorantly simple.
Because, sir, you shall see I am a poet,
No less than cook, and that I find you want
A special service here, an antimasque,
I'll fit you with a dish out of the kitchen,
Such, as I think, will take the present palates,
A metaphorical dish ! and do but mark

---

    [8] *The goodly bole being got, &c.*] Milton treads rather closely
upon the heels of Jonson here :
      " The fig tree that——
        In Malabar or Decan spreads her arms
        Branching so broad and long, that in the ground
        The bended twigs take root, and daughters grow
        About the mother tree, a pillar'd shade
        High over-arch'd, and echoing walks between."
                          Par. Lost, ix. 1100.

How a good wit may jump with you. Are you
    ready, child ?
(Had there been masque, or no masque, I had made it.)
Child of the boiling-house !

Enter Boy.

Boy. Here, father.
Cook. Bring forth the pot. It is an olla podrida.
But I have persons to present the meats.
Poet. Persons !
Cook. Such as do relish nothing but *di stato*,
But in another fashion, than you dream of,
Know all things the wrong way, talk of the affairs,
The clouds, the cortines, and the mysteries
That are afoot, and from what hands they have them,
The master of the elephant, or the camels :
What correspondencies are held ; the posts
That go, and come, and know almost their minutes,
All but their business : therein, they are fishes ;
But have their garlic, as the proverb says.
They are our Quest of Enquiry after news.
Poet. Together with their learned authors ?
Boy. Yes, sir.
And of the epicœne gender, hees, and shees :
Amphibion Archy is the chief.
Cook. Good boy !
The child is learned too : note but the kitchen !
Have you put him into the pot, for garlic ?
Boy. One in his coat shall stink as strong as he, sir,
And his friend Giblets with him.
Cook. They are two,
That give a part of the seasoning.
Poet. I conceive
The way of your gallimaufry.
Cook. You will like it,
When they come pouring out of the pot together.
Boy. O, if the pot had been big enough !

Cook. What then, child ?

Boy. I had put in the elephant, and one camel,
At least, for beef.

Cook. But, whom have you for partridge ?

Boy. A brace of dwarfs, and delicate plump birds.

Cook. And whom for mutton, and kid ?

Boy. A fine laced mutton,[9]
Or two ; and either has her frisking husband :
That reads her the Corranto, every week.
Grave master Ambler, news-master o' Paul's,
Supplies your capon ; and grown captain Buz,
His emissary, under-writes for Turkey ;
A gentleman of the Forest presents pheasant,
And a plump poulterer's wife, in Grace's street,
Plays hen with eggs in the belly, or a coney,
Choose which you will.

Cook. But where's the bacon, Tom ?

Boy. Hogrel the butcher, and the sow his wife,
Are both there.

Cook. It is well ; go dish them out.
Are they well boil'd ?

Boy. Podrida !

Poet. What's that, rotten ?

Cook. O, that they must be.   There's one main
          ingredient
We have forgot, the artichoke.

Boy. No, sir ;
I have a fruiterer, with a cold red nose
Like a blue fig, performs it.

Cook. The fruit looks so.
Good child, go pour them out, shew their concoction.
They must be rotten boil'd ; the broth's the best on't,
And that's the dance : the stage here is the charger.
And, brother poet, though the serious part

---

[9] *A fine laced mutton.*] A cant term for a wanton. Some of the
characters mentioned in this speech, the author subsequently introduced into the *Staple of News.*

Be yours, yet, envy not the cook his art.
Poet. Not I : *nam lusus ipse Triumphus amat.*

Here the ANTIMASQUE *is danced by the persons described, coming out of the pot.*

Poet. Well, now, expect the scene itself; it opens!

The island of DELOS *is discovered, the* Masquers *sitting in their several sieges. The heavens opening, and* APOLLO, *with* MERCURY, *some of the* Muses, *and the goddess* HARMONY, *make the music : the while the island moves forward,* PROTEUS *sitting below, and* APOLLO *sings.*

SONG.

Apol. *Look forth, the shepherd of the seas,*
And of the ports that keep'st the keys,
And to your Neptune tell,
His Albion, prince of all his isles,
For whom the sea and land so smiles,
Is home returned well.

Grand Cho. *And be it thought no common cause,*
That, to it, so much wonder draws,
And all the heavens consent,
With Harmony, to tune their notes,
In answer to the public votes,
That for it up were sent.

It was no envious step-dame's rage,
Or tyrant's malice of the age,
That did employ him forth :
But such a wisdom that would prove
By sending him their hearts, and love,
That else might fear his worth.

By this time, the island hath joined itself with the shore : and PROTEUS, PORTUNUS, and SARON come
8   D

forth ; and go up singing to the state, while the
Masquers take time to land.

SONG.

Pro. *Ay, now the pomp of Neptune's triumph shines !*
      And all the glories of his great designs
      Are read, reflected, in his son's return !

Por. *How all the eyes, the looks, the hearts here burn*
      At his arrival.

Sar.   *These are the true fires*
      Are made of joys !

Pro.   *Of longing !*

Por.   *Of desires !*

Sar. *Of hopes !*

Pro.   *Of fears !*

Por.   *No intermitted blocks.*

Sar. *But pure affections, and from odorous stocks !*

Cho. *'Tis incense all, that flames,*
      And these materials scarce have names !

Pro. *My king looks higher, as he scorn'd the wars*
      Of winds, and with his trident touch'd the stars;
      There is no wrinkle in his brow, or frown,
      But as his cares he would in nectar drown,
      And all the silver-footed nymphs were drest
      To wait upon him, to the Ocean's feast.

Por. *Or, here in rows upon the banks were set,*
      And had their several hairs made into net
      To catch the youths in, as they come on shore.

Sar. *How, Galatea sighing ! O, no more,*
      Banish your fears.

Por.   *And, Doris, dry your tears.*
      ALBION *is come.*

Pro.   *And Haliclyon too,*[1]
      That kept his side, as he was charg'd to do,
      With wonder.

---

[1] *And Haliclyon too.*] The duke of Buckingham, lord high ad-
miral.

Sar.	*And the Syrens have him not.*
Por.	*Though they no 'practice, nor no arts forgot,*
	That might have won him, or by charm, or song.
Pro.	*Or laying forth their tresses all along*
	Upon the glassy waves.
Por.	*Then diving.*
Pro.	*Then,*
	Up with their heads, as they were mad of men.
Sar.	*And there the highest-going billows crown,*
	Until some lusty sea-god pull'd them down.
Cho.	*See, he is here!*
Pro.	*Great master of the main,*
	Receive thy dear, and precious pawn again.
Cho.	*Saron, Portunus, Proteus bring him thus,*
	Safe, as thy subjects' wishes gave him us:
	And of thy glorious triumph let it be
	No less a part, that thou their loves dost see,
	Than that his sacred head's return'd to thee.

This sung, the island goes back, whilst the Upper Chorus takes it from them, and the Masquers prepare for their figure.

Cho.	*Spring all the Graces of the age,*
	And all the Loves of time:
	Bring all the pleasures of the stage,
	And relishes of rhyme:
	Add all the softnesses of courts,
	The looks, the laughters, and the sports:
	And mingle all their sweets and salts,
	That none may say, the Triumph halts.

Here the Masquers dance their Entry.

Which done, the first prospective of a maritime palace, or the house of OCEANUS, *is discovered, with loud music.*

And the other above is no more seen.

Poet. Behold the palace of Oceanus !
Hail, reverend structure ! boast no more to us
Thy being able all the gods to feast ;
We've seen enough ; our Albion was thy guest.

Then follows the MAIN DANCE.

*After which, the second prospect of the sea is shown, to
the former music.*

Poet. Now turn and view the wonders of the deep,
Where Proteus' herds, and Neptune's orcs do keep,
Where all is plough'd, yet still the pasture's green,
The ways are found, and yet no paths are seen.

There PROTEUS, PORTUNUS, SARON, *go up to the*
Ladies *with this* SONG.

Pro.   *Come, noble nymphs, and do not hide*
        The joys for which you so provide.
Sar.   *If not to mingle with the men,*
        What do you here ? go home agen.
Por.   *Your dressings do confess,*
        By what we see so curious parts
        Of Pallas' and Arachne's arts,
             That you could mean no less.
Pro.   *Why do you wear the silk-worm's toils,*
        Or glory in the shell-fish' spoils,
        Or strive to shew the grains of ore,
        That you have gather'd on the shore,
             Whereof to make a stock
        To graft the greener emerald on,
        Or any better-water'd stone ?
Sar.   *Or ruby of the rock ?*
Pro.   *Why do you smell of amber-grise,*
        Of which was formed Neptune's niece,
        The queen of Love ; unless you can,
        Like sea-born Venus, love a man ?

Sar.   *Try, put yourselves unto't.*
Cho.   *Your looks, your smiles, and thoughts that meet,*
       Ambrosian hands, and silver feet,
        Do promise you will do't.

     The REVELS *follow.*

*Which ended, the fleet is discovered, while the three
      cornets play.*

   Poet. 'Tis time, your eyes should be refresh'd at
   length
With something new, a part of Neptune's strength
See yond' his fleet, ready to go or come,
Or fetch the riches of the ocean home,
So to secure him, both in peace and wars,
Till not one ship alone, but all be stars.
                    [*A shout within.*

Re-enter the Cook, *followed by a number of* Sailors.

   Cook. I've another service for you, brother Poet;
a dish of pickled sailors, fine salt sea-boys, shall
relish like anchovies, or caveare, to draw down a cup
of nectar, in the skirts of a night.
   Sail. Come away, boys, the town is ours; hey for
Neptune, and our young master!
   Poet. He knows the compass, and the card,
While Castor sits on the main yard,
And Pollux too, to help your hales;
And bright Leucothoë fills your sails:
Arion sings, the dolphins swim,
And all the way, to gaze on him.

    The ANTIMASQUE *of* Sailors.

*Then the last Song to the whole music, five lutes, three
      cornets, and ten voices.*

Song.

Pro. *Although we wish the triumph still might last*
For such a prince, and his discovery past;
Yet now, great lord of waters, and of isles,
Give Proteus leave to turn unto his wiles.

Por. *And, whilst young Albion doth thy labours ease,*
Dispatch Portunus to thy ports.

Sar.   *And Saron to thy seas:*
To meet old Nereus, with his fifty girls,
From aged Indus laden home with pearls,
And Orient gums, to burn unto thy name.

Grand Cho. *And may thy subjects' hearts be all on*
flame,
Whilst thou dost keep the earth in firm estate,
And 'mongst the winds, dost suffer no debate,
But both at sea, and land, our powers increase,
With health and all the golden gifts of peace.

The last Dance.

WITH WHICH THE WHOLE ENDED.

PAN'S ANNIVERSARY:

OR THE

SHEPHERD'S HOLYDAY.

AS IT WAS PRESENTED AT COURT BEFORE
KING JAMES, 1625.

THE INVENTORS, INIGO JONES; BEN JONSON.

PAN'S ANNIVERSARY, &c.] This Masque, which was probably presented on New Year's day, was the last that James witnessed, as he died on the twenty-seventh of March following. It only appears in the fol. 1641, and was printed after Jonson's death.

PAN'S ANNIVERSARY.

The SCENE *Arcadia.*

The Court being seated, enter three Nymphs, *strewing several sorts of flowers, followed by an old* SHEPHERD, *with a censer and perfumes.*

1 *Nymph.*

THUS, thus begin the yearly rites
 Are due to Pan on these bright nights;
 His morn now riseth, and invites
 To sports, to dances, and delights:
  All envious and profane, away,
  This is the shepherd's holyday.

2 *Nym.* Strew, strew the glad and smiling ground
  With every flower, yet not confound
  The primrose drop, the spring's own
   spouse,
  Bright day's-eyes, and the lips of cows,
   The garden-star, the queen of May,
   The rose, to crown the holyday.

3 *Nym.* Drop, drop your violets, change your hues,
  Now red, now pale, as lovers use,
  And in your death go out as well,
  As when you lived unto the smell:
   That from your odour all may say,
   This is the shepherd's holyday.

Shep. Well done, my pretty ones, rain roses still,
Until the last be dropt: then hence ; and fill
Your fragrant prickles[1] for a second shower.
Bring corn-flag, tulips, and Adonis' flower,
Fair ox-eye, goldy-locks, and columbine,
Pinks, goulands, king-cups, and sweet sops-in-wine,
Blue hare-bells, pagles, pansies, calaminth,
Flower-gentle, and the fair-hair'd hyacinth,
Bring rich carnations, flower-de-luces, lilies,
The checqued, and purple-ringed daffodillies,
Bright crown-imperial, kingspear, holyhocks,
Sweet Venus-navel, and soft lady-smocks,
Bring too some branches forth of Daphne's hair,
And gladdest myrtle for these posts to wear,
With spikenard weav'd, and marjoram between,
And starr'd with yellow-golds, and meadows-queen,
That when the altar, as it ought, is drest,
More odour come not from the phœnix' nest ;
The breath thereof Panchaia may envy,
The colours China,[2] and the light the sky.

Loud Music.

The Scene opens, and the Masquers *are discovered sitting about the Fountain of Light, with the* Musicians, *attired like the Priests of Pan, standing in the work beneath them.*

Enter a Fencer, *flourishing.*

Fen. Room for an old trophy of time ; a son of
the sword, a servant of Mars, the minion of the
muses, and a master of fence ! One that hath shown

---

[1] *Your fragrant* prickles.] So the gardeners still call the light
open wicker baskets, in which flowers are brought to market.
[2] *The colours China.*] This is the earliest allusion that I have
found to the beautiful colouring of this ware ; which now began to
make its appearance in the shops, or, as they were called, China-
houses of the capital.

his quarters, and played his prizes at all the games of Greece in his time; as fencing, wrestling, leaping, dancing, what not? and hath now usher'd hither, by the light of my long sword, certain bold boys of Bœotia, who are come to challenge the Arcadians at their own sports, call them forth on their own holy-day, and dance them down on their own green-swarth.

Shep. 'Tis boldly attempted, and must be a Bœotian enterprise, by the face of it, from all the parts of Greece else, especially at this time, when the best, and bravest spirits of Arcadia, called together by the excellent Arcas, are yonder sitting about the Fountain of Light, in consultation of what honours they may do to the great Pan, by increase of anniversary rites, fitted to the music of his peace.

Fen. Peace to thy Pan, and mum to thy music, swain: there is a tinker of Thebes a coming, called Epam, with his kettle, will make all Arcadia ring of him: What are your sports for the purpose? say, if singing, you shall be sung down; if dancing, danced down. There is no more to be done with you, but know what; which it is; and you are in smoke, gone, vapoured, vanished, blown, and, as a man would say, in a word of two syllables, nothing.

Shep. This is short, though not so sweet. Surely the better part of the solemnity here will be dancing.

Fen. Enough: they shall be met with instantly in their own sphere, the sphere of their own activity, a dance. But by whom, expect: no Cynætheian, nor Satyrs; but, as I said, boys of Bœotia, things of Thebes, (the town is ours, shepherd) mad merry Greeks, lads of life, that have no gall in us, but all air and sweetness. A tooth-drawer is our foreman, that if there be but a bitter tooth in the company, it may be called out at a twitch: he doth command any man's teeth out of his head upon the point of his poniard; or tickles them forth with his riding rod: he draws teeth a horse-back in full speed, yet he will dance a foot, he hath given his word: he is yeoman of the mouth to the whole brotherhood, and is charged to see their gums be clean, and their breath sweet, at a minute's warning. Then comes my learned Theban, the tinker, I told you of,[3] with his kettle drum, before and after, a master of music, and a man of metal, he beats the march to the tune of Ticklefoot, Pam, Pam, Pam, brave Epam with a Nondas. That's the strain.

Shep. A high one!

Fen. Which is followed by the trace, and tract of an excellent juggler, that can juggle with every joint about him, from head to heel. He can do tricks with his toes, wind silk, and thread pearl with them, as nimble a fine fellow of his feet, as his hands: for there is a noble corn-cutter, his companion, hath so pared and finified them——Indeed, he hath taken it into his care, to reform the feet of all, and fit all their footing to a form! only one splay foot in the company, and he is a bellows-mender, allowed, who hath the looking to all of their lungs by patent, and by his place is to set that leg afore still, and with his puffs, keeps them in breath, during pleasure: a tinder-

---

[3] *Then comes my learned Theban, the tinker, I told you of.*] In *Lear*, the poor old king says,

"I'll talk a word with this same learned Theban."

On which Steevens observes, "Ben Jonson, in his Masque of *Pan's Anniversary*, has introduced a tinker, whom he calls a learned Theban, *perhaps* in ridicule of this passage." The ridicule (if ridicule there be) must be in the word *learned*, for (though Steevens was ignorant of it) the tinker actually was a Theban: as he was also a *master of music*, the epithet does not seem to be very much out of its place. But, "perhaps," Jonson laid the scene of this grave Antimasque in Greece, that he might have an opportunity of "ridiculing Shakspeare;" and this I take to be the case, as *Thebes* is not particularly celebrated for the musical talents of its tinkers. The commentators should consider this well.

box-man, to strike new fire into them at every turn, and where he spies any brave spark that is in danger to go out, ply him with a match presently.

Shep. A most politic provision !

Fen. Nay, we have made our provisions beyond example, I hope. For to these, there is annexed a clock-keeper, a grave person, as Time himself, who is to see that they all keep time to a nick,[4] and move every elbow in order, every knee in compass. He is to wind them up, and draw them down, as he sees cause : then is there a subtle shrewd bearded sir, that hath been a politician, but is now a maker of mouse-traps, a great inginer yet : and he is to catch the ladies' favours in the dance, with certain cringes he is to make ; and to bait their benevolence. Nor can we doubt of the success, for we have a prophet amongst us of that peremptory pate, a tailor or master-fashioner, that hath found it out in a painted cloth, or some old hanging, (for those are his library,) that we must conquer in such a time, and such a half time ; therefore bids us go on cross-legg'd, or however thread the needles of our own happiness, go through stitch with all, unwind the clew of our cares ; he hath taken measure of our minds, and will fit our fortune to our footing. And to better assure us, at his own charge, brings his philosopher with him, a great clerk, who, they say, can write, and it is shrewdly suspected but he can read too. And he is to take the whole dances from the foot by brachygraphy, and so make a memorial, if not a map of the business. Come forth, lads, and do your own turns.

The Bœotians *enter for the* ANTIMASQUE, *which is Danced,*

After which,

[4] *To a* nick,] i. e. what Shakspeare calls "a jar o' the clock."

Fen. How like you this, shepherd ? was not this gear gotten on a hólyday ?

Shep. Faith, your folly may deserve pardon, because it hath delighted : but beware of presuming, or how you offer comparison with persons so near deities : Behold where they are that have now forgiven you, whom should you provoke again with the like, they will justly punish that with anger, which they now dismiss with contempt.   Away !

[They retire.

To the Masquers.

And come, you prime Arcadians forth, that taught
   By Pan the rites of true society,
From his loud music all your manners wrought,
   And made your commonwealth a harmony,
Commending so to all posterity
   Your innocence from that fair fount of light,
As still you sit without the injury
   Of any rudeness, folly can, or spite :
Dance from the top of the Lycæan mountain,
   Down to this valley, and with nearer eye
Enjoy, what long in that illumin'd fountain
   You did far off, but yet with wonder, spy.

HYMN I.

I Nym. *Of Pan we sing, the best of singers, Pan,*
      That taught us swains how first to tune
        our lays,
      And on the pipe more airs than Phœbus can.

Cho.   *Hear, O you groves, and hills resound his*
      praise.

2 Nym. *Of Pan we sing, the best of leaders, Pan,*
      That leads the Naiads and the Dryads
        forth ;
      And to their dances more than Hermes can.

Cho.   *Hear, O you groves, and hills resound his worth.*

3 Nym.   *Of Pan we sing, the best of hunters, Pan,*
          That drives the hart to seek unused ways,
          And in the chase more than Sylvanus can.
Cho.   *Hear, O you groves, and hills resound his praise.*

2 Nym.   *Of Pan we sing, the best of shepherds, Pan,*
          That keeps our flocks and us, and both leads forth,
          To better pastures than great Pales can.
Cho.   *Hear, O you groves, and hills resound his worth.*
    And while his powers and praises thus we sing,
    The valleys let rebound, and all the rivers ring.

The Masquers descend, and dance their Entry.

HYMN II.

Pan is our All, by him we breathe, we live,
  We move, we are; 'tis he our lambs doth rear,
Our flocks doth bless, and from the store doth give
  The warm and finer fleeces that we wear.
      He keeps away all heats and colds,
      Drives all diseases from our folds;
      Makes every where the spring to dwell,
      The ewes to feed, their udders swell;
      But if he frown, the sheep, alas!
      The shepherds wither, and the grass.

Cho. *Strive, strive to please him then, by still increasing thus*
The rites are due to him, who doth all right for us.

THE MAIN DANCE.

HYMN III.

If yet, if yet,
Pan's orgies you will further fit,
See where the silver-footed fays do sit,
The nymphs of wood and water ;
Each tree's and fountain's daughter !
Go take them forth, it will be good
To see them wave it like a wood,
And others wind it like a flood ;
In springs,
And rings,
Till the applause it brings,
Wakes Echo from her seat,
The closes to repeat.

Ech.   *The closes to repeat.*

Echo the truest oracle on ground,
Though nothing but a sound.

Ech.   *Though nothing but a sound.*

Beloved of Pan the valleys queen.

Ech.   *The valleys queen.*

And often heard, though never seen.

Ech.   *Though never seen.*

Here the REVELS.

After which re-enter the Fencer.

Fen. Room, room, there; where are you, shepherd ? I am come again, with my second part of my bold bloods, the brave gamesters ; who assure you by me, that they perceive no such wonder in all is done here, but that they dare adventure another trial. They look for some sheepish devices here in Arcadia, not these, and therefore a hall ! a hall ! they demand.

Shep. Nay, then they are past pity, let them come, and not expect the anger of a deity to pursue them, but meet them. They have their punishment with their fact : they shall be sheep.

Fen. O spare me, by the law of nations, I am but their ambassador.

Shep. You speak in time, sir.

The THEBANS *enter for the* 2 ANTIMASQUE, *which danced,*

Shep. Now let them return with their solid heads, and carry their stupidity into Bœotia, whence they brought it, with an emblem of themselves, and their country. This is too pure an air for so gross brains.

                                  [They retire.

To the Nymphs.
End you the rites, and so be eas'd
Of these, and then great Pan is pleas'd.

HYMN IV.

Great Pan, the father of our peace and pleasure,
    Who giv'st us all this leisure,
Hear what thy hallow'd troop of herdsmen pray
    For this their holyday,
And how their vows to thee they in Lycæum pay.

Cho. So may our ewes receive the mounting rams,
And we bring thee the earliest of our lambs :
So may the first of all our fells be thine,
And both the beestning of our goats and kine ;
    As thou our folds dost still secure,
    And keep'st our fountains sweet and pure ;
Driv'st hence the wolf, the tod,[5] the brock,
Or other vermin from the flock.
That we, preserv'd by thee, and thou observ'd by us,
May both live safe in shade of thy lov'd Mænalus.

Shep. Now each return unto his charge,
        And though to-day you've liv'd at large,

        [5] *The* tod,] i. e. the fox. WHAL.

And well your flocks have fed their fill,
Yet do not trust your hirelings still.
See yond' they go, and timely do
The office you have put them to;
But if you often give this leave,
Your sheep and you they will deceive.

THUS IT ENDED.

THE MASQUE OF OWLS,
AT KENELWORTH.

PRESENTED BY THE GHOST OF CAPTAIN COX,
MOUNTED ON IIIS HOBBY-HORSE, 1626.

THE MASQUE OF OWLS, &c.] From the second folio. This trifle is not a *Masque*, nor could it have been so termed by the author: it is, in fact, a mere monologue, a *Lecture on Heads;* which, such as it is, probably gave the first hint to G. A. Stevens, for his amusing exhibition, of that name.

Of captain Cox I know no more than Jonson tells. Queen Elizabeth had been entertained at Kenelworth by the "great earl of Leicester," in 1575. To make her time pass as agreeably as possible, the bears were brought in, and baited with great applause! There was also a burlesque representation of a battle, from some old romance, in which captain Cox, who appears to have been some well-known humourist, valiantly bestirred himself. A description of this part of the Entertainment was written and published at the time, in a " Letter from a freend Officer attendant in the court, unto his freend a citizen and merchaunt of London." To this letter, which is written in a most uncouth style by a pedantic coxcomb of the name of Laneham, under an affectation of humour, Jonson perpetually alludes.

THE MASQUE OF OWLS.

Enter captain Cox, *on his Hobby-horse.*[1]

OOM! room! for my horse will wince,
    If he come within so many yards of a
        prince;
    And though he have not on his wings,
    He will do strange things.
He is the Pegasus that uses
To wait on Warwick Muses;
And on gaudy-days he paces
Before the Coventry Graces;
For to tell you true, and in rhyme,
He was foal'd in queen Elizabeth's time,
When the great earl of Lester
In this castle did feast her.
  Now, I am not so stupid
To think, you think me a Cupid,
Or a Mercury that sit him;
Though these cocks here would fit him:

---

[1] The captain enters on, or rather in, the paste-board hobby-horse used by the morris-dancers of the county, whom Jonson calls the Warwickshire Muses, and capers round the circle to make room, according to the usual practice. This little *jeu-d'esprit* formed perhaps an episode in some amusement of a more extensive nature, for it could scarcely occupy ten minutes. It is not easy to say before whom it was played. The first couplet speaks of the Prince, and, from a subsequent passage, it would seem to be the prince of Wales: but there was none at this period: add too, that the earl of Leicester (if he was the possessor of Kenelworth castle) died in 1626; so that the date is probably too late, by a year.

But a spirit very civil,
Neither poet's god, nor devil,
An old Kenelworth fox,
The ghost of captain Cox,
For which I am the bolder,
To wear a cock on each shoulder.
   This captain Cox, by St. Mary,
Was at Bullen with king Ha-ry;
And (if some do not vary)
Had a goodly library,[2]

---

[2] His library is given at great length, by the author of the " Letter." It is curious and amusing. "And fyrst Captain Cox, an od man I promiz yoo: by profession a mason, and that right skilfull; very cunning in fens, (fencing) and hardy as Gavin; for his tonsword hangs at hiz tablz eend; great oversight hath he in matters of storie: For az for *King Arthurz* book, *Huan of Burdiaus*, the foour sons of *Aymon*, *Bevys of Hampton*, *The Squyre* of lo degree, *The Knight of Courtesy*, and *the Lady Faguell*, *Frederik of Gene*, *Syr Eglamoour*, *Syr Tryamoour*, *Syr Lamwell*, *Syr Isenbras*, *Syr Gawyn*, *Olyver of the Castle*, *Lucres and Curialus*, *Virgil's Life*, *the Castle of Ladiez*, *the Wido Edyth*, *the King and the Tanner*, *Frier Rous*, *Howleglas*, *Gargantua*, *Robin Hood*, *Adam Bel*, *Clim of the Clough*, and *William of Cloudsley*, *the Churl and the Burd*, the *Seven Wise Masters*, the *Wife* lapt in a *Morels skin*, the *Sak full of Nuez*, the *Seargeaunt* that became a *Fryar*, *Skogan*, *Collyn Clout*, *the Fryar and the Boy*, *Elynor Rumming*, and the *Nutbrooun Maid*, with many moe than I rehearz here: I beleeve hee have them all at hiz fingers endz.—

"Then in Philosophy, both morale and naturale, I think he be az naturally overseen: beside *Poetrie* and *Astronomie*, and oother hid *Sciencez*, as I may gesse by the omberzt of his books: whereof part, az I remember, The *Shepherdz Kalender*, *The Ship of Foalz*, Danielz Dreamz, the *Booke of Fortune*, *Stans puer ad Mensam*, The hy *wey* to the Spitl-house, *Julian of Brainford's Testament*, *The Castle of Love*, the *Booget of Demaunds*, the *Hundred merry Talez*, the *Booke of Riddels*, the *Seaven Sororz of Wemen*, the *Prooud Wives Pater-Noster*, the *Chapman* of a *Peniworth* of *Wit:* Beside his Auncient Playz, *Yooth* and *Charitee*, *Hikskorner*, *Nugizee*, *Impacient Poverty*, and herewith *Doctor Boordz Breviary* of *Health*. What shoold I rehearz heer, what a Bunch of Ballets and Songs, all auncient; az *Broom broom on Hil*, *So wo is me begon*, *truly lo*, *Over a Whinny Meg*, *Hey ding a ding*, *Bony lass upon a green*, *My bony on gave me a bek*, *By a*

By which he was discerned
To be one of the learned,
To entertain the queen here,
When last she was seen here.
And for the town of Coventry
To act to her sovereignty.
But so his lot fell out,
That serving then a-foot,
And being a little man ;
When the skirmish began
'Twixt the Saxon and the Dane,
(From thence the story was ta'en)
He was not so well seen
As he would have been o' the queen.
Though his sword were twice so long
As any man's else in the throng ;
And for his sake, the play
Was call'd for the second day.
But he made a vow
(And he performs it now)
That were he alive or dead,

bank as I lay: and a hundred more he hath fair wrapt up in parch-
ment, and bound with a whip-cord.   And as for Almanaks of An-
tiquitee (a point for *Ephemeridees*), I ween he can sheaw from *Jasper
Laet* of *Antwerp* unto *Nostradam* of *Frauns*, and thens untoo oour
John Securiz of *Salsbury*.   To stay ye no longer heer in, I dare say
he hath az fair a Library for theez sciencez, and as many goodly
monuments both in prose and poetry, and at afternoonz can talk az
much without book az ony inholder betwixt *Brainford* and Bagshot,
what degree soever he be."———

The letter-writer evidently meant to raise a smile at the Captain's
expense ; but there is no occasion for it.   The list shews him to
have been a diligent and successful collector of the domestic literature of his country, and so far he is entitled to praise.   Some of the
fugitive pieces here mentioned are now lost ; one of them however,
the *Hundred Merry Tales*, which has long set the Shakspeare commentators by the ears, has partly been recovered within these few
days, pasted into the binding of an old book.   It is now in Mr.
Bindley's possession, and proves to be a collection of jests, of no
great novelty or value.

Hereafter it should never be said
But captain Cox would serve on horse
For better or for worse,
If any prince came hither,
And his horse should have a feather ;
Nay such a prince it might be
Perhaps he should have three.
    Now, sir, in your approach,
The rumbling of your coach
Awaking me, his ghost,
I come to play your host ;
And feast your eyes and ears,
Neither with dogs nor bears,[3]
Though that have been a fit
Of our main-shire wit,
In times heretofore,
But now, we have got a little more.
    These then that we present
With a most loyal intent,
And, as the author saith,
No ill meaning to the catholic faith,
Are not so much beasts, as fowls,
But a very nest of owls,
And natural, so thrive I,
I found them in the ivy,
A thing, that though I blunder'd at,
It may in time be wonder'd at,
If the place but affords
Any store of lucky birds,
As I make them to flush,
Each owl out of his bush.
    Now, these owls, some say, were men,
And they may be so again,

---

[3] *Neither with* dogs *nor* bears.] This alludes to the following
passage in the *Letter*. "On the syxth day of her Majestyes cum-
ming, a great sort of bandogs whear thear tyed in the utter cooart,
and *thyrteen bears* in the inner," &c. See Massinger, vol. i. p. 44.

If once they endure the light
Of your highness' sight :
For bankrupts, we have known
Rise to more than their own,
With a little-little savour
Of the prince's favour ;
But as you like their tricks,
I'll spring them, they are but six.

HEY, OWL FIRST ! [4]

This bird is London-bred,
As you may see by his horn'd head.
And had like to have been ta'en
At his shop in Ivy-lane,
Where he sold by the penny
Tobacco as good as any ;
But whether it did provoke
His conscience, he sold smoke ;
Or some other toy he took,
Towards his calling to look :
He fled by moon-shine thence ;
And broke for sixteen pence.

HEY, OWL SECOND !

This too, the more is the pity,
Is of the breed of the same city ;
A true owl of London
That gives out he is undone,
Being a cheesemonger,
By trusting two of the younger
Captains, for the hunger
Of their half-starv'd number ;

[4] *Hey, Owl first !*] Here the captain probably produced, from beneath the foot-cloth of the hobby-horse, a block ridiculously dressed or painted to correspond with the description.

Whom since they have shipt away :
And left him *God to pay*,[5]
With those ears for a badge
Of their dealing with his Madge.

HEY, OWL THIRD !

A pure native bird [6]
This, and though his hue
Be not Coventry blue,
Yet is he undone
By the thread he has spun ;
For since the wise town
Has let the sports down
Of may-games and morris,
For which he right sorry is ;
Where their maids and their makes,[7]
At dancings and wakes,
Had their napkins and posies,
And the wipers for their noses,
And their smocks all-be-wrought
With his thread which they bought :

---

[5] God to pay.]   A cant term for a hopeless debt, nothing.   See *Epig.* xii.

[6] *A* pure native *bird*,] i. e. a puritan of Coventry, whose zeal in putting down may-poles and hobby-horses had injured the manufactory of blue thread, (the chief staple of the town,) of which a great consumption was made in ornamenting napkins, scarfs, &c. "I have heard," an old writer, W. Stafford, says, "that the chief trade of Coventry, was heretofore in making *blew thred*, and then the towne was riche ever upon that trade in maner onely, and now our thredde comes all from beyond sea: wherefore that trade of Coventry is decaied, and thereby the towne likewise." This appeared long before *Owl the third* was hatched; so that the *wise town* must have suffered from more causes than the loss of its rural sports.

[7] *Where their maids and their* makes,] i. e. *mates*.   So Chaucer :

"God shelde soche a lordes wife to take
Another man to husbonde, or to *make*."   WHAL.

It now lies on his hands,
And having neither wit nor lands,
Is ready to hang or choke him,
In a skein of that that broke him.

HEY, OWL FOURTH !

Was once a bankrupt of worth ;
And having run a shifting-race,
At last by money, and grace,
Got him a serjeant's place,
And to be one of chace.
A full fortnight was not spent,
But out comes the parliament,
Takes away the use of his mace,
And left him in a worse than his first case.

HEY, OWL FIFTH !

But here was a defeat,
Never any so great,
Of a Don, a Spanish reader,
Who had thought to have been the leader,
Had the match gone on,
Of our ladies one by one,
And triumph'd our whole nation,
In his rodomant fashion :
But now since the breach,
He has not a scholar to teach.

HEY, OWL SIXTH !

The bird bringer-up is a knight,
But a passionate wight,
Who, since the act against swearing,
(The tale's worth your hearing)
In this short time's growth
Hath at twelve-pence an oath,
For that, I take it, is the rate,
Sworn himself out of his estate.

THE THIRD OWL VARIED.

A crop-ear'd scrivener, this,
Who when he heard but the whis-
per of monies to come down,
Fright got him out of town
With all the bills and bands
Of other men's in his hands,
And cried, who will, drive the trade,
Since such a law they had made :
It was not he that broke,
Two i' the hundred spoke.
Nor car'd he for the curse,
He could not hear much worse,
He had his ears in his purse.

THE FORTUNATE ISLES,

AND THEIR UNION.

CELEBRATED IN A MASQUE DESIGNED FOR THE
COURT, ON THE TWELFTH-NIGHT, 1626.

Hic choreæ, cantusque vigent.

THE FORTUNATE ISLES.] From the second folio. Charles (now king) seems to have been so much pleased with the main Masque of *Neptune's Triumph*, presented two years before, as to call for it again, with another introduction, by way of Antimasque. This was the poet's first exhibition before his new sovereign, and it did not discredit him; for there is a considerable degree of humour, as well as satire, in the part of Johphiel; the latter of which must have been fully felt and enjoyed at a period when men were hourly bury-ing white wands in the ground, to catch fairies; and muttering prayers in woods, to render sylphs and salamanders visible!

Evil days were now come upon Jonson: some months before this Masque was written, he had been struck with the palsy, from which he never recovered: his old complaint the dropsy, too, in-creased about the same time; and, as he says himself, *fixed his muse to the bed and boards, as she had never been.* Though no symp-toms of decay be apparent in the present Entertainment, yet it is necessary to mention these circumstances; as the poet's enemies, while they watch for the opportunity of triumphing in the abate-ment of his powers, anxiously keep his maladies out of sight.

THE FORTUNATE ISLES.

His Majesty being set,

Enter, running, JOHPHIEL, *an airy spirit, and (according to the Magi) the intelligence of Jupiter's sphere :*[1] *attired in light silks of several colours, with wings of the same, a bright yellow hair, a chaplet of flowers, blue silk stockings, and pumps, and gloves, with a silver fan in his hand.*

Johphiel.

IKE a lightning from the sky,
    Or an arrow shot by Love,
Or a bird of his let fly ;
    Be't a sparrow, or a dove :
With that winged haste, come I,
    Loosed from the sphere of Jove,
        To wish good-night
        To your delight.

[1] *Johphiel, an airy spirit, and (according to the Magi) the Intelligence of Jupiter's sphere.*] Jonson is so accurate in all his positions (however unimportant they may appear in themselves) that it can scarcely be doubted that he had authority for the rank of Johphiel. I will not question the assertion of the " Magi ;" but Agrippa (also a wise-man) affirms that " Johphiel is one of the presiding angels in the Intelligible World, and that he reigns in the sphere of the zodiac." This seems a pretty wide command ! The name of the spirit of the "sphere of Jupiter, is Zadkiel." *Occ. Phil.* b. 2. c. xiii.

Nothing in Jonson is done at random. Whatever was the subject of his verse, he came to it with a mind fully furnished, and

Enter Merefool, *a melancholic student, in bare and worn clothes, shrowded under an obscure cloke, and the eves of an old hat.*

Mere. [*fetching a deep sigh.*] Oh, ho!

Johp. In Saturn's name, the father of my lord,
What over-charged piece of melancholy
Is this, breaks in between my wishes thus,
With bombing sighs?

Mere. No! no intelligence!
Not yet! and all my vows now nine days old!
Blindness of fate! puppies had seen by this time;
But I see nothing that I should, or would see!
What mean the brethren of the Rosy-cross,
So to desert their votary?

Johp. O! 'tis one
Hath vow'd himself unto that airy order,
And now is gaping for the fly they promised him.
I'll mix a little with him for my sport.   [*Steps aside.*

Mere. Have I both in my lodging and my diet,
My clothes, and every other solemn charge,
Observed them, made the naked boards my bed,

what appears, at first sight, the mere sportiveness of invention, will be found, upon falling into the track of his studies, (which is seldom my lot,) to be the result of laborious and excursive reading. In the *Alchemist*, for example, the directions given to Abel, for insuring the prosperity of his shop,

> "—— On the east side of your shop, aloft,
> Write Mathlai, Tarmiel, and Baraborat;
> Upon the north part, Rael, Velel, Thiel,"

Vol. iv. p. 39.

have probably been regarded as a mere play of fancy; but they appear to be derived from the very depths of magical science. "*Angeli secundi cœli regnantes die Mercurii, quos advocari oportet a quatuor mundi partibus:*

> *Ad Orientem:*
> *Mathlai, Tarmiel, Baraborat.*
> *Ad Septentrionem:*
> *Thiel, Rael, Velel, &c.*

Elem. Magica Petri de Albana.

A faggot for my pillow, hungred sore !
    Johp. And thirsted after them !
    Mere. To look gaunt, and lean !
    Johp. Which will not be.
    Mere. Who's that ?—Yes, and outwatch'd,
Yea, and outwalked any ghost alive
In solitary circle, worn my boots,
Knees, arms, and elbows out !
    Johp. Ran on the score !
    Mere. That have I—who suggests that ?—and for
      more
Than I will speak of, to abate this flesh,
And have not gain'd the sight——
    Johp. Nay, scarce the sense.
    Mere. Voice, thou art right—of any thing but a cold
Wind in my stomach.
    Johp. And a kind of whimsie——
    Mere. Here in my head, that puts me to the
      staggers,
Whether there be that brotherhood, or no.
    Johp. Believe, frail man, they be ; and thou shalt
      see.
    Mere. What shall I see ?
    Johp. Me.
    Mere. Thee ! where ?
    Johp. [*comes forward.*] Here, if you
Be master Merefool.
    Mere. Sir, our name is Merryfool,
But by contraction Merefool.
    Johp. Then are you
The wight I seek ; and, sir, my name is Johphiel,
Intelligence to the sphere of Jupiter,
An airy jocular spirit, employ'd to you
From father Outis.
    Mere. Outis ! who is he ?[2]

  [2] Outis ! *who is he ?*] *Outis* is Greek for no-body ; here is an
allusion to the trick Ulysses put on Polyphemus when he had shut

8   F

Johp. Know ye not Outis? then you know no-
   body :—
The good old hermit, that was said to dwell
Here in the forest without trees, that built
The castle in the air, where all the brethren
Rhodostaurotic live. It flies with wings,
And runs on wheels; where Julian de Campis[3]
Holds out the brandish'd blade.

him in his cave, and asked him what his name was, which Ulysses
said was *Outis.* WHAL.

[3] —————— *Where Julian de Campis*
  Holds out the brandish'd blade.] For my knowledge of this
person, I am indebted to the kindness and activity of my friend,
F. Cohen, who rummaged him out from a world of forgotten lumber
in the old German language.

 " *Send Brieff oder Bericht an alle welche von der Newen Brü-
derschafft des Ordens vom Rozen Creutz gennant, etwas gesehen oder
von andern per modum discursus der sachen beschaffenheit vernommen.*

 " *Es sind viel die im schranken lauffen, etliche aber gewinnen nur
das kleinot, darumb ermahne ich,*
     Julianus de Campis,
      OGDCRFE,
*dass diejenigen welche von einer glücklichen direction und gewünschtes
impression guberniret worden, sich nicht durch ihrer selbst eigenen
diffidens oder uppigheit unartiges judiciren wendig lassen.*

 " *Milita bonam militiam, servans fidem, et accipies coronam gloriæ.*
 " *Gedruckt im Jahr* 1615."

 "A Letter Missive, or account addressed to all those who have
[as yet] read any thing concerning the New Fraternity, entitled the
order of the Rosy Cross, or who have become acquainted with the
matter by the verbal relations of others.

 " Many enter the cabinet, but few acquire the treasure.   Therefore I,
     Julianus de Campis,
      OGDCRFE,
warn all who wish to be guided by a happy direction and desirable
impression, not to suffer themselves to be misled by their own mis-
trust, or by the loose judgment of forward people.

 " Printed in the year 1615."

 It is probable that this Julian de Campis (an assumed name)
was among the earliest writers on this fantastic subject, and that
Jonson derived some information from his Letter Missive. Mr.

Mere. Is't possible
They think on me ?
Johp. Rise, be not lost in wonder,
But hear me : and be faithful. All the brethren
Have heard your vows, salute you, and expect you,
By me, this next return. But the good father
Has been content to die for you.
Mere. For me ?
Johp. For you. Last New-year's-day, which some
   give out,
Because it was his birth-day, and began
The year of jubilee, he would rest upon it,
Being his hundred five and twentieth year :
But the truth is, having observ'd your genesis,
He would not live, because he might leave all
He had to you.
Mere. What had he ?

Cohen, however, assures me that there is nothing in it respecting
" the brandished blade."

It is somewhat singular that the origin of the Rosicrucians should
not have been discovered. Neither Paracelsus nor Agrippa, (daring
dreamers as both were,) has any approaches to this singular sect,
which, as far as can be discovered, did not spring to light till the
end of the sixteenth century. It seems not unreasonable to conjecture that the folly had birth in one of those hot-beds, so pro-
lific of

   "———— all monstrous, all prodigious things,
   Gorgons and hydras, and chimæras dire,"

a German lodge of Free Masons : thus much, at least, is certain,
that they pretend to the *brandished blade*, which is even now one of
their hieroglyphics.

A curious disquisition, I will not say a profitable one, might be
written on this subject, on which nothing satisfactory has hitherto
appeared. The Count de Gabalis wisely broke off just in time to
hide his utter ignorance of it ; indeed, he only refines upon the rude
visions of Paracelsus ; and Gabriel Naudé, who wrote expressly on
the Rosicrucians, is loose and declamatory, and has little to the
purpose. He notices, however, a work entitled " *Speculum Sophis-
ticum Rhodostauroticum*," which our poet had perhaps seen.—But I
forget—*satque superque.*

Johp. Had! an office,
Two, three, or four.
   Mere. Where?
   Johp. In the upper region;
And that you'll find.   The farm of the great customs,
Through all the ports of the air's intelligences;
Then constable of the castle Rosy-cross:
Which you must be, and keeper of the keys
Of the whole Kabal, with the seals; you shall be
Principal secretary to the stars;
Know all the signatures and combinations,
The divine rods, and consecrated roots:
What not? Would you turn trees up like the wind,
To shew your strength? march over heads of armies,
Or points of pikes, to shew your lightness? force
All doors of arts, with the petard of your wit?
Read at one view all books? speak all the languages
Of several creatures? master all the learnings
Were, are, or shall be? or, to shew your wealth,
Open all treasures, hid by nature, from
The rock of diamond, to the mine of sea-coal?
Sir, you shall do it.
   Mere. But how?
   Johp. Why, by his skill,
Of which he has left you the inheritance,
Here in a pot; this little gallipot
Of tincture, high rose tincture.   There's your order,
You will have your collar sent you, ere't be long.
   Mere. I look'd, sir, for a halter, I was desperate.
   Johp. Reach forth your hand.
   Mere. O, sir, a broken sleeve
Keeps the arm back, as 'tis in the proverb.
   Johp. Nay,
For that I do commend you; you must be poor
With all your wealth, and learning.   When you have
      made
Your glasses, gardens in the depth of winter,

Where you will walk invisible to mankind,
Talk with all birds and beasts in their own language,
When you have penetrated hills like air,
Dived to the bottom of the sea like lead,
And risse again like cork, walk'd in the fire,
An 'twere a salamander, pass'd through all
The winding orbs, like an Intelligence,
Up to the empyreum, when you have made
The world your gallery, can dispatch a business
In some three minutes, with the antipodes,
And in five more, negotiate the globe over;
You must be poor still.

 Mere. By my place I know it.

 Johp. Where would you wish to be now, or what
   to see,
Without the Fortunate Purse to bear your charges,
Or Wishing Hat? I will but touch your temples,
The corners of your eyes, and tinct the tip,
The very tip o' your nose, with this collyrium,
And you shall see in the air all the ideas,
Spirits, and atoms, flies, that buz about
This way, and that way, and are rather admirable,
Than any way intelligible.

 Mere. O, come, tinct me,
Tinct me; I long; save this great belly, I long!
But shall I only see?

 Johp. See, and command
As they were all your varlets, or your footboys:
But first you must declare, (your Greatness must,
For that is now your style,) what you would see,
Or whom.

 Mere. Is that my style? my Greatness, then,
Would see king Zoroastres.

 Johp. Why, you shall;
Or any one beside. Think whom you please;
Your thousand, your ten thousand, to a million:
All's one to me, if you could name a myriad.

Mere. I have named him.

Johp. You've reason.

Mere. Ay, I have reason;
Because he's said to be the father of conjurors,
And a cunning man in the stars.

Johp. Ay, that's it troubles us
A little for the present : for, at this time,
He is confuting a French almanack,
But he will straight have done, have you but patience;
Or think but any other in mean time,
Any hard name.

Mere. Then Hermes Trismegistus.

Johp. O, ὁ τρισμέγιστος ! why, you shall see him,
A fine hard name.   Or him, or whom you will,
As I said to you afore.   Or what do you think
Of Howleglass, instead of him ?

Mere. No, him
I have a mind to.

Johp. O, but Ulen-spiegle,
Were such a name !⁴—but you shall have your longing.
What luck is this, he should be busy too !
He is weighing water but to fill three hour-glasses,
And mark the day in penn'orths like a cheese,
And he has done. 'Tis strange you should name him
Of all the rest! there being Jamblicus,
Or Porphyry, or Proclus, any name
That is not busy.

Mere. Let me see Pythagoras.

Johp. Good.

Mere. Or Plato.

Johp. Plato is framing some ideas,
Are now bespoken, at a groat a dozen,
Three gross at least : and for Pythagoras,
He has rashly run himself on an employment,
Of keeping asses from a field of beans ;

---

⁴ ——— *O, but* Ulen-spiegle
Were such a name.]   See vol. iv. p. 58.

And cannot be stav'd off.
 Mere. Then, Archimedes.
 Johp. Yes, Archimedes!
 Mere. Ay, or Æsop.
 Johp. Nay,
Hold your first man, a good man, Archimedes,
And worthy to be seen; but he is now
Inventing a rare mouse-trap with owl's wings
And a cat's-foot, to catch the mice alone :
And Æsop, he is filing a fox-tongue,
For a new fable he has made of court :
But you shall see them all, stay but your time,
And ask in season; things ask'd out of season
A man denies himself. At such a time
As Christmas, when disguising is on foot,
To ask of the inventions, and the men,
The wits and the ingines that move those orbs !—
Methinks you should inquire now after Skelton,
Or master Skogan.
 Mere. Skogan! what was he?
 Johp. O, a fine gentleman, and master of arts,
Of Henry the fourth's time, that made disguises
For the king's sons, and writ in ballad-royal
Daintily well.
 Mere. But wrote he like a gentleman?
 Johp. In rhyme, fine tinkling rhyme, and flowing
   verse,
With now and then some sense! and he was paid for't,
Regarded and rewarded ; which few poets
Are now-a-days.
 Mere. And why?
 Johp. 'Cause every dabbler
In rhyme is thought the same :—but you shall see him.
Hold up your nose. [*Anoints his eyes and temples.*
 Mere. I had rather see a Brachman,
Or a Gymnosophist yet.
 Johp. You shall see him, sir,

Is worth them both : and with him domine Skelton,
The worshipful poet laureat to king Harry,
And *Tityre tu* of those times. Advance, quick Skogan,
And quicker Skelton, shew your crafty heads,
Before this heir of arts, this lord of learning,
This master of all knowledge in reversion !

Enter SKOGAN *and* SKELTON, *in like habits as
they lived.*[5]

Skog. Seemeth we are call'd of a moral intent,
If the words that are spoken as well now be meant.
Johp. That, master Skogan, I dare you ensure.
Skog. Then, son, our acquaintance is like to endure.
Mere. A pretty game ! like Crambo ; master
      Skogan,
Give me thy hand : thou art very lean, methinks,

---

[5] Enter Skogan and Skelton in *like habits as they lived,*] i. e. in
the dress they wore while they were alive. This puts an end to the
grave difficulties and graver doubts of M. Mason, Steevens, and
Malone, as to the exclamation of Hamlet,

" My father, in like habit as he lived,"

meaning, in the clothes which he usually wore. The idea of Steevens, that a ghost who once puts on armour, can never exchange
it afterwards for any thing more light and comfortable, is very
good.

In the lines which follow, Jonson imitates the language of Skogan and Skelton. The former (Henry Skogan) lived in the time of
Henry IV., and, as Stowe says, sent a *ballad* to the young prince
(Shakspeare's Hal) and his brothers, "while they were at supper in
the Vintry, amongst the merchants." This is the *ballad-royal* of
which our poet speaks : it was not very well timed, it must be
allowed ; and if we may judge from the opening stanza, moral as it
is, it was not much better tuned :

" My noble sonnes and eke my Lords deare,
      I your father called unworthily,
Send unto you this ballad following here,
      Written with mine owne hand full rudely."

I have no knowledge of his " disguises." If *moral* Skogan (for
this was his usual appellation) wrote any things of this nature, they
were probably religious pieces, Mysteries and Moralities.

Is't living by thy wits?
  Skog. If it had been that,
My worshipful son, thou hadst ne'er been so fat.
  Johp. He tells you true, sir.   Here's a gentleman,
My pair of crafty clerks, of that high caract,
As hardly hath the age produced his like.
Who not content with the wit of his own times,
Is curious to know yours, and what hath been.
    Mere.   Or is, or shall be.
    Johp.   Note his latitude.
    Skel.   *O, vir amplissimus,*
           Ut scholis dicimus,
           Et gentilissimus!
  Johp. The question-*issimus*
Is, should he ask a sight now, for his life;
I mean a person, he would have restored
To memory of these times, for a play-fellow,
Whether you would present him with an Hermes,
Or with an Howleglass?
    Skel.   An Howleglass
           To come to pass
           On his father's ass;
           There never was,
           By day, nor night,
           A finer sight
           With feathers upright
           In his horned cap,
           And crooked shape,
           Much like an ape,
           With owl on fist,
           And glass at his wrist.
  Skog. Except the four knaves entertain'd for the
      guards
Of the kings and the queens that triumph in the
      cards.
  Johp. Ay, that were a sight and a half, I confess,
To see 'em come skipping in, all at a mess!

Skel.   *With Elinor Rumming,*
          To make up the mumming; [6]
          That comely Gill,
          That dwelt on a hill,
          But she is not grill:—
          Her face all bowsy,
          Droopy and drowsy,
          Scurvy, and lousy,
          Comely crinkled,
          Wondrously wrinkled,
          Like a roast pig's ear
          Bristled with hair.

Skog. Or, what do you say to Ruffian Fitz-Ale?
Johp. An excellent sight, if he be not too stale.
But then we can mix him with modern Vapors,
The child of tobacco, his pipes, and his papers.

Mere. You talk'd of Elinor Rumming, I had rather
See Ellen of Troy.

[6] *With* Elinor Rumming,
    To make up the mumming, &c.] These are Skelton's own verses
in his ballad on *Eleanor Rumming*, the old ale-wife. WHAL.

Jonson was evidently fond of Skelton, and frequently imitates his
short titupping style, which is not his best. I know Skelton only
by the modern edition of his works, dated 1736. But from this
stupid publication I can easily discover that he was no ordinary
man. Why Warton and the writers of his school rail at him so
vehemently, I know not; he was perhaps the best scholar of his
day, and displays, on many occasions, strong powers of description,
and a vein of poetry that shines through all the rubbish which
ignorance has spread over it. He flew at high game, and therefore
occasionally called in the aid of vulgar ribaldry to mask the direct
attack of his satire. This was seen centuries ago, and yet we are
now instituting a process against him for rudeness and indelicacy!
" By what means," says Grange, (who wrote about the beginning
of Elizabeth's reign,) " could Skelton, that laureat poet, have uttered
his mind so well at large, as thorowe his cloke of mery conceytes, as
in his *Speake Parrot, Ware the Hawke, The Tunning of Elinor
Rumming, Why come ye not to the Court,* &c. Yet what greater
sense or better matter can be, than is in this ragged rhyme con-
tayned? Or who would have hearde his fault so playnely told him,
if not in such gibyng sorte?" *The Golden Aphroditis.*

Johp. Her you shall see :
But credit me,
That Mary Ambree
(Who march'd so free
To the siege of Gaunt,
And death could not daunt,
As the ballad doth vaunt,[7])
Were a braver wight,
And a better sight.
Skel. Or Westminster Meg,[8]
With her long leg,
As long as a crane ;
And feet like a plane :
With a pair of heels,
As broad as two wheels ;
To drive down the dew,
As she goes to the stew :
And turns home merry,
By Lambeth ferry.
Or you may have come
In, Thomas Thumb,
In a pudding fat
With doctor Rat.
Johp. Ay, that ! that ! that !
We'll have 'em all,
To fill the hall.

---

[7] *As the* ballad *doth vaunt.*] The ballad, of which the first stanza follows, is re-published in Percy's *Reliques*, vol. ii. p. 218.

"When captains courageous, whom death colde not daunte,
Did march to the siege of the cittye of Gaunte,
They mustred their souldiers by two and by three,
And foremost in battle was *Mary Ambree.*"

[8] *Or Westminster Meg.*] There is a penny story-book of this tremendous virago, who performed many wonderful exploits about the time that Jack the Giant-killer flourished. She was buried, as all the world knows, in the cloisters of Westminster abbey, where a huge stone is still pointed out to the Whitsuntide visitors as her grave-stone.

The ANTIMASQUE *follows,*

Consisting of these twelve persons, HOWLEGLASS, *the four* Knaves, *two* Ruffians, (FITZ-ALE *and* VAPOR,) ELINOR RUMMING, MARY AMBREE, LONG MEG *of Westminster,* TOM THUMB, *and* doctor RAT.

They DANCE, *and withdraw.*

Mere. What, are they vanish'd ! where is skipping
  Skelton ?
Or moral Skogan ? I do like their shew,
And would have thank'd them, being the first grace
The company of the Rosy-cross hath done me.
  Johp. The company o' the Rosy-cross, you
  widgeon !
The company of [the] players.[9] Go, you are,
And will be still your self, a Merefool, in :
And take your pot of honey here, and hogs-grease,
See who has gull'd you, and make one.
          [*Exit* MEREFOOL.
Great king,
Your pardon, if desire to please have trespass'd.
This fool should have been sent to Anticyra,
The isle of Ellebore, there to have purg'd,
Not hoped a happy seat within your waters.—
Hear now the message of the Fates, and Jove,
On whom these Fates depend, to you, as Neptune
The great commander of the seas and isles.
That point of revolution being come,
When all the Fortunate Islands should be join'd,
MACARIA one, and thought a principal,
That hitherto hath floated, as uncertain
Where she should fix her blessings, is to-night

 [9] *The company of [the] players.*] Professional actors, as has been already observed, were sometimes employed in the Antimasques, more especially where they were of a very grotesque and ridiculous nature.

Instructed to adhere to your Britannia :
That where the happy spirits live, hereafter
Might be no question made, by the most curious,
Since the MACARII come to do you homage,
And join their cradle to your continent.

Here the·scene opens, and the Masquers *are discovered
sitting in their several sieges. The air opens above,
and* APOLLO, *with* HARMONY, *and the* Spirits *of*
Music *sing, the while the Island moves forward,*
PROTEUS *sitting below, and hearkening.*

SONG.

*Look forth, the shepherd of the seas,
And of the ports that keep the keys,
    And to your Neptune tell,
Macaria, prince of all the isles,
Wherein there nothing grows but smiles,
    Doth here put in, to dwell.*

*The winds are sweet and gently blow,
But Zephyrus, no breath they know,
    The father of the flowers :
By him the virgin violets live,
And every plant doth odours give,
    As new, as are the hours.*

Cho. *Then, think it not a common cause,
    That to it so much wonder draws,
        And all the heavens consent,
    With harmony to tune their notes,
    In answer to the public votes,
        That for it up were sent.*

By this time, the island having joined itself to the
    shore, PROTEUS, PORTUNUS, and SARON come forth,
    and go up singing to the state, while the Masquers
    take time to rank themselves.

Song.

Pro. *Ay, now, the heights of Neptune's honours shine,*
  And all the glories of his greater style
  Are read, reflected in this happiest isle.
Por. *How both the air, the soil, the seat combine*
  To speak it blessed !
Sar.   *These are the true groves*
  Where joys are born.
Pro.   *Where longings,*
Por.   *And where loves !*
Sar. *That live !*
Pro.   *That last !*
Por.   *No intermitted wind*
  Blows here, but what leaves flowers or fruit behind.
Cho.*'Tis odour all that comes !*
  And every tree doth give his gums.
Pro. *There is no sickness, nor no old age known*
  To man, nor any grief that he dares own.
  There is no hunger here, nor envy of state,
  Nor least ambition in the magistrate.
  But all are even hearted, open, free,
  And what one is, another strives to be.
Por. *Here, all the day, they feast, they sport, and spring,*
  Now dance the Graces' hay ; now Venus ring :
  To which the old musicians play and sing.
Sar. *There is Arion, tuning his bold harp,*
                  From flat to sharp,
Por. *And light Anacreon,*
 · *He still is one !*
Pro.   *Stesichorus there, too,*
  That Linus and old Orpheus doth outdo
  To wonder.
Sar.   *And Amphion ! he is there.*
Por.   *Nor is Apollo dainty to appear*
  In such a quire, although the trees be thick,
Pro. *He will look in, and see the airs be quick,*

And that the times be true.

Por.   *Then, chanting,*

Pro.   *Then,*

Up with their notes, they raise the prince of men,

Sar. *And sing the present prophesy that goes,*
Of joining the bright Lily and the Rose.

Cho. *See.! all the flowers,*

Pro   *That spring the banks along,*
Do move their heads unto that under song.

Cho. *Saron, Portunus, Proteus, help to bring*
Our primrose in, the glory of the spring ;
And tell the daffodil, against that day,
That we prepare new garlands fresh as May,
And interweave the myrtle and the bay.

This sung, the island goes back, whilst the Upper
Chorus takes it from them, and the Masquers
prepare for their figure.

Cho.   *Spring all the graces of the age,*
      And all the loves of time;
   Bring all the pleasures of the stage,
      And relishes of rhyme.
   Add all the softnesses of courts,
      The looks, the laughters, and the sports ;
   And mingle all their sweets, and salts,
      That none may say, the triumph halts.

The Masquers dance their E<small>NTRY</small>, or F<small>IRST</small>
D<small>ANCE</small>.

Which done, the first prospective, a maritime palace, or
the house of O<small>CEANUS</small> *is discovered to loud music.*

The other above is no more seen.

Johp. Behold the palace of Oceanus !
Hail, reverend structure ! boast no more to us
Thy being able all the gods to feast ;
We saw enough ; when Albion was thy guest.

Here the MEASURES.

After which, the second prospective, a sea, is shown
to the former music.

Johp. Now turn, and view the wonders of the
    deep,
Where Proteus' herds, and Neptune's orcs do keep,
Where all is plough'd, yet still the pasture's green;
New ways are found, and yet no paths are seen.

Here PROTEUS, PORTUNUS, SARON, *go up to the*
Ladies *with this* SONG.

Pro. *Come, noble nymphs, and do not hide*
        The joys for which you so provide :
Sar. *If not to mingle with the men,*
        What do you here? Go home agen.
Por.   *Your dressings do confess,*
        By what we see, so curious parts
        Of Pallas, and Arachne's arts,
            That you could mean no less.
Pro. *Why do you wear the silk-worm's toils,*
        Or glory in the shell-fish' spoils ;
        Or strive to shew the grains of ore
        That you have gather'd on the shore,
            Whereof to make a stock
        To graft the greener emerald on,
        Or any better water'd stone,
Sar.   *Or ruby of the rock.*
Pro. *Why do you smell of amber-grise,*
        Of which was formed Neptune's niece,
        The queen of love; unless you can,
        Like sea-born Venus, love a man?
Sar.   *Try, put yourselves unto't.*

Cho. *Your looks, your smiles, and thoughts that meet,*
        Ambrosian hands, and silver feet,
            Do promise you will do't.

The REVELS follow.

Which ended, the fleet is discovered, while the three cornets play.

Johp. 'Tis time, your eyes should be refresh'd at length
With something new, a part of Neptune's strength,
See yond', his fleet, ready to go or come,
Or fetch the riches of the Ocean home,
So to secure him, both in peace and wars,
Till not one ship alone, but all be stars.

Then the last

SONG.

Pro. *Although we wish the glory still might last*
Of such a night, and for the causes past:
Yet now, great lord of waters, and of isles,
Give Proteus leave to turn unto his wiles.
Por. *And whilst young Albion doth thy labours ease,*
Dispatch Portunus to the ports.
Sar. *And Saron to the seas,*
To meet old Nereus, with his fifty girls,
From aged Indus laden home with pearls,
And orient gums, to burn unto thy name.

Cho. *And may thy subjects' hearts be all on flame,*
Whilst thou dost keep the earth in firm estate,
And 'mongst the winds dost suffer no debate;
But both at sea, and land, our powers increase,
With health, and all the golden gifts of peace.

After which they danced their last DANCE.

AND THUS IT ENDED.

8   G

LOVE'S TRIUMPH THROUGH CALLIPOLIS.

Performed in a Masque at Court, 1630. By
his Majesty, with the Lords and
Gentlemen assisting.

The Inventors, Ben Jonson; Inigo Jones.

Quando magis dignos licuit spectare triumphos ?

LOVE'S TRIUMPH THROUGH CALLIPOLIS.] From the small edition in 4to. 1630, which differs in no material point from the second folio. In this, which was the Queen's Masque, the King was a performer; in that which follows, (the King's Masque,) she returned the compliment. It does not appear that either *Love's Triumph*, or *Chloridia*, which follows it, was given to the press by Jonson: the latter is not dated, but was printed for the same bookseller, Thomas Walkley, as the former.

LOVE'S TRIUMPH.

To make the Spectators understanders.

HEREAS, all Representations, especially those of this nature in court, public spectacles, either have been, or ought to be, the mirrors of man's life, whose ends, for the excellence of their exhibitors (as being the donatives of great princes to their people) ought always to carry a mixture of profit with them, no less than delight; we, the inventors, being commanded from the KING to think on something worthy of his majesty's putting in act, with a selected company of his lords and gentlemen, called to the assistance; for the honour of his court, and the dignity of that heroic love, and regal respect born by him to his unmatchable lady and spouse, the queen's majesty, after some debate of cogitation with ourselves,[1] resolved on this following argument.

First, that a person, *boni ominis*, of a good character, as Euphemus, sent down from heaven to Callipolis, which is understood the city of Beauty or Goodness, should come in; and, finding her majesty there enthroned, declare unto her, that Love, who was wont to be respected as a special deity in court,

[1] *After some debate with ourselves, &c.*] This is worth notice, as it seems to prove that up to this late period, nearly thirty years from the commencement of their connection, nothing had happened to interrupt the good understanding between Inigo Jones and Jonson.

and tutelar god of the place, had of late received an advertisement, that in the suburbs, or skirts of Callipolis, were crept in certain sectaries, or depraved lovers, who neither knew the name, or nature of love rightly, yet boasted themselves his followers, when they were fitter to be called his furies : their whole life being a continued vertigo, or rather a torture on the wheel of love, than any motion either of order or measure. When suddenly they leap forth below, a mistress leading them, and with antic gesticulation and action, after the manner of the old pantomimi, they dance over a distracted comedy of love, expressing their confused affections, in the scenical persons and habits of the four prime European nations.

> A glorious boasting lover.
> · A whining ballading lover.
> An adventurous romance lover.
>
> A phantastic umbrageous lover.
> A bribing corrupt lover.
> A froward jealous lover.
>
> A sordid illiberal lover.
> A proud scornful lover.
> An angry quarrelling lover.
>
> A melancholic despairing lover.
> An envious unquiet lover.
> A sensual brute lover.

All which, in varied intricate turns, and involved mazes, exprest, make the ANTIMASQUE : *and conclude the exit, in a circle.*

EUPHEMUS *descends singing.*

Joy, joy to mortals, the rejoicing fires
Of gladness smile in your dilated hearts !
Whilst love presents a world of chaste desires,
Which may produce a harmony of parts !

Love is the right affection of the mind,
  The noble appetite of what is best :
Desire of union with the thing design'd,
  But in fruition of it cannot rest.

The father Plenty is, the mother Want,[2]
  Plenty the beauty which it wanteth draws ;
Want yields itself ; affording what is scant :
  So both affections are the union's cause.

But rest not here.   For love hath larger scopes,
  New joys, new pleasures, of as fresh a date
As are his minutes : and in him no hopes
  Are pure, but those he can perpetuate.
                    [He goes up to the state.

To you, that are by excellence a queen !
  The top of beauty ! but of such an air,
As only by the mind's eye may be seen
  Your interwoven lines of good and fair !

Vouchsafe to grace love's triumph here to-night,
  Through all the streets of your Callipolis ;
Which by the splendor of your rays made bright,
  The seat and region of all beauty is.

Love in perfection longeth to appear,
  But prays of favour he be not call'd on,
Till all the suburbs and the skirts be clear
  Of perturbations, and th' infection gone.

Then will he flow forth, like a rich perfume
  Into your nostrils ! or some sweeter sound
Of melting music, that shall not consume
  Within the ear, but run the mazes round.

  [2] *The father Plenty is, the mother Want.*]   This allegory is a fiction of Plato, in his *Symposium.* WHAL.
  Whalley was not aware of the existence of the 4to. edition. There Jonson gives the names *Porus* and *Penia.*

Here the Chorus walk about with their censers.

Cho. *Mean time, we make lustration of the place,*
  And, with our solemn fires and waters prove
  T'have frighted hence the weak diseased race
  Of those were tortured on the wheel of love.

  The Glorious, Whining, the Adventurous fool,
  Fantastic, Bribing, and the Jealous ass.
  The Sordid, Scornful, and the Angry mule,
  The Melancholic, Dull, and Envious mass.

Grand Cho. *With all the rest, that in the sensual*
  school
  Of lust, for their degree of brute may pass;
  All which are vapour'd hence.
  No loves, but slaves to sense;
  Mere cattle, and not men.
  Sound, sound, and treble all our joys agen,
  Who had the power and virtue to remove
  Such monsters from the labyrinth of love.

The scene opens and discovers a prospect of the
  sea. The Triumph is first seen afar off, and led
  in by Amphitrite, the wife of Oceanus, with four
  sea gods attending her, Nereus, Proteus,
  Glaucus, Palæmon.

The Triumph[3] consisted of fifteen Lovers, and as
  many Cupids, who rank themselves seven and
  seven on a side, with each a Cupid before him,

---

[3] *The Triumph, &c.*] The approach of this Triumph, (that is
the procession, or grand entry of the Masquers crowned with chap-
lets of roses, laurel, and all the rich adornments of victory, and
ushered in by a blaze of torches,) must have afforded a magnificent
spectacle. Indeed, the whole of this masque is creditable to the
fancy of the inventors; who appear to have consulted the splendour
of the show more than the usual concomitants of poetry, music, and
dancing.

with a lighted torch, and the middle person (which is his Majesty) placed in the centre.[4]

Amph. *Here stay a while: this, this,*
The temple of all beauty is !
Here, perfect lovers, you must pay
First fruits ; and on these altars lay
(The ladies' breasts,) your ample vows,
Such as love brings, and beauty best allows !

Cho. *For love without his object soon is gone :*
Love must have answering love to look upon.

Amph. *To you, best judge then of perfection !*

Euph. *The queen of what is wonder in the place !*

Amph. *Pure object of heroic love, alone !*

Euph. *The centre of proportion !—*

Amph.   *Sweetness !*

Euph.   *Grace!*

Amph. *Deign to receive all lines of love in one.*

Euph. *And by reflecting of them fill this space.*

Cho. *Till it a circle of those glories prove,*
Fit to be sought in beauty, found by love.

[4] If the reader is curious to know who presented the respective lovers, he may learn it from the following arrangement as given by the author.

1. The provident.	Marquess of HAMILTON.
2. The judicious.	Lord Chamberlain.
3. The secret.	Earl of HOLLAND.
4. The valiant.	Earl of CARNARVON.
5. The witty.	Earl of NEWPORT.
6. The jovial.	Viscount DONCASTER.
7. The secure.	Lord STRANGE.

15. THE HEROICAL.   The KING.

8. The substantial.	Sir WILLIAM HOWARD.
9. The modest.	Sir ROBERT STANLEY.
10. The candid.	Sir WILLIAM BROOK.
11. The courteous.	Master GORING.
12. The elegant.	Master RALEGH.
13. The rational.	Master DIMOCK.
14. The magnificent.	Master ABERCROMY.

Semi-cho. *Where love is mutual, still*
              All things in order move.
Semi-cho. *The circle of the will*
              Is the true sphere of love.
Cho.   *Advance, you gentler Cupids, then, advance,*
              Andshew your just perfections in your dance.

The Cupids dance their dance ; and the Masquers
              their Entry.

Which done, EUCLIA, or a fair glory, appears in the
heavens, singing an applausive SONG, or Pæan of
the whole, which she takes occasion to ingeminate
in the second chorus, upon the sight of a work of
Neptune's, being a hollow rock, filling part of the
sea-prospect, whereon the MUSES sit.

HYMN.

Euc. *So love emergent out of chaos brought*
              The world to light !
         And gently moving on the waters, wrought
              All form to sight !

              Love's appetite
              Did beauty first excite :
              And left imprinted in the air
              Those signatures of good and fair,
Cho. *Which since have flow'd, flow'd forth upon the*
              sense
         To wonder first, and then to excellence,
         By virtue of divine intelligence !

The Ingemination.

              And Neptune too,
              Shews what his waves can do :
              To call the Muses all to play,
              And sing the birth of Venus' day,

Cho. *Which from the sea flow'd forth upon the sense,*
       To wonder first, and next to excellence,
       By virtue of divine intelligence!

Here follow the REVELS.

Which ended, the scene changeth to a garden, and
 the heavens opening, there appear four new persons,
 in form of a Constellation, sitting; or a new Aste-
 rism, expecting VENUS, whom they call upon with
 this

SONG.

JUPITER, JUNO, GENIUS, HYMEN.

Jup. *Haste, daughter Venus, haste and come away,*
Jun. *All powers that govern marriage, pray*
          That you will lend your light,
Gen. *Unto the constellation of this night.*
Hym. *Hymen.*
Jun. *And Juno.*
Gen. *And the Genius call.*
Jup. *Your father Jupiter.*
Grand Cho. *And all*
          That bless or honour holy nuptial.

VENUS here appears in a cloud, and passing through
 the Constellation, descendeth to the earth, when
 presently the cloud vanisheth, and she is seen sitting in a throne.

Ven.   *Here, here I present am*
              Both in my girdle, and my flame;
              Wherein are woven all the powers
              The Graces gave me, or the Hours,
              My nurses once, with all the arts
              Of gaining, and of holding hearts:
                 And these with I descend.
              But, to your influences, first commend
                 The vow, I go to take
              On earth, for perfect love and beauty's sake.

Her song ended, and she rising up to go to the queen, the throne disappears : in place of which, there shooteth up a palm-tree with an imperial crown on the top ; from the root whereof, lilies and roses twining together, and embracing the stem, flourish through the crown ; which she in the SONG with the CHORUS describes.

Grand Cho. *Beauty and Love, whose story is mysterial,*
In yonder palm-tree, and the crown imperial,
Do from the Rose and Lily, so delicious,
Promise a shade, shall ever be propitious
To both the kingdoms. But to Britain's Genius
The snaky rod, and serpents of Cyllenius
Bring not more peace than these, who so united be
By Love, as with it earth and heaven delighted be.
And who this king and queen would well historify,
Need only speak their names ; these them will glorify :
MARY *and* CHARLES, *Charles with his Mary named*
        are,
And all the rest of loves or princes famed are.

After this, they DANCE their going out.

AND THUS IT ENDED.

CHLORIDIA.

RITES TO CHLORIS AND HER NYMPHS.

PERSONATED IN A MASQUE AT COURT. BY THE
QUEEN'S MAJESTY, AND HER LADIES,
AT SHROVE-TIDE, 1630.

The Inventors, BEN JONSON; INIGO JONES.

Unius tellus ante coloris erat.

CHLORIDIA.] From the undated 4to. but probably printed in 1630 : it is also in the fol. 1641. See the observations on *Love's Triumph*. No mention of Jones occurs in the 4to. edition of this Masque ; though his name is found in the folio.

CHLORIDIA.

HE King and Queen's majesty having given their command for the invention of a new argument, with the whole change of the scene, wherein her majesty, with the like number of her ladies, purposed a presentation to the king; it was agreed, it should be the celebration of some rites done to the goddess Chloris, who, in a general council of the gods, was proclaimed goddess of the flowers; according to that of Ovid, in the Fasti,

——*Arbitrium tu Dea floris habe.*

And was to be stellified on earth, by an absolute decree from Jupiter, who would have the earth to be adorn'd with stars, as well as the heaven.

Upon this hinge the whole invention moved.

The ornament which went about the scene, was composed of foliage, or leaves heighten'd with gold, and interwoven with all sorts of flowers, and naked children, playing and climbing among the branches; and in the midst a great garland of flowers, in which was written, CHLORIDIA.

The curtain being drawn up, the scene is discovered, consisting of pleasant hills, planted with young trees, and all the lower banks adorned with flowers. And from some hollow parts of those hills, fountains come gliding down; which, in the far-off landscape, seemed all to be converted to a river.

Over all a serene sky, with transparent clouds,

giving a great lustre to the whole work; which did imitate the pleasant Spring.

When the spectators had enough fed their eyes with the delights of the scene, in a part of the air, a bright cloud begins to break forth; and in it is sitting a plump boy, in a changeable garment, richly adorned, representing the mild ZEPHYRUS. On the other side of the scene, in a purplish cloud, appeareth the SPRING, a beautiful maid, her upper garment green, under it a white robe wrought with flowers; a garland on her head.

Here ZEPHYRUS begins his dialogue, calling her forth, and making narration of the gods' decree at large, which she obeys, pretending it is come to earth already; and there begun to be executed by the king's favour, who assists with all bounties, that may be either urged as causes or reasons of the Spring.

1 SONG.

Zeph.   *Come forth, come forth, the gentle Spring,*
          And carry the glad news I bring,
             To earth, our common mother :
          It is decreed by all the gods,
          That heaven of earth shall have no odds,
             But one shall love another.

          Their glories they shall mutual make,
          Earth look on heaven, for heaven's sake,
             Their honours shall be even :
          All emulation cease, and jars,
          Jove will have earth to have her stars
             And lights, no less than heaven.

Spring. *It is already done, in flowers*
          As fresh and new as are the hours,
             By warmth of yonder sun :
          But will be multiplied on us,
          If from the breath of Zephyrus
             Like favour we have won.

Zeph.   *Give all to him : His is the dew,*
        The heat, the humour,
Spring.   *—All the true*
        Beloved of the Spring !
Zeph.   *The sun, the wind, the verdure !*
Spring.   *—All*
        That wisest nature cause can call
        Of quick'ning any thing.

At which ZEPHYRUS passeth away through the air,
and the SPRING descendeth to the earth ; and is
received by the NAIADES, or Napeæ, who are the
nymphs, fountains, and servants of the season.

2 SONG.

Naïades. *Fair maid, but are you come to dwell,*
        And tarry with us here?
Spring. *Fresh fountains, I am come to tell*
        A tale in yond' soft ear,
        Whereof the murmur will do well ;
        If you your parts will bear.
Naïades. *Our purlings wait upon the Spring.*
Spring. *Go up with me, then ; help to sing*
        The story to the king.

Here the SPRING goes up, singing the argument, to
the king, and the NAÏADES follow with the close.

Spring. *Cupid hath ta'en offence of late,*
        At all the gods, that of the state,
        And in their council, he was so deserted,
        Not to be call'd unto their guild,
        But slightly pass'd by as a child.
Naïades.*Wherein he thinks his honour was perverted.*

Spring. *And though his mother seek to season,*
        And rectify his rage with reason,

8   H

> *By shewing he lives yet under her command,*
>   *Rebellious he doth disobey,*
>   *And she hath forced his arms away.*

Naïades. *To make him feel the justice of her hand.*

> *Whereat the boy, in fury fell,*
>   *With all his speed, is gone to hell,*
>   *There to excite and stir up jealousy.*
>   *To make a party 'gainst the gods,*
>   *And set heaven, earth, and hell at odds.*

Naïades. *And raise a chaos of calamity.*

The SONG ended, the Nymphs fall into a dance, to
their voices and instruments, and so return into
the scene.

The ANTIMASQUE.

A part of the under-ground opening, out of it enter a
Dwarf *post from hell, riding on a curtal, with
cloven feet, and two* Lacqueys : *these dance, and
make the first entry of the Antimasque. He alights
and speaks.*

Dwarf. Hold my stirrup, my one lacquey ; and
look to my curtal, the other ; walk him well, sirrah,
while I expatiate myself here in the report of my
office. Oh, the Furies! how I am joyed with the
title of it! Postillion of hell! yet no Mercury; but
a mere cacodæmon, sent hither with a packet of
news! news! never was hell so furnished of the
commodity of news! Love hath been lately there,
and so entertain'd by Pluto and Proserpine, and all
the grandees of the place, as it is there perpetual
holyday ; and a cessation of torment granted, and
proclaimed for ever ! Half-famish'd Tantalus is fallen
to his fruit, with that appetite, as it threatens to undo
the whole company of costard-mongers ; and has a
river afore him, running excellent wine. Ixion is
loosed from his wheel, and turn'd dancer, does

nothing but cut capreols, fetch friskals, and leads lavoltos with the Lamiæ! Sisyphus has left rolling the stone, and is grown a master-bowler; challenges all the prime gamesters, parsons in hell, and gives them odds; upon Tityus's breast, that (for six of the nine acres) is counted the subtlest bowling-ground in all Tartary.[1] All the Furies are at a game call'd nine-pins, or keils, made of old usurers' bones, and their souls looking on with delight, and betting on the game! Never was there such freedom of sport. Danaus' daughters have broke their bottomless tubs, and made bonfires of them. All is turn'd triumph there. Had hell-gates been kept with half that strictness, as the entry here has been to-night, Pluto would have had but a cold court, and Proserpine a thin presence, though both have a vast territory. We had such a stir to get in, I, and my curtal, and my two lacqueys, all ventured through the eye of a Spanish needle, we had never come in else, and that was by the favour of one of the guard who was a woman's tailor, and held ope the passage.—Cupid by commission hath carried Jealousy from hell, Disdain, Fear, and Dissimulation, with other goblins, to trouble the gods. And I am sent after, post, to raise TEMPEST, WINDS, LIGHTNINGS, THUNDER, RAIN, and SNOW, for some new exploit they have against the earth, and the goddess Chloris, queen of the flowers, and mistress of the Spring. For joy of which, I will return to myself, mount my bidet, in a dance; and curvet upon my curtal.

Here he mounts his curtal, and with his lacqueys, danceth forth as he came in.

[1] *Is counted the* subtlest *bowling-ground in all Tartary,*] i. e. the smoothest, finest: the expression occurs in Shakspeare:

"Like to a bowl upon a *subtle* ground." *Coriolanus,* Act v.
WHAL.

Second ENTRY.

Cupid, Jealousy, Disdain, Fear, and Dissimulation dance together.

Third ENTRY.

The queen's dwarf,[2] richly apparelled, as a prince
of hell, attended by six infernal spirits, he first
danceth alone, and then the spirits, all expressing
their joy for Cupid's coming among them.

Fourth ENTRY.

Here the scene changeth into a horrid storm ; out
of which enters the nymph Tempest, with four
Winds ; they dance.

---

[2] *The queen's dwarf.*] Jeffrey Hudson. He was born at Oak-
ham, in Rutlandshire. His father, who kept the duke of Buckingham's " baiting-bulls," and was, as Fuller says, a very proper man,
broad shouldered and broad chested, presented him to the Duchess
when he was nine years old, and scarcely a foot and a-half in height.
In 1626, he was served up to the king and queen, then upon a visit
to Burleigh, in a cold pye ; and subsequently taken to Whitehall,
where he became the queen's page, and entered into the diversions
of the court.

It is probable that he played *Tom Thumb* in the preceding
Masque, in which Evans, the gigantic porter, in the character of
Dr. Rat, to the inexpressible delight of the spectators, produced
him out of his pocket.

But Jeffrey played a part in more serious affairs. He was sent
some time after this, to France, to fetch a midwife for the queen ;
and on his return was captured by a Dunkirk privateer. On the
breaking out of the civil war, he held a commission in the cavalry,
and followed his mistress to France. Here he had a dispute with
a Mr. Crofts, a young gentleman of family, which ended in a challenge. Crofts came to the field armed with a squirt :—this only
served to exasperate matters ; and a real duel ensued, in which
Jeffrey shot his antagonist dead upon the spot. For this, (Fuller
says,) he was imprisoned.

·· He returned to England after the Restoration, and was involved
in some trouble on account of what was called the Popish Plot.
He died about 1683.

Fifth ENTRY.

Lightnings, three in number, their habits glistering expressing that effect, in their motion.

Sixth ENTRY.

Thunder alone dancing the tunes to a noise, mixed, and imitating thunder.

Seventh ENTRY.

Rain, presented by five persons, all swollen, and clouded over, their hair flagging, as if they were wet, and in their hands balls full of sweet water, which, as they dance, sprinkle all the room.

Eighth ENTRY.

Seven with rugged white heads and beards, to express Snow, with flakes on their garments, mixed with hail. These having danced, return into the stormy scene, whence they came.

Here, by the providence of Juno, the Tempest on an instant ceaseth; and the scene is changed into a delicious place, figuring the BOWER OF CHLORIS, wherein an arbour feigned of goldsmith's-work, the ornament of which was born up with termes of satyrs, beautified with festoons, garlands, and all sorts of fragrant flowers. Beyond all this, in the sky a-far off, appeared a rainbow : in the most eminent place of the Bower, sat the goddess CHLORIS, accompanied with fourteen nymphs,[5] their

[5] The names of the Masquers, who personated the Nymphs, are thus given by the poet, arranged as they sat in the BOWER.

1. Countess of CARLISLE.	2. Countess of CARNARVON.
3. Countess of BERKSHIRE.	4. M. PORTER.
5. Countess of NEWPORT.	6. M. DOR. SAVAGE.

15. The QUEEN.

7. Countess of OXFORD.	8. Lady HOWARD.
9. Lady ANNE CAVENDISH.	10. M. ELIZ. SAVAGE.
11. Lady PENELOPE EGERTON.	12. M. ANNE WESTON.
13. Lady STRANGE.	14. M. SOPHIA CARY.

apparel white, embroidered with silver, trimmed at the shoulders with great leaves of green, embroidered with gold, falling one under the other. And of the same work were their bases, their headtires of flowers, mixed with silver and gold, with some sprigs of ægrets among, and from the top of their dressing, a thin veil hanging down.

All which beheld, the Nymphs, Rivers, *and* Fountains, *with the* Spring, *sung this rejoicing Song.*

3 Song.

Grand Cho. *Run out, all the floods, in joy, with your silver feet,*
  And haste to meet
  The enamour'd Spring,
For whom the warbling fountains sing :
  The story of the flowers,
  Preserved by the Hours ;
At Juno's soft command, and Iris' showers ;
Sent to quench jealousy, and all those powers
Of Love's rebellious war :
Whilst Chloris sits a shining star
To crown, and grace our jolly song, made long,
To the notes that we bring, to glad the Spring.

Which ended, the Goddess and her Nymphs descend the degrees into the room, and dance the Entry of the Grand Masque.

After this, another Song *by the same persons as before.*

4 Song.

Grand Cho. *Tell a truth, gay Spring, let us know*
  What feet they were, that so
  Impress'd the earth, and made such various flowers to grow.

Spring. *She that led, a queen was at least,*
   Or a goddess 'bove the rest :
  And all their graces in herself exprest.

Grand Cho. *O, 'twere a fame to know her name!*
   Whether she were the root;
  Or they did take th' impression from her foot.

  The Masquers *here dance their second Dance.*

Which done, the farther prospect of the scene
changeth into air, with a low landscape, in part
covered with clouds : and in that instant, the heaven
opening, JUNO and IRIS are seen ; and above them
many airy spirits, sitting in the clouds.

    5 SONG.

Juno. *Now Juno, and the air shall know,*
  The truth of what is done below
  From our discoloured bow.
    Iris, what news?
Iris. *The air is clear, your bow can tell,*
  Chloris renown'd, Spight fled to hell ;
  The business all is well,
    And Cupid sues.
Juno. *For pardon ! Does he ?*
Iris.   *He sheds tears*
  More than your birds have eyes.
Juno.   *The gods have ears :*
  Offences made against the deities
  Are soon forgot.—
Iris.   *If who offends be wise.*

Here, out of the earth ariseth a Hill, and on the
top of it a globe, on which FAME is seen standing
with her trumpet in her hand ; and on the hill are
seated four persons, presenting POESY, HISTORY,
ARCHITECTURE, and SCULPTURE; who together with

the Nymphs, Floods, and Fountains, make a full
choir; at which FAME begins to mount, and moving
her wings flieth, singing, up to heaven.

Fame. *Rise, golden Fame, and give thy name a birth.*
Cho.   *From great and generous actions done on earth.*
Fame. *The life of Fame is action.*
Cho.   *Understood,*
       That action must be virtuous, great, and good.
Fame. *Virtue itself by Fame is oft protected,*
       And dies despised—
Cho.   *Where the Fame's neglected.*[4]
Fame. *Who hath not heard of Chloris, and her*
           bower,
       Fair Iris' act, employ'd by Juno's power,
       To guard the Spring, and prosper every flower,
       Whom jealousy and hell thought to devour?
Cho.   *Great actions oft obscured by time, may lie,*
       Or envy——
Fame.   *But they last to memory.*
Poesy. *We that sustain thee, learned Poesy,*
Hist. *And I her sister, severe History,*
Archi. *With Architecture, who will raise thee high,*
Sculp. *And Sculpture, that can keep thee from to die.*[5]
Cho.   *All help to lift thee to eternity.*
Juno. *And Juno through the air doth make thy way.*
Iris. *By her serenest messenger of day.*

[4] *Where the Fame's neglected.*] This sentiment has occurred
more than once before. It is from Tacitus: *Contemptu famæ con-
temni virtutem.*

[5] *From to die,*] i. e. from death. A very elegant Grecism; απο
του θανειν: and which our poets have employed in our language
with singular strength and beauty. Thus Spenser:

"Be sure that nought may save thee *from to die.*" WHAL.

The Grecism is, as Whalley says, very elegant; in our language
the expression is a mere barbarism, feeble, ungraceful, and un-
grammatical.

Fame. *Thus Fame ascends, by all degrees, to heaven,*
And leaves a light, here, brighter than the
seven.

Grand Cho. *Let all applaud the sight.*
Air first, that gave the bright
Reflections, day or night!
. With these supports of Fame,
That keep alive her name!
The beauties of the Spring.
Founts, Rivers, every thing:
From the height of all,
To the waters fall,
Resound and sing
The honours of his Chloris, to the king.
Chloris, the queen of flowers;
The sweetness of all showers;
The ornament of bowers:
The top of paramours.

FAME being hidden in the clouds, the hill sinks, and
the heaven closeth.

The MASQUERS dance with the LORDS.

AND THUS IT ENDED.

E have now reached the scene of contention between our poet and Inigo Jones. Till this period they appear to have lived in sufficient harmony. The writer of Jones's life, in the *Biographia Britannica*, says, that the quarrel broke out soon after 1609, and continued to the death of Jonson; this is the eternal echo : and I am weary of repeating that it is utterly false and groundless. The first symptoms of disaffection, on the poet's side, appear in the *Tale of a Tub*, written in 1633, and from the language there used, it is more than probable that the quarrel originated not with him, but his associate.

If the reader has looked through these Masques, he must have noticed the friendly solicitude of Jonson to put forward the talents of this man : this was the more important, as the first attempts of Jones had been somewhat unsuccessful. In 1605-6, he was employed on a Masque, prepared for the king's entertainment, at Oxford. "The machinery and stages," (says my author) "were chiefly constructed by one Mr. Jones, a great traveller, who undertook to furnish them with rare devices, but performed very little to what was expected." *Lel. Col.* vol. ii. 646. He was not more fortunate at Cambridge, where he was employed on the machinery for the representation of *Ajax*. Till the death of Prince Henry, then, in 1612, nothing but kindness appears on the part of Jonson. In that year, or the next, Jones went abroad, and pursued his studies in Italy for several years ; yet Jonson is ridiculously charged with attacking him in *Bartholomew Fair*, which was brought out in 1614. No mention of his name occurs in any part of our poet's works, (though the Master of the Revels says he was employed in the *Prince's Masque*,) till 1625, when he joined in the production of *Pan's Anniversary*. Another interval of five years took place, before he was called upon again, when, as Jonson says, they met by the king's command, and consulted together on the construction of *Love's Triumph* and *Chloridia*. During this long period, not a murmur of discontent appears to have escaped Jonson. Why then is it taken for granted that the quarrel which followed the exhibition of the last piece, originated solely with him ? Even in the description of the scenery, which evidently proceeded from Jonson, there is a visible anxiety to recommend it to favour.

But what, after all, occasioned the breach? Dr. Aikin, in that worthless compilation, the *General Biography*, is pleased to insinuate that it arose from our author's envy of Inigo's poetry! The only poetry, I believe, of which the architect was ever known to be guilty, is a little piece of five stanzas, written in 1610, and prefixed to the first edition of *Coryat's Crudities*. I will subjoin the best of them, that the reader may form some idea of the transcendent excellence of those verses which disturbed the tranquillity of Jonson for more than twenty years!

> " Enough of this ; all pens in this doe travell
> To track thy steps, who, Proteus like, dost varie
> Thy shape to place, the home-borne muse to gravell,
> For though in Venice thou not long didst tarie,
> Yet thou the Italian soul so soone couldst steale,
> As in that time thou eat'st but one good meale."

It seems reasonable to suppose that *Chloridia* was not so well received as *Love's Triumph*. Ben's share in it, as a poet, was not very important, nor, to say the truth, very remarkable either for harmony or expression. In the construction of the fable, both took part alike ; but Inigo chose to fasten on the verse, and to attribute their want of success solely to its demerits, while he arrogated to himself a more than ordinary portion of applause for his skill in painting the scenery. He had a fair field before him : he was rich and popular ; his associate was sick, confined to "the bed and boards," and in want of every thing. Jones was, besides, as vain as Jonson was proud ; as arrogant as Jonson was overbearing ; he was also extremely petulant. Pennant claims him for a countryman on the strength of his " violent passions ;"[1] and we know, from the charges carried up by the Commons to the House of Lords against him, that his language was of the most insolent kind. Jonson, however, bore it for two years, when he wrote, in 1633, the ridiculous *Motion of Squire Tub of Totten ;* and, as this perhaps did not silence his adversary, two years afterwards he drew up, and handed about, in private, the verses which Whalley reprinted among the *Epigrams*. To prevent the necessity of recurring to this disagreeable subject, I shall give them here.

The first notice of them appears in Howel's *Letters*.

"I thank you for the last *regalo* you gave me at your *Museum*, and for the good company. I heard you censured[2] lately at court,

---

[1] *Tour in Wales*, vol. ii. p. 150.

[2] *I heard you censured lately at court*.] It might be so ; but the validity of the assertion depends upon the character of Howel's informer, *a good hand*, as he calls him just below. One thing, however, is certain, that the king had listened, some time before, and, as far as appears, without displeasure, to an attack upon Inigo

that you have lighted too foul upon sir Inigo, and that you write with a porcupine's quill, dipt in too much gall: excuse me that I am so free with you, it is because I am in no common way of friendship,

"Your's, &c.

"*May* 3, 1635."   "J. H.

This letter, which is directed "to his honoured friend and father, M. Ben Johnson," having failed of effect, he wrote a second, bearing date July 5, 1635, in which he repeats his allusion to the porcupine's quill, and, after deprecating the asperity of the satire on the "royal architect," concludes thus: "If your spirit will not let you retract, yet you shall do well to repress any more copies of the satire; for to deal plainly with you, you have lost some ground at court by it; and as I hear from a good hand, the King, who hath so great a judgment in poetry, (as in all other things else,) is not well pleased therewith. Dispense with this.

"Your respectful son and servitor.
"J. H."

In consequence, perhaps, of this remonstrance, Jonson recalled, and destroyed every copy (as he probably thought) of his satire, for not a line of it was found among his papers: but there is in some minds a perverse passion for perpetuating the memory of enmities, which no sense of propriety can subdue. A copy, most probably secreted by a person of this description, fell into the hands of Mr. Vertue, who communicated it, as a great favour, to Whalley, by whom it was sent to the press. Thus, in despite of the author, this wretched squabble has reached posterity.

(Coronel Vitruvius) in a masque prepared solely for his entertainment, and presented by one who would, on no account, have hazarded a word that was likely to give him offence. See p. 134.

AN EXPOSTULATION[1]

WITH INIGO JONES.

ASTER Surveyor, you that first began
From thirty pounds in pipkins, to the
man
You are : from them leap'd forth an
architect,
Able to talk of Euclid, and correct
Both him and Archimede ; damn Archytas,
The noblest inginer that ever was :
Control Ctesibius, overbearing us
With mistook names,[2] out of Vitruvius ;
Drawn Aristotle on us, and thence shewn
How much Architectonice is your own :
Whether the building of the stage, or scene,
Or making of the properties it mean,

---

[1] *An Expostulation.*] That some part of this may have proceeded from Jonson I am not prepared to question; but it has
assuredly been much corrupted or interpolated. The fifth line
could not be written by our poet, who was much too good a judge
of accent to give this for a verse.

[2] *With mistook names, &c.*] A Mr. Webb, related to Jones,
published some account of him, in imitation, as it seems to me, of
sir Thomas Urquhart's *Life of the Admirable Crichton.* In this
ridiculous rhapsody we are told, that " Mr. Jones was not only proclaimed by public acclamation the Vitruvius of England, but of all
Christendom ; that his abilities in all human sciences, surpassed
most of his age ; that he was a perfect master of the mathematics,
and had some insight into the two learned languages," &c. &c.
The fact is, that he knew scarcely any thing of either. He was a
good scene painter, a better machinist, and an incomparable architect. I give Jonson full credit for what he says of his antagonist's
mistakes.

Vizors, or antics; or it comprehend
Something your sur-ship doth not yet intend.
By all your titles, and whole style at once,
Of tireman, mountebank, and justice Jones,
I do salute you : are you fitted yet ?
Will any of these express your place, or wit ?
Or are you so ambitious 'bove your peers,
You'd be an Assinigo by your ears ?
Why much good do't you ; be what part you will,
You'll be, as Langley said, "an Inigo still."
What makes your wretchedness to bray so loud
In town and court ? are you grown rich, and proud ?
Your trappings will not change you, change your
       mind;
No velvet suit you wear will alter kind.
A wooden dagger is a dagger of wood,
.Nor gold, nor ivory haft can make it good.
What is the cause you pomp it so, I ask ?
And all men echo, you have made a masque.
I chime that too, and I have met with those
That do cry up the machine, and the shows ;
The majesty of Juno in the clouds,
And peering forth of Iris in the shrouds ;
The ascent of lady Fame, which none could spy,
Not they that sided her, dame Poetry,[3]
Dame History, dame Architecture too,
And goody Sculpture, brought with much ado
To hold her up : O shows, shows, mighty shows !
The eloquence of masques ! what need of prose,
Or verse, or prose, t'express immortal you ?
You are the spectacles of state, 'tis true,

[3] *Th' ascent of lady Fame, which none could spy,*
   Not they that sided her, dame Poetry.] This alludes to the
scenery and decorations of *Chloridia*. As these were the Surveyor's province, it is possible those here referred to were so injudiciously contrived or ordered, as to occasion the sarcasms of our
poet. WHAL.

Court-hieroglyphics, and all arts afford,
In the mere perspective of an inch-board;
You ask no more than certain politic eyes,
Eyes, that can pierce into the mysteries
Of many colours, read them, and reveal
Mythology, there painted on slit deal.
Or to make boards to speak! there is a task!
Painting and carpentry are the soul of masque.
Pack with your pedling poetry to the stage,
This is the money-got, mechanic age.
To plant the music where no ear can reach,
Attire the persons, as no thought can teach
Sense, what they are; which by a specious, fine
Term of [you] architects, is call'd Design;
But in the practised truth, destruction is
Of any art, beside what he calls his.
Whither, O whither will this tireman grow?
His name is Σκηνοποιος, we all know,
The maker of the properties, in sum,
The scene, the engine; but he now is come
To be the music-master; tabler too;
He is, or would be, the main *Dominus Do-
All* of the work,[4] and so shall still for Ben,
Be Inigo, the whistle, and his men.
He's warm on his feet, now he says; and can
Swim without cork: why, thank the good queen
    Anne.[5]
I am too fat to envy, he too lean

[4] *He is, or would be, the main* Dominus Do-
All *of the work.*] This is no forced description of Inigo's manner. In the Declaration of the Commons, already noticed, in behalf of the parishioners of St. Gregory, they complain that " the said Inigo Jones would not undertake the work (of re-edifying the church) unless he might be, as he termed it, *sole monarch,* or might have the *principality* thereof," &c. What follows is still more offensive.

[5] *Why, thank the good queen* Anne.] Consort to James I., who appointed Inigo Jones her architect. WHAL.

To be worth envy; henceforth I do mean
To pity him, as smiling at his feat
Of lantern-lerry, with fuliginous heat
Whirling his whimsies, by a subtilty
Suck'd from the veins of shop-philosophy.
What would he do now, giving his mind that way,
In presentation of some puppet-play,
Shou'd but the king his justice-hood employ,
In setting forth of such a solemn toy?
How wou'd he firk, like Adam Overdo,[6]
Up and about; dive into cellars too,
Disguised, and thence drag forth Enormity,
Discover Vice, commit Absurdity:
Under the moral, shew he had a pate
Moulded or strok'd up to survey a state!
O wise surveyor, wiser architect,
But wisest Inigo; who can reflect
On the new priming of thy old sign-posts,
Reviving with fresh colours the pale ghosts
Of thy dead standards; or with marvel see
Thy twice conceived, thrice paid for imagery;
And not fall down before it, and confess
Almighty Architecture, who no less
A goddess is, than painted cloth, deal board,
Vermillion, lake, or crimson can afford
Expression for; with that unbounded line,
Aim'd at in thy omnipotent design!
What poesy e'er was painted on a wall,

---

[6] *How wou'd he firk, like Adam Overdo,*

Up and about, &c.] This line is of some importance, inasmuch as it quite destroys the established opinion that Lantern Leatherhead was meant for Inigo Jones. "Old Ben," as Mr. Malone truly observes, "generally spoke out," and he was, here, sufficiently angry to identify him with that character, to which not only his allusion to *Bartholomew Fair*, but his mention of a puppet play, directly led: and we may confidently assure ourselves that he would have done it, had, what he is so often charged with, been ever in his contemplation.

That might compare with thee ? what story shall,
Of all the worthies, hope t' outlast thy own,
So the materials be of Purbeck stone ?
Live long the feasting-room ! and ere thou burn
Again, thy architect to ashes turn ;
Whom not ten fires, nor a parliament, can
With all remonstrance, make an honest man.[7]

TO A FRIEND.

An Epigram of INIGO JONES.

IR Inigo doth fear it, as I hear,[8]
And labours to seem worthy of this fear ;
That I should write upon him some sharp
    verse,

[7] *Whom not ten fires, nor a parliament, can
With all* remonstrance, *make an honest man.*] Jones, by some
arbitrary proceedings, had subjected himself to the censures of parliament ; and this seems to refer to the affair between him and the
parishioners of St. Gregory in London. In order to execute his
design of repairing St. Paul's cathedral, he demolished part of the
church of St. Gregory adjoining to it ; upon which the parishioners
presented a *Remonstrance* to the parliament against him : but that
affair did not come to an issue, till some time after the writing of
this satire. WHAL.
   The question is, when it began. The *Remonstrance* was not
even presented to Parliament till three years after Jonson's death,
and could scarcely have been in contemplation at the date of this
satire, 1635. There are many difficulties in the way of those who
make Jonson the author of the whole of this piece.
   [8] *Sir Inigo doth fear it, &c.*] This is undoubtedly Jonson's, and
this seems to shew that nothing had been hitherto written against
Jones. The learned writers of the *Biographia Britannica*, in their
zeal to criminate Jonson, strangely mistake the sense of the ninth
line,
         "If thou art so desirous to be read,"
" which," they say, " alludes to some attempt of the architect in the
poetical way," whereas, it merely means, if you are so desirous to
be noticed, hope not for it from me ; but, &c.

8   I

Able to eat into his bones, and pierce
The marrow. Wretch ! I quit thee of thy pain,
Thou'rt too ambitious, and dost fear in vain :
The Lybian lion hunts no butterflies ;
He makes the camel and dull ass his prize.
If thou be so desirous to be read,
Seek out some hungry painter, that, for bread,
With rotten chalk or coal, upon the wall,
Will well design thee to be view'd of all,
That sit upon the common draught or strand ;
Thy forehead is too narrow for my brand.

To Inigo Marquis Would-be.

A Corollary.

UT 'cause thou hear'st the mighty king of Spain
Hath made his Inigo marquis, would'st thou
fain
Our Charles should make thee such ? 'twill not be-
come
All kings to do the self-same deeds with some :
Besides, his man may merit it, and be
A noble honest soul : what's this to thee ?
He may have skill, and judgment to design
Cities and temples, thou a cave for wine,
Or ale ; he build a palace, thou the shop,
With sliding windows, and false lights a-top :
He draw a forum with quadrivial streets ;
Thou paint a lane where Tom Thumb Jeffrey meets.[9]
He some Colossus, to bestride the seas,
From the fam'd pillars of old Hercules :
Thy canvas giant at some channel aims,
Or Dowgate torrents falling into Thames ;

---

[9] *Thou paint a lane, &c.,*] i. e. just wide enough to allow of the
meeting of Tom Thumb and Jeffrey Hudson.

And stradling shews the boys' brown paper fleet
Yearly set out there, to sail down the street :
Your works thus differing, much less so your style,
Content thee to be Pancridge earl the while,[1]
An earl of show ; for all thy worth is show :
But when thou turn'st a real Inigo,
Or canst of truth the least entrenchment pitch,
We'll have thee styled the Marquis of Towerditch.

[1] *Content thee to be Pancridge earl the while,*] i. e. one of the "Worthies" who annually rode to Mile End, or the Artillery Ground, in the ridiculous procession called *Arthur's Shew.* There can be no doubt, however, that Inigo Jones really aspired to the elevation mentioned in the first couplet. Sir Francis Kinaston, (the translator of Chaucer's *Troilus and Cressida,* into Latin,) in his *Cynthiades,* 1642, says :

> " Meantime imagine that Newcastle coles,
> Which, as sir Inigo saith, have perisht Paules,
> And by the skill of *Marquis Would-be Jones,*
> 'Tis found the smockes salt did corrupt the stones."

Other notices of this might be produced :—but enough, and more than enough, has been said of this foolish quarrel, little honourable to either party, and which, now that Jonson appears not to have been the aggressor, not to have sought " every occasion of injury," not to have lived in " constant hostility," &c., may be dismissed without much regret to the oblivion from which it was dragged by the misdirected industry of my predecessor.

LOVE'S WELCOME.

THE KING'S ENTERTAINMENT AT WELBECK, IN NOTTINGHAMSHIRE,

A House of the Right Honourable William, Earl of Newcastle, Viscount Mansfield, Baron of Botle and Bolsover, &c.

At his going into Scotland, 1633.

Love's Welcome (or, as it is called in the folio, the King's Entertainment, &c.)] In the spring of 1633, Charles, in an interval of tranquillity, resolved to make a progress into the northern part of his kingdom, and to be solemnly crowned in Scotland, which he had not seen since he was two years old. His journey was a perpetual triumph, the great families of the counties through which he passed feasting him on his way. None of the nobility and gentry, however, seem to have equalled the earl of Newcastle in the magnificence of their hospitality. "When he passed (says lord Clarendon) through Nottinghamshire, both the King and Court were received and entertained by the earl of Newcastle, and at his own proper expense, in such a wonderful manner and in such an excess of feasting as had scarce ever before been known in England ; and would be still thought very prodigious, if the same noble person had not, within a year or two afterwards, made the King and Queen a more stupendous Entertainment ; which, God be thanked, though possibly it might too much whet the appetite of others to excess, no man ever after imitated." *Hist. of the Rebellion.* The duchess, in the *Life of the Duke of Newcastle*, speaks of it modestly enough. "When his majesty (her Grace says) was going into Scotland to be crowned, he took his way through Nottinghamshire ; and lying at Worksep manor, hardly two miles distant from Welbeck where my lord then was, my lord invited his Majesty thither to dinner, which he was graciously pleased to accept of. This entertainment cost my lord between four and five thousand pounds." p. 183.

On this occasion our poet was called on, to prepare one of those little compliments, which, in those days, were supposed to grace, and, as it were, vivify the feast. The object was merely to introduce, in a kind of Antimasque, a course at Quintain, performed by the gentlemen of the county, neighbours to this great earl, in the guise of rustics, in which much awkwardness was affected, and much real dexterity probably shewn. Whatever it was, however, it afforded considerable amusement to the king and his attendants ; a fact recorded by the duchess with no little complacency in the memoirs of her family.

This Entertainment, with that which immediately follows it, is shuffled in among the translations, towards the close of the folio, 1641. It is evidently given in a very imperfect manner ; but there is no other copy.

LOVE'S WELCOME, ETC.

His Majesty *being set at Dinner,*

Music :

The Passions, DOUBT *and* LOVE, *enter with the Affections,* JOY, DELIGHT, *&c. and sing this*

SONG.

Doubt.

WHAT *softer sounds are these salute the ear,*
From the large circle of the hemisphere,
As if the centre of all sweets met here !
Love. *It is the breath and soul of every thing,*
Put forth by earth, by nature, and the spring,
To speak the welcome, welcome of the king.

Chorus of Affections. *The joy of plants, the spirit of flow'rs,*
The smell and verdure of the bow'rs,
The waters murmur, with the show'rs,
Distilling on the new fresh hours ;
The whistling winds and birds that sing
The welcome of our great, good king :
Welcome, O welcome, is the general voice,
Wherein all creatures practise to rejoice.
[A pause. Music again.

Love. When was old Sherwood's head more
     quaintly curl'd ?
Or look'd the earth more green upon the world ?
Or nature's cradle more enchased and purl'd ?
When did the air so smile, the wind so chime,
As quiristers of season, and the prime ?
    Doubt. If what they do, be done in their due time.

Cho. of Affections. *He makes the time for whom 'tis*
        done,
    From whom the warmth, heat, life begun ;
    Into whose fostering arms do run
    All that have being from the sun.
    Such is the fount of light, the king,
    The heart that quickens every thing,
And makes the creatures language all one voice,
In welcome, welcome, welcome to rejoice :
Welcome is all our song, is all our sound,
The treble part, the tenor, and the ground.

After Dinner.

    The King *and the* Lords *being come down, and
ready to take horse, in the crowd were discovered two
notorious persons, whose names were* ACCIDENCE *and*
FITZALE, *men of business, as by their eminent dressing
and habits did soon appear.*
    *One in a costly cassock of black buckram girt unto
him, whereon was painted* party-per pale :

On the one side,   On the other side,

Noun,		*Adverb,*		
Pronoun,	*declined.*	*Conjunction,*	*undeclined.*	
Verb,		*Preposition,*		
Participle,		*Interjection,*		

*With his hat, hatband, stocking, and sandals suited,
and marked A, B, C, &c.*

The other in a taberd, or herald's coat, of azure *and*
gules *quarterly changed, of buckram ; limned with
yellow, instead of gold, and pasted over with old records of the two shires, and certain fragments of the
forest, as a coat of antiquity and president, willing to
be seen, but hard to be read, and as loth to be understood, without the interpreter who wore it : for the
wrong end of the letters were turned upward, therefore
was a label fixed,* To the curious prier, *advertising :*

> *Look not so near, with hope to understand ;
> Out-cept, sir, you can read with the left-hand.*

Acci. By your fair leave, gentlemen of the court ;
for leave is ever fair, being asked ; and granted, is as
light, according to our English proverb, *Leave is
light.* Which is the king, I pray you ?

Fitz. Or rather the king's lieutenant ? for we have
nothing to say to the king, till we have spoken with
my lord lieutenant.

Acci. Of Nottinghamshire.

Fitz. And Derbyshire, for he is both. And we
have business to both sides of him, from either of the
counties.

Acci. As far as his command stretches.

Fitz. Is this he ?

Acci. This is no great man by his timber, as we
say in the forest ; by his thewes he may.[1] I'll venture
a part of speech, two or three at him, to see how he
is declined.—My lord, pleaseth your good lordship,
I am a poor neighbour, here, of your honour's, in the
country.

Fitz. Master A. B. C. Accidence, my good lord,
school-master of Mansfield, the painful instructor of

---

[1] *By his* thewes *he may,*] i. e. by his manners, accomplishments.
Shakspeare, in *Henry IV.* "Care I for the *thewes*," &c., seems to
use it in the sense of sinews, which, after all, may be the genuine
word.

our youth in their country elements, as appeareth by the sign of correction in his hat, with the trust of the town pen-and-inkhorn, committed to the surety of his girdle, from the whole corporation.

Acci. This is the more remarkable man, my very good lord ; father Fitz-Ale, herald of Derby, light and lanthorn of both counties ; the learned antiquary of the north ; conserver of the records of either forest, as witnesseth the brief taberd, or coat-armour he carries, being an industrious collection of all the written or reported wonders of the Peak.

> Saint Anne of Buxton's boiling well,
> Or Elden, bottomless, like hell :
> Poole's Hole, or Satan's sumptuous Arse.
> (Surreverence) with the mine-men's farce.
> Such a light and metall'd dance
> Saw you never yet in France.
> And by lead-men for the nones,
> That turn round like grindlestones ;
> Which they dig out fro' the dells,
> For their bairns' bread, wives and sells :
> Whom the whetstone sharps to eat,
> And cry milstones are good meat.
> He can fly o'er hills and dales,
> And report you more odd tales
> Of our outlaw Robin Hood,
> That revell'd here in Sherewood,
> And more stories of him show,
> (Though he ne'er shot in his bow)
> Than men or believe, or know.

> *Fitz.* Stint, stint your court,
>   Grow to be short,
>   Throw by your clatter,
>   And handle the matter :
>   We come with our peers,
>   And crave your ears,

To present a wedding,
Intended a bedding,
  Of both the shires.
Father Fitz-Ale
Hath a daughter stale
In Derby town,
Known up and down
  For a great antiquity :
And Pem she hight,
A solemn wight
As you should meet
In any street,
  In that ubiquity.
Her he hath brought,
As having sought
By many a draught
Of ale and craft,
With skill to graft
In some old stock
Of the yeoman block,
And forest-blood
Of old Sherewood.
And he hath found
Within the ground,
At last no shrimp,
Whereon to imp
His jolly club,
But a bold Stub
O' the right wood,
A champion good ;
  Who here in place
Presents himself,
Like doughty elf
  Of Greenwood chase.

Here STUB *the bridegroom presented himself, being*
apparelled in a yellow canvas doublet, cut, a green

*jerkin and hose, like a ranger; a Monmouth cap,
with a yellow feather, yellow stockings and shoes;
for being to dance, he would not trouble himself with
boots.*

Fitz.   Stub of Stub-hall,
         Some do him call;
         But most do say,
         He's Stub will stay
             To run his race,
         Not run away.
Acci.   At Quintain he,
         In honour of this bridaltee,
         Hath challeng'd either wide countee;
         Come Cut and Long-tail: for there be
         Six bachelors as bold as he,
         Adjuting to his companee,
         And each one hath his livery.
Fitz.   Six Hoods they are, and of the blood,
         They tell of ancient Robin Hood.

Enter RED-HOOD.

         Red-hood, the first that doth appear
         In stamel.[2]
Acci.   Scarlet is too dear.

Enter GREEN-HOOD.

Fitz.   Then Green-hood.
Acci.   He's in Kendal-green,
         As in the forest-colour seen.

[2] *Red-hood, the first that doth appear
In* stamel,] i. e. a kind of red, inferior both in quality and price
to scarlet. Thus Fletcher:

   "To see a handsome, young, fair enough, and well-mounted
        wench
   Humble herself in an old *stamel* petticoat."
                              Woman Hater, Act iv. Scene 2.

And our author, a little after, describes the bride-maids drest in
stamel petticoats, after the cleanliest country guise. WHAL.

Enter BLUE-HOOD.

Fitz. Next Blue-hood is, and in that hue
Doth vaunt a heart as pure and true
As is the sky; give him his due.
Acci. Of old England the yeoman blue.

Enter TAWNY-HOOD.

Fitz. Then Tawny fra' the kirk that came.
Acci. And cleped was the abbot's man.

Enter MOTLEY-HOOD.

Fitz. With Motley-hood, the man of law.

Enter RUSSET-HOOD.

Acci. And Russet-hood keeps all in awe.
Bold bachelors they are, and large,
And come in at the country charge;
Horse, bridles, saddles, stirrups, girts,
All reckon'd o' the country skirts!
And all their courses, miss or hit,
Intended are for the shire-wit,
And so to be received. Their game
Is country sport, and hath a name
From the place that bears the cost,
Else all the fat i' the fire were lost.
Go, captain Stub, lead on, and show
What house you come on by the blow
You give sir Quintain, and the cuff
You scape o' the sand-bag's counterbuff.[3]
                                    [*Flourish.*

---

[3] *Go, captain Stub, lead on, and shew*
What house you come on by the blow
You give sir Quintain, *and the cuff*
You scape o' th' sand-bag's counterbuff.] The diversion here
mentioned is thus described by Dr. Kennet: "They set up a post
perpendicularly in the ground, and then placed a slender piece of
timber on the top of it on a spindle, with a board nailed to it on
one end, and a bag of sand on the other. Against this board they

STUB'S COURSE.

Acci. O well run, yeoman Stub !
 Thou hast knock'd it like a club,
  And made sir Quintain know,
 By this his race so good,
 He himself is also wood,
  As by his furious blow. [*Flourish.*

RED-HOOD'S COURSE.

Fitz. Bravely run, Red-hood,
  There was a shock
 To have buff'd out the blood
  From aught but a block. [*Flourish.*

GREEN-HOOD'S COURSE.

Acci. Well run, Green-hood, got between,
 Under the sand-bag he was seen,
 Lowting low, like a forester green.
Fitz. He knows his tackle, and his treen.
       [*Flourish.*

BLUE-HOOD'S COURSE.

Acci. Give the old England yeoman his due,
 He has hit sir Quintain just in the qu—
 Though that be black, yet he is blue.
 It is a brave patch and a new ! [*Flourish.*

TAWNY-HOOD'S COURSE.

Fitz. Well run, Tawny, the abbot's churl,
  His jade gave him a jerk,
 As he would have his rider hurl
  His hood after the kirk.

rode with spears. Dr. Plot writes, that he saw it at Deddington in
Oxfordshire, where only strong staves were used : which violently
bringing about the bag of sand, if they made not good speed away,
it struck them on the neck, and shoulders, and sometimes perhaps
knocked them off their horses." *Paroch. Antiq.* WHAL.

But he was wiser, and well beheft,
For this is all that he hath left. [*Flourish.*

MOTLEY-HOOD'S COURSE.

Fitz. Or the saddle turn'd round, or the girts brake :
For low on the ground, woe for his sake!
· The law is found.
Acci. Had his pair of tongues not so much good,
To keep his head in his motley hood,
  [Safefrom the ground ?⁴]   [*Flourish.*

RUSSET-HOOD'S COURSE.

Fitz. Russet ran fast, though he be thrown.
Acci. He lost no stirrup, for he had none.
Fitz. His horse it is the herald's weft.
Acci. No, 'tis a mare, and hath a cleft.⁵
Fitz. She is country-borrow'd, and no vail,
Acci. But's hood is forfeit to Fitz-Ale.

Here ACCIDENCE *did break them off, by calling them
to the dance, and to the bride, who was dressed like an
old May-lady, with scarfs, and a great wrought hand-
kerchief, with red and blue, and other habiliments :
Six maids attending on her, attired with buckram bride-
laces begilt, white sleeves, and stammel petticoats, drest
after the cleanliest country guise ; among whom* mistress ALPHABET, master ꞏ ACCIDENCE'S *daughter, did
bear a prime sway.*

*The two bride-squires, the cake-bearer and the bowl-
bearer, were in two yellow leather doublets, and russet*

---

⁴ [*Safe from the ground.*] A line is lost in this place, and I
have merely put in brackets what I conceive the sense of it to have
been.

⁵ *And hath a cleft.*] This passage is quoted by Mr. Todd to illustrate the meaning of *clefts*, "a term in farriery for a disease of the
pasterns." This is very innocently done ; nevertheless, I would
advise the substitution of another example, for the present is unluckily not to the purpose.

*hose, like two twin clowns prest out for that office, with
livery hats and ribands.*

Acci. Come to the bride ; another fit
   Yet show, sirs, of your country wit,
   But of your best. Let all the steel
   Of back and brains fall to the heel ;
   And all the quicksilver in the mine
   Run in the foot-veins, and refine
   Your firk-hum jerk-hum to a dance,
   Shall fetch the fiddles out of France,
   To wonder at the horn-pipes here,
   Of Nottingham and Derbyshire.
Fitz. With the phant'sies of hey-troll,
   Troll about the bridal bowl,
   And divide the broad bride cake,
   Round about the bride's-stake.
Acci. With, Here is to the fruit of Pem,
Fitz. Grafted upon Stub his stem,
Acci. With the Peakish nicety,
Fitz. And old Sherewood's vicety.

The last of which words were set to a tune, and
sung to the bagpipe, and measure of their dance ;
the clowns and company of spectators drinking and
eating the while.

SONG.

Let's sing about, and say, Hey troll,
Troll to me the bridal bowl,
And divide the broad bride-cake,
Round about the bride's-stake.
With, Here is to the fruit of Pem,
Grafted upon Stub his stem,
With the Peakish nicety,
And old Sherewood's vicety.
But well danced Pem upon record,
Above thy yeoman, or May-lord.

Here it was thought necessary they should be broken off, by the coming in of a GENTLEMAN, an officer or servant of the lord lieutenant's, whose face had put on, with his clothes, an equal authority for the business.

Gent. Give end unto your rudeness : know at length
Whose time and patience you have urg'd, the KING'S.
Whom if you knew, and truly, as you ought,
'Twould strike a reverence in you, ev'n to blushing.
That King whose love it is to be your parent !
Whose office and whose charge, to be your pastor !
Whose single watch defendeth all your sleeps !
Whose labours are your rests ! whose thoughts and cares
Breed your delights, whose business all your leisures !
And you to interrupt his serious hours
With light, impertinent, unworthy objects,
Sights for yourselves, and savouring your own tastes !
You are to blame. Know your disease, and cure it.
Sports should not be obtruded on great monarchs,
But wait when they will call for them as servants,
And meanest of their servants, since their price is
At highest, to be styl'd, but of their pleasures !
—Our King is going now to a great work,
Of highest love, affection, and example,
To see his native country, and his cradle,
And find those manners there, which he suck'd in
With nurse's milk, and parent's piety.
O sister Scotland ! what hast thou deserved
Of joyful England, giving us this king !
What union (if thou lik'st) hast thou not made,
In knitting for Great Britain such a garland,
And letting him to wear it, such a king
As men would wish, that knew not how to hope
His like, but seeing him ! a prince that's law

8   K

Unto himself; is good for goodness sake,
And so becomes the rule unto his subjects !
That studies not to seem or to shew great,
But be : nor drest for others eyes and ears,
With vizors and false rumours, but makes fame
Wait on his actions, and thence speak his name.
O bless his goings-out, and comings-in,
Thou mighty God of heaven ! lend him long
Unto the nations, which yet scarcely know him,
Yet are most happy by his government.
Bless his fair bedmate, and their certain pledges,
And never may he want those nerves in fate ;
For sure succession fortifies a state.
Whilst he himself is mortal, let him feel
Nothing about him mortal in his house ;
Let him approve his young increasing Charles,
A loyal son ; and take him long to be
An aid, before he be a successor.
Late come that day that heaven will ask him from us !
Let our grand-children, and their issue, long
Expect it, and not see it.   Let us pray,
That fortune never know to exercise
More power upon him, than as Charles his servant,
And his Great Britain's slave : ever to wait
Bondwoman to the GENIUS of this state.

THUS IT ENDED.

LOVE'S WELCOME.

THE KING AND QUEEN'S ENTERTAINMENT

AT BOLSOVER,

AT THE EARL OF NEWCASTLE'S, THE

30TH OF JULY, 1634.

LOVE'S WELCOME.]. The King (as was observed before) was so well pleased with the Entertainment at Welbeck, that he sent the earl of Newcastle word, the Queen was resolved to make a progress with him into the north, and he therefore desired him to prepare the same amusement for her which had given him such satisfaction in the preceding year. " Which, (says her Grace,) my lord accordingly did, and endeavoured for it with all possible care and industry, sparing nothing that might add splendour to that feast, which both their Majesties were pleased to honour with their presence. Ben Jonson he employed in fitting such scenes and speeches as he could best devise, and sent for all the gentry of the country to come and wait on their Majesties. This entertainment he made at Bolsover Castle, in Derbyshire, some five miles distant from Welbeck, and resigned Welbeck for their Majesties lodging. It cost him in all between fourteen and fifteen thousand pounds." *Life of the Duke of Newcastle.* p. 184.

It is probable that the course at the Quintain was repeated ; what we have here, was exhibited, not at the dinner, but at the *banquet*, a kind of dessert, which was usually served up in an open room. This little piece is wretchedly given in the folio.

LOVE'S WELCOME, ETC.

The King and Queen being set at banquet, this SONG
was sung by two tenors and a bass.

Full Cho.

F Love be call'd a lifting of the sense
To knowledge of that pure intelligence,
Wherein the soul hath rest and residence,
    1 Ten. *When weret he senses in such*
        order placed?

2 Ten. *The Sight, the Hearing, Smelling, Touching,*
        Taste,
    All at one banquet?

Bas. *Would it ever last!*

1 Ten. *We wish the same: who set it forth thus?*

Bas. *Love!*

2 Ten. *But to what end, or to what object?*

Bas. *Love!*

1 Ten. *Doth Love then feast itself?*

Bas. *Love will feast Love.*

2 Ten. *You make of Love a riddle, or a chain,*
    A circle, a mere knot; untie't again.

Bas. *Love is a circle, both the first and last*
    Of all our actions, and his knot's, too, fast.

1 Ten. *A true love knot will hardly be untied:*
    And if it could, who would this pair divide?

Bas. *God made them such, and Love.*

2 Ten.   *Who is a ring*
    The likest to the year of any thing,

1 Ten. *And runs into itself.*

Bas. *Then let us sing,*
And run into one sound.

Cho. *Let Welcome fill*
Our thoughts, hearts, voices, and that one word
thrill
Through all our language, Welcome, Welcome
still!

1 Ten. *Could we put on the beauty of all creatures*
2 Ten. *Sing in the air, and notes of nightingales,*
1 Ten. *Exhale the sweets of earth, and all her fea-*
tures,
2 Ten. *And tell you, softer than in silk, these tales;*
Bas. *Welcome should season all for taste.*

Cho. *And hence,*
At every real banquet to the sense,
Welcome, true welcome, fill the compliments.

After the Banquet,

The King *and* Queen *being retired, were entertained*
with a Dance *of* Mechanics.

Enter Coronel Vitruvius *speaking to some without.*

Vit. Come forth, boldly put forth, in your holiday
clothes, every mother's son of you. This is the
king and queen's majestical holiday. My lord has it
granted from them; I had it granted from my lord;
and do give it unto you *gratis*, that is, *bona fide*, with
the faith of a surveyor, your coronel Vitruvius. Do
you know what a surveyor is now? I tell you, a
supervisor. A hard word that; but it may be
softened, and brought in, to signify something. An
overseer! one that overseeth you. A busy man!
and yet I must seem busier than I am, as the poet

sings, but which of them I will not now trouble
myself to tell you.

Enter captain SMITH, (or VULCAN,) *with three* Cyclops.

O captain Smith! or hammer-armed Vulcan! with
your three sledges, you are our music, you come a
little too tardy, but we remit that to your polt-foot,
we know you are lame. Plant yourselves there, and
beat your time out at the anvil. Time and Measure
are the father and mother of music, you know, and
your coronel Vitruvius knows a little.

Enter CHESIL *the carver;* MAUL *the free-mason;*
squire SUMMER *the carpenter;* TWYBIL *his man.*

O Chesil, our curious carver! and master Maul our
free-mason; squire Summer our carpenter; and
Twybil his man; stand you four there, in the second
rank, work upon that ground.

Enter DRESSER *the plumber;* QUARREL *the glazier;*
FRET *the plaisterer;* BEATER *mortar-man.*

And you, Dresser the plumber; Quarrel the glazier;
Fret the plaisterer; and Beater the mortar-man: put
all you on in the rear; as finishers in true footing,
with tune and measure. Measure is the soul of a
dance, and tune the tickle-foot thereof. Use holiday
legs, and have 'em; spring, leap, caper, and gingle:
pumps and ribands shall be your reward, till the
soles of your feet swell with the surfeit of your light
and nimble motion. [*Here they began to dance.*
Well done, my musical, arithmetical, geometrical
gamesters! or rather my true mathematical boys! it
is carried in number, weight, and measure, as if the
airs were all harmony, and the figures a well-timed
proportion! I cry still, deserve holidays, and have
'em. I'll have a whole quarter of the year cut out

for you in holidays, and laced with statute-tunes and dances, fitted to the activity of your tressels, to which you shall trust, lads, in the name of your Iniquo Vitruvius,[1] Hey for the lily, for, and the blended rose.

Here the dance ended, and the Mechanics *retired.*

The King and Queen had a second banquet set down before them from the clouds by two Loves, Eros and Anteros : one as the king's, the other as the queen's, differenced by their garlands only; his of white and red roses, the other of lilies interweaved, gold, silver, purple, &c., with a bough of palm in his hand cleft a little at the top; they were both armed and winged; with bows and quivers, cassocks, breeches, buskins, gloves and perukes alike.   They stood silent a while, wondering at one another, till at last the lesser of them began to speak.

Er. Another Cupid !

An. Yes, your second self,
A son of Venus, and as mere an elf
And wag as you.

Er. Eros ?

An. No, Anteros :
Your brother Cupid, yet not sent to cross,
Or spy into your favours here at court.

Er. What then ?

An. To serve you, brother, and report
Your graces from the queen's side to the king's,
In whose name I salute you.

Er. Break my wings
I fear you will.

----

[1] *Iniquo Vitruvius.*]   This miserable pun upon Inigo, is copied by the poet's friend, Philip, earl of Pembroke, in some angry remarks upon Jones, written in the margin of his work on *Stonehenge.*

An. O be not jealous, brother !
What bough is this ?
   Er. A palm.
   An. Give't me.
   Er. Another
You may have.
   An. I will this.   *[Snatches at the palm.*
   Er. Divide it.
        [He divides it, and gives ANTEROS *a part.*
   An. So,
This was right brother-like ! the world will know
By this one act, both natures. You are Love,
I Love, again. In these two spheres we move,
Eros and Anteros.
   Er. We have cleft the bough,
And struck a tally of our loves too now.
   An. I call to mind the wisdom of our mother
Venus, who would have Cupid have a brother——
   Er. To look upon and thrive. Me seems I grew
Three inches higher since I met with you.
It was the counsel that the oracle gave
Your nurses, the glad Graces, sent to crave
Themis' advice. You do not know, quoth she,
The nature of this infant. Love may be
Brought forth thus little, live awhile alone,
But ne'er will prosper, if he have not one
Sent after him to play with, such another
As you are, Anteros, our loving brother.
   An. Who would be always planted in your eye ;
For love by love increaseth mutually.
   Er. We either, looking on each other, thrive.
   An. Shoot up, grow galliard——
   Er. Yes, and more alive !
   An. When one's away, it seems we both are less.
   Er. I was a dwarf, an urchin, I confess,
Till you were present.
   An. But a bird of wing,

Now fit to fly before a queen or king.

Er. I have not one sick feather since you came,
But turn'd a jollier Cupid,

An. Than I am.

Er. I love my mother's brain, could thus provide
For both in court, and give us each our side,
Where we might meet.

An. Embrace.

Er. Circle each other.

An. Confer and whisper.

Er. Brother with a brother.

An. And by this sweet contention for the palm,
Unite our appetites, and make them calm.

Er. To will, and nill one thing.

An. And so to move
Affection in our wills, as in our love.

Er. It is the place, sure, breeds it, where we are.

An. The king and queen's court, which is circular,
And perfect.

Er. The pure school that we live in,
And is of purer love, a discipline.[2]

Enter PHILALETHES.

No more of your poetry, pretty Cupids, lest presuming on your little wits, you profane the intention of your service. The place, I confess, wherein (by the providence of your mother Venus) you are now planted, is the divine school of Love : an academy or court, where all the true lessons of Love are thoroughly read and taught. The reasons, the pro-

---

[2] We have already had this fable in the *Tilting at a Marriage*. There is not much to be said of it here. In fact, these effusions, which attended the king in his progresses, and which perhaps came upon him unexpectedly, are merely little artifices of love and duty on the part of the noble hosts, to keep their sovereign with them as long as possible, and should not be too rigorously judged : they are, as Jonson says, "suddenly thought upon."

portions and harmony, drawn forth in analytic tables, and made demonstrable to the senses. Which if you, brethren, should report, and swear to, would hardly get credit above a fable, here, in the edge of Derbyshire, the region of ale, because you relate in rhyme. O that rhyme is a shrewd disease, and makes all suspected it would persuade. Leave it, pretty Cupids, leave it. Rhyme will undo you, and hinder your growth and reputation in court, more than any thing beside, you have either mentioned or feared. If you dabble in poetry once, it is done of your being believed or understood here. No man will trust you in this verge, but conclude you for a mere case of canters, or a pair of wandering gipsies.

Return to yourselves, little deities, and admire the miracles you serve, this excellent king and his unparalleled queen, who are the canons, the decretals, and whole school-divinity of Love. Contemplate and study them. Here shall you read Hymen, having lighted two torches, either of which inflame mutually, but waste not. One love by the other's aspect increasing, and both in the right lines of aspiring. The Fates spinning them round and even threads, and of their whitest wool, without brack or purl. Fortune and Time fettered at their feet with adamantine chains, their wings deplumed, for starting from them. All amiableness in the richest dress of delight and colours courting the season to tarry by them, and make the idea of their felicity perfect; together with the love, knowledge, and duty of their subjects perpetual. So wisheth the glad and grateful client, seated here, the overjoyed master of the house; and prayeth that the whole region about him could speak but his language. Which is, that first the people's love would let that people know their own happiness, and that knowledge could confirm their duties to an admiration of your sacred persons ; descended, one from the most peaceful, the other the most warlike, both your pious and just progenitors ; from whom, as out of peace, came strength, and " out of the strong came sweetness ;" so in you joined by holy marriage, in the flower and ripeness of years, live the promise of a numerous succession to your sceptres, and a strength to secure your own islands, with their own ocean, but more your own palm-branches, the types of perpetual victory. To which, two words be added, a zealous *Amen*, and ever rounded with a crown of *Welcome*. Welcome, welcome !

EPIGRAMS.

BOOK I.

EPIGRAMS.] From the folio of 1616. The Collection is there called Book I., from which it may be collected, that Jonson intended, at the period of its appearance, to make a further selection. It is to be lamented, on many accounts, that he subsequently changed his purpose. The character of the illustrious nobleman, to whom this manly and high-spirited dedication is addressed, must be looked for in the history of the times.

It may be necessary to admonish the reader not to take up these poems with the general expectation of finding them terminate in a point of wit. This, indeed, is the modern construction of the word; but this was never Jonson's: by Epigram he meant nothing more than a short poem, chiefly restricted to one idea, and equally adapted to the delineation and expression of every passion incident to human life. The work is, in short, an Anthology, and may occasionally remind those who are studious of antiquity, of the collections which pass under that name.

TO THE GREAT EXAMPLE OF HONOUR AND VIRTUE,

THE MOST NOBLE

WILLIAM EARL OF PEMBROKE,

LORD CHAMBERLAIN, ETC.

My Lord,

WHILE you cannot change your merit, I dare not change your title: it was that made it, and not I. Under which name, I here offer to your lordship the ripest of my studies, my Epigrams; *which, though they carry danger in the sound, do not therefore seek your shelter ; for, when I made them, I had nothing in my conscience, to expressing of which I did need a cipher. But, if I be fallen into those times, wherein, for the likeness of vice, and facts, every one thinks another's ill deeds objected to him ; and that in their ignorant and guilty mouths, the common voice is, for their security,* Beware the poet ! *confessing therein so much love to their diseases, as they would rather make a party for them, than be either rid, or told of them ; I must expect, at your Lordship's hand, the protection of truth and liberty, while you are constant to your own goodness. In thanks whereof, I return you the honour of leading forth so many good and great names (as my verses mention on the better part) to their remembrance with posterity. Amongst whom, if I have praised unfortunately any one that doth not deserve ; or, if all answer not, in all numbers, the pictures I have made of them ;*

*I hope it will be forgiven me, that they are no ill pieces,
though they be not like the persons. But I foresee a
nearer fate to my book than this, that the vices therein
will be owned before the virtues, (though there I have
avoided all particulars, as I have done names,) and
some will be so ready to discredit me, as they will
have the impudence to belie themselves: for if I meant
them not, it is so. Nor can I hope otherwise. For
why should they remit any thing of their riot, their
pride, their self-love, and other inherent graces, to consider truth or virtue, but, with the trade of the world,
lend their long ears against men they love not; and
hold their dear mountebank or jester in far better condition than all the study, or studiers of humanity?
For such, I would rather know them by their visards
still, than they should publish their faces, at their
peril, in my theatre,[1] where Cato, if he lived, might
enter without scandal.*

Your Lordship's

most faithful honourer,

BEN JONSON.

---

[1] *In my theatre,*] i. e. in the ensuing collection of epigrams.
This would not have deserved mention, had not Oldys, in his MS.
notes to Langbaine, gravely produced the passage to prove that
Jonson was "master of a play-house!" "He (Ben) mentions
something of his *theatre* to the earl of Pembroke, before his epigrams." So men sometimes read !

EPIGRAMS.

I.

To the Reader.

PRAY thee, take care, that tak'st my
    book in hand,
To read it well; that is, to under-
    stand.

II.

To my Book.

IT will be look'd for, Book, when some but see
    Thy title, Epigrams, and named of me,
    Thou shouldst be bold, licentious, full of gall,
Wormwood, and sulphur, sharp, and tooth'd withal;
Become a petulant thing, hurl ink, and wit,
As madmen stones; not caring whom they hit.
Deceive their malice, who could wish it so;
And by thy wiser temper, let men know
Thou art not covetous of least self-fame,
Made from the hazard of another's shame;
Much less, with lewd, profane, and beastly phrase,
To catch the world's loose laughter, or vain gaze.

S   L

He that departs with his own honesty
For vulgar praise, doth it too dearly buy.

III.

To my Bookseller.

THOU that mak'st gain thy end, and wisely well,
Call'st a book good, or bad, as it doth sell,
Use mine so too; I give thee leave: but crave,
For the luck's sake, it thus much favour have,
To lie upon thy stall, till it be sought;
Not offer'd, as it made suit to be bought;
Nor have my title-leaf on posts or walls,
Or in cleft-sticks, advanced to make calls
For termers, or some clerklike serving-man,
Who scarce can spell th' hard names; whose knight
    less can.
If, without these vile arts, it will not sell,
Send it to Bucklers-bury, there 'twill well.[2]

IV.

To King James.

NOW, best of kings, dost thou a sceptre bear![3]
How, best of poets, dost thou laurel wear!
But two things rare the Fates had in their store,
And gave thee both, to shew they could no more.

[2] *Send it to* Bucklers-bury, *there 'twill well.*] "The whole street (Stow says) called *Buckle's-bury*, on both the sides throughout, is possessed of grocers and apothecaries." So that there must have been a terrible consumption of poetry, and, of course, a never-failing demand for it. "The pepperers," also, it appears from the same authority, mightily affected this street.

[3] *How, best of kings, &c.*] "Dr. Hurd," Whalley says in the margin of his copy, "has severely but justly reprehended Jonson

For such a poet, while thy days were green,
Thou wert, as chief of them are said t' have been.
And such a prince thou art, we daily see,
As chief of those still promise they will be.
Whom should my muse then fly to, but the best
Of kings, for grace ; of poets, for my test ?

for the gross adulation in these verses." Reprehensions of adulation come with a good grace from Hurd, it must be confessed !
But why this outcry against our poet ? His epigram was probably
written soon after the accession of James, and when this good
prince had surely given little cause for complaint to any one. With
respect to his boyish poetry, of which I presume Hurd never read
a line, it is really creditable to his talents. Some of the Psalms
are better translated by him than they were by Milton at his years ;
and surrounded as he was by the hirelings of Elizabeth, who betrayed his mother, and only waited for the word to do as much by
him, it is greatly to his honour that he turned his studies to so good
an account. But why, let me ask again, this eternal outcry against
Jonson ? Hurd had not very far to look for those who flattered
much more grossly than Jonson, without his plea for it. James
was his munificent patron, and gratitude, which none felt more
ardently than our poet, might excuse some little exaggeration of
praise.—But what extraordinary inducement had Shakspeare for his
adulation ? Hurd never asked himself this question. What plea
had Drummond, or his friend Alexander (Lord Stirling) for their
gross sycophancy ? The latter has a panegyric on James for a
sonnet greatly inferior to any thing which his majesty had written
at the date of this Epigram, in which he says,

> " He, prince, or poet, more than man doth prove ! "

and, after a deal of fulsome rant, concludes thus :

> " But all his due who can afford him then ?
> A God of poets, and a king of men ! "

And this is addressed to the queasy Drummond, who is so grievously
scandalized at the "insincerity" of his " dear friend " Jonson. I
trust that the reader will not be mortified at discovering that our
author has partners in his delinquency : a fact that never appears
to have been suspected by those who write against him.

V.

On the Union.

HEN was there contract better driven by Fate,
Or celebrated with more truth of state ?
  The world the temple was, the priest a king,
The spoused pair two realms, the sea the ring.

VI.

To Alchemists.

F all you boast of your great art be true ;
  Sure, willing poverty lives most in you.

VII.

On the new Hot-house.[4]

HERE lately harbour'd many a famous whore,
A purging bill, now fix'd upon the door,
  Tells you it is a hot-house ; so it may,
And still be a whore-house : they're synonyma.

VIII.

On a Robbery.

IDWAY robb'd Duncote of three hundred
          pound,
    Ridway was ta'en, arraign'd, condemn'd to
          die ;

---

[4] A bagnio. Thus Shakspeare : " Now she professes a *hot-house,*
which I think is a very ill house too." *Measure for Measure.*

But, for this money, was a courtier found,
    Begg'd Ridway's pardon : Duncote now doth cry,
" Robb'd both of money, and the law's relief,
    The courtier is become the greater thief."

IX.

TO ALL TO WHOM I WRITE.

AY none whose scatter'd names honour my
        book,
    For strict degrees of rank or title look :
'Tis 'gainst the manners of an epigram ;
And I a poet here, no herald am.

X.

TO MY LORD IGNORANT.

HOU call'st me POET, as a term of shame ;
    But I have my revenge made, in thy name.

XI.

ON SOMETHING, THAT WALKS SOMEWHERE.

T court I met it, in clothes brave enough,
    To be a courtier ; and looks grave enough,
    To seem a statesman : as I near it came,
It made me a great face ; I ask'd the name.
A Lord, it cried, buried in flesh and blood,
And such from whom let no man hope least good,
For I will do none ; and as little ill,
For I will dare none : Good Lord, walk dead still.

XII.

ON LIEUTENANT SHIFT.

SHIFT, here in town, not meanest amongst
    squires,
    That haunt Pickt-hatch, Marsh-Lambeth, and
    White-friars,[5]
Keeps himself, with half a man, and defrays
The charge of that state, with this charm, god pays.[6]
By that one spell he lives, eats, drinks, arrays
Himself: his whole revenue is, god pays.
The quarter-day is come; the hostess says,
She must have money: he returns, god pays.
The tailor brings a suit home; he it says,
Looks o'er the bill, likes it: and says, god pays.
He steals to ordinaries; there he plays
At dice his borrow'd money: which, god pays.
Then takes up fresh commodities, for days;
Signs to new bonds; forfeits; and cries, god pays.
That lost, he keeps his chamber, reads essays,
Takes physic, tears the papers: still, god pays.
Or else by water goes, and so to plays;

[5] *That haunt Pickt-hatch, Marsh-Lambeth, and White-friars.*]
The respective resorts of debauchees, thieves, and fraudulent
debtors.
    [6] *God pays.*] The impudent plea for charity, or rather for run-
ning in debt, advanced by disbanded soldiers, of whom there were
many at this period, and more who pretended to be such. The
expression occurs in the *London Prodigal*, in a passage much to the
purpose:
        Sir Arthur. I am a soldier and a gentleman.
        Lace. I neither doubt your valour nor your love,
    But there be some that bear a soldier's form,
    That swear by him they never think upon:
    Go swaggering up and down from house to house,
    Crying, *god pays.*"
For *says* (tries) see vol. v. p. 163.

Calls for his stool, adorns the stage : god pays.
To every cause he meets, this voice he brays:
His only answer is to all, god pays.
Not his poor cockatrice but he betrays
Thus ; and for his letchery scores, god pays.
But see ! the old bawd hath serv'd him in his trim,
Lent him a pocky whore.—She hath paid him.

XIII.

To Doctor Empiric.

HEN men a dangerous disease did 'scape,
Of old, they gave a cock to Æsculape :[7]
Let me give two, that doubly am got free ;
From my disease's danger, and from thee.

XIV.

To William Camden.

AMDEN! most reverend head, to whom I owe
All that I am in arts, all that I know;[8]
(How nothing's that?) to whom my country
owes
The great renown, and name wherewith she goes !
Than thee the age sees not that thing more grave,
More high, more holy, that she more would crave.

---

[7] *They gave a cock to Æsculape.*] The last request which Socrates made to his friends was, that they would offer this popular sacrifice for him. This has led some to imagine that the poison had begun to take effect, and that he was become light-headed. He was quite as rational as his critics ; and, in perfect consistency with his creed, viewed his death as a *recovery* to life.

[8] Camden, *most reverend head, to whom I owe*
All that I am in arts, all that I know.] Camden was our poet's master at Westminster-school ; and gratitude has led him

What name, what skill, what faith hast thou in
    things !
What sight in searching the most antique springs !
What weight, and what authority in thy speech !
Men scarce can make that doubt, but thou canst
    teach.
Pardon free truth, and let thy modesty,
Which conquers all, be once o'ercome by thee.
Many of thine, this better could, than I ;
But for their powers, accept my piety.

XV.

ON COURT-WORM.

ALL men are worms; but this no man.   In
    silk
    'Twas brought to court first wrapt, and white
    as milk ;
Where, afterwards, it grew a butterfly,
Which was a caterpillar : so 'twill die.[9]

to make a proper acknowledgment for his care and pains in teaching him, both by this epigram, and the dedication of *Every Man in his Humour* to him. WHAL.

    These are not the only places in which Camden is mentioned with respect. In the *King's Entertainment*, Jonson terms him "the glory and light of the kingdom," and in the *Masque of Queens*, he introduces him with similar commendation. No man ever possessed a more warm and affectionate heart than this great poet, whose name is made synonymous with envy and ingratitude, by every desperate blockhead who reprints an old play or a poem.

[9] ————————————————— *in silk*

    'Twas brought to court, &c.] Pope had this epigram in his thoughts when he wrote his Epistle to Arbuthnot :

        " Let Sporus tremble. What, that thing of silk !
        Sporus, that mere white curd of ass's milk."

But he has confounded the metaphor, which is preserved by Jonson with equal accuracy and beauty.

XVI.

To Brainhardy.

HARDY, thy brain is valiant, 'tis confest,
  Thou more; that with it every day dar'st jest
  Thy self into fresh brawls : when, call'd upon,
Scarce thy week's swearing brings thee off, of one.
So in short time, thou art in arrearage grown
Some hundred quarrels, yet dost thou fight none ;
Nor need'st thou : for those few, by oath releast,
Make good what thou dar'st do in all the rest.
Keep thy self there, and think thy valour right ;
He that dares damn himself, dares more than fight.

XVII.

To the learned Critic.

MAY others fear, fly, and traduce thy name,
  As guilty men do magistrates ; glad I,
  That wish my poems a legitimate fame,
  Charge them, for crown, to thy sole censure hie.
And but a sprig of bays, given by thee,
Shall outlive garlands, stol'n from the chaste tree.[1]

XVIII.

To my mere English censurer.

TO thee, my way in Epigrams seems new,
  When both it is the old way, and the true.
  Thou say'st, that cannot be ; for thou hast
      seen

---

[1] *Shall outlive garlands stolen from the* chaste tree,] i. e. the
laurel ; Daphne, rather than consent to the desires of Apollo, being
changed into that tree. WHAL.

Davis, and Weever,[2] and the best have been,
And mine come nothing like.   I hope so : Yet,
As theirs did with thee, mine might credit get,
If thou'dst but use thy faith, as thou didst then ;
When thou wert wont t' admire, not censure men.
Prithee believe still, and not judge so fast,
Thy faith is all the knowledge that thou hast.

XIX.

ON SIR COD THE PERFUMED.

HAT Cod can get no widow, yet a knight,
I scent the cause : he wooes with an ill sprite.[3]

[2] ——————— *For thou hast seen*
Davis, *and* Weever.] *Davis* was the author of a collection of epigrams called *the Scourge of Folly:* he was by profession a writing-master, and chiefly taught in the university of Oxford.   He was a contemporary of Jonson, and has an epigram addressed to him. *Weever* was the author of a work in folio, which is called *Funeral Monuments*, and is a miscellany of epitaphs, and inscriptions, collected from ancient monuments in various parts of the kingdom. WHAL.

[3] *He wooes with an ill sprite.*]   A play on the double meaning of the last word, an evil genius or spirit, and a stinking breath.   To this last sense of sprite, young Knowell alludes in the inflated panegyric with which he puzzles and plays upon master Stephen : " A wight that hitherto, his every step hath left the stamp of a *great foot* behind him, as every word the savour of a *strong spirit.*"   The name of the person to whom this epigram is addressed is borrowed from the *cod* or little purse in which civet and other perfumes were kept in the poet's days.

In the *Woman's Prize*, Livia says to her lover,

" Hold this certain—
    Selling, which is a sin unpardonable,
    Of counterfeit *cods*, or musty English crocus,
    Switches, or stones for the tooth-ach, sooner finds me
    Than that drawn fox Moroso."   A. i. S. 2.

Upon which Mr. Weber observes : " In some MS. notes which have been procured for me, *cod* is explained, a pillow, a belly.   I

XX.

To the same.

THE expense in odours is a most vain sin,
Except thou could'st, sir Cod, wear them
within.

XXI.

On Reformed Gamester.

LORD, how is Gamester chang'd! his hair close
cut,[4]
His neck fenced round with ruff, his eyes half
shut!
His clothes two fashions off, and poor! his sword
Forbid his side, and nothing, but the word,
Quick in his lips! Who hath this wonder wrought?
The late ta'en bastinado.   So I thought.
What several ways men to their calling have!
The body's stripes, I see, the soul may save.

XXII.

On my first daughter.

HERE lies, to each her parent's ruth,
Mary, the daughter of their youth;
Yet all heaven's gifts being heaven's due,
It makes the father less to rue.

am afraid the allusion is not so delicate." The writer's fears are
about as ideal as those of Mr. Steevens, from whom this miserable
cant is adopted; his ignorance, however, here, as well as every
where else, is sufficiently real: what did he suppose Livia to mean?
Counterfeit cods are spurious or adulterate civet-bags, and nothing
more.
    [4] —— *his hair close cut, &c.*]   These are the characteristic

At six months end she parted hence
With safety of her innocence ;
Whose soul heaven's Queen, whose name she bears,[5]
In comfort of her mother's tears,
Hath placed amongst her virgin-train :
Where while that, severed, doth remain,
This grave partakes the fleshly birth ;
Which cover lightly, gentle earth !

XXIII.

To John Donne.[6]

ONNE, the delight of Phœbus and each Muse,
Who, to thy one, all other brains refuse ;
Whose every work, of thy most early wit,
Came forth example, and remains so, yet :
Longer a knowing than most wits do live,
And which no affection praise enough can give !
To it, thy language, letters, arts, best life,
Which might with half mankind maintain a strife ;

marks of a puritan, which Gamester was now become. The *word* was the cant phrase for the Scripture, which was profanely applied to every incident of life. This is an epigram of all times.

[5] *Whose soul heaven's* Queen, *whose name she bears,*] i. e. the virgin *Mary;* this seems to have been written, when our poet was a convert to the church of Rome. WHAL.

There is both pathos and beauty in this little piece : Jonson appears to have been a most kind and affectionate parent, and if, as Fuller says, he did not always meet with an equal return of duty and love, those who denied it to him have the greater sin. It is here the proper place to observe that our poet is by far the best writer of epitaphs that this country ever possessed.

[6] *John Donne.*] The celebrated Dean of St. Paul's. His character is excellently given in this affectionate memorial of his virtues ; indeed, no one knew him better, or valued him more justly than Jonson. The domestic life of this eminent man is admirably written by Izaak Walton ; and a severe, though not unjust, estimate of his poetical merits will be found in Dr. Johnson's Life of Cowley.

All which I meant to praise, and yet I would ;
But leave, because I cannot as I should !

XXIV.

To the Parliament.

THERE'S reason good, that you good laws
should make :
Men's manners ne'er were viler, for your sake.

XXV.

On sir Voluptuous Beast.

WHILE Beast instructs his fair and innocent
wife,
In the past pleasures of his sensual life,
Telling the motions of each petticoat,
And how his Ganymede mov'd, and how his goat,
And now her hourly her own cucquean makes,
In varied shapes, which for his lust she takes :
What doth he else, but say, Leave to be chaste,
Just wife, and to change me, make woman's haste !

XXVI.

On the Same.

THAN his chaste wife though Beast now know
no more,
He adulters still : his thoughts lie with a
whore.

XXVII.

ON SIR JOHN ROE.[7]

IN place of scutcheons that should deck thy
        herse,
    Take better ornaments, my tears and verse.
If any sword could save from Fates', Roe's could ;
    If any Muse outlive their spight, his can ;
If any friends' tears could restore, his would ;
    If any pious life ere lifted man
To heaven ; his hath : O happy state ! wherein
We, sad for him, may glory, and not sin.

XXVIII.

ON DON SURLY.

DON Surly, to aspire the glorious name
    Of a great man, and to be thought the same,
    Makes serious use of all great trade he knows.
He speaks to men with a rhinocerote's nose,[8]
Which he thinks great ; and so reads verses too :
And that is done, as he saw great men do.

---

[7] *On sir John Roe.*] Probably the son of sir Thomas Roe, knt.,
an eminent merchant of London, who after passing with distinguished credit through every municipal honour, died full of years
and good works about 1570.   This worthy citizen, whose charity
was directed by his piety to the most useful purposes, left four sons,
who appear to have trod in the footsteps of their father.
    [8] *He speaks to men with a rhinocerote's nose,*] i. e. I believe, with
a nose elate, or curled up into a kind of sneer, scornfully, contemptuously.   This, at least, is the meaning of the expression in
Martial's lively address to his book :

> *Nescis, heu nescis dominæ fastidia Romæ,*
> `  ` *Crede mihi, nimium Martia turba sapit;*
> *Majores nusquam ronchi, juvenesque senesque,*
> `    ` *Et pueri nasum Rhinocerotis habent !*   lib. i. 4.

He has tympanies of business in his face,
And can forget men's names, with a great grace.
He will both argue, and discourse in oaths,
Both which are great : and laugh at ill-made clothes ;
That's greater, yet : to cry his own up neat.
He doth at meals, alone, his pheasant eat,
Which is·main greatness ; and at his still board,
He drinks to no man : that's, too, like a lord.
He keeps another's wife, which is a spice
Of solemn greatness ; and he dares, at dice,
Blaspheme God greatly ; or some poor hind beat,
That breathes in his dog's way : [9] and this is great.
Nay more, for greatness sake, he will be one
May hear my epigrams, but like of none.
SURLY, use other arts, these only can
Style thee a most great fool, but no great man.

XXIX.

TO SIR ANNUAL TILTER.

ILTER, the most may admire thee, though
            not I ;
        And thou, right guiltless, may'st plead to it,
            Why ?
For thy late sharp device.   I say 'tis fit
All brains, at times of triumph, should run wit :
For then our water-conduits do run wine ;
But that's put in, thou'lt say.   Why, so is thine.

---

[9] *That* breathes *in his dog's way.*]   "Breathes (Whalley says) is
intended to express what Shakspeare means when he describes
such as 'breathe in their watering.'"   There is no end to this nonsense, since Steevens first set it abroach.   I have already relieved
Shakspeare from the obloquy of so filthy a meaning (vol. ii. p. 32,)
and to take away every possible plea for its being charged upon him
again, I will now add the following decisive passage.   The words
of Shakspeare are : "They call drinking deep dying scarlet, and
when you breathe in your watering," (stop to take breath in your

XXX.

To Person Guilty.

GUILTY, be wise; and though thou know'st
  the crimes
  Be thine, I tax, yet do not own my rhymes:
'Twere madness in thee, to betray thy fame,
And person to the world, ere I thy name.

XXXI.

On Banks the Usurer.

BANKS feels no lameness of his knotty gout,
  His monies travel for him in and out:
  And though the soundest legs go every day,
He toils to be at hell, as soon as they.

XXXII.

On sir John Roe.[1]

WHAT two brave perils of the private sword
  Could not effect, nor all the Furies do,
  That self-divided Belgia did afford;
  What not the envy of the seas reach'd to,

draught,) "they cry *hem!* and bid you play it off." The parallel
passage follows:
  "Fill Will his beaker, he will never flinch
   To give a full quart pot the emptie pinch.
   He'll looke unto your *waters* well enough,
   And hath an eye that no man leaves a snuffe:
   A pox of piece-meale drinking! William sayes,
   Play it away; will have no stoppes and stayes;
   Blown drink is odious," &c. *S. Rowland,* Sat. 6.
  [1] Jonson appears to have sincerely loved and lamented this ex-

The cold of Mosco, and fat Irish air,
　His often change of clime, though not of mind,
All could not work ; at home, in his repair,
　Was his blest fate, but our hard lot to find.
Which shews, wherever death doth please t' appear,
Seas, sérenes,[2] swords, shot, sickness, all are there.

XXXIII.

To the Same.

'LL not offend thee with a vain tear more,
　Glad-mention'd Roe ; thou art but gone
　　before,
Whither the world must follow : and I, now,
Breathe to expect my When, and make my How.

cellent person, of whose actions I can give the reader no account
He seems to have followed the business of a merchant-venturer at
first, like his father, and subsequently, in imitation of many gallant
spirits in those days, to have embarked in the wars of the Nether-
lands.　He died, however, in peace, at home.

　Among Whalley's loose papers, I find another memorial of our
author's regard for him.　It seems to be taken from the blank
leaf of a Persius, with which he had presented him.　Why Whalley
chose to give us vile English instead of copying the elegant Latin
of the original, I cannot tell.

　" To sir John Roe, his most approved friend, this his love and
delight, the most learned of satirists, PERSIUS, with a most learned
commentary, is consecrated by Ben. Jonson, who willingly, deservedly, gives and dedicates it.　Nor is a parent more to be preferred by me than a friend."

　[2] *Seas*, sérenes, *&c.*] i. e. a blast of warm air; a blight, or mildew,
vol. iii. p. 248.　The most miserable pun on record, (which yet was
repeated at every table in Paris,) was made by the marquis of
Bievre on this word.　Mad. d'Angivilliers had a favourite *serin*, (a
canary-bird,) and the marquis, on coming into her drawing-room,
gravely put on his hat, with this notable piece of wit : " I beg your
ladyship's pardon—but I am afraid of the serein !"　The marquis
was a great reader of Joe Miller—so were not the French in general :
his second wit therefore was in high request.

8　　　　　　　　　　　M

Which if most gracious heaven grant like thine,
Who wets my grave,[3] can be no friend of mine.

XXXIV.

OF DEATH.

HE that fears death, or mourns it, in the just,
Shews of the Resurrection little trust.

XXXV.

TO KING JAMES.

WHO would not be thy subject, James, t' obey
A prince that rules by' example, more than
    sway?
Whose manners draw, more than thy powers con-
    strain.
And in this short time of thy happiest reign,
Hast purg'd thy realms, as we have now no cause
Left us of fear, but first our crimes, then laws.
Like aids 'gainst treasons who hath found before,
And than in them, how could we know God more?
First thou preserved wert our king to be;
And since, the whole land was preserv'd for thee.[4]

---

[3] *Who wets my grave, &c.*] This is a beautiful little valediction;
there is a simple grandeur of thought, a high moral dignity in all
the addresses of Jonson, (for there are more to come) to this distinguished family, which does no less honour to them than to the
poet.
   [4] *And since the whole land was preserv'd for thee.*] This epigram
was probably written in 1604, as the last allusion is to the plague,
which broke out in London soon after the death of Elizabeth. The
" treasons " spoken of just above, are probably those of the Gow-
ries and sir Walter Raleigh.

XXXVI.

To the Ghost of Martial.

MARTIAL, thou gav'st far nobler epigrams
    To thy Domitian, than I can my James;
    But in my royal subject I pass thee,
Thou flatter'dst thine, mine cannot flatter'd be.

XXXVII.

On Cheveril the lawyer.

NO cause, nor client fat, will Cheveril leese,
    But as they come, on both sides he takes
        fees,
And pleaseth both : for while he melts his grease,
For this ; that wins, for whom he holds his peace.

XXXVIII.

To Person Guilty.

GUILTY, because I bade you late be wise,[5]
    And to conceal your ulcers, did advise,
    You laugh when you are touch'd, and long
        before
Any man else, you clap your hands and roar,
And cry, *good ! good !* this quite perverts my sense,
And lies so far from wit, 'tis impudence.
Believe it, GUILTY, if you lose your shame,
I'll lose my modesty, and tell your name.

   [5] GUILTY, *because I bade you* late *be wise.*] See Epig. XXX.
This is an excellent epigram ; replete with strong sense, and keen
observation of mankind.

XXXIX.

On old Colt.

OR all night-sins, with others' wives unknown,
Colt now doth daily penance in his own.

XL.

On Margaret Ratcliffe.

M ARBLE, weep, for thou dost cover
A dead beauty underneath thee,
R ich as nature could bequeath thee :
G rant then, no rude hand remove her.
A ll the gazers on the skies
R ead not in fair heaven's story,
E xpresser truth, or truer glory,
T han they might in her bright eyes.

R are as wonder was her wit ;
A nd, like nectar, ever flowing :
T ill time, strong by her bestowing,
C onquer'd hath both life and it ;
L ife, whose grief was out of fashion
I n these times.   Few so have rued
F ate in a brother.   To conclude,[6]
F or wit, feature, and true passion,
E arth, thou hast not such another.

[6] ———— *Few so have rued*
Fate in a brother.] Of this lady, Margaret Ratcliffe, I can give
the reader no information. She was probably a collateral branch
of the family of the earl of Sussex, for the marriage of whose
daughter Jonson wrote the beautiful Masque of the *Hue and Cry
after Cupid.* From a subsequent Epigram I collect that she had
five brothers, of whom she had the misfortune to lose four ; two in
the field, in Ireland, and two by sickness, in the Low Countries.

XLI.

ON GIPSY.

GIPSY, new bawd, is turn'd physician,
And gets more gold than all the college can :
Such her quaint practice is, so it allures,
For what she gave, a whore ; a bawd, she cures.

XLII.

ON GILES AND JOAN.

WHO says that Giles and Joan at discord be ?
Th' observing neighbours no such mood can
see.
Indeed, poor Giles repents he married ever ;
But that his Joan doth too. And Giles would never,
By his free-will, be in Joan's company :
No more would Joan he should. Giles riseth early,
And having got him out of doors is glad ;
The like is Joan : but turning home is sad ;
And so is Joan. Oftimes when Giles doth find
Harsh sights at home, Giles wisheth he were blind ;
All this doth Joan : or that his long-yearn'd life
Were quite out-spun ; the like wish hath his wife.
The children that he keeps, Giles swears are none
Of his begetting ; and so swears his Joan.
In all affections she concurreth still.
If now, with man and wife, to will and nill
The self-same things,[7] a note of concord be :
I know no couple better can agree !

Jonson had reason, therefore, to say that few had *rued* such fate in their relations.

[7] ——— *to will and nill*
  The self-same things, &c.] *Idem velle atque nolle, ea demum amicitia est.*

XLIII.

TO ROBERT EARL OF SALISBURY.[8]

HAT need hast thou of me, or of my muse,
    Whose actions so themselves do celebrate ?
    Which should thy country's love to speak
        refuse,
Her foes enough would fame thee in their hate.
Tofore, great men were glad of poets ; now,
    I, not the worst, am covetous of thee :
Yet dare not to my thought least hope allow
    Of adding to thy fame ; thine may to me,
When in my book men read but Cecil's name,
    And what I write thereof find far, and free
From servile flattery, common poets' shame,
    As thou stand'st clear of the necessity.

---

[8] *Robert earl of Salisbury.*] Younger son of lord Burleigh. He and his elder brother, William, were both created earls in the same day. Robert in the morning ; to give his descendants precedency of those of William.

"This man," Walpole says, "who had the fortune or misfortune" (why misfortune ? but this poor stuff was meant for wit) "to please both Elizabeth and James the First ; who like the son of the duke of Lerma had the uncommon fate of succeeding his own father as prime minister, and who unlike that son of Lerma did not, though treacherous to every body else, supplant his own father, is sufficiently known ; his public story may be found in all our histories, his particular in the Biographia." *Cat. of Royal and Noble Authors.* In none of these, however, did Walpole look for the "story" of this eminent statesman ; but in the ignorant, impure, and scandalous reports of the Weldons, Peytons, and other puritanical disseminators of falsehood, as better suited to the base and envious nature of his own spirit. When the time shall come for Walpole himself to be added to the number of "noble authors," by a sterner biographer than Mr. Parke, he will, if fairly represented, be found to be one of the most odious and contemptible of the whole "Catalogue."

XLIV.

ON CHUFFE, BANKS *the Usurer's Kinsman.*

CHUFFE, lately rich in name, in chattels,
    goods,
    And rich in issue to inherit all,
Ere blacks were bought for his own funeral,
Saw all his race approach the blacker floods :
He meant they thither should make swift repair,
When he made him executor, might be heir.

XLV.

ON MY FIRST SON.

FAREWELL, thou child of my right hand, and
    joy ; [9]
    My sin was too much hope of thee, lov'd boy :
Seven years thou wert lent to me, and I thee pay,
Exacted by thy fate, on the just day.

[9] *Farewell*, thou child of my right hand, *and joy.*] The expression here must be explained : *thou child of my right hand* shews us his son's name was *Benjamin ;* that word being usually taken as a compound of two Hebrew words, which imply that meaning. But some modern commentators more justly interpret the word *Benjamin* to signify the *son of days*, or *of old age. Benjamin* was the youngest son, and probably born when his father was advanced in years. WHAL.

My predecessor seems to write without reading what he is about to explain. The title declares the Epitaph to be written on *his first son;* Benjamin, says the critic, was the *youngest son*, and probably born when the father was advanced in years ! This is sad trifling; but Whalley appears to me to have contented himself, upon all occasions, with second-hand authorities, which are commonly worse than none at all. In one of the spiteful attempts made to injure Jonson by his " friend " Drummond, he relates the following anecdote, which he had (he says) from the poet's own mouth. " While the plague raged in London, he was on a visit with Camden, at the house of sir Robert Cotton, in the country. Here he saw, in

O, could I lose all father, now ! for why,
Will man lament the state he should envy ?
To have so soon scaped world's, and flesh's rage,
And, if no other misery, yet age !
Rest in soft peace, and ask'd, say here doth lie
BEN JONSON his best piece of poetry :
For whose sake henceforth all his vows be such,
As what he loves may never like too much.

XLVI.

TO SIR LUCKLESS WOO-ALL.

S this the sir, who, some waste wife to win,
A knight-hood bought, to go a wooing in ?
'Tis Luckless, he that took up one on band
To pay at's day of marriage.   By my hand
The knight-wright's cheated then ! he'll never pay :
Yes, now he wears his knighthood every day.

a dream, his eldest son, with the mark of a bloody cross (the token
of the plague) on his forehead. Alarmed at this, he prayed to God
for him, and went in the morning to Camden's room, and told him
what he had seen. Camden desired him not to be dejected, for
that it was merely the creation of his own fears : but there came a
letter from his wife, to inform him that the child was dead of the
plague. Jonson added, that his son appeared to him of a manly
stature, and of such growth as he thought he would be at the Resurrection." There is enough in this narrative to convince any one
but the vile calumniator who reports it, that the fond father was
not, as he asserts, void of all religion :—but to the purpose of the
note. The plague broke out in 1603, the child was then in his
seventh year ; he was born, therefore, in 1596, when Jonson, instead
of being "advanced in years," was just turned of two and twenty !
    The last couplet contains a pretty allusion to the cheerless ad-
vice of Martial, in one of his melancholy moods :

> *Si vitare velis accrba quædam,*
> *Et tristes animi cavere morsus,*
> *Nulli te facias nimis sodalem,*
> *Gaudebis minus, at minus dolebis.*

XLVII.

To the Same.

IR LUCKLESS, troth, for luck's sake pass by
one;
 He that wooes every widow, will get none.

XLVIII.

On Mungril Esquire.

IS bought arms Mung' not liked ; for his first
day
 Of bearing them in field, he threw 'em away ;[1]
And hath no honour lost, our duellists say.

XLIX.

To Playwright.

LAYWRIGHT me reads, and still my verses
damns,
 . He says I want the tongue of epigrams ;
I have no salt, no bawdry he doth mean ;[2]
For witty, in his language, is obscene.

---

[1] ——————— *For his first day*
Of bearing them in field, *he threw 'em away.*] The arms were
usually pourtrayed upon the shield; so that on his entering into
battle, he flung away his shield, that he might not be encumbered
in his flight. This marks him for his cowardice. WHAL.
 Jonson might have thrown his epigram after Mungril's arms,
with no more loss of credit than the other of honour.
 [2] *I have no salt, no bawdry he doth mean.*] This expression
sufficiently justifies Pope's emendation of the passage in *Hamlet*,
"I remember one said there were no *salts* in the lines to make the
matter *savoury*." The old copies read *sallets*, which being akin to
nonsense is, according to custom, replaced in the text by the last

Playwright, I loath to have thy manners known
In my chaste book; profess them in thine own.

L.

To sir Cod.

LEAVE, Cod, tobacco-like, burnt gums to take,
Or fumy clysters, thy moist lungs to bake:
Arsenic would thee fit for society make.

LI.

To King James.

*Upon the happy false rumour of his death, the two
and twentieth day of March,* 1606.[3]

WHAT we thy loss might know, and thou our love,
Great heaven did well to give ill fame free
wing;
Which though it did but panic terror prove,
And far beneath least pause of such a king;

editors;—though, as Mr. Steevens adds, "the alteration of Pope
may be, in some measure, supported by the following passage in
Decker's *Satiromastix*—"a prepared troop of gallants, who shall
distaste every *unsalted* line in their fly-blown comedies." If the
change be *in some measure* supported by this quotation, it is altogether fixed by the line above, of which none of the commentators
take the slightest notice.

[3] The best comment upon this little piece is to be found in
Winwood's State Papers, in a letter from Mr. Chamberlaine to that
minister, dated April 5th, 1606; from which it appears that Jonson has not exaggerated the common feeling, which was the more
alive as the story came so quickly upon the discovery of the Gun-
powder Plot. The report was that the king had been stabbed
with a poisoned knife, at Woking, in Surrey, where he was hunting.

Yet give thy jealous subjects leave to doubt,
  Who this thy scape from rumour gratulate,
No less than if from peril; and devout,
  Do beg thy care unto thy after-state.
For we, that have our eyes still in our ears,
Look not upon thy dangers, but our fears.

LII.

To Censorious Courtling.

OURTLING, I rather thou should'st utterly
  Dispraise my work, than praise it frostily :
  When I am read, thou feign'st a weak ap-
    plause,
As if thou wert my friend, but lack'dst a cause.
This but thy judgment fools : the other way
Would both thy folly and thy spite betray.

Mr. Lodge has also a letter on the subject from the earl of Kent
to the earl of Shrewsbury, of which a part is subjoined.

"My very hon'ble good Lo. I received yesterday yor hon'able
and frendley lines by John Sibley, whereby it pleased yor L^p to
adv'tise me of the untruthe of those bruits spread abroad of so
horrible a treason against his Maj^{ties} precious life. Theis false
bruits come very speedily not only to the Privie Councell at the
Corte, and so to London, but also into theis parts, and not onlike,
into a great p'te of the kingdom. All thother daye being Sondaye,
we here knew nothinge certenly to the contrary but that the worst
might be feared : but the greater astonishment this sudden fearefull
rumour hath ev'y where occasioned, the more sing'lar comfort and
joye will now redounde to ev'ie true harted subject by the report
of his Maties safetie, for wch they shall have so just cause to sounde
forth God's praise, together with incessant prayers for his Highnes
longe happie and prosperous raigne ov^r us." Wilson's account of
the confusion and dismay which took place on this occasion, is
given in yet stronger language.

LIII.

To Oldend Gatherer.

ONG-GATHERING Oldend, I did fear thee
        wise,
    When having pill'd a book which no man buys,
Thou wert content the author's name to lose :
But when, in place, thou didst the patron's choose,
It was as if thou printed hadst an oath,
To give the world assurance thou wert both ;
And that, as puritans at baptism do,
Thou art the father, and the witness too.
For, but thyself, where, out of motley, 's he⁴
Could save that line to dedicate to thee ?

LIV.

On Cheveril.

HEVERIL cries out my verses libels are ;
    And threatens the Star-chamber, and the Bar.
    What are thy petulant pleadings, Cheveril, then,
That quit'st the cause so oft, and rail'st at men ?

LV.

To Francis Beaumont.

OW I do love thee, Beaumont, and thy Muse,
    That unto me dost such religion use !
    How I do fear myself, that am not worth
The least indulgent thought thy pen drops forth !

----

⁴ *Where, out of motley, 's he, &c.*] i. e. where out of a motley, or
fool's coat is he, &c. In other words, who but a fool ?—Whalley
seems to have strangely mistaken this simple expression.

At once thou mak'st me happy, and unmak'st;
And giving largely to me, more thou tak'st!
What fate is mine, that so itself bereaves?
What art is thine, that so thy friend deceives?
When even there, where most thou praisest me,
For writing better, I must envy thee.[5]

LVI.

ON POET-APE.

OOR Poet-ape,[6] that would be thought our chief,
    Whose works are e'en the frippery of wit,
From brokage is become so bold a thief,
   As we, the robb'd, leave rage, and pity it.
At first he made low shifts, would pick and glean,
   Buy the reversion of old plays ; now grown

---

[5] *When even there, where most thou praisest me,*
   For writing better, I must envy thee.] This short poem is an answer to a letter, which Beaumont, then in the country with Fletcher, sent to Jonson, together with two unfinished comedies. The letter is an excellent one, and proves the interesting frankness and cordiality in which "the envious and malignant Ben" lived with his brother poets. The passage to which the text more immediately applies is the following :

   ———————————— "Fate once again
Bring me to thee, who canst make smooth and plain
The way of knowledge for me, and then I,
(Who have no good but in thy company,)
Protest it will my greatest comfort be,
To acknowledge all I have to flow from thee.
Ben, when these scenes are perfect, we'll taste wine,
I'll drink thy muse's health, thou shalt quaff mine.

[6] *Poor Poet-ape, &c.*] Mr. Chalmers will *take it on his death* that the person here meant is Shakspeare ! Who can doubt it? For my part, I am persuaded, that Groom Idiot in the next epigram is also Shakspeare ; and, indeed, generally, that he is typified by the words "fool and knave," so exquisitely descriptive of him, wherever they occur in Jonson.

To a little wealth, and credit in the scene,
    He takes up all, makes each man's wit his own :
And, told of this, he slights it.   Tut, such crimes
    The sluggish gaping auditor devours ;
He marks not whose 'twas first : and after-times
    May judge it to be his, as well as ours.
Fool ! as if half eyes will not know a fleece
From locks of wool, or shreds from the whole piece.

LVII.

ON BAWDS AND USURERS.

F, as their ends, their fruits were so, the same,
    Bawdry and Usury were one kind of game.

LVIII.

TO GROOM IDIOT.

DIOT, last night, I pray'd thee but forbear
    To read my verses ; now I must to hear :
    For offering with thy smiles my wit to grace,
Thy ignorance still laughs in the wrong place.
And so my sharpness thou no less disjoints,
Than thou didst late my sense, losing my points.
So have I seen at Christmas-sports, one lost,
And hood-wink'd, for a man embrace a post.

LIX.

ON SPIES.

PIES, you are lights in state, but of base stuff,
    Who, when you've burnt your selves down to
            the snuff,
Stink, and are thrown away.   End fair enough.

LX.

To William lord Mounteagle.[7]

O, what my country should have done (have
    raised
    An obelisk, or column to thy name,
Or, if she would but modestly have praised
    Thy fact, in brass or marble writ the same)
I, that am glad of thy great chance, here do !
    And proud, my work shall out-last common
      deeds,
Durst think it great, and worthy wonder too,
    But thine, for which I do't, so much exceeds !
My country's parents I have many known ;
But, saver of my country, THEE alone.

---

[7] *To William lord Mounteagle.*] This was the nobleman who received the remarkable letter about the gun-powder plot, taken notice of by our historians, and which gave the first apprehensions of what was then contriving. WHAL.

Many angry attacks have been made on James for assuming to himself the merit of discovering the import of this letter ; of which Cecil takes the credit in an excellent official paper to sir Charles Cornwallis, (*Winwood Mem.* vol. ii. p. 170,) but surely without much cause. The fact seems to be that Cecil allowed the king (who was always tenacious of his own sagacity) to imagine that he had detected the latent meaning of the letter. Cecil was the most shrewd, and James the most simple and unsuspicious of mortals :— there is, therefore, not the smallest reason to believe that the king meant to mislead the parliament, or that he thought otherwise than he spoke. We deceive ourselves grossly, if we assume that all which is known now was known at the time when the event took place. Cecil's letter was a sealed letter to the parliament and the nation ; and, after all, we have only the minister's word for his share in the discovery. The hint to lord Mounteagle, which was given to him by his sister, Mary Parker, wife of Thomas Habington, and mother of the amiable and virtuous author of *Castora*, was not the only one conveyed to the earl of Salisbury on this mysterious business.

LXI.

To Fool, or Knave.

WHY praise or dispraise is to me alike ;
One doth not stroke me, nor the other strike.

LXII.

To fine lady Would-be.

FINE madam Would-be, wherefore should you
        fear,
    That love to make so well, a child to bear ?
The world reputes you barren : but I know
Your pothecary, and his drug, says no.
Is it the pain affrights ? that's soon forgot.
Or your complexion's loss ? you have a pot,
That can restore that. Will it hurt your feature ?
To make amends, you are thought a wholesome
        creature.
What should the cause be ? oh, you live at court ;
And there's both loss of time, and loss of sport,
In a great belly : Write then on thy womb,
" Of the not born, yet buried, here's the tomb."

LXIII.

To Robert earl of Salisbury.

WHO can consider thy right courses run,
    With what thy virtue on the times hath won,
    And not thy fortune ? who can clearly see
The judgment of the king so shine in thee ;
And that thou seek'st reward of thy each act,
Not from the public voice, but private fact ?

Who can behold all envy so declined
By constant suffering of thy equal mind;
And can to these be silent, Salisbury,
Without his, thine, and all time's injury?
Curst be his Muse, that could lie dumb, or hid
To so true worth, though thou thy self forbid.

LXIV.

To the same.

Upon the Accession of the Treasurership to him.[8]

NOT glad, like those that have new hopes, or suits,
With thy new place, bring I these early fruits
Of love, and, what the golden age did hold
A treasure, art; contemn'd in the age of gold.
Nor glad as those, that old dependents be,
To see thy father's rites new laid on thee.
Nor glad for fashion; nor to shew a fit
Of flattery to thy titles; nor of wit.
But I am glad to see that time survive,
Where merit is not sepulcher'd alive;
Where good men's virtues them to honours bring,
And not to dangers: when so wise a king
Contends to have worth enjoy, from his regard,
As her own conscience, still, the same reward.

[8] Enough has been said already of the character of this eminent statesman; but it may not be amiss, on the present occasion, to enumerate the periods of his successive honours. He was born June 1, 1563, knighted in 1591; sworn of the privy council in the following August, and in 1596 appointed principal secretary of state. In 1599 he was made master of the court of wards, and in the same year sent to France to negotiate a peace between that country and Spain. On the accession of king James, 1603, he was created baron Cecil, and viscount Cranborn, and in 1605, earl of Salisbury. In 1608, (which is therefore the date of this epigram,) he was created LORD HIGH TREASURER; and in this post he died May 24, 1612.

8   N

These, noblest Cecil, labour'd in my thought,
Wherein what wonder see thy name hath wrought !
That whilst I meant but thine to gratulate,
I have sung the greater fortunes of our state.

LXV.

TO MY MUSE.

WAY, and leave me, thou thing most abhorr'd,
   That hast betray'd me to a worthless lord ;
   Made me commit most fierce idolatry
To a great image through thy luxury :
Be thy next master's more unlucky muse,
And, as thou'st mine, his hours and youth abuse,
Get him the time's long grudge, the court's ill will;
And reconcil'd, keep him suspected still.
Make him lose all his friends ; and, which is worse,
Almost all ways to any better course.
With me thou leav'st an happier muse than thee,
And which thou brought'st me, welcome poverty :
She shall instruct my after-thoughts to write
Things manly, and not smelling parasite.
But I repent me : stay—Whoe'er is raised,
For worth he has not, he is tax'd not praised.

LXVI.

TO SIR HENRY CARY.[9]

HAT neither fame, nor love might wanting be
   To greatness, Cary, I sing that and thee ;
   Whose house, if it no other honour had,
In only thee, might be both great and glad :

[9] *Sir Henry Cary.*]   First lord Falkland, and father of the celebrated Lucius lord Falkland, who acted so conspicuous and noble

Who, to upbraid the sloth of this our time,
Durst valour make, almost, but not a crime.
Which deed I know not, whether were more high,
Or, though more happy, it to justify
Against thy fortune ; when no foe, that day,
Could conquer thee, but chance, who did betray.
Love thy great loss, which a renown hath won,
To live when Broeck not stands, nor Roor doth run :[1]

a part in the Rebellion. Sir Henry was also a very distinguished
character as a statesman and soldier. He had been master of the
Jewel Office to Elizabeth, was made a knight of the Bath at the
creation of prince Henry, and soon after lord deputy of Ireland.
The intimacy of Jonson with this family (for he was much endeared
to the son as well as father) is not a little to his credit ; but, indeed,
this great poet, who is represented by Steevens and his followers
as little better than an obscure garretteer, lived on terms of
honourable familiarity with all the genius, worth, and rank of his
age.

[1] " The castle and river (Jonson says) near where he was taken."
It appears from a letter of sir Thomas Edmonds (resident Ambassador with the Archduke, at Brussels) that while Spinola was
engaged in securing the passage of the Roer by the erection of a
battery, an attempt was made to surprise the covering party by
count Maurice. The action was short but severe, and in the end,
the count was obliged to retreat. Some officers of rank fell on
each side, and Spinola made some prisoners, " among whom," sir
Thomas says, " were certain English gentlemen, whereof the principal are *sir Henry Carey,* and Mr. Radcliffe, brother to sir John
Radcliffe, (and to *Margaret,*) and one captain Pigot." *Winwood's
Mem.* vol. ii. 145. This letter is dated 21st October, 1605; and
the action took place a few days before.

The capture of sir Henry Carey seems to have been viewed by
the Spanish court as a matter of considerable moment, and it required all the influence of Cecil, and all the dexterity of sir Charles
Cornwallis, our ambassador at Madrid, to procure his release. " In
conclusion," sir Charles writes to the earl of Salisbury, " I moved
him (the duke of Lerma) for sir Henry Carey; saying ' I was there-
unto sollicited by the entreatie of many honourable personages
that wished well to the state ; and by some fair ladies, whom I
knew his Excellencie would be apt to favour. I delivered his
valuable estate, and the hard course taken against him. .And lastly
told what between the Conde de Villa Longa and me, had been
agreed to be done in his favour, whereat he smyled, and desired he

Love honours, which of best example be,
When they cost dearest, and are done most free.
Though every fortitude deserves applause,
It may be much, or little, in the cause.
He's valiant'st, that dares fight, and not for pay;
That virtuous is, when the reward's away.

LXVII.

TO THOMAS EARL OF SUFFOLK.[2]

SINCE men have left to do praiseworthy things,
Most think all praises flatteries : but truth
  brings
That sound and that authority with her name,
As, to be raised by her, is only fame.
Stand high, then, Howard, high in eyes of men,
High in thy blood, thy place ; but highest then,
When, in men's wishes, so thy virtues wrought,
As all thy honours were by them first sought :
And though design'd to be the same thou art,
Before thou wert it, in each good man's heart.
Which, by no less confirm'd, than thy king's choice,
Proves that is God's, which was the people's voice.

might be put in further memorie of it, which by God's grace shall
not be omitted.' " This was in June, 1606; but it required yet
many conferences before his liberty was procured.

  [2] *To Thomas earl of Suffolk.*] He was so created by James I.
in 1603, and bore several great offices of state. In the 12th year
of the same king, he was constituted lord high treasurer ; and it is
not improbable but this epigram was addressed to him on his promotion to that high station. WHAL.

  The epigram has a much earlier date than Whalley assigns it.
It was probably written upon his accession to the title of Suffolk,
when he was also appointed lord chamberlain.

LXVIII.

ON PLAYWRIGHT.

PLAYWRIGHT convict of public wrongs to
   men,
   Takes private beatings, and begins again.
Two kinds of valour he doth shew at once ;
Active in's brain, and passive in his bones.

LXIX.

TO PERTINAX COB.

COB, thou nor soldier, thief, nor fencer art,
   Yet by thy weapon liv'st! thou hast one good
      part.

LXX.

TO WILLIAM ROE.

WHEN nature bids us leave to live, 'tis late
   Then to begin, my Roe ! He makes a state
   In life, that can employ it ; and takes hold
On the true causes, ere they grow too old.
Delay is bad, doubt worse, depending worst ;
Each best day of our life escapes us, first :[3]

---

[3] *Each best day of our life escapes us first.*]   From Virgil :
   " *Optima quæque dies miseris mortalibus ævi
      Prima fugit.*"

William Roe was probably the brother of the person to whose
memory the epigrams at pp. 158, 160, and 161 are consecrated.
I have already remarked on the solemn tone which the poet assumes
in all his addresses to this family.

Then, since we, more than many, these truths know;
Though life be short, let us not make it so.   .

LXXI.

On Court Parrot.

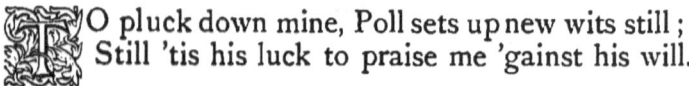O pluck down mine, Poll sets up new wits still;
　　Still 'tis his luck to praise me 'gainst his will.

LXXII.

To Courtling.

GRIEVE not, Courtling, thou art started up
　　A chamber-critic, and doth dine, and sup
　　At madam's table, where thou mak'st all wit
Go high, or low, as thou wilt value it.
'Tis not thy judgment breeds thy prejudice,
Thy person only, Courtling, is the vice.

LXXIII.

To Fine Grand.[4]

HAT is't, Fine Grand, makes thee my friend-
　　　　ship fly,
　　Or take an Epigram so fearfully,
As 'twere a challenge, or a borrower's letter?
The world must know your greatness is my debtor.
Imprimis, Grand, you owe me for a jest
I lent you, on mere acquaintance, at a feast.

---

[4] Randolph has imitated this Epigram in his *Pedlar;* a forgotten
piece, from which Dodsley took the plot, and something more than
the plot, of his *Toy-shop.*

Item, a tale or two some fortnight after ;
That yet maintains you, and your house in laughter.
Item, the Babylonian song you sing ;
Item, a fair Greek poesy for a ring,
With which a learned madam you bely.
Item, a charm surrounding fearfully
Your *partie-per-pale* picture, one half drawn
In solemn cyprus, th' other cobweb lawn.
Item, a gulling imprese for you, at tilt.
Item, your mistress' anagram, in your hilt.
Item, your own, sew'd in your mistress' smock.
Item, an epitaph on my lord's cock,
In most vile verses, and cost me more pain,
Than had I made 'em good, to fit your vein.
Forty things more, dear Grand, which you know true,
For which, or pay me quickly', or I'll pay you.

LXXIV.

To Thomas Lord Chancellor Egerton.

WHILST thy weigh'd judgments, Egerton, I
     hear,
     And know thee then a judge, not of one year ;
Whilst I behold thee live with purest hands ;
That no affection in thy voice commands ;
That still thou'rt present to the better cause ;
And no less wise than skilful in the laws ;
Whilst thou art certain to thy words, once gone,
As is thy conscience, which is always one :
The Virgin, long since fled from earth, I see,
To our times return'd, hath made her heaven in thee.[5]

[5] *The Virgin, long since fled from earth, I see,*
To our times return'd, hath made her heaven in thee.] This is
high praise ; but it is not bestowed at random ; and it comes from
one who knew and judged him well.
This great man was the natural son of sir Richard Egerton, of

LXXV.

On Lippe the Teacher.

 CANNOT think there's that antipathy
'Twixt puritans and players, as some cry ;
Though Lippe, at Paul's, ran from his text
    away,
To inveigh 'gainst plays, what did he then but play?

Ridley, Cheshire, by Alice, daughter of Mr. Sparke, also of Cheshire. He was born in 1539, sent to Oxford when he was about 17, and thence to Lincoln's Inn. In 1584 he was appointed Solicitor General, and two years afterwards, he was made Master of the Rolls, which office he held together with that of Lord Keeper until the accession of James I., 1603, when he was advanced to the dignity of baron of Ellesmere, and constituted Lord High Chancellor of England. In 1610 he was created viscount Brackley, and died at York House in the Strand, 15th March, 1617, having on the third of that month obtained the king's leave, after long and earnest importunity, to resign the great seal. He was in his seventy-eighth year.

His person, as to its exterior, was so grave and dignified, that many people, Fuller says, have gone to the Chancery on purpose only to see his venerable garb, and were highly pleased at so acceptable a spectacle. But his interior presented a subject of higher admiration. "His apprehension was keen and ready ; his judgment deep and sound, his reason clear and comprehensive, his elocution eloquent and easy. As a lawyer he was prudent in council, extensive in information, honest in principle, so that while he lived he was excelled by none ; and when he died, he was lamented by all." *Coll. Peerage*, vol. iii. p. 190.

Jonson has some allusions to the Ode to Lollius, who was very far from an Egerton:

> " *Consulque non unius anni*
>   *Sed quoties bonus atque fidus*
>   *Judex honestum prætulit utili," &c.*

LXXVI.

ON LUCY, COUNTESS OF BEDFORD.

THIS morning, timely rapt with holy fire,[6]
   I thought to form unto my zealous Muse,
   What kind of creature I could most desire,
To honour, serve, and love ; as poets use.
I meant to make her fair, and free, and wise,
   Of greatest blood, and yet more good than great ;
I meant the day-star should not brighter rise,
   Nor lend like influence from his lucent seat.
I meant she should be courteous, facile, sweet,
   Hating that solemn vice of greatness, pride ;
I meant each softest virtue there should meet,
   Fit in that softer bosom to reside.
Only a learned, and a manly soul
   I purposed her ; that should, with even powers,
The rock, the spindle, and the sheers control
   Of Destiny, and spin her own free hours.
Such when I meant to feign, and wish'd to see,
My Muse bade, Bedford write, and that was she !

LXXVII.

TO ONE THAT DESIRED ME NOT TO NAME HIM.

BE safe, nor fear thyself so good a fame,
   That, any way, my book should speak thy
      name :
For, if thou shame, rank'd with my friends, to go,
I'm more ashamed to have thee thought my foe.

[6] *This morning, timely rapt with holy fire.*] The English language, rich as it is in effusions of this kind, does not furnish a complimentary poem that for delicacy of sentiment, and beauty of diction, can at all be compared with this exquisite epigram ; which has yet the further merit of being consonant to truth. See vol. vii. p. 18.

LXXVIII.

To Hornet.

HORNET, thou hast thy wife drest for the
          stall,
    To draw thee custom : but herself gets all.

LXXIX.

To Elizabeth, countess of Rutland.

WHAT poets are far rarer births than kings,[7]
    Your noblest father proved; like whom,
          before,
Or then, or since, about our Muses' springs,
    Came not that soul exhausted so their store.
Hence was it, that the Destinies decreed
    (Save that most masculine issue of his brain)
No male unto him ; who could so exceed
    Nature, they thought, in all that he would feign.
At which, she happily displeased, made you:
    On whom, if he were living now, to look,
He should those rare, and absolute numbers view,
    As he would burn, or better far his book.

[7] *That poets are far rarer births than kings,*
    Your noblest father prov'd.] This lady, wife to Roger earl of
Rutland, was daughter to sir Philip Sidney, by his wife Frances,
only daughter to sir Francis Walsingham, secretary of state to
queen Elizabeth. It is necessary to know such trivial circumstances, as, in these smaller poems, their chief merit often consists
in the turns of thought which allude to them. Whal.
    It is somewhat singular that Whalley should entertain this
opinion, and yet that this should be almost the only person whom
he has noticed. This celebrated lady, who was also the patroness
of Donne and Daniel, and to whom Jonson wrote other verses,
died before these poems were published. The "masculine issue"
of her father was the *Arcadia.*

LXXX.

OF LIFE AND DEATH.

THE ports of death are sins; of life, good deeds;
Through which our merit leads us to our
meeds.
How wilful blind is he, then, that would stray,
And hath it, in his powers, to make his way !
This world death's region is, the other life's ;
And here, it should be one of our first strifes,
So to front death, as men might judge us past it :
For good men but see death, the wicked taste it.

LXXXI.

TO PROWLE, THE PLAGIARY.

FORBEAR to tempt me, Prowle, I will not show
A line unto thee, till the world it know ;
Or that I've by two good sufficient men,
To be the wealthy witness of my pen :[8]
For all thou hear'st, thou swear'st thyself didst do.
Thy wit lives by it, Prowle, and belly too.
Which, if thou leave not soon, though I am loth,
I must a libel make, and cozen both.

LXXXII.

ON CASHIERED CAPTAIN SURLY.

SURLY'S old whore in her new silks doth swim :
He cast, yet keeps her well ! No ; she keeps
him.

---

[8] *To be the* wealthy witness *of my pen.*] This is a pure Latinism:
testis locuples is the phrase for a full and sufficient evidence. WHAL.

LXXXIII.

To a Friend.

O put out the word, whore, thou dost me woo,
Throughout my book.   Troth, put out woman
too.

LXXXIV.

To Lucy countess of Bedford.

ADAM, I told you late, how I repented,
    I ask'd a lord a buck, and he denied me ;
    And, ere I could ask you, I was prevented :
For your most noble offer had supplied me.
Straight went I home ; and there, most like a poet,
    I fancied to myself, what wine, what wit
I would have spent ; how every muse should know it,
    And Phœbus' self should be at eating it.
O, madam, if your grant did thus transfer me,[9]
Make it your gift !   See whither that will bear me.

LXXXV.

To sir Henry Goodyere.

OODYERE, I'm glad,[1] and grateful to report,
    Myself a witness of thy few days sport ;
    Where I both learn'd, why wise men hawking
        follow,
And why that bird was sacred to Apollo :

----

[9] *O, madam, if your* grant, *&c.*]   She had probably offered him
a warrant for one : the object of the epigram seems to be that it
should be sent home to him.
   [1] Goodyere, *I'm glad, &c.*]   Sir Henry Goodyere, to whom this

She doth instruct men by her gallant flight,
That they to knowledge so should tower upright,
And never stoop, but to strike ignorance;
Which if they miss, yet they should re-advance
To former height, and there in circle tarry,
Till they be sure to make the fool their quarry.
Now, in whose pleasures I have this discerned,
What would his serious actions me have learned ?

and the following epigram are addressed, was a gentleman of great
probity and virtue, and much respected by the men of genius in
our author's age. There was great intimacy between him and Dr.
Donne, whose letters to sir Henry Goodyere make up the greatest
part of the collection published by the Doctor's son. WHAL.

Sir Henry had a fine seat at Polesworth, in Warwickshire, where
Jonson, much to his satisfaction, appears to have passed some time
with him.

"To the honour of this sir Henry," Camden says, "a knight
memorable for his virtues, an affectionate friend of his made this
tetrastich." There is certainly more affection than poetry in it:

> "An Ill yeare of a Goodyere us bereft
> Who, gone to God, much lack of him here left
> Full of good gifts of body and of mind,
> Wise, comely, learned, eloquent, and kind."
>
> *Remains*, 341.

Sir Henry joined the band of wits who amused themselves with
the simple vanity of Coryat. He was not much of a poet: and I
give the following extract merely because it serves to illustrate a
passage relating to the "trunk" in the Masque of *Love Restored*,
vol. vii. p. 202.

> "If any think Tom dull and heavy, know
> The court and city's mirth cannot be so;
> Who thinks him light, ask them who had the task,
> To beare him *in a tronke* unto the maske."

In the page just referred to, there is an omission that I now wish
to supply. The old copy reads "which made me once think of a
trunk, but that I would not imitate so catholic a coxcomb as Coryat,
and make a case: uses." The last words appearing unintelligible,
were thrown to the bottom of the page. I now think I see the
author's meaning, and that the defect may be thus remedied: "I
would not imitate so catholic a coxcomb as Coryat, and make a
case (i. e. a pair) *of asses.*"

LXXXVI.

To the Same.

WHEN I would know thee, Goodyere, my
        thought looks
        Upon thy well-made choice of friends, and
        books ;
Then do I love thee, and behold thy ends
In making thy friends books, and thy books friends:
Now I must give thy life and deed, the voice
Attending such a study, such a choice ;
Where, though 't be love that to thy praise doth move,
It was a knowledge that begat that love.

LXXXVII.

On captain Hazard, the cheater.[2]

TOUCH'D with the sin of false play in his punk,
        Hazard a month forswore his, and grew drunk,
        Each night, to drown his cares ; but when the
        gain
Of what she had wrought came in, and waked his brain,
Upon the accompt, hers grew the quicker trade :
Since when he's sober again, and all play's made.

LXXXVIII.

On English Monsieur.

WOULD you believe, when you this Monsieur
        see,
        That his whole body should speak French, not
        he ?

---

[2] *On captain Hazard, the* cheater,] i. e. the gamester. The terms

That so much scarf of France, and hat, and feather,
And shoe, and tye, and garter, should come hither,
And land on one whose face durst never be
Toward the sea, farther than half-way tree ?[3]
That he, untravell'd, should be French so much,
As Frenchmen in his company should seem Dutch ?
Or had his father, when he did him get,
The French disease, with which he labours yet ?
Or hung some Monsieur's picture on the wall,
By which his dam conceived him, clothes and all ?
Or is it some French statue ? no : 't doth move,
And stoop, and cringe.   O then, it needs must prove
The new French tailor's motion, monthly made,
Daily to turn in Paul's, and help the trade.

LXXXIX.

To Edward Allen.[4]

F Rome so great, and in her wisest age,
Fear'd not to boast the glories of her stage,
As skilful Roscius, and grave Æsop, men,
Yet crown'd with honours, as with riches, then ;
Who had no less a trumpet of their name,
Than Cicero, whose every breath was fame :

were synonymous in Jonson's age, and perhaps have been so in
every age since. Whal.

  [3] *Farther than* half-way tree.] In the way to Dover, in the
poet's time, 'tis probable some remarkable tree might be standing
in the road about half way thither. Whal.

  [4] *To Edward Allen.*] The fame of this celebrated actor yet lives
in these verses of our author, and in those of his contemporary
poets : but a more durable monument of his name and goodness,
is existing in Dulwich-college, near London, of which he was the
munificent and pious founder. Whal.

  Two things may be collected from this excellent epigram, first,
that Jonson had other acquaintance on the stage than Shakspeare,
and secondly, that when he spoke of " some better natures among

How can so great example die in me,
That, Allen, I should pause to publish thee ?
Who both their graces in thy self hast more
Out-stript, than they did all that went before :
And present worth in all dost so contract,
As others speak, but only thou dost act.
Wear this renown.   'Tis just, that who did give
So many poets life, by one should live.

XC.

ON MILL, MY LADY'S WOMAN.

WHEN Mill first came to court, th' unprofiting
        fool,
    Unworthy such a mistress, such a school,
Was dull, and long ere she would go to man :
At last, ease, appetite, and example wan
The nicer thing to taste her lady's page ;
And, finding good security in his age,
Went on : and proving him still day by day,
Discern'd no difference of his years, or play.
Not though that hair grew brown, which once was
        amber,
And he, grown youth, was call'd to his lady's chamber ;
Still Mill continued : nay, his face growing worse,
And he removed to gentleman of the horse,

the players, who had been drawn in to abuse him," he did not, as
Messrs. Steevens and Malone are pleased to suggest, necessarily
mean that great poet.

Hurd has two or three pages of vapid pomposity, to prove that
doctus, applied, by Horace, to Roscius, ought to be translated
skilful, and not learned. Jonson, who had ten times Hurd's learning, without a tithe of his pedantry, had done it in one word.   Of
this, however, no notice is taken !   The verse which Jonson had
in view, is in the Epistle to Augustus :

    Quæ gravis Æsopus, quæ doctus *Roscius egit.*

Mill was the same.   Since, both his body and face
Blown up; and he (too unwieldy for that place)
Hath got the steward's chair; he will not tarry
Longer a day, but with his Mill will marry :
And it is hop'd, that she, like Milo, wull
First bearing him a calf, bear him a bull.

XCI.

To sir Horace Vere.[5]

WHICH of thy names I take, not only bears
    A Roman sound, but Roman virtue wears,
    Illustrious Vere, or Horace; fit to be
Sung by a Horace, or a Muse as free ;
Which thou art to thyself : whose fame was won
In the eye of Europe, where thy deeds were done,
When on thy trumpet she did sound a blast,
Whose relish to eternity shall last.
I leave thy acts, which should I prosecute
Throughout, might flattery seem ; and to be mute

    [5] *To sir* Horace Vere.]   He was created lord Tilbury, and was
the famous general in the Low Country wars in the reign of queen
Elizabeth.   Many of the nobility at that time served under him.
WHAL.
    Sir Horace was grandson of John Vere, fifteenth earl of Ox-
ford.   He was a celebrated warrior, as well as his elder brother,
sir Francis.   Fuller, in his quaint but forcible manner, says, that
" he had more meekness, and as much valour as his brother; so
pious, that he first made his peace with God before he went out to
war with man."
    Rowland Whyte (in a letter to the earl of Shrewsbury, dated
Court, 7th Nov. 1607,) says, "sir Horacio Vere shall marry w^{th}in
these eight days, one Mrs. Hoby, a widdow, sister to sir John
Tracey; a fine, comely, well graced gentelwoman."   To this lady,
who outlived sir Horace nearly forty years, the Parliament confided
the care of the younger children of their unfortunate sovereign.
They could not be in better hands, for she was "a person of excellent character."   Sir Horace was created Lord Vere of Tilbury in
1625, being, as Fuller says, the first baron made by Charles I.

8   O

To any one, were envy ; which would live
Against my grave, and time could not forgive.
I speak thy other graces, not less shown,
Nor less in practice ; but less mark'd, less known :
Humanity, and piety, which are
As noble in great chiefs, as they are rare ;
And best become the valiant man to wear,
Who more should seek men's reverence, than fear.

XCII.

THE NEW CRY.

RE cherries ripe ! and strawberries ! be gone ;
Unto the cries of London I'll add one.
Ripe statesmen, ripe ! they grow in every
          street ;
At six and twenty, ripe.   You shall them meet,
And have them yield no savour, but of state.
Ripe are their ruffs, their cuffs, their beards, their gait,
And grave as ripe, like mellow as their faces.
They know the states of Christendom, not the places ;
Yet they have seen the maps, and bought 'em too,
And understand them, as most chapmen do.
The councils, projects, practices they know,
And what each prince doth for intelligence owe,
And unto whom ; they are the almanacks,
For twelve years yet to come, what each state lacks.
They carry in their pockets Tacitus,
And the Gazetti, or Gallo-Belgicus ;
And talk reserv'd, lock'd up, and full of fear,
Nay, ask you, how the day goes, in your ear ;
Keep a Star-chamber sentence close twelve days,
And whisper what a Proclamation says.
They meet in sixes, and at every mart,
Are sure to con the catalogue by heart ;

Or every day, some one at Rimee's looks,
Or Bill's,[6] and there he buys the names of books.
They all get Porta, for the sundry ways
To write in cipher, and the several keys,
To ope the character; they've found the slight
With juice of limons, onions, piss, to write;
To break up seals, and close them : and they know,
If the States make [not] peace, how it will go
With England.   All forbidden books they get,
And of the powder-plot, they will talk yet :
At naming the French king their heads they shake,
And at the Pope and Spain slight faces make;
Or 'gainst the bishops, for the brethren rail,
Much like those brethren; thinking to prevail
With ignorance on us, as they have done
On them : and therefore do not only shun
Others more modest, but contemn us too,
That know not so much state, wrong, as they do.

XCIII.

To sir John Radcliffe.

OW like a column, Radcliffe, left alone[7]
For the great mark of virtue, those being gone
Who did, alike with thee, thy house up-bear,
Stand'st thou, to shew the times what you all were ?

---

[6] *Some one at* Rimee's *looks,*
Or Bill's————
They all get Porta.] The two first were booksellers in that
age : the last was the famous Neapolitan, *Johannes Baptista Porta,*
who has a treatise extant in Latin, *De furtivis literarum notis, vulgo
de Ziferis,* printed at Naples 1563.   He died 1615.   WHAL.

[7] *How like a column, Radcliffe, &c.*]   This epigram (a very admirable one) is addressed to the surviving brother of Margaret'
Radcliffe. (See Epig. xl.) It undoubtedly furnished Edwards
with the model for his affecting sonnet, *On a Family Picture,* which

Two bravely in the battle fell and died,[*]
Upbraiding rebels' arms, and barbarous pride :
And two that would have fall'n as great as they,
The Belgic fever ravished away.
Thou, that art all their valour, all their spirit,
And thine own goodness to encrease thy merit,
Than whose I do not know a whiter soul,
Nor could I, had I seen all nature's roll,
Thou yet remain'st, unhurt in peace or war,
Though not unprov'd ; which shews thy fortunes are
Willing to expiate the fault in thee,
Wherewith, against thy blood, they' offenders be.

the reader will find subjoined, and which may be counted among the best of this polished and amiable man.

ON A FAMILY PICTURE.

"When pensive on that portraiture I gaze,
  Where my four brothers round about me stand,
  And four fair sisters smile with graces bland,
The goodly monument of happier days ;

And think how soon insatiate death, who preys
  On all, has cropt the rest with ruthless hand ;
  While only I survive of all that band,
Which one chaste bed did to my father raise :

It seems that like a column left alone,
  The tottering remnant of some splendid fane,
  Scaped from the fury of the barbarous Gaul,
And wasting time which has the rest o'erthrown,
  Amidst our house's ruins I remain
  Single, unpropt, and nodding to my fall."

It is melancholy to add to the little history of Sir J. Radcliffe's family, that this "column" also, this "great mark of virtue," fell, not many years afterwards, like "the rest." That valiant and generally beloved gentleman (Weever says,) sir John Radcliffe, lieutenant colonell, was slaine fighting against the French in the isle of Rhee, the 29th of October, in the year of our Lord, 1627.

  [*] In Ireland.

XCIV.

To Lucy countess of Bedford, with master Donne's Satires.[8]

UCY, you brightness of our sphere, who are,
Life of the Muses' day, their morning star !
If works, not authors, their own grace should
    look,
Whose poems would not wish to be your book ?
But these, desired by you, the maker's ends
Crown with their own : Rare poems ask rare
    friends.
Yet satires, since the most of mankind be
Their unavoided subject, fewest see ;
For none e'er took that pleasure in sin's sense,
But, when they heard it tax'd, took more offence.
They then, that living where the matter's bred,
Dare for these poems yet both ask, and read,
And like them too ; must needfully, though few,
Be of the best, and 'mongst those best are you :
Lucy, you brightness of our sphere, who are
The Muses' evening, as their morning star !

---

[8] Daniel, who has a poem addressed to the countess, terms her
"learned ;" undoubtedly she was a most accomplished lady, and
skilled in a variety of arts, not much studied by the females of
those days.   Sir Thomas Roe has a letter to her, in which he speaks
of her proficiency in the knowledge of ancient medals ; and sir
William Temple mentions her with applause in his Essay on the
gardens of Epicurus, for "projecting the most perfect figure of a
garden that he ever saw."   Granger attempts to be severe on her
bounty to the poets ; but as Drayton, Donne, Daniel, and our
author were among the number, her liberality seems to be nearly as
secure from censure as her judgment.

It is pleasing to mark the habitual kindness with which Jonson
recommends his friend's works, and the ingenious mode in which
he compliments his patroness for desiring to have a copy of the
Satires.

XCV.

TO SIR HENRY SAVILE.

F, my religion safe, I durst embrace
That stranger doctrine of Pythagoras,
I should believe, the soul of Tacitus
In thee, most weighty Savile lived to us :
So hast thou render'd him in all his bounds,
And all his numbers, both of sense and sounds.
But when I read that special piece restored,
Where Nero falls, and Galba is adored,
To thine own proper I ascribe then more,
And gratulate the breach I griev'd before ;
Which fate, it seems, caus'd in the history,
Only to boast thy merit in supply.
O, would'st thou add like hand to all the rest !
Or, better work ! were thy glad country blest,
To have her story woven in thy thread ;[9]
Minerva's loom was never richer spread.

---

[9] ———— *were thy glad country blest,*
　To have her story woven in thy thread.] It was then imagined,
that sir Henry Savile intended to have compiled a general history
of England ; but he gave over the design, and engaged in the
excellent edition of Chrysostom, which he afterwards published.
WHAL.

There is no date to this epigram ; but it must have been written
after 1604, as he did not receive the honour of knighthood till that
year, and before 1613, in which year his magnificent edition of
Chrysostom's Works, 8 vol. fol. appeared, which Jonson would not
have omitted to mention. Sir Henry was one of the most learned
men of that learned age, and published many valuable works, which
raised his reputation no less abroad than at home. The translation of which Jonson speaks was published long before the death
of Elizabeth, to whom it was dedicated : to this he appended a
large body of notes, in which the breaks in the original are occasionally supplied with great ingenuity. He was admirably skilled
in the history of this country, and collected and printed the tracts
of many of the best ancient writers on the subject ; if, therefore,

For who can master those great parts like thee,
That liv'st from hope, from fear, from faction free ?
Thou hast thy breast so clear of present crimes,
Thou need'st not shrink at voice of after-times ;
Whose knowledge claimeth at the helm to stand ;
But wisely thrusts not forth a forward hand,
No more than Salust in the Roman state :
As then his cause, his glory emulate.
Although to write be lesser than to do,
It is the next deed, and a great one too.
We need a man that knows the several graces
Of history, and how to apt their places ;
Where brevity, where splendor, and where height,
Where sweetness is required, and where weight ;
We need a man can speak of the intents,[1]
The councils, actions, orders, and events
Of state, and censure them ; we need his pen
Can write the things, the causes, and the men :

he really designed, as Whalley says, to compile a general history of
England, we have to lament that one so well qualified for the task
found cause to lay it aside.

Sir Henry was warden of Merton College, Oxford, and provost
of Eton.   Aubrey says that he was a severe governour, and that
the scholars hated him for his austerity : but all governors were
severe in those days.   The worst of him was that " he could not
abide witts :"—" If a young scholar was recommended to him for
a good witt, Out upon him ! he would say, I'll have nothing to do
with him—if I wold look for witts I wold go to Newgate, there be
the witts."   *Letters by Eminent Persons*, vol. ii. p. 525.

Aubrey has other complaints ; but his idle stories are the mere
gossip of the day.—Sir Henry Savile was, after all, every thing that
Jonson describes him to be ; and we may securely acquiesce in the
opinion of bishop Montague, that he was "a magazine of learning,
whose memory will be honourable amongst not only the wise, but
the righteous for ever."

[1] *We need a man can speak of the intents,*

The councils, actions, orders, and events, &c.]   These are the es-
sentials of history, and are laid down by Cicero (*de Oratore*, lib. ii,)
as what a good historian should be capable of treating : this sentiment is taken from thence.   WHAL.

But most we need his faith (and all have you,)
That dares not write things false, nor hide things true.[2]

XCVI.

TO JOHN DONNE.

HO shall doubt, Donne, whêre I a poet be,[3]
When I dare send my Epigrams to thee ?
That so alone canst judge, so alone dost make :
And in thy censures, evenly, dost take
As free simplicity, to disavow,
As thou hast best authority t' allow.
Read all I send; and if I find but one
Mark'd by thy hand, and with the better stone,
My title's seal'd. Those that for claps do write,
Let pui'nees', porters', players' praise delight,
And till they burst, their backs, like asses, load :
A man should seek great glory, and not broad.

XCVII.

ON THE NEW MOTION.

EE you yond' Motion ? not the old fa-ding,
Nor captain Pod, nor yet the Eltham thing ;[4]
But one more rare, and in the case so new :
His cloak with orient velvet quite lined through ;

---

[2] *That dares not, &c.*] This is the primary feature of a good historian, according to Cicero : " *Ne quid falsi dicere audeat, ne quid veri non audeat.*"

[3] *Who shall doubt, Donne, whêre I a poet be.*] This contraction of the interrogative *whether*, seems peculiar to the poet. WHAL.

Whalley is greatly mistaken ; it is common to them all. Jonson has no peculiarities.

[4] *Nor captain Pod, nor yet the* Eltham thing.] *Pod* has been mentioned before as the master of a puppet-show: the *Eltham*

His rosy ties and garters so o'erblown,
By his each glorious parcel to be known!
He wont was to encounter me aloud,
Where-e'er he met me, now he's dumb, or proud.
Know you the cause? he has neither land nor lease,
Nor bawdy stock that travels for increase,
Nor office in the town, nor place in court,
Nor 'bout the bears, nor noise to make lords sport.
He is no favourite's favourite, no dear trust
Of any madam, hath need o' squires, and must.
Nor did the king of Denmark him salute,[5]
When he was here; nor hath he got a suit,
Since he was gone, more than the one he wears.
Nor are the queen's most honour'd maids by th' ears
About his form.   What then so swells each limb?
Only his clothes have over-leaven'd him.

XCVIII.

TO SIR THOMAS ROE.[6]

THOU hast begun well, Roe, which stand well to,
And I know nothing more thou hast to do.

thing is alluded to in the *Silent Woman;* "The perpetual motion is here, and not at Eltham." WHAL.

For *fa-ding*, see vol. vii. p. 226.

[5] *Nor did the king of Denmark, &c.*] Christian IV., who visited this country in 1606. See vol. vi. p. 470.

[6] *Sir Thomas Roe.*] Grandson of sir Thomas Roe, and nephew of the sir John, and William Roe already mentioned. "In this great man," Granger truly says, "the accomplishments of the scholar, the gentleman, and the statesman, were eminently united. During his residence in the Mogul's court, he zealously promoted the trading interest of this kingdom, for which the East India Company was greatly indebted to him. In his embassy to the Grand Signior, he collected many valuable Greek and Oriental manuscripts, which he presented to the Bodleian Library, to which he left his valuable collection of coins. The fine Alexandrian MS. of the

He that is round within himself, and straight,[7]
Need seek no other strength, no other height ;
Fortune upon him breaks herself, if ill,
And what would hurt his virtue, makes it still.
That thou at once then nobly may'st defend
With thine own course the judgment of thy friend,
Be always to thy gather'd self the same ;
And study conscience more than thou would'st fame.
Though both be good, the latter yet is worst,
And ever is ill got without the first.

XCIX.

To the Same.

WHAT thou hast kept thy love, encreas'd thy
    will,
    Better'd thy trust to letters ; that thy skill ;
Hast taught thyself worthy thy pen to tread,
And that to write things worthy to be read :
How much of great example wert thou, Roe,
If time to facts, as unto men would owe ?

Greek Bible which Cyrill, the patriarch of Constantinople, presented
to Charles I. was procured by his means. This was afterwards
published by Dr. Grabe. His speech, at the council-table, against
debasing the coin in the reign of Charles, gained him the highest
reputation. His curious and interesting 'Negotiations' were first
published by the Society for promoting Learning, 1740, fol."

    Sir Thomas was the son of Robert Roe : he was born in 1580,
and, about the close of Elizabeth's reign, was made esquire of the
body to that princess. He was knighted by James in 1604, and
in 1614 appointed, at the request of the East India Company, ambassador to the Mogul : he continued at his court four years, and
was dismissed with extraordinary honours. He died after a very
active and useful life in 1644, and was buried in Woodford church,
Essex.

    [7] *He that is round, &c.*] From Horace :

        ———— *totus teres atque rotundus,*
    In quem manca ruit fortuna, &c.

But much it now avails, what's done, of whom :
The self-same deeds, as diversly they come,
From place or fortune, are made high or low,
And e'en the praiser's judgment suffers so.
Well, though thy name less than our great ones be,
Thy fact is more : let truth encourage thee.

C.

ON PLAYWRIGHT.[8]

LAYWRIGHT, by chance, hearing some toys
      I'd writ,
    Cry'd to my face, they were th' elixir of wit :
And I must now believe him ; for to-day,
Five of my jests, then stolen, past him a play.

CI.

INVITING A FRIEND TO SUPPER.

O-NIGHT, grave sir, both my poor house and I
    Do equally desire your company :
    Not that we think us worthy such a guest,
But that your worth will dignify our feast,

---

[8] *On Playwright.*] This epigram is said by Stephen Jones (the person so judiciously selected by the booksellers to prepare the new edition of the *Biographia Dramatica*) to have been written on the appearance of Ford's *Ladies' Trial.* "Ben Jonson (he says) a *bitter enemy of Ford's*, charges the latter with having stolen a character in this play from him.

    " Playwright (i. e. Ford) hearing," &c.

Mr. Jones has not here the usual apology for his stupidity,—that "he found it so in the former edition ;" for Read, though Macklin's forgery lay before him, was too well acquainted with dates to adopt it. The fact is, that the *Ladies' Trial* did not appear till two years after Jonson's death, while the epigram to which it is here said to have given birth, was published two and twenty, and

With those that come; whose grace may make that
    seem
Something, which else could hope for no esteem.
It is the fair acceptance, sir, creates
The entertainment perfect, not the cates.
Yet shall you have, to rectify your palate,
An olive, capers, or some better sallad
Ushering the mutton; with a short legg'd hen,
If we can get her, full of eggs, and then,
Limons, and wine for sauce : to these, a coney
Is not to be despair'd of for our money ;
And though fowl now be scarce, yet there are clerks,
The sky not falling, think we may have larks.
I'll tell you of more, and lie, so you will come :
Of partridge, pheasant, woodcock, of which some
May yet be there ; and godwit if we can ;
Knat, rail, and ruff too.   Howsoe'er, my man
Shall read a piece of Virgil, Tacitus,[9]
Livy, or of some better book to us,

probably written two and thirty years before! All this Mr. Jones
must have found stated in the very paper from which he copied
the epigram ; and all this he chose to conceal from an itch become
quite epidemic among the low scribblers of his caste, to insult the
memory of Jonson.   The assertion that this great poet was *the
bitter enemy of Ford*, is an echo of the profligate falsehood of Weber,
who is not afraid to declare, that it is proved by *indisputable docu-
ments !* whereas the only memorial of any passage whatever between
Ford and Jonson, now known to exist, is a very friendly elegy by
the former, "ON THE DEATH OF THE BEST OF ENGLISH POETS, BEN
JONSON." It is mortifying to contend with such a "case of asses ;"
—but they must not be suffered to kick at the ashes of Jonson with
impunity.

[9] —— *Howsoe'er my man*
    Shall read a piece of Virgil, &c.] Richard Brome, his servant,
whom he had apparently instructed in Latin, whose talents justify
his master's pains, and whose good qualities warrant his affection.
Jonson had Juvenal in view here :

    Nostra dabunt alios hodie convivia ludos ;
    Conditor Iliados cantabitur, atque Maronis
    Altisoni dubiam facientia carmina palmam. Sat. 11.

Of which we'll speak our minds, amidst our meat ;
And I'll profess no verses to repeat :
To this if aught appear, which I not know of,
That will the pastry, not my paper, show of.
Digestive cheese, and fruit there sure will be ;
But that which most doth take my muse and me,
Is a pure cup of rich Canary wine,
Which is the Mermaid's now, but shall be mine :[1]
Of which had Horace or Anacreon tasted,
Their lives, as do their lines, till now had lasted.
Tobacco, nectar, or the Thespian spring,
Are all but Luther's beer, to this I sing.
Of this we will sup free, but moderately,
And we will have no Pooly', or Parrot by ;
Nor shall our cups make any guilty men :
But at our parting, we will be, as when
We innocently met. No simple word,
That shall be utter'd at our mirthful board,
Shall make us sad next morning ; or affright
The liberty, that we'll enjoy to-night.

---

[1] *Which is the* Mermaid's *now, but shall be mine.*] The *Mermaid*, a tavern in Bread-street, at that time frequented by our author, and his poetical friends Beaumont and Fletcher, and the reigning wits of the age. WHAL.
This is from Horace's *Invitation to Virgil :*

> *Nardi parvus onyx eliciet cadum*
> *Qui nunc Sulpiciis accubet horreis,*
> *Spes donare novas largus, &c.*

But the plan of the whole is from a little poem of Martial, lib. x. epig. 48, of which it has many incidental imitations, particularly of the concluding lines :

> *De Nomentana vinum sine fæce lagena,*
> *Quæ bis Frontino consule plena fuit.*
> *Accedent sine felle joci, nec mane timenda*
> *Libertas, et nil quod tacuisse velis :*
> *De Prasino conviva meus, Venetoque loquatur ;*
> *Nec facient quenquam pocula nostra reum.*

CII.

To WILLIAM EARL OF PEMBROKE.

I DO but name thee, Pembroke, and I find
It is an epigram on all mankind;
    Against the bad, but of, and to the good :
Both which are ask'd, to have thee understood.
Nor could the age have miss'd thee, in this strife
Of vice and virtue, wherein all great life
Almost is exercised ; and scarce one knows,
To which, yet, of the sides himself he owes.
They follow virtue for reward to-day ;
To-morrow vice, if she give better pay :
And are so good, and bad, just at a price,
As nothing else discerns the virtue' or vice.
But thou, whose noblêsse keeps one stature still,[2]
And one true posture, though besieged with ill
Of what ambition, faction, pride can raise ;
Whose life, even they that envy it, must praise ;
That art so reverenced, as thy coming in,
But in the view, doth interrupt their sin ;
Thou must draw more : and they that hope to see
The commonwealth still safe, must study thee.

CIII.

To MARY LADY WROTH.[3]

H OW well, fair crown of your fair sex, might he
That but the twilight of your sprite did see,
    And noted for what flesh such souls were fram'd,
Know you to be a Sidney, though unnam'd ?

---

[2] *But thou whose* noblêsse, *&c.,*] i. e. nobleness, nobility. A
word which we have very improvidently suffered to become obsolete.
[3] *To Mary* lady Wroth.] She was a woman of genius, and wrote

And being nam'd, how little doth that name
Need any muse's praise to give it fame ?
Which is itself the imprese of the great,
And glory of them all, but to repeat !
Forgive me then, if mine but say you are
A Sidney ; but in that extend as far
As loudest praisers, who perhaps would find
For every part a character assign'd :
My praise is plain, and wheresoe'er profest,
Becomes none more than you, who need it least.

CIV.

To Susan countess of Montgomery.[4]

ERE they that nam'd you, prophets ? did they see,
            Even in the dew of grace, what you would be?
Or did our times require it, to behold
A new Susanna, equal to that old ?
Or, because some scarce think that story true,
To make those faithful did the Fates send you,

a romance called *Urania*, printed in folio, 1621 ; she was wife to
sir Robert Wroth, of Durance, in the county of Middlesex, and
daughter to Robert earl of Leicester, a younger brother of sir
Philip Sidney. WHAL.

    [4] *To Susan* countess of Montgomery.] Wife to Philip earl of
Montgomery, and grand-daughter to William lord Burleigh. WHAL.

    This accomplished and excellent woman, who appeared in most
of Jonson's Masques at court, has been more than once noticed.
She was a lady of strict piety and virtue, and wrote a little treatise
called *Eusebia, expressing briefly the Soul's praying robes*, 1620.

    It is much to the credit, or the good fortune of " that memorable
simpleton," as Walpole calls him, Philip Herbert, to have married
in succession two wives of such distinguished worth. His second,
as the reader knows, was the high-born and high-spirited daughter
of George earl of Cumberland, widow of Richard Sackville earl of
Dorset.

And to your scene lent no less dignity
Of birth, of match, of form, of chastity ?
Or, more than born for the comparison
Of former age, or glory of our own,
Were you advanced, past those times, to be
The light and mark unto posterity ?
Judge they that can : here I have raised to show,
A picture, which the world for yours must know,
And like it too ; if they look equally :
If not, 'tis fit for you, some should envy.

CV.

To Mary lady Wroth.

MADAM, had all antiquity been lost,
All history seal'd up, and fables crost,
That we had left us, nor by time, nor place,
Least mention of a Nymph, a Muse, a Grace,
But even their names were to be made anew,
Who could not but create them all from you ?
He, that but saw you wear the wheaten hat,
Would call you more than Ceres, if not that ;
And drest in shepherd's tire, who would not say
You were the bright Œnone, Flora, or May ?
If dancing, all would cry, the Idalian queen
Were leading forth the Graces on the green ;
And armed to the chase, so bare her bow
Diana' alone, so hit, and hunted so.
There's none so dull, that for your style would
    ask,
That saw you put on Pallas' plumed cask ;
Or, keeping your due state, that would not cry,
There Juno sat, and yet no peacock by :
So are you nature's index, and restore,
In yourself, all treasure lost of the age before.

CVI.

To sir Edward Herbert.[5]

F men get name for some one virtue ; then,
What man art thou, that art so many men,
All-virtuous Herbert ! on whose every part
Truth might spend all her voice, fame all her art ?
Whether thy learning they would take, or wit,
Or valour, or thy judgment seasoning it,
Thy standing upright to thyself, thy ends
Like straight, thy piety to God, and friends :
Their latter praise would still the greatest be,
And yet they, all together, less than thee.

CVII.

To captain Hungry.

O what you come for, captain, with your news ;
That's sit and eat : do not my ears abuse.
I oft look on false coin to know't from true ;
Not that I love it more than I will you.

[5] *Sir Edward Herbert.*] Lord Herbert of Cherbury. He was a person of great learning and of many excellent qualities as a statesman, a gentleman, and a scholar. This was all that was known of him at the period when this epigram appeared ; but he subsequently fell into strange contradictions : with great professions of piety he openly disavowed all belief in a divine revelation, and yet persuaded himself that his own prayers were audibly answered from heaven ! He was advanced to the dignity of baron of the kingdom of Ireland, in 1625, and in 1631 was created lord Herbert of Cherbury in Shropshire, a favour which he repaid by joining the enemies of his sovereign, on the breaking out of the civil war. His death took place in 1648. "He died (Aubrey says) very serenely ; asked what it was o'clock, and then, sayed he, 'an hour hence I shall depart!' He then turned his head to the other side, and expired."

Tell the gross Dutch those grosser tales of yours,
How great you were with their two emperours ;
And yet are with their princes : fill them full
Of your Moravian horse, Venetian bull.
Tell them, what parts you've ta'en, whence run
    away,
What states you've gull'd, and which yet keeps you'
    in pay.
Give them your services, and embassies
In Ireland, Holland, Sweden ; pompous lies !
In Hungary and Poland, Turky too ;
What at Ligorne, Rome, Florence you did do :
And, in some year, all these together heap'd,
For which there must more sea and land be leap'd,
If but to be believed you have the hap,
Than can a flea at twice skip in the map.
Give your young statesmen (that first make you
    drunk,
And then lye with you, closer than a punk,
For news) your Villeroys, and Silleries,
Ianins, your Nuncios, and your Tuilleries,
Your Archdukes agents, and your Beringhams,
That are your words of credit.　Keep your names
Of Hannow, Shieter-huissen, Popenheim,
Hans-spiegle, Rotteinberg, and Boutersheim,
For your next meal ; this you are sure of.　Why
Will you part with them here unthriftily ?
Nay, now you puff, tusk, and draw up your chin,
Twirl the poor chain you run a-feasting in.—
Come, be not angry, you are Hungry ; eat :
Do what you come for, captain ; there's your meat.

CVIII.

TO TRUE SOLDIERS.[6]

STRENGTH of my country, whilst I bring to view
    Such as are miscall'd captains, and wrong you,
And your high names ; I do desire that thence
Be nor put on you, nor you take offence.
I swear by your true friend, my muse, I love
Your great profession, which I once did prove ;
And did not shame it with my actions then,
No more than I dare now do with my pen.
He that not trusts me, having vow'd thus much,
But's angry for the captain, still ; is such.[7]

[6] *To true soldiers.*] We have this epigram in the *Apologetical Dialogue*, printed at the end of the *Poetaster :* and it seems to have been written as a kind of compensation for the character of captain Tucca, in that play. WHAL.

This was written before the *Poetaster.* Could not Whalley see that it alluded to the *captain* in the preceding epigram ? If there was any soldier stupid enough to take the character of Tucca as a reflection on the army, he was not to be reclaimed to sense by the power of verse. Jonson produced the epigram in his *Apology* to shew that he entertained no disrespectful opinion of the profession of a soldier. In a word, it is impossible to read that comedy, and listen to the complaints which the men of arms and of law are said to have made on the occasion, without discovering that they were more captious than just, and that the poet himself was the calumniated person.

[7] ———— —— *is* such,] i. e. is the captain Hungry whom I have just satirized. The observation is well-timed.

CIX.

To sir Henry Nevil.[8]

WHO now calls on thee, Nevil, is a muse,
    That serves not fame, nor titles; but doth
    chuse
Where virtue makes them both, and that's in thee:
Where all is fair beside thy pedigree.

[8] *To sir* Henry Nevil.] Son to Edward lord Abergavenny: he succeeded his father in the title in 1622, and died in December, 1641. Holland, in his additions to *Camden's Britannia*, mentions a place in Berkshire, called Bilingsbere, the inhabitation of sir Henry Nevil, issued from the lord Abergavenny. WHAL.

Surely Whalley has mistaken the person to whom this is addressed, or confounded two different characters. The sir Henry Neville of the poet was the son of sir H. Neville of Billingbear, by Elizabeth, a daughter of sir John Gresham. He was a very distinguished statesman, and much employed by the Queen, to whom he was introduced by Cecil. He was connected with the secretary by marriage; but he was less indebted to this for his promotion at court than to his own merits: "being," as Mr. Lodge says, "a person of great wisdom and integrity." He was sent ambassador to France in 1599, whence he returned in the following year, time enough, unfortunately for his future peace and prosperity, to be implicated in the wild treason of the earl of Essex. He was committed to the Tower, "which," says Cecil to sir Ralph Winwood, "being rather matter of form than substance, if any of his friends should have industriously opposed, it had been the ready way to have forced a course of more severity." What more was to be feared, I know not, but he was heavily fined; and his release from the Tower did not take place till some months after the accession of James. That he had really been in some danger, may be collected from the following passage:

> " Thou rather striv'st the matter to possess,
>   And elements of honour, than the dress;
>   To make *thy lent life* good against the fates,
>   And thence," &c.

But though restored to liberty, he was not advanced, as was generally expected. " All men (sir Henry Wotton says) contemplate sir Henry Neville for the future secretary; some saying that

Thou art not one seek'st miseries with hope,
Wrestlest with dignities, or feign'st a scope
Of service to the public, when the end
Is private gain, which hath long guilt to friend.
Thou rather striv'st the matter to possess,
And elements of honour, than the dress ;
To make thy lent life good against the fates :
And first to know thine own state, then the state's ;
To be the same in root thou art in height ;
And that thy soul should give thy flesh her weight.
Go on, and doubt not what posterity,
Now I have sung thee thus, shall judge of thee.
Thy deeds unto thy name will prove new wombs,
Whilst others toil for titles to their tombs.

it is but deferred till the return of the queen (Anne, who was then at Bath) that she may be allowed a hand in his introduction!" James, however, had strong prepossessions against him, which no interest could overcome, and the little remainder of this able statesman's life (for his correspondence is among the best in Winwood's collection) passed in dejection and comparative obscurity. It is to the honour of Jonson's steady friendship, that he liberally praises, and commends to the notice of posterity a worthy man depressed by two sovereigns, by each of whom he was himself favoured and patronized.

Sir Henry died 1615. He married Anne, daughter of sir Henry Killigrew of Cornwall ; by whom he had seven sons, whose descendants yet enjoy the family seat of their great ancestor.

CX.

To Clement Edmonds,

on his Cæsar's Commentaries observed and translated.[9]

NOT Cæsar's deeds, nor all his honours won,
    In these west parts,[1] nor, when that war was
        done,
The name of Pompey for an enemy,
Cato's to boot ; Rome, and her liberty,
All yielding to his fortune, nor, the while,
To have engraved these acts with his own style,
And that so strong and deep, as't might be thought
He wrote with the same spirit that he fought ;
Nor that his work lived in the hands of foes,
Unargued then, and yet hath fame from those ;
Not all these, Edmonds, or what else put to,
Can so speak Cæsar, as thy labours do.
For where his person lived scarce one just age,
And that midst envy and parts ; then fell by rage :
His deeds too dying, but in books, whose good
How few have read ! how fewer understood !
Thy learned hand and true Promethean art,
As by a new creation, part by part,
In every counsel, stratagem, design,
Action, or engine, worth a note of thine,
To all future time not only doth restore
His life, but makes, that he can die no more.

    [9] *To* Clement Edmonds, *on his Cæsar's Commentaries.*] Of this learned gentleman, who bore several public offices, during the reigns of queen Elizabeth and James I., the reader has an account in the *Athenæ Oxoniensis.* WHAL.

    This, and the following poem were prefixed, with other commendatory verses, to *Observations upon Cæsar's Commentaries: by Clement Edmundes, Remembrancer of the city of London.* fol.

    [1] —— *In these west parts,*] i. e. in Gaul and Britain. WHAL.

CXI.

To the Same. On the Same.

WHO, Edmonds, reads thy book, and doth not
  see
 What the antique soldiers were, the modern
  be?
Wherein thou shew'st, how much the later are
Beholding to this master of the war;
And that in action there is nothing new,
More, than to vary what our elders knew;
Which all but ignorant captains will confess;
Nor to give Cæsar this, makes ours the less.
Yet thou, perhaps, shalt meet some tongues will
  grutch,
That to the world thou should'st reveal so much,
And thence deprave thee and thy work: to those
Cæsar stands up, as from his urn late rose,
By thy great help; and doth proclaim by me,
They murder him again, that envy thee.

CXII.

To a weak gamester in poetry.

WITH thy small stock, why art thou venturing
  still,
 At this so subtle sport, and play'st so ill?
Think'st thou it is mere fortune, that can win,.
Or thy rank setting? that thou dar'st put in
Thy all, at all: and whatsoe'er I do,
Art still at that, and think'st to blow me' up too?
I cannot for the stage a drama lay,
Tragic or comic; but thou writ'st the play.

I leave thee there, and giving way, intend
An epic poem ; thou hast the same end.
I modestly quit that, and think to write,
Next morn, an ode ; thou mak'st a song ere night.
I pass to elegies ; thou meet'st me there :
To satires ; and thou dost pursue me.   Where,
Where shall I scape thee ? in an epigram ?
O, thou cry'st out, that is my proper game.
Troth, if it be, I pity thy ill luck ;
That both for wit and sense so oft dost pluck,
And never art encounter'd, I confess ;
Nor scarce dost colour for it, which is less.
Prithee, yet save thy rest ; give o'er in time :
There's no vexation that can make thee prime.[2]

CXIII.

To sir Thomas Overbury.[3]

O Phœbus make me worthy of his bays,
    As but to speak thee, Overbury, 's praise :
    So where thou liv'st, thou mak'st life under-
        stood,
Where, what makes other great, doth keep thee good !

[2] *There's no vexation that can make thee* prime.] This is an excellent little poem ; the allusion to a set at *primero*, which pervades
the whole of it, is supported with equal spirit and ingenuity.
    One of sir John Harington's "epigrams," or, as Jonson called
them, "narrations," contains "the story of Marcus' life at primero."
In this the various accidents of the game are detailed with great
dulness and prolixity. A short specimen taken at random, will
shew how closely our author has kept to the terms of the game.

> "But Marcus never can *encounter* right,
>   Yet drew two aces, and for further spight
>   Had *colour for it*, with a hopeful *draught*,
>   But not *encountered*, it avail'd him naught."

[3] *Sir Thomas Overbury*.] This epigram was probably written
about 1610, when sir Thomas returned from his travels, and fol-

I think, the fate of court thy coming crav'd,
That the wit there and manners might be sav'd :
For since, what ignorance, what pride is fled !
And letters, and humanity in the stead !
Repent thee not of thy fair precedent,
Could make such men, and such a place repent :
Nor may any fear to lose of their degree,
Who' in such ambition can but follow thee.

CXIV.

To mistress Philip Sidney.[4]

MUST believe some miracles still be,
When Sidney's name I hear, or face I see :
For Cupid, who at first took vain delight
In mere out-forms, until he lost his sight,

lowed the fortunes of Carr with a zeal and integrity worthy of a
better fate. That sir Thomas was poisoned in the Tower by the
infamous countess of Essex is well known; but it has been, and
indeed still may be made a question, whether Carr himself was
privy to this atrocious fact. It is said that his opposition to the
marriage between his friend and the divorced countess made it ex-
pedient to remove him from court, and that while Rochester (Carr)
intreated the king to bestow an embassy upon him, he secretly
instigated Overbury to refuse the charge. It would seem, however,
from Winwood's State Papers (vol. iii. pp. 447, 453, 475,) that the
refusal originated with sir Thomas himself, who was of a lofty and
unmanageable spirit. However it might be, James was justly
irritated; the destined victim was committed to the Tower, and the
catastrophe followed with fatal speed.

Overbury was of an ancient family in Warwickshire. He was
born in 1581, came to court to push his fortune in 1604, was
knighted in 1608, and died in 1613. He was highly accomplished,
and, as Granger truly remarks, was " possessed of parts, learning,
and judgment, beyond his years."

[4] Daughter of that great statesman, sir Francis Walsingham,
many years principal secretary to queen Elizabeth, and widow of
sir Philip Sidney. Walsingham died poor, so that his daughter,
who was also his heiress, brought little to her husband besides her
beauty and her virtues.

Hath changed his soul, and made his object you :
Where finding so much beauty met with virtùe,
He hath not only gain'd himself his eyes,
But, in your love, made all his servants wise.

CXV.

ON THE TOWN'S HONEST MAN.

YOU wonder who this is, and why I name
Him not aloud, that boasts so good a fame :
Naming so many too! but this is one,
Suffers no name, but a description ;
Being no vicious person, but the Vice
About the town ; and known too, at that price.
A subtle thing that doth affections win
By speaking well o' the company it's in.
Talks loud and bawdy, has a gather'd deal
Of news and noise, to sow out a long meal.
Can come from Tripoly,[5] leap stools, and wink,
Do all that longs to the anarchy of drink,
Except the duel : can sing songs and catches ;
Give every one his dose of mirth : and watches
Whose name's unwelcome to the present ear,
And him it lays on ;—if he be not there.
Tells of him all the tales itself then makes ;
But if it shall be question'd, undertakes,
It will deny all ; and forswear it too ;
Not that it fears, but will not have to do
With such a one : and therein keeps its word.
'Twill see its sister naked, ere a sword.
At every meal, where it doth dine or sup,
The cloth's no sooner gone, but it gets up,
And shifting of its faces, doth play more

---

[5] *Can come from* Tripoly,]i. e. can jump, and do feats of activity :
see the *Silent Woman*. WHAL.

Parts than the Italian could do, with his door.[6]
Acts Old Iniquity, and in the fit
Of miming, gets the opinion of a wit.
Executes men in picture; by defect,
From friendship, is its own fame's architect :
An inginer in slanders of all fashion,
That, seeming praises, are yet accusations.
Described it's thus : defined would you it have?
Then, the town's Honest Man's her errant'st knave.

CXVI.

To sir WILLIAM JEPHSON.

JEPHSON, thou man of men, to whose lov'd
name,
All gentry yet owe part of their best flame :
So did thy virtue inform, thy wit sustain
That age, when thou stood'st up the master-brain :
Thou wert the first mad'st merit know her strength,
And those that lack'd it, to suspect at length,
'Twas not entail'd on title : that some word
Might be found out as good, and not " my lord :"
That nature no such difference had imprest
In men, but every bravest was the best;

[6] ——— *Doth play more*
Parts than the Italian *could do, with his door.*] An allusion to
an *Italian*, then well known for his performances and tricks of art :
the person meant, I believe, is taken notice of in king James's
Dæmonology, and is there called *Scoto:* " The devil will learn them
many juglary tricks at cards, dice, and such like, to deceive mens
senses thereby, and such innumerable false practics, which are
proved by over many in this age ; as they who are acquainted with
that Italian called *Scoto*, yet living, can report." Lib. i. p. 105.
Old Iniquity, means the character called the Vice, in our ancient
Moralities : it has a place in our author's comedy, *The Devil is an
Ass.* WHAL.
This is an excellent piece, full of strong sense, and just satire.
It will serve for all times.

That blood not minds, but minds did blood adorn;
And to live great was better than great born.
These were thy knowing arts : which who doth now
Virtuously practise, must at least allow
Them in, if not from thee, or must commit
A desperate solœcism in truth and wit.   '

CXVII.

ON GROINE.

GROINE, come of age, his state sold out of
          hand
     For's whore : Groine doth still occupy his land.

CXVIII.

ON GUT.

GUT eats all day and letchers all the night,
     So all his meat he tasteth over twice ;
     And striving so to double his delight,
He makes himself a thorough-fare of vice.
Thus, in his belly, can he change a sin,
Lust it comes out, that gluttony went in.

CXIX.

TO SIR RALPH SHELTON.[7]

NOT he that flies the court for want of clothes,
     At hunting rails, having no gift in oaths,
     Cries out 'gainst cocking, since he cannot bet,
Shuns press—for two main causes, pox and debt,

     [7] This is the person who engaged with Mr. Hayden, in the mad

·With me can merit more, than that good man,
Whose dice not doing well, to a pulpit ran.—
No, Shelton, give me thee, canst want all these,
But dost it out of judgment, not disease ;
Dar'st breathe in any air ; and with safe skill,
Till thou canst find the best, choose the least ill.
That to the vulgar canst thyself apply,
Treading a better path, not contrary ;
And in their error's maze thine own way know :
Which is to live to conscience, not to show.
He that, but living half his age, dies such,[8]
Makes the whole longer than 'twas given him, much.

CXX.

An Epitaph on Salathiel Pavy, a child of Queen Elizabeth's chapel.

EEP with me, all you that read
  This little story :
And know, for whom a tear you shed
  Death's self is sorry.

frolic of rowing up Fleet ditch to Holborn, celebrated, page 233 ;
but I know nothing more of him.
 [8] *He that, but living half his age, dies such,*
  Makes the whole longer than 'twas given him, much.]
   Qui sic vel medio finitus vixit in ævo
   Longior huic facta est quam data vita fuit.
        Mart. lib. viii. 27.

 [9] *Salathiel Pavy.*] The subject of this beautiful epitaph acted
in *Cynthia's Revels,* and in the *Poetaster,* 1600 and 1601, in which
year he probably died. The poet speaks of him with interest and
affection, and it cannot be doubted that he was a boy of extraordinary talents. Many of the children of St. Paul's, as well as of
the queen's chapel, evinced great powers on the stage, at a very
early period of life, and not a few of them became the pride and
ornament of it in riper years.
 Our times have witnessed several attempts to bring children (pert

'Twas a child that so did thrive
        In grace and feature,
As heaven and nature seem'd to strive
        Which own'd the creature.
Years he number'd scarce thirteen
        When fates turn'd cruel,
Yet three fill'd zodiacs had he been
        The stage's jewel ;
And did act, what now we moan,
        Old men so duly,
As, sooth, the Parcæ thought him one,
        He play'd so truly.
So, by error to his fate [1]
        They all consented ;

boys and girls) upon the stage, as prodigies, which have all terminated, as might reasonably be expected, in disappointment and
disgrace. It should be recollected that the " children " of the old
theatre were strictly educated, and that they were opposed only to
one another. Nothing so monstrous ever entered into the thoughts
of the managers of those days as taking infants from the cock-horse,
and setting them to act with men and women.—And yet it would
be unjust, perhaps, to attribute the present encouragement of this
degrading exhibition wholly to the managers : if they took advantage of the gross folly of that many-headed beast, the town, and
indulged its vitiated taste, they did little more than their precarious situation seemed to warrant.—Let not Mr. Kemble, however, be defrauded of his due praise: but for his judicious and well-
timed humour in arranging the characters of the *Provoked Husband*
in such a manner as to place the absurdity of the attempt in the
most glaring light, that forward baby, Miss Mudie, would have
disgraced and delighted all London for the season, instead of
being sent back to her dirt pies, and her doll, after a single exposure.

[1] *So*, by error *to his fate*
    They all consented, &c.]

> *Ille ego sum Scorpus, clamosi gloria Circi,*
>   *Plausus, Roma, tui, deliciæque breves ;*
> *Invida quem Lachesis raptum trieteride nona,*
>   *Dum numerat palmas, credidit esse senem.*

                                        Mart. lib. x. epig. 53.

Lachesis (Dr. Jortin observes) did not take away Scorpus out of

But viewing him since, alas, too late !
    They have repented ;
And have sought, to give new birth,
    In baths to steep him ;
But being so much too good for earth,
    Heaven vows to keep him.

CXXI.

To Benjamin Rudyerd.[2]

RUDYERD, as lesser dames to great ones use,
My lighter comes to kiss thy learned muse ;
Whose better studies while she emulates,
She learns to know long difference of their states.

envy, but *by mistake*. She concluded that one who had gained so
many prizes at the chariot-races was an old man, and in consequence of this *error*, took him in the flower of youth. I fancy,
therefore, that Martial wrote,

" *Inscia quem Lachesis*," &c.   *Tracts*, vol. ii. p. 273.

There can be no doubt that Jonson read *Inscia;* and it seems
highly probable that Jortin was led to the emendation by this
epitaph, which was always well known.

  [2] Sir Benjamin Rudyerd (for subsequently to the writing of this
epigram, he received the honour of knighthood) was, as Granger
says, "an accomplished gentleman, and an elegant scholar." It
is no small proof of his worth, that he lived on terms of intimacy
with the earl of Pembroke, to whose poetical trifles his own were
subjoined, in a little volume which came out in 1660.

In the troubles which led to the usurpation of the Parliament,
sir Benjamin took an active part, and spoke often on the side of
moderation and justice, particularly on the question of excluding
the bishops from the Upper House. He was the last person who
held the office of " Surveyor of the Court of Wards and Liveries,"
and, when that court was abolished in 1646, received a grant of
land and money as a compensation for his place. He died in 1658,
and, as may be conjectured from his epitaph, which he wrote himself, in the practice of that piety and virtue which had formed the

Yet is the office not to be despised,
If only love should make the action prized ;
Nor he for friendship can be thought unfit,
That strives his manners should precede his wit.

CXXII.

To the Same.

F I would wish for truth, and not for show,
The aged Saturn's age and rites to know ;
If I would strive to bring back times, and try
The world's pure gold, and wise simplicity ;
If I would virtue set as she was young,
And hear her speak with one, and her first tongue ;
If holiest friendship, naked to the touch,
I would restore, and keep it ever such ;
I need no other arts, but study thee :
Who prov'st all these were, and again may be.

CXXIII.

To the Same.

RITING thyself, or judging others writ,
I know not which thou'st most, candor, or
                    wit :
But both thou hast so, as who affects the state
Of the best writer and judge, should emulate.

consolation of his life. There is a beautiful and touching simplicity in the second of these epigrams, which cannot be too highly
praised.

CXXIV.

Epitaph on Elizabeth, L. H.[3]

WOULD'ST thou hear what man can say
 In a little ? reader, stay.
  Underneath this stone doth lie
As much beauty as could die :
Which in life did harbour give
To more virtue than doth live.
 If at all she had a fault,
Leave it buried in this vault.
One name was Elizabeth,
The other let it sleep with death :
Fitter, where it died, to tell,
Than that it lived at all.   Farewell !

---

[3] *Elizabeth, L. H.*] Of this lady I can say nothing. If Jonson desired to keep her name secret, he has apparently succeeded; and yet he could scarcely mean to do this, as he has involved it, in some measure, with her history, in the last couplet. A luckier guesser, or a better historian, than I pretend to be, may one day hit upon it. But what is the import of this nameless tribute to beauty and virtue ? " To be read by bare inscriptions, (says sir Thomas Brown,) to hope for eternity by ænigmatical epithets, or initial letters, to be studied by antiquaries who we were, and have new names given us like some of the mummies, are cold consolations to the student of perpetuity, even by everlasting languages," or, as in the case before us, by everlasting verse.

Addison, after drawing a beautiful picture of good humour, innocence, and piety, in the person of Sophronia, adds that he "cannot conclude his essay better than by a short epitaph written by Ben Jonson, with a spirit which nothing could inspire but such an object as he had been describing.

   " Underneath this stone doth lie
   As much beauty as could die :
   Which in life did harbour give
   To more virtue than doth live." *Spec.* No. xxxiii.

I must observe here that, in the *Spectator* this passage is very incorrectly given. In a work so universally read, the utmost care should be taken to preserve the integrity of the text.

To sir WILLIAM UVEDALE.

UVEDALE, thou piece of the first times, a man
Made for what nature could, or virtue can ;
Both whose dimensions lost, the world might
  find
Restored in thy body, and thy mind !
Who sees a soul in such a body set,
Might love the treasure for the cabinet.
But I, no child, no fool, respect the kind,
The full, the flowing graces there enshrined ;
Which, would the world not miscall 't flattery,
I could adore almost to idolatry !

CXXVI.

To his LADY,

THEN MISTRESS CARY.[4]

RETIRED, with purpose your fair worth to
             praise,
      Mongst Hampton shades, and Phœbus' grove
             of bays,
I pluck'd a branch ; the jealous god did frown,
And bade me lay th' usurped laurel down :
Said I wrong'd him, and, which was more, his love.
I answer'd, Daphne now no pain can prove.
Phœbus replied, Bold head, it is not she :
Cary my love is, Daphne but my tree.

[4] Mistress *Cary.*]   The usual term in the poet's days for an unmarried woman, or miss : Of her husband, sir William Uvedale,
knt. I can say nothing but that he was of Wickham, in the county
of Southampton.

CXXVII.

To Esme lord Aubigny.[5]

S there a hope that man would thankful be,
      If I should fail in gratitude to thee,
         To whom I am so bound, loved Aubigny ?
No, I do therefore call posterity
Into the debt ; and reckon on her head,
How full of want, how swallow'd up, how dead
I and this muse had been, if thou hadst not
Lent timely succours, and new life begot :
So all reward or name, that grows to me
By her attempt, shall still be owing thee.
And than this same I know no abler way
To thank thy benefits : which is, to pay.

CXXVIII.

To William Roe.[6]

OE, and my joy to name, thou'rt now to go,
      Countries and climes, manners and men to
         know,
To extract and choose the best of all these known,
And those to turn to blood, and make thine own.

[5] *Esme lord Aubigny.*] Brother to the duke of Lenox, whom he succeeded in title and estate. He has been already noticed.

[6] *William Roe.*] Younger brother, or perhaps cousin, of sir Thomas Roe. (epig. 98.) This gentleman seems to have gone abroad in a mercantile or diplomatic capacity ; but with the activity and energy inherent in this distinguished family, he subsequently entered on the profession of arms, and probably served under Gustavus Adolphus. A few years of hardship, however, gave him enough of campaigning, and he returned to the pursuits of his youth. " William Roe (Howell writes to his friend at Brussels) is returned from the wars ; but he is grown lame in one of his arms, so he hath no mind to bear *arms* any more ; he confesseth himself

May winds as soft as breath of kissing friends,
Attend thee hence ; and there may all thy ends,
As the beginnings here, prove purely sweet,
And perfect in a circle always meet !
So when we, blest with thy return, shall see
Thyself, with thy first thoughts brought home by thee;
We each to other may this voice inspire ;
This is that good Æneas, past through fire,
Through seas, storms, tempests ; and, embark'd for
         hell,
Came back untouch'd.   This man hath travell'd well.

CXXIX.

To Mime.

THAT not a pair of friends each other see,
         But the first question is, When one saw thee?
         That there's no journey set or thought upon,
To Brentford, Hackney, Bow, but thou mak'st one ;
That scarce the town designeth any feast
To which thou'rt not a week bespoke a guest ;
That still thou'rt made the supper's flag, the drum,
The very call, to make all others come :
Think'st thou, Mime, this is great ? or that they strive
Whose noise shall keep thy miming most alive,
Whilst thou dost raise some player from the grave,
Out-dance the babion, or out-boast the brave[7]

to be an egregious fool to leave his mercership for a musket."
Lib. ii. lett. 62.
    [7] *Or out-boast the brave,*] i. e. the bravo, the ruffian ; some well
known bully of the time.   Cokely, Pod, and Gue, mentioned just
below, were masters of motions, or puppet-shows, and exhibitors
at Bartholomew Fair.   The strong sense and indignant satire of
this little poem might yet be turned to account if the parasite could
feel shame, or the table-buffoon be awakened to a sense of honour
by the pity, scorn, and insulting applause with which his degrading
fooleries are received.

Or, mounted on a stool, thy face doth hit
On some new gesture, that's imputed wit ?
O, run not proud of this.   Yet take thy due.
Thou dost out-zany Cokely, Pod ; nay, Gue :
And thine own Coryat too ; but,—would'st thou see,
Men love thee not for this ; they laugh at thee.

CXXX.

To Alphonso Ferrabosco, on his book.[8]

O urge, my loved Alphonso, that bold fame
   Of building towns, and making wild beasts
         tame,
Which music had; or speak her own effects,
That she removeth cares, sadness ejects,
Declineth anger, persuades clemency,
Doth sweeten mirth, and heighten piety,
And is to a body, often, ill inclined,
No less a sovereign cure, than to the mind ;
T' allege, that greatest men were not asham'd,
Of old, even by her practice to be fam'd ;

[8] *To* Alphonso Ferrabosco, *on his book.*] This person, descended
of Italian parents, was born at Greenwich in Kent : he was much
admired, both at home and abroad, for his excellent compositions,
and fancies, as they were then called, in music ; he was principally
employed in setting the songs to music in our poet's masques.
Whal.

Jonson appears to have had an extraordinary regard and affection for this excellent composer. He delights to mention him
upon all occasions ; and in the *Masque of Hymen*, hurried away by
his feelings, he interrupts the strain of applause in which he was
describing Alphonso's exertions, with a genuine burst of tenderness,
"Virtuous friend ! take well this abrupt testimony : It cannot be
flattery in me, who never did it to great ones ; and less than love
and truth it is not where it is done out of knowledge !"

The learned reader will observe that Jonson had in view Horace's
admirable description of the office of the ancient Chorus, in the
opening of this epigram.

To say indeed, she were the soul of heaven,
That the eighth sphere, no less than planets seven,
Moved by her order, and the ninth more high,
Including all, were thence call'd harmony ;
I yet had utter'd nothing on thy part,
When these were but the praises of the art :
But when I have said, the proofs of all these be
Shed in thy songs ; 'tis true : but short of thee.

CXXXI.

TO THE SAME.[9]

WHEN we do give, Alphonso, to the light,
A work of ours, we part with our own right ;
For then, all mouths will judge, and their
own way :
The learn'd have no more privilege than the lay.
And though we could all men, all censures hear,
We ought not give them taste we had an ear.
For if the humorous world will talk at large,
They should be fools, for me, at their own charge.
Say this or that man they to thee prefer ;
Even those for whom they do this, know they err :

[9] TO THE SAME.] The "Book" from which the composer probably expected a large harvest of praise seems to have met with
some ungentle critic, and Jonson writes this sensible and manly
epigram to his friend, to qualify the excess of his disappointment
and mortification. I know not the person meant, unless it be
Morley, who is mentioned as dissatisfied with some of his compositions by Peacham :—but I will give the passage :
 "Alphonso Ferrabosco the father, while he lived, for judgment
and depth of skill, as also his son now living, was inferior to none.
What he did was most elaborate and profound, and pleasing in
aire ; though master Thomas Morley censureth him otherwise.
That of his, *I saw my ladie weeping*, and the *Nightingale*, upon
which dittie master Bird and he in a friendly emulation exercised
their invention, cannot be bettered for sweetnesse of aire, or depth
of judgment." *Compleat Gent.* 1622.

And would (being ask'd the truth) ashamed say,
They were not to be nam'd on the same day.
Then stand unto thyself, nor seek without
For fame, with breath soon kindled, soon blown out.

CXXXII.

To Mr. Joshua Silvester.[1]

F to admire were to commend, my praise
    Might then both thee, thy work and merit
        raise :
But as it is, (the child of ignorance,
And utter stranger to all air of France,)

---

[1] *To Mr.* Joshua Silvester.] His translation of the French poem of *Du Bartas on the Creation*, was esteemed to be well done ; but he had little genius or invention of his own. In a censure of the poets, ascribed to Drayton, we have his character given in the following verses :

> " And *Silvester*, who, from the French more weak,
>   Made Bartas of his six days labour speak
>   In natural English : who, had he there stay'd,
>   He had done well ; and never had bewray'd
>   His own invention to have been so poor,
>   Who still wrote less, in striving to write more." Whal.

This epigram was written some years before the folio 1616 appeared, being prefixed to the 4to. edition of Silvester's Du Bartas, which came out in 1605. Jonson declares his ignorance of French, so that his praise must be confined to the poetical merits of the translator, who was pretty generally supposed to have gone beyond his original. When Jonson became acquainted with the French language, and was able to compare the two works, he then discovered, as he told Drummond, that Silvester had not been sufficiently faithful : this censure, however, must be understood with a reference to his own ideas of translation, and we know what they were, from the majority of his professed versions.

Ritson appears to have strangely misunderstood the passage in Drummond. He says, it was Ben Jonson's opinion, " that Silvester's translation of Du Bartas was not well done, and that he wrote his verses before he understood to confer." *Bibliographica Poetica,*

How can I speak of thy great pains, but err ?
Since they can only judge, that can confer.
Behold ! the reverend shade of Bartas stands
Before my thought, and, in thy right, commands
That to the world I publish for him, this ;
Bartas doth wish thy English now were his.
So well in that are his inventions wrought,
As his will now be the translation thought,
Thine the original ; and France shall boast,
No more those maiden glories she hath lost.

CXXXIII.

ON THE FAMOUS VOYAGE.[2]

NO more let Greece her bolder fables tell
    Of Hercules, or Theseus going to hell,
    Orpheus, Ulysses ; or the Latin muse,
With tales of Troy's just knight, our faiths abuse.

p. 356.   But the HE refers to Jonson not to Silvester, whose knowledge of French was never questioned.
    The translation is now little known : an unlucky quotation of
Dryden,

        Nor, with Du Bartas, "bridle up the floods"
        And " periwig with wool the baldpate woods,"

serves as an apology for consigning it to ridicule and neglect ;
Silvester wanted taste rather than poetry, and he has many shining
passages.   Goffe, who had a marvellous love for uncouth and ex-
travagant phraseology, has imitated the line above, with noble
emulation, in his *Courageous Turke :*

    "Who set the world on flame ? How now, ye heavens,
        Grow you so proud as to put on curl'd lockes,
        And clothe yourselves in periwigs of fire ! "

    [2] Of this " Voyage," undertaken, as I have already observed,
in a mad frolic, and celebrated in no very sane one, I shall only
say that more humour and poetry are wasted on it than it deserves.
As a picture of a populous part of London, it is not without some
interest, and might admit of a few remarks ; but I dislike the sub-

We have a Shelton, and a Heyden got,[3]
Had power to act, what they to feign had not.
All that they boast of Styx, of Acheron,
Cocytus, Phlegethon, ours have proved in one;
The filth, stench, noise: save only what was there
Subtly distinguish'd, was confused here.
Their wherry had no sail too; ours had ne'er one:
And in it, two more horrid knaves than Charon.
Arses were heard to croak instead of frogs;
And for one Cerberus, the whole coast was dogs.
Furies there wanted not; each scold was ten,
And for the cries of ghosts, women and men,
Laden with plague-sores, and their sins, were heard,
Lash'd by their consciences, to die affeard.
Then let the former age with this content her,
She brought the poets forth, but ours th' adventer.

THE VOYAGE ITSELF.

 SING the brave adventure of two wights,
And pity 'tis, I cannot call them knights:
One was; and he for brawn and brain right able
To have been styled of king Arthur's table.
The other was a squire, of fair degree;
But, in the action, greater man than he,
Who gave, to take at his return from hell,
His three for one.   Now, lordlings, listen well.

ject, and shall therefore leave the reader, who will not follow my
example, and pass lightly over it, to the annotations of Whalley.

[3] *We have a* Shelton *and a* Heyden *got.*] The names of the
persons who embarked in this enterprize. The first, I suppose, is
sir *Ralph Shelton*, to whom the 119th epigram is addressed. The
latter is probably sir Christopher Heyden, to whom Davis, in his
Scourge of Folly, p. 191, addresses an epigram. WHAL.

Yet Jonson says, in the opening of the *Voyage*, that the "latter"
was *a squire*.

It was the day, what time the powerful moon [4]
Makes the poor Bankside creature wet it's shoon,
In its own hall; when these, (in worthy scorn
Of those, that put out monies, on return
From Venice, Paris, or some inland passage
Of six times to and fro, without embassage,
Or him that backward went to Berwick, or which
Did dance the famous morris unto Norwich)
At Bread-street's Mermaid having dined, and merry,
Proposed to go to Holborn in a wherry:
A harder task, than either his to Bristo',
Or his to Antwerp. Therefore, once more, list ho'.

A dock there is, that called is Avernus,
Of some Bridewell, and may, in time concern us
All, that are readers: but, methinks, 'tis odd,
That all this while I have forgot some god,
Or goddess to invoke, to stuff my verse;
And with both bombast style and phrase, rehearse
The many perils of this port, and how
Sans help of Sibyl, or a golden bough,
Or magic sacrifice, they past along!—
Alcides, be thou succouring to my song.
Thou hast seen hell, some say, and know'st all nooks
          there,
Canst tell me best, how ever Fury looks there,
And art a god, if fame thee not abuses,
Always at hand, to aid the merry muses.
Great club-fist, though thy back and bones be sore
Still, with thy former labours; yet, once more,
Act a brave work, call it thy last adventry:
But hold my torch, while I describe the entry
To this dire passage. Say, thou stop thy nose;
'Tis but light pains: indeed, this dock's no rose.

---

[4] *It was the day, what time the* powerful moon,] i. e. a spring
tide, when the river frequently overflows its banks. WHAL.
    The persons alluded to in the next lines are William Kempe,
Taylor the water-poet, and Coryat.

In the first jaws appear'd that ugly monster,
Ycleped mud, which, when their oars did once stir,
Belch'd forth an air as hot, as at the muster
Of all your night-tubs, when the carts do cluster,
Who shall discharge first his merd-urinous load :
Thorough her womb they make their famous road,
Between two walls; where, on one side, to scare men,
Were seen your ugly centaurs, ye call carmen,
Gorgonian scolds, and Harpies : on the other
Hung stench, diseases, and old filth, their mother,
With famine, wants, and sorrows many a dozen,
The least of which was to the plague a cousin.
But they unfrighted pass, though many a privy
Spake to them louder, than the ox in Livy;[5]
And many a sink pour'd out her rage anenst 'em,
But still their valour and their virtue fenc'd 'em,
And on they went, like Castor brave and Pollux,
Ploughing the main.   When, see (the worst of all
        lucks)
They met the second prodigy, would fear a
Man, that had never heard of a Chimæra.
One said, 'twas bold Briareus, or the beadle,
Who hath the hundred hands when he doth meddle,
The other thought it Hydra, or the rock
Made of the trull that cut her father's lock :[6]
But coming near, they found it but a li'ter,
So huge, it seem'd they could by no means quite her.

---

[5] *Than the* ox *in* Livy.] *Jam alia vulgata miracula erant, hastam Martis Præneste suâ sponte promotam :* bovem in Siciliâ locutum, *Liv.* l. xxiv. cap. 10. Though I believe the poet here refers to the following passage of the same author ; *Inter cætera prodigia, quæ plurima fuisse traduntur, bovem Cn. Domitii consulis locutum,* Roma, cave tibi, *refertur.*   Epit. lib. xxxv.   WHAL.

[6] ———————— *Or the rock Made of the* trull *that cut her father's* lock.] He means *Scylla,* who *cut off the hair* of her father Nisus : but Ovid tells us she was changed into a bird called Ciris.   The old poets seem to have confounded two different stories together.   WHAL.

Back, cried their brace of Charons : they cried, No,
No going back; on still, you rogues, and row.
How hight the place ?   A voice was heard, Cocy-
    tus.
Row close then, slaves.   Alas ! they will beshite us.
No matter, stinkards, row.   What croaking sound
Is this we hear ? of frogs? No, guts wind-bound,
Over your heads : well, row.   At this a loud
Crack did report itself, as if a cloud
Had burst with storm, and down fell, *ab excelsis,*
Poor Mercury, crying out on Paracelsus,
And all his followers, that had so abused him ;
And in so shitten sort, so long had used him :
For (where he was the god of eloquence,
And subtilty of metals) they dispense
His spirits now in pills, and eke in potions,
Suppositories, cataplasms, and lotions.—
But many moons there shall not wane, quoth he,
In the mean time, let them imprison me,
But I will speak, and know I shall be heard,
Touching this cause, where they will be affeard
To answer me : and sure, it was the intent
Of the grave fart, late let in parliament,[7]
Had it been seconded, and not in fume
Vanish'd away : as you must all presume
Their Mercury did now.   By this, the stem
Of the hulk touch'd, and, as by Polypheme
The sly Ulysses stole in a sheep-skin,
The well-greased wherry now had got between,
And bade her farewell sough unto the lurden :
Never did bottom more betray her burden;
The meat-boat of bear's-college, Paris-garden,
Stunk not so ill ; nor, when she kiss'd, Kate Arden.

---

[7] ———————— *And sure it was th' intent*
  Of the grave fart, *late let in parliament.*] An accident of this
kind happened about this time, which, it seems, was the occasion
of much mirth among the wits.   See the *Alchemist.*   WHAL.

Yet one day in the year, for sweet 'tis voist,
And that is when it is the Lord Mayor's foist.

By this time had they reach'd the Stygian pool,
By which the masters swear, when on the stool
Of worship, they their nodding chins do hit
Against their breasts.   Here, several ghosts did flit
About the shore, of farts but late departed,
White, black, blue, green, and in more forms out-
    started,
Than all those *atomi* ridiculous
Whereof old Democrite, and Hill Nicholas,[8]
One said, the other swore, the world consists.
These be the cause of those thick frequent mists
Arising in that place, through which, who goes,
Must try the unused valour of a nose :
And that ours did.   For, yet, no nare was tainted,
Nor thumb, nor finger to the stop acquainted,
But open, and unarm'd, encounter'd all :
Whether it languishing stuck upon the wall,
Or were precipitated down the jakes,
And after, swam abroad in ample flakes,
Or that it lay heap'd like an usurer's mass,
All was to them the same, they were to pass,
And so they did, from Styx to Acheron,
The ever-boiling flood ; whose banks upon
Your Fleet-lane Furies, and hot cooks do dwell,
That with still-scalding steams, make the place hell.
The sinks ran grease, and hair of meazled hogs,
The heads, houghs, entrails, and the hides of dogs :
For, to say truth, what scullion is so nasty,
To put the skins and offal in a pasty ?

[8] *Whereof old* Democrite, *and* Hill Nicholas.]   "*Nicholas Hill*
was a fellow of St. John's college in Oxford : he adopted the
notions of Democritus about atoms, and was a great patron of the
Corpuscular philosophy.   The book he published on this subject
is entituled *Philosophia Epicurea, Democritana, Theophrastica, pro-*
posita simpliciter, non edocta.   Par. 1601."   A. WOOD.

Cats there lay divers had been flea'd and roasted,
And after mouldy grown, again were toasted,
Then selling not, a dish was ta'en to mince 'em,
But still, it seem'd, the rankness did convince 'em,
For, here they were thrown in with th' melted pewter,
Yet drown'd they not : they had five lives in future.

But 'mongst these Tiberts,[9] who do you think there
     was ?
Old Banks the jugler, our Pythagoras,
Grave tutor to the learned horse ; both which,
Being, beyond sea, burned for one witch,
Their spirits transmigrated to a cat :
And now, above the pool, a face right fat,
With great gray eyes, it lifted up, and mew'd ;
Thrice did it spit ; thrice dived : at last it view'd
Our brave heroës with a milder glare,
And in a piteous tune, began.   How dare
Your dainty nostrils, in so hot a season,
When every clerk eats artichokes and peason,
Laxative lettuce, and such windy meat,
Tempt such a passage ?   When each privy's seat
Is fill'd with buttock, and the walls do sweat
Urine and plaisters, when the noise doth beat
Upon your ears, of discords so unsweet,
And outcries of the damned in the Fleet ?
Cannot the Plague-bill keep you back, nor bells
Of loud Sepulchre's, with their hourly knells,
But you will visit grisly Pluto's hall ?
Behold where Cerberus, rear'd on the wall
Of Holborn-height (three serjeants' heads) looks o'er,
And stays but till you come unto the door !
Tempt not his fury, Pluto is away :
And madam Cæsar, great Proserpina,

---

[9] *But 'mongst these* Tiberts,] i. e. *cats.* The name given to them
in the old story book of *Reynard the Fox. Banks,* who follows in
the next line, was a fellow who shewed a horse about that time,
famous for his tricks. WHAL.

Is now from home; you lose your labours quite,
Were you Jove's sons, or had Alcides' might.
They cry'd out, Puss.   He told them he was Banks,
That had so often shew'd them merry pranks.
They laugh'd, at his laugh-worthy fate ; and past
The triple-head without a sop.   At last,
Calling for Rhadamanthus, that dwelt by,
A soap-boiler ; and Æacus him nigh,
Who kept an ale-house ; with my little Minos,
An ancient purblind fletcher, with a high nose ;
They took them all to witness of their action :
And so went bravely back without protraction.

In memory of which most liquid deed,
The city since hath raised a pyramid ;
And I could wish for their eternized sakes,
My Muse had plough'd with his, that sung A-JAX.[1]

---

[1] *My Muse had plough'd with his, that sung A-jax.*] Sir John
Harington, author of the treatise called, *Misacmos,* or the *Meta-
morphosis of A-jax.* WHAL.

THE END OF THE EPIGRAMS.

THE FOREST.

R

THE FOREST.] From the folio, 1616. Between this and the poem which now concludes the Epigrams, Whalley foisted in several compositions under that title, which appeared long after the publication of the volume. This was injudiciously done, for as the date of the folio was well known, it tended to confound the idea of time, and to mislead the general reader. Several of the pieces given by Whalley under the head of Epigrams, closed by the author in 1616, were written by him as late as 1630.

THE FOREST.

I.

WHY I WRITE NOT OF LOVE.

SOME act of Love's bound to rehearse,
I thought to bind him in my verse :
Which when he felt, Away, quoth he,
Can poets hope to fetter me ?
It is enough, they once did get
Mars and my mother, in their net :
I wear not these my wings in vain.
With which he fled me ; and again,
Into my rhymes could ne'er be got
By any art : then wonder not,
That since, my numbers are so cold,
When Love is fled, and I grow old.

II.

TO PENSHURST.[1]

THOU art not, Penshurst, built to envious
show
Of touch or marble ;[2] nor canst boast a row
Of polish'd pillars, or a roof of gold :
Thou hast no lantern, whereof tales are told ;

[1] *To Penshurst.*] This place is pleasantly situated near the banks

Or stair, or courts ; but stand'st an ancient pile,
And these grudg'd at, art reverenced the while.
Thou joy'st in better marks, of soil, of air,
Of wood, of water ; therein thou art fair.
Thou hast thy walks for health, as well as sport :
Thy mount, to which thy Dryads do resort,
Where Pan and Bacchus their high feasts have made,
Beneath the broad beech, and the chestnut shade ;
That taller tree, which of a nut was set,
At his great birth, where all the Muses met.[3]

of the Medway ; it was the ancient seat of sir Stephen Pencestre,
warden of the Cinque Ports, and Constable of Dover Castle, in the
reign of Henry III., and was granted by Edward VI. to sir William
Sidney and his heirs :—having been forfeited to the crown by the
rebellion of sir R. Fane, its last proprietor.

  [2] *Thou art not, Penshurst, built to envious show*
  Of touch *or* marble.] The common kind of black marble
frequently made use of in funeral monuments, was then called by
this name ; so Weaver, giving the account of a tomb at Hamp-
stead :

        " Under a fair monument of *marble and touch*," &c.

From its solidity and firmness it was used also as the test of gold :
in this sense it occurs in Shakspeare :

        " Ah ! Buckingham, now do I ply the *touch*."
                            Richard III. Act iv. sc. 2.

And from this use of it, the name itself was taken. It seems to be
the same with that anciently called *basalt*. WHAL.

  [3] *At his great* birth, *where all the Muses met*,] i. e. sir Philip Sidney's, who was born at Penshurst in Kent. WHAL.
  Sir Philip Sidney was born 29th November, 1554. " That taller
tree," produced from an acorn, planted on his birth-day, and which
has been the theme of many poets, is no longer standing. It is
said to have been felled by mistake in 1768 ; a wretched apology,
if true, and, in a case of such notoriety, scarcely possible. Waller,
in one of his poems, written at Penshurst, where he amused himself with falling in love, has an allusion to this oak :

        " Go, boy, and carve this passion on the bark
          Of yonder tree, which stands the sacred mark
          Of noble Sidney's birth," &c.

On which the commentator on his poems observes that though no
tradition of the circumstance remained in the family, yet the obser-

There, in the writhed bark, are cut the names
Of many a sylvan, taken with his flames;
And thence the ruddy satyrs oft provoke
The lighter fauns, to reach thy lady's oak.[4]
Thy copse, too, named of Gamage, thou hast there,[5]
That never fails to serve thee season'd deer,
When thou wouldst feast, or exercise thy friends.
The lower land, that to the river bends,
Thy sheep, thy bullocks, kine, and calves do feed;
The middle grounds thy mares and horses breed.
Each bank doth yield thee conies; and the tops
Fertile of wood, Ashore and Sydneys copp's,
To crown thy open table, doth provide
The purpled pheasant, with the speckled side:
The painted partridge lies in ev'ry field,
And for thy mess is willing to be kill'd.

vation of Cicero on the Marian oak might not unaptly be applied to it. "*Manet vero et semper manebit. Sata est enim ingenio: Nullius autem agricolæ cultu stirps tam diuturna quam poetæ versu seminari potest.*" *De leg.* lib. i.

About a century after the date of Waller's verses, this oak was still standing, and the ingenious Mr. F. Coventry wrote the following lines under its shade:

> "Stranger kneel here! to age due homage pay
> When great Eliza held Britannia's sway
> My growth began,—the same illustrious morn,
> Joy to the hour! saw gallant Sidney born.
> He perish'd early; I just stay behind
> An hundred years; and lo! my clefted rind,
> My wither'd boughs foretell destruction nigh;
> We all are mortal; oaks and heroes die."

[4] ——— *thy lady's oak.*] There is an old tradition that a lady Leicester (the wife undoubtedly of sir Robert Sidney) was taken in travail under an oak in Penshurst park, which was afterwards called *my Lady's oak.*

[5] *Thy copse, too, named of* Gamage.] "This coppice is now called lady Gamage's bower; it being said that Barbara Gamage, countess of Leicester, used to take great delight in feeding the deer therein from her own hands." *Dug. Baron.* This lady was daughter and heiress of John Gamage of Coytie, in Glamorganshire, and the first wife of sir Robert.

And if the high-swoln Medway fail thy dish,
Thou hast thy ponds, that pay thee tribute fish,
Fat aged carps that run into thy net,
And pikes, now weary their own kind to eat,
As loth the second draught or cast to stay,
Officiously at first themselves betray.
Bright eels that emulate them, and leap on land,
Before the fisher, or into his hand.
Then hath thy orchard fruit, thy garden flowers,
Fresh as the air, and new as are the hours.
The early cherry, with the later plum,
Fig, grape, and quince, each in his time doth come:
The blushing apricot, and woolly peach
Hang on thy walls, that every child may reach.
And though thy walls be of the country stone,
They're rear'd with no man's ruin, no man's groan;
There's none, that dwell about them, wish them down;
But all come in, the farmer and the clown;
And no one empty-handed, to salute
Thy lord and lady, though they have no suit.
Some bring a capon, some a rural cake,
Some nuts, some apples; some that think they make
The better cheeses, bring them; or else send
By their ripe daughters, whom they would commend
This way to husbands; and whose baskets bear
An emblem of themselves in plum, or pear.
But what can this (more than express their love)
Add to thy free provisions, far above
The need of such? whose liberal board doth flow,
With all that hospitality doth know!
Where comes no guest, but is allow'd to eat,[6]
Without his fear, and of thy lord's own meat:

---

[6] *Where comes no guest, but is allow'd to eat,*
   Without his fear, and of thy lord's own meat, &c.] This, and
what follows, may appear a strange topic for praise to those who
are unacquainted with the practice of those times. But, in fact,
the liberal mode of hospitality here recorded, was almost peculiar

Where the same beer and bread, and self-same wine,
That is his lordship's, shall be also mine.
And I not fain to sit (as some this day,
At great men's tables) and yet dine away.
Here no man tells my cups ; nor standing by,
A waiter, doth my gluttony envỳ :
But gives me what I call, and lets me eat,
He knows, below, he shall find plenty of meat ;
Thy tables hoard not up for the next day,
Nor, when I take my lodging, need I pray
For fire, or lights, or livery ; all is there ;
As if thou then wert mine, or I reign'd here :
There's nothing I can wish, for which I stay.
That found king James, when hunting late, this way,
With his brave son, the prince ; they saw thy fires
Shine bright on every hearth, as the desires
Of thy Penates had been set on flame,
To entertain them ; or the country came,
With all their zeal, to warm their welcome here.
What (great, I will not say, but) sudden chear

to this noble person. The great, indeed, dined at long tables (they
had no other in their vast halls) and permitted many guests to sit
down with them ; but the gradations of rank and fortune were
rigidly maintained, and the dishes grew visibly coarser as they re-
ceded from the head of the table. No reader of our old poets can
be ignorant of the phrase, *below the salt;* but it may not be generally
known that in some countries the custom yet prevails. It is the
natural consequence of feudal manners ; and the scene between the
patron and the client which excited the caustic indignation of
Juvenal, is daily renewed in many parts of Russia, and in the whole
of Poland. In England the system was breaking up when Jonson
wrote, and he notices it with his usual good sense. It is to the
honour of Penshurst that the observation was made there.

Herrick, who abounds in imitations of Jonson, whom he loved
and admired, has copied many passages of this and the following
poem, in his *Panegyrick to sir L. Pemberton.* Here is one of them :

    " No, no, thy bread, thy wine, thy jocund beere
        Is not reserv'd for Trebius here,
      But all, who at thy table seated are,
        Find equal freedom, equal fare," &c.

Didst thou then make'em! and what praise was heap'd
On thy good lady, then! who therein reap'd
The just reward of her high huswifry;
To have her linen, plate, and all things nigh,
When she was far; and not a room, but drest,
As if it had expected such a guest!
These, Penshurst, are thy praise, and yet not all.
Thy lady's noble, fruitful, chaste withal.
His children thy great lord may call his own; [7]
A fortune, in this age, but rarely known.
They are, and have been taught religion; thence
Their gentler spirits have suck'd innocence.
Each morn, and even, they are taught to pray,
With the whole household, and may, every day,
Read in their virtuous parents' noble parts,
The mysteries of manners, arms, and arts.
Now, Penshurst, they that will proportion thee
With other edifices, when they see
Those proud ambitious heaps, and nothing else,
May say, their lords have built, but thy lord dwells.

III.

To sir Robert Wroth.

OW blest art thou, canst love the country, Wroth,
     Whether by choice, or fate, or both!
        And though so near the city, and the court, [8]
Art ta'en with neither's vice nor sport:

---

[7] *Thy great lord, &c.*] Robert Sidney, the second son of sir Henry Sidney, and brother of sir Philip, was knighted for his gallant behaviour at the battle of Zutphen, 1586; advanced to the dignity of baron Sidney of Penshurst by James, created viscount Lisle in 1605, and finally promoted to the earldom of Leicester in 1618. He is not flattered in these pleasing lines; for his character was truly excellent.

[8] *And though so near the city and the court.*] The seat of sir

That at great times, art no ambitious guest
    Of sheriff's dinner, or mayor's feast.
Nor com'st to view the better cloth of state,
    The richer hangings, or crown-plate ;
Nor throng'st (when masquing is) to have a sight
    Of the short bravery of the night ;
To view the jewels, stuffs, the pains, the wit
    There wasted, some not paid for yet !
But canst at home, in thy securer rest,
    Live, with unbought provision blest ;
Free from proud porches, or the gilded roofs,
    'Mongst lowing herds, and solid hoofs :
Along the curled woods, and painted meads,
    Through which a serpent river leads
To some cool courteous shade, which he calls his,
    And makes sleep softer than it is.
Or if thou list the night in watch to break,
    A-bed canst hear the loud stag speak,
In spring, oft roused for thy master's sport,
    Who for it makes thy house his court ;
Or with thy friends, the heart of all the year
    Divid'st, upon the lesser deer :
In Autumn, at the partridge mak'st a flight,
    And giv'st thy gladder guests the sight ;
And in the winter, hunt'st the flying hare,
    More for thy exercise, than fare ;
While all that follow, their glad ears apply
    To the full greatness of the cry :
Or hawking at the river, or the bush,[9]
    Or shooting at the greedy thrush,

Robert Wroth was at Durance, in Middlesex. James was a frequent guest there.

[9] *Or hawking at the river,*] i. e. for the greater game, which frequented it. This, which was the afternoon's amusement, is noticed by many of our old writers. *Sir Topas* was much attached to it, if we may trust Chaucer :

      " He couth hunt at the wild dere
        And ride an *hawking by the rivere,*" &c.

Thou dost with some delight the day out-wear,
  Although the coldest of the year !
The whilst the several seasons thou hast seen
  Of flowery fields, of cop'ces green,
The mowed meadows, with the fleeced sheep,
  And feasts, that either shearers keep ;
The ripened ears, yet humble in their height,
  And furrows laden with their weight ;
The apple-harvest, that doth longer last ;
  The hogs return'd home fat from mast ;
The trees cut out in log, and those boughs made
  A fire now, that lent a shade !
Thus Pan and Sylvan having had their rites,
  Comus puts in for new delights ;
And fills thy open hall with mirth and cheer,
  As if in Saturn's reign it were ;
Apollo's harp, and Hermes' lyre resound,
  Nor are the Muses strangers found.
The rout of rural folk come thronging in,
  (Their rudeness then is thought no sin)
Thy noblest spouse affords them welcome grace ;[1]
  And the great heroes of her race
Sit mixt with loss of state, or reverence.
  Freedom doth with degree dispense.
The jolly wassal walks the often round,
  And in their cups their cares are drown'd :
They think not then, which side the cause shall
      leese,
  Nor how to get the lawyer fees.
Such and no other was that age of old,
  Which boasts t' have had the head of gold.

Again :
      " These fauconers upon a fair rivere
        That with the hawkis han the heron slaine."
                                Franklin's Tale.

  [1] *Thy noblest spouse, &c.*] This accomplished and learned lady
has been already mentioned as the niece of sir Philip Sidney.

And such, since thou canst make thine own content,
　Strive, Wroth, to live long innocent.
Let others watch in guilty arms, and stand
　The fury of a rash command,
Go enter breaches, meet the cannon's rage,
　That they may sleep with scars in age;
And shew their feathers shot, and colours torn,
　And brag that they were therefore born.
Let this man sweat, and wrangle at the bar,
　For every price, in every jar,
And change possessions oftner with his breath,
　Than either money, war, or death :
Let him, than hardest sires, more disinherit,
　And each where boast it as his merit,
To blow up orphans, widows, and their states ;
　And think his power doth equal fate's.
Let that go heap a mass of wretched wealth,
　Purchased by rapine, worse than stealth,
And brooding o'er it sit, with broadest eyes,
　Not doing good, scarce when he dies.
Let thousands more go flatter vice, and win,
　By being organs to great sin;
Get place and honour, and be glad to keep
　The secrets that shall break their sleep:
And so they ride in purple, eat in plate,
　Though poison, think it a great fate.
But thou, my Wroth, if I can truth apply,
　Shalt neither that, nor this envy :
Thy peace is made; and when man's state is well,
　'Tis better, if he there can dwell.
God wisheth none should wreck on a strange shelf :
　To him man's dearer, than t' himself,[2]
And howsoever we may think things sweet,
　He always gives what he knows meet;

---

[2] *God wisheth none should wreck on a strange* shelf:
　To him man's dearer than t' himself.] The sentiment, with the

Which who can use is happy : Such be thou.
  Thy morning's and thy evening's vow
Be thanks to him, and earnest pray'r, to find
  A body sound, with sounder mind ;
To do thy country service, thy self right ;
  That neither want do thee affright,
Nor death ; but when thy latest sand is spent,
  Thou may'st think life a thing but lent.[3]

IV.

To the World.

A Farewell for a Gentlewoman, virtuous and noble.

ALSE world, good-night ! since thou hast
      brought
    That hour upon my morn of age,
  Henceforth I quit thee from my thought,
    My part is ended on thy stage.

Do not once hope that thou canst tempt
  A spirit so resolv'd to tread
Upon thy throat, and live exempt
  From all the nets that thou canst spread.

following verses, is taken from that celebrated passage in the 10th
satire of Juvenal :

> *Permittes ipsis expendere Numinibus, quid*
> *Conveniat nobis, rebusque sit utile nostris ;*
> *Nam pro jucundis aptissima quæque dabunt dii.*
> *Carior est illis homo, quam sibi——*
> *Orandum est, ut sit mens sana in corpore sano.*

A *shelf*, or *shelve*, is a bank of sand.   Whal.
  [3] *Thou may'st think life a thing but lent.*]   This is a very beautiful
Epode, honourable alike to the writer, and the subject of it.   How
nobly do Jonson's lines rise above the common addresses of his
age ! he is familiar with decorum, and moral with dignity ; while his
unbounded command of classic images gives a force to his language,
which renders his description of the humblest object interesting.

I know thy forms are studied arts,
   Thy subtle ways be narrow straits;
Thy courtesy but sudden starts,
   And what thou call'st thy gifts are baits.

I know too, though thou strut and paint,
   Yet art thou both shrunk up, and old;
That only fools make thee a saint,
   And all thy good is to be sold.

I know thou whole art but a shop
   Of toys and trifles, traps and snares,
To take the weak, or make them stop:
   Yet art thou falser than thy wares.

And knowing this should I yet stay,
   Like such as blow away their lives,
And never will redeem a day,
   Enamour'd of their golden gyves?

Or having 'scaped shall I return,
   And thrust my neck into the noose,
From whence so lately, I did burn,
   With all my powers, my self to loose?

What bird, or beast is known so dull,
   That fled his cage, or broke his chain,
And tasting air and freedom, wull
   Render his head in there again?

If these who have but sense, can shun
   The engines, that have them annoy'd;
Little for me had reason done,
   If I could not thy gins avoid.

Yes, threaten, do. Alas, I fear
   As little, as I hope from thee:
I know thou canst nor shew, nor bear
   More hatred, than thou hast to me.

My tender, first, and simple years
    Thou didst abuse, and then betray ;
Since stirr'dst up jealousies and fears,
    When all the causes were away.

Then in a soil hast planted me,
    Where breathe the basest of thy fools ;
Where envious arts professed be,
    And pride and ignorance the schools :

Where nothing is examin'd, weigh'd,
    But as 'tis rumour'd, so believed ;
Where every freedom is betray'd,
    And every goodness tax'd or grieved.

But what we're born for, we must bear :
    Our frail condition it is such,
That what to all may happen here,
    If't chance to me, I must not grutch.

Else I my state should much mistake,
    To harbour a divided thought
From all my kind ; that for my sake,
    There should a miracle be wrought.

No, I do know that I was born
    To age, misfortune, sickness, grief :
But I will bear these with that scorn,
    As shall not need thy false relief.

Nor for my peace will I go far,
    As wanderers do, that still do roam ;
But make my strengths, such as they are,
    Here in my bosom, and at home.

V.

SONG.

To Celia.

COME, my Celia, let us prove,[4]
    While we may, the sports of love;
    Time will not be ours for ever:
    He at length our good will sever.
Spend not then his gifts in vain.
Suns that set, may rise again;
But if once we lose this light,
'Tis with us perpetual night.
Why should we defer our joys?
Fame and rumour are but toys.
Cannot we delude the eyes
Of a few poor houshold spies;
Or his easier ears beguile,
So removed by our wile?
'Tis no sin love's fruit to steal,
But the sweet theft to reveal:
To be taken, to be seen,
These have crimes accounted been.

VI.

To the Same.

KISS me, sweet: the wary lover
    Can your favours keep, and cover,
    When the common courting jay
    All your bounties will betray.
Kiss again: no creature comes.
Kiss, and score up wealthy sums

[4] *Come, my Celia, &c.*] This beautiful song is to be found in

On my lips thus hardly sundred,
While you breathe.   First give a hundred,
Then a thousand, then another
Hundred, then unto the other
Add a thousand, and so more :
Till you equal with the store,
All the grass that Rumney yields,
Or the sands in Chelsea fields,
Or the drops in silver Thames,
Or the stars that gild his streams,
In the silent Summer-nights,
When youths ply their stolen delights ;
That the curious may not know
How to tell 'em as they flow,
And the envious, when they find
What their number is, be pined.

VII.

SONG.

THAT.WOMEN ARE BUT MEN'S SHADOWS.

OLLOW a shadow, it still flies you,
   Seem to fly it, it will pursue :
   So court a mistress, she denies you ;
   Let her alone, she will court you.
Say are not women truly, then,
Styl'd but the shadows of us men ?

At morn and even shades are longest ;
   At noon they are or short, or none :
So men at weakest, they are strongest,
   But grant us perfect, they're not known.

the *Fox.* See vol. iii. p. 247. Whalley says, " this, and the following are translations from Catullus." Translations, they certainly
are not ; but very elegant and happy imitations of particular passages in that poet.

Say are not women truly, then,
Styl'd but the shadows of us men ?

VIII.

SONG.

To SICKNESS.

WHY, Disease, dost thou molest
Ladies, and of them the best ?
Do not men enow of rites
To thy altars, by their nights
Spent in surfeits ; and their days,
And nights too, in worser ways ?
    Take heed, Sickness, what you do,
I shall fear you'll surfeit too.
Live not we, as all thy stalls,
Spittles, pest-house, hospitals,
Scarce will take our present store ?
And this age will build no more.
    'Pray thee, feed contented then,
Sickness, only on us men ;
Or if it needs thy lust will taste
Woman-kind ; devour the waste
Livers, round about the town.
    But, forgive me,—with thy crown
They maintain the truest trade,
And have more diseases made.·
    What should yet thy palate please ?
Daintiness, and softer ease,
Sleeked limbs, and finest blood ?
If thy leanness love such food,
There are those, that for thy sake,
Do enough ; and who would take
Any pains ; yea, think it price,
To become thy sacrifice.

8   S

That distill their husband's land
In decoctions; and are mann'd
With ten emp'rics, in their chamber,
Lying for the spirit of amber.
That for the oil of talc dare spend
More than citizens dare lend[5]
Them, and all their officers.
That to make all pleasure theirs,
Will by coach, and water go,
Every stew in town to know;
Dare entail their loves on any,
Bald or blind, or ne'er so many:
And for thee at common game,
Play away health, wealth, and fame.
  These, Disease, will thee deserve;
And will long, ere thou should'st starve,
On their beds, most prostitute,
Move it, as their humblest suit,
In thy justice to molest
None but them, and leave the rest.

IX.

SONG.

To CELIA.[6]

DRINK to me, only with thine eyes,
    And I will pledge with mine;
    Or leave a kiss but in the cup,
    And I'll not look for wine.
The thirst, that from the soul doth rise,
    Doth ask a drink divine:

---

[5] *That for the* oil of talc *dare spend*
  More than citizens dare lend.] See vol. iv. p. 90. Whalley has
strangely confounded this cosmetic with a nauseous unction for the
tick in sheep.
  [6] No part of Jonson has been so frequently quoted as this song,

But might I of Jove's nectar sup,
I would not change for thine.

which, pleasing as it is, is not superior to many others scattered
through his works.

"I was surprised, (Cumberland says) the other day to find our
learned poet Ben Jonson had been poaching in an obscure collection of love letters, written by the sophist Philostratus in a very
rhapsodical stile, merely for the purpose of stringing together a
parcel of unnatural far-fetched conceits, more calculated to disgust
a man of Jonson's classical taste, than to put him upon the humble
task of copying them, and then fathering the translation. The little
poem he has taken from this despicable sophist is now become a
very popular song." *Observer*, No. lxxiv.

Cumberland, who reasoned very loosely, was hardly aware, I
think, of the extraordinary compliment he was paying Jonson in
this passage. But why should he be *surprised?*—Did we not know
that he was directed to Philostratus by a more skilful and excursive finger than his own, we might perhaps be *surprised* at finding
the critic there; but they must have a very imperfect acquaintance
with Jonson who are unprepared to meet with him in any volume
which antiquity has bequeathed to us. It need not follow that our
poet admired every writer that he read : he might not, perhaps,
have judged more favourably of Philostratus than Mr. Cumberland, or, rather, Dr. Bentley; yet he had the address to turn
him to some account : but to the quotations; which, it must be
added, are translated without much apparent knowledge of the
original.

"Εμοι δε μονοις προπινε τοις ομμασιν. Ει δε βουλει, τοις χειλεσι
προσφερουσα, πληρου φιληματων το εκπωμα, και ούτως διδου." "Drink
to me with thine eyes only—Or, if thou wilt, putting the cup to thy
lips, fill it with kisses, and so bestow it upon me." *Lett.* xxiv.

"Εγω, επειδαν ιδω σε, διψω, και το εκπωμα κατεχων, και το μεν ου
προσαγω τοις χειλεσι, σου δε οιδα πινων." "I, as soon as I behold
thee, thirst, and taking hold of the cup, do not indeed apply that
to my lips for drink, but thee." *Lett.* xxv. This is by no means
the sense. It was not thus that Jonson read Philostratus.

"Πεπομφα σοι στεφανον ρoδων, ου σε τιμων, (και τουτο μεν γαρ)
αλλ' αυτοις τι χαριζομενος τοις ροδοις, ίνα μη μιρανδη." "I sent thee
a rosy wreath, not so much honouring thee (though this also is in
my thoughts) as bestowing favour upon the roses, that so they
might not be withered." *Lett.* xxx.

"Ει δε βουλει τι φιλω χαριζεσθαι, τα λειψανα αυτων αντιπεμψον,
μηκετι πνεοντα ροδον μονον αλλα και σου." "If thou wouldst do a
kindness to thy lover, send back the reliques of the roses (I gave

I sent thee late a rosy wreath,
　　Not so much honouring thee,
As giving it a hope, that there
　　It could not wither'd be.
But thou thereon didst only breathe,
　　And sent'st it back to me :
Since when it grows, and smells, I swear,
　　Not of itself, but thee.

x.

PRÆLUDIUM.[7]

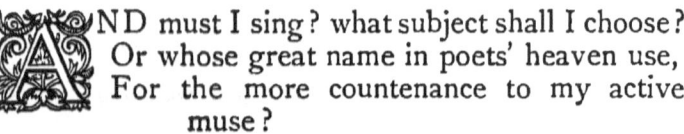ND must I sing? what subject shall I choose?
　　Or whose great name in poets' heaven use,
　　For the more countenance to my active
　　　　muse ?

Hercules ? alas, his bones are yet sore,
With his old earthly labours : t' exact more,
Of his dull godhead, were sin.　I'll implore

thee) no longer smelling of themselves only, but of thee." *Lett.*
xxxi.
　　Mr. Cumberland is quite scandalized at the omission of the
poet's acknowledgments to Philostratus : this is very natural in so
scrupulous a borrower as himself; but he ought to have known that
this was not the practice of Jonson's times.
　　It is a little singular that the artful arrangement of this song
(which is peculiar to our poet) should have escaped the critics.
Cumberland divides it into four stanzas ; so do the ingenious
authors of the *Anthology*, who, from the incorrect manner in which
they have given it, evidently overlooked the construction.
　　[7] This Præludium, (which is merely sportive) together with the
admirable Epode, to which it forms an introduction, must have
been among the earliest of Jonson's works, since both are prefixed
to a volume of rare occurrence (obligingly communicated to me by
T. Hill, Esq.) called "Love's Martyr, or Rosalin's complaint.
Allegorically shadowing the truth of Love in the constant fate of
the Phœnix and Turtle—now first translated out of the venerable
Italian Torquato Cæliano, by Robert Chester, to which are added
some new compositions of several writers, 1601." The Epode is

Phœbus.　No, tend thy cart still.　Envious day
Shall not give out that I have made thee stay,
And founder'd thy hot team, to tune my lay.

Nor will I beg of thee, Lord of the vine,
To raise my spirits with thy conjuring wine,
In the green circle of thy ivy twine.

Pallas, nor thee I call on, mankind maid,
That at thy birth, mad'st the poor smith afraid,
Who with his axe, thy father's midwife plaid.

Go, cramp dull Mars, light Venus, when he snorts,
Or with thy tribade trine, invent new sports ;
Thou nor thy looseness with my making sorts.

Let the old boy, your son, ply his old task,
Turn the stale prologue to some painted mask ;
His absence in my verse, is all I ask.

Hermes, the cheater, shall not mix with us,
Though he would steal his sisters' Pegasus,
And rifle him ; or pawn his petasus.

immediately followed by " the Phœnix analyzed," and the " Ode "
given below (*) both, as it would seem, by our author, though his
name does not appear to them.
　Till the discovery of this volume, of which Whalley apparently
knew nothing, these poems could scarcely be considered as intelligible.　Shakspeare, Marston, and Chapman united with Jonson in this commendation of the Phœnix, and " consecrated their
verses (the Preface says) to the love and merit of the true noble
knight, sir John Salisburie."

---

*THE PHŒNIX ANALYSED.

Now after all, let no man
　　Receive it for a fable,
　　If a bird so amiable
Do turn into a woman.

Nor all the ladies of the Thespian lake,
Though they were crush'd into one form, could make
A beauty of that merit, that should take

Or, by our Turtle's augure,
  That nature's fairest creature
  Prove of his mistress' feature
But a bare type and figure.

Ode ενθουσιαστικη.

Splendor! O more than mortal
For other forms come short all,
Of her illustrious brightness
As far as sin's from lightness.

Her wit as quick and sprightful
As fire, and more delightful
Than the stolen sports of lovers,
When night their meeting covers.

Judgment, adorn'd with learning
Doth shine in her discerning,
Clear as a naked vestal
Closed in an orb of crystal.

Her breath for sweet exceeding
The Phœnix' place of breeding,
But mix'd with sound, transcending
All nature of commending.

Alas then whither wade I
In thought to praise this lady,
When seeking her renowning
My self am so near drowning?

Retire, and say her graces
Are deeper than their faces,
Yet she's not nice to show them,
Nor takes she pride to know them.

My muse up by commission ; no, I bring
My own true fire : now my thought takes wing,
And now an Epode to deep ears I sing.

XI.

EPODE.

OT to know vice at all, and keep true state,
        Is virtue and not fate :
    Next to that virtue, is to know vice well,
        And her black spite expel.
Which to effect (since no breast is so sure,
        Or safe, but she'll procure
Some way of entrance) we must plant a guard
        Of thoughts to watch, and ward
At the eye and ear, the ports unto the mind,
        That no strange, or unkind
Object arrive there, but the heart, our spy,
        Give knowledge instantly,
To wakeful reason, our affections' king :
        Who, in th' examining,
Will quickly taste the treason, and commit
        Close, the close cause of it.
'Tis the securest policy we have,
        To make our sense our slave.
But this true course is not embraced by many :
        By many ! scarce by any.
For either our affections do rebel,
        Or else the sentinel,
That should ring larum to the heart, doth sleep ;
        Or some great thought doth keep
Back the intelligence, and falsly swears,
        They are base, and idle fears
Whereof the loyal conscience so complains.
        Thus, by these subtile trains,

Do several passions invade the mind,
  And strike our reason blind,
Of which usurping rank, some have thought love
  The first ; as prone to move
Most frequent tumults, horrors, and unrests,
  In our enflamed breasts :
But this doth from the cloud of error grow,
  Which thus we over-blow.
The thing they here call Love, is blind desire,
  Arm'd with bow, shafts, and fire ;
Inconstant, like the sea, of whence 'tis born,
  Rough, swelling, like a storm :
With whom who sails, rides on the surge of fear,
  And boils, as if he were
In a continual tempest. Now, true love
  No such effects doth prove ;
That is an essence far more gentle, fine,
  Pure, perfect, nay divine ;
It is a golden chain let down from heaven,
  Whose links are bright and even,
That falls like sleep on lovers, and combines
  The soft, and sweetest minds
In equal knots : this bears no brands, nor darts,
  To murder different hearts,
But in a calm, and god-like unity,
  Preserves community.
O, who is he, that, in this peace, enjoys
  The elixir of all joys ?
A form more fresh than are the Eden bowers,
  And lasting as her flowers :
Richer than Time, and as time's virtue rare [8]
  Sober, as saddest care ;
A fixed thought, an eye untaught to glance :
  Who, blest with such high chance

---

[8] *And as time's virtue rare.*] *Truth*, which is said proverbially
to be the daughter of *Time*. WHAL.

Would, at suggestion of a steep desire,
    Cast himself from the spire
Of all his happiness? But soft : I hear
    Some vicious fool draw near,
That cries, we dream, and swears there's no such thing,
    As this chaste love we sing.
Peace, Luxury,[9] thou art like one of those
    Who, being at sea, suppose,
Because they move, the continent doth so.
    No, Vice, we let thee know,
Though thy wild thoughts with sparrow's wings do flie,
    Turtles can chastly die ;
And yet (in this t'express our selves more clear)
    We do not number here
Such spirits as are only continent,
    Because lust's means are spent :
Or those, who doubt the common mouth of fame,
    And for their place and name,
Cannot so safely sin : their chastity
    Is mere necessity.
Nor mean we those, whom vows and conscience
    Have fill'd with abstinence :
Though we acknowledge, who can so abstain,
    Makes a most blessed gain.
He that for love of goodness hateth ill,
    Is more crown-worthy still,
Than he, which for sin's penalty forbears ;
    His heart sins, though he fears.
But we propose a person like our Dove,
    Graced with a Phœnix' love ;

---

[9] *Peace, luxury,*] i. e. *lust.* It is simply the Fr. *luxure*, then in general use. On this trite word, Steevens (under the name of Collins) has poured out, for the benefit of the youthful readers of Shakspeare, pages of the grossest indecency.
       —— " *verbis, nudum olido stans*
    Fornice mancipium quibus abstinet !"

A beauty of that clear and sparkling light,
　　　Would make a day of night,
And turn the blackest sorrows to bright joys;
　　　Whose odorous breath destroys
All taste of bitterness, and makes the air
　　　As sweet as she is fair.
A body so harmoniously composed,
　　　As if nature disclosed
All her best symmetry in that one feature!
　　　O, so divine a creature,
Who could be false to? chiefly, when he knows
　　　How only she bestows
The wealthy treasure of her love on him;
　　　Making his fortunes swim
In the full flood of her admired perfection?
　　　What savage, brute affection,
Would not be fearful to offend a dame
　　　Of this excelling frame?
Much more a noble, and right generous mind,
　　　To virtuous moods inclin'd,
That knows the weight of guilt;[1] he will refrain
　　　From thoughts of such a strain,
And to his sense object this sentence ever,
　　　"Man may securely sin, but safely never."

---

[1] *That knows the weight of guilt, &c.*] This is from Seneca, the
tragedian:

> *Quid pœna presens consciæ mentis pavor,*
> *Animusque culpa plenus, et semet timens:*
> *Scelus aliqua tutum, nulla securum tulit.*

XII.

EPISTLE

To Elizabeth countess of Rutland.[2]

MADAM,

HILST that for which all virtue now is sold,
And almost every vice, almighty gold,
That which, to boot with hell, is thought
    worth heaven
And for it, life, conscience, yea souls are given,
Toils, by grave custom, up and down the court,
To every squire, or groom, that will report
Well or ill, only all the following year,
Just to the weight their this day's presents bear;
While it makes huishers serviceable men,
And some one apteth to be trusted then,
Though never after; whiles it gains the voice
Of some grand peer, whose air doth make rejoice
The fool that gave it; who will want and weep,
When his proud patron's favours are asleep;
While thus it buys great grace, and hunts poor fame;
Runs between man and man; 'tween dame and dame;
Solders crack'd friendship; makes love last a day;
Or perhaps less: whilst gold bears all this sway,
I, that have none to send you, send you verse.
A present which, if elder writs rehearse
The truth of times, was once of more esteem,
Than this our gilt, nor golden age can deem,
When gold was made no weapon to cut throats,
Or put to flight Astrea, when her ingòts

---

[2] *Elizabeth countess of Rutland.*] The lady to whom the 79th
epigram is addressed, daughter of sir Philip Sidney, and wife of
Roger Manners, fifth earl of Rutland. She died before the appearance of this volume, as did her husband.

Were yet unfound, and better placed in earth,[3]
Than here, to give pride fame, and peasants birth.
But let this dross carry what price it will
With noble ignorants, and let them still
Turn upon scorned verse their quarter-face :
With you, I know, my offering will find grace.
For what a sin 'gainst your great father's spirit,
Were it to think, that you should not inherit
His love unto the Muses, when his skill
Almost you have, or may have when you will ?
Wherein wise nature you a dowry gave,
Worth an estate, treble to that you have.
Beauty I know is good, and blood is more ;
Riches thought most ; but, madam, think what
    store
The world hath seen, which all these had in trust,
And now lie lost in their forgotten dust.
It is the Muse alone, can raise to heaven,
And at her strong arm's end, hold up, and even,
The souls she loves.   Those other glorious notes,
Inscribed in touch or marble, or the coats
Painted, or carv'd upon our great men's tombs,
Or in their windows, do but prove the wombs
That bred them, graves : when they were born they
    died,
That had no muse to make their fame abide.
How many equal with the Argive queen,
Have beauty known, yet none so famous seen ?
Achilles was not first, that valiant was,
Or, in an army's head, that lock'd in brass

---

[3] ———— *when her ingòts*
Were yet unfound, and better placed in earth, &c.]

      " *Aurum irrepertum et sic melius situm*
        Cum terra celet, spernere fortior
          Quàm cogere humanos in usus
            Omne sacrum rapiente dextra."   HOR.

Gave killing strokes.   There were brave men before
Ajax, or Idomen,[4] or all the store
That Homer brought to Troy ; yet none so live,
Because they lack'd the sacred pen could give
Like life unto them.   Who heav'd Hercules
Unto the stars, or the Tyndarides ?
Who placed Jason's Argo in the sky,
Or set bright Ariadne's crown so high ?
Who made a lamp of Berenice's hair,
Or lifted Cassiopeia in her chair,
But only poets, rapt with rage divine ?
And such, or my hopes fail, shall make you shine.
You, and that other star, that purest light,
Of all Lucina's train, Lucy the bright ;[5]

[4] ——*There were brave men before*
Ajax, or Idomen.]   The sentiment is from Horace, lib. iv. 9.

> *Vixere fortes ante Agamemnona*
> *Multi ; sed omnes illacrymabiles*
> *Urgentur, ignotique longa*
> *Nocte, carent quia vate sacro.*   WHAL.

[5] *You, and that other star, that purest light*
Of all Lucina's train, Lucy *the bright.*]   This, I presume, was
Lucy countess of Bedford, to whom our author hath addressed
some epigrams, and who was particularly celebrated by Dr. Donne.
If what follows in the succeeding lines must be applied to him,
one would imagine some little misunderstanding was then subsist-
ing between him and the poet ; though from the verses which
Donne and Jonson have mutually wrote to each other, it appears
there was always a very friendly correspondence between them.
WHAL.

No doubt of it : but Whalley is mistaken in the person here
meant, who is not Donne but Daniel.   There is no necessity for
wantonly stirring up new enmities, since Jonson is already charged
with more than he ever felt ; and it is certain that he was at this
time, and continued to the end of his life, the affectionate friend
and admirer of Donne.

That there was no cordiality between our poet and Daniel seems
probable, and he here gives the reason of it.   Daniel "envied"
him.   A little retrospect into his history may shew, perhaps, that
the assertion (setting aside the undoubted veracity of Jonson) has
nothing improbable in it.   Daniel was born in 1562.   At the age

Than which a nobler heaven itself knows not ;
Who, though she have a better verser got,

of seventeen he was admitted a commoner of Magdalen Hall, Oxford, where he continued three years.   In 1582 he came to London, and was recommended to the court through the interest of
his brother-in-law, " the resolute John Florio."   On the death of
Spenser, in 1599, he succeeded to the Laureatship ; in other words,
he became the court poet, and as such, was called on to furnish the
complimentary poems, pageants, masques, &c., incidental to the
situation.   He seems, therefore, not unnaturally, to have experienced
some uneasiness when, soon after the accession of James I., Jonson was called upon to prepare the Masques of that gay period.
This appears to be *the very head and front* of our poet's offending,
unless it be added, that though he always thought and called Daniel
" a good and honest man," he entertained no very lofty opinion of
his style of poetry.

Daniel, however, numbered among his friends and patrons, the
most distinguished characters of both sexes ; and it appears that he
was not wanting in remonstrating against the attempt to supersede
him, nor in using the interest which his talents and virtues had
procured, to be permitted to resume what he probably considered
as the duties of his office.   In the dedication of *the Vision of the
Twelve Goddesses*, 1604, to the countess of Bedford, he expresses
his thankfulness " for her preferring him to the queen, for this employment."   The dedication is, in itself, sufficiently captious and
querulous, and seems pointed, in some measure, at our poet.   He
was also called on to assist in the solemnity of creating Henry,
prince of Wales ; when he wrote the masque or rather pageant of
*Tethys' Festival.**

But Daniel's spirits were wounded, and he could not apparently
brook the rising favour of his younger competitor.   About a year

---

* I take the earliest opportunity of correcting a mistake respecting this "Solemnitie."   It is stated, vol. vii. p. 148, that the *Masque
of Oberon* was performed before the prince on the 5th of June,
1610.   I have since been enabled to ascertain, by the kindness of
Mr. Cohen, that the masque performed on that day was the *Tethys*
of Daniel, to which therefore the description of the Master of the
Ceremonies must be referred.   The *Masque of Oberon* was probably
presented, as it is printed, after the *Barriers*, on the sixth day, or
Thursday.   The machinery of *Tethys* was furnished by Inigo Jones,
and the accompaniments must have been very splendid.   The
poet's part was the least important, and consisted of little more
than some pretty songs.

Or poet, in the court-account, than I,
And who doth me, though I not him, envẏ,

after the publication of his first Masque, he printed his *Philotas*,
with a dedication, in verse, to prince Henry, of which it is scarcely
possible to read without emotion the simple and affecting conclusion :

" And I, although among the latter train
    And least of those that sung unto this land,
Have borne my part, though in an humble strain,
    And pleased the gentler that did understand.

" And never had my harmless pen at all
    Distain'd with any loose immodesty,
Nor ever noted to be touch'd with gall,
    To aggravate the worst man's infamy.

" But still have done the fairest offices
    To virtue and the time : yet nought prevails,
And all our labours are without success,
    For either favour or our virtue fails.

" And therefore since I have outliv'd the date
    Of former grace, acceptance, and delight,
I would my lines late born beyond the fate
    Of her spent line,* had never come to light !

" So had I not been tax'd for wishing well,
    Nor now mistaken by the censuring stage,
Nor in my fame and reputation fell,
    Which I esteem more than what all the age
Or th' earth can give : But years hath done this wrong,
To make me write too much, and live too long."

He could not be beyond five and forty at this period of de-
spondency : he remained, however, about the court for some time
longer, probably till about 1615, in which year, Jonson, who was still
rising in reputation, obtained a fixed salary for his services, when
this amiable man retired to Somersetshire, commenced farmer, and
passed the remainder of his days in privacy, piety, and peace.

Daniel was highly esteemed by queen Anne, and to this Jonson
alludes in the text, while his great patron was James. Still, however, there seems no adequate cause for any hostility against Jonson, if he only made a fair advantage of his superior talents for the
drama ; for which, it must be confessed, his rival wanted both

---

* *Of her spent line,*] i. e. of queen Elizabeth's.

Yet for the timely favours she hath done,
To my less sanguine muse, wherein she hath won
My grateful soul, the subject of her powers,
I have already used some happy hours,
To her remembrance ; which when time shall bring
To curious light, to notes I then shall sing,
Will prove old Orpheus' act no tale to be :
For I shall move stocks, stones, no less than he.
Then all that have but done my Muse least grace,[6]
.Shall thronging come, and boast the happy place
|They hold in my strange poems, which, as yet,
|Had not their form touch'd by an English wit.
There, like a rich and golden pyramed,
Born up by statues, shall I rear your head
Above your under-carved ornaments,
And shew how to the life my soul presents
Your form imprest there : not with tickling rhymes,
Or common-places, filch'd, that take these times,
But high and noble matter, such as flies
From brains entranced, and fill'd with extasies ;
Moods, which the godlike Sidney oft did prove,
And your brave friend and mine so well did love.
Who, wheresoe'er he be——

The rest is lost.

energy and fancy, and which indeed, he laments, just above, that
he ever attempted.
   [6] *Then all that have but done my Muse least grace,*
      Shall thronging come.] This intimates a design the poet had of
celebrating the ladies of his native country.   WHAL.
   See vol. vii. p. 139.

XIII.

EPISTLE.

To Katharine lady Aubigny.[7]

'T IS grown almost a danger to speak true
    Of any good mind, now; there are so few.
    The bad, by number, are so fortified,
    As what they have lost t' expect, they dare
        deride.
So both the prais'd and praisers suffer; yet,
For others ill ought none their good forget.
I therefore, who profess myself in love
With every virtue, wheresoe'er it move,
And howsoever; as I am at feud
With sin and vice, though with a throne endued;
And, in this name, am given out dangerous
By arts, and practice of the vicious,
Such as suspect themselves, and think it fit,
For their own capital crimes, to indict my wit; ·
I that have suffer'd this; and though forsook
Of fortune, have not alter'd yet my look,
Or so myself abandon'd, as because
Men are not just, or keep no holy laws
Of nature and society, I should faint;
Or fear to draw true lines, 'cause others paint:
I, madam, am become your praiser; where,
If it may stand with your soft blush, to hear
Yourself but told unto yourself, and see
In my chàracter what your features be,

---

[7] *Lady Aubigny.*] This lady has been already noticed. She was the daughter and sole heir of sir Gervase Clifton, and was married to lord Aubigny in 1607. The connection with a family so deservedly dear to James I. as the Stewarts, procured a peerage for her father, who was created in the following year, baron Clifton, of Leighton Bromswold, in Nottinghamshire.

8   T

You will not from the paper slightly pass:
No lady, but at some time loves her glass.
And this shall be no false one, but as much
Remov'd, as you from need to have it such.
Look then, and see your self—I will not say
Your beauty, for you see that every day;
And so do many more: all which can call
It perfect, proper, pure, and natural,
Not taken up o' the doctors, but as well
As I, can say and see it doth excel;
That asks but to be censured by the eyes:
And in those outward forms, all fools are wise.
Nor that your beauty wanted not a dower,
Do I reflect.   Some alderman has power,
Or cozening farmer of the customs, so
To advance his doubtful issue, and o'erflow
A prince's fortune: these are gifts of chance,
And raise not virtue; they may vice enhance.
My mirror is more subtle, clear, refined,
And takes and gives the beauties of the mind;
Though it reject not those of fortune: such
As blood, and match.   Wherein, how more than
        much
Are you engaged to your happy fate,
For such a lot! that mixt you with a state
Of so great title, birth, but virtue most,
Without which all the rest were sounds, or lost.
'Tis only that can time and chance defeat:
For he that once is good, is ever great.   .
Wherewith then, madam, can you better pay
This blessing of your stars, than by that way
Of virtue, which you tread?   What if alone,
Without companions? 'tis safe to have none.
In single paths dangers with ease are watch'd;
Contagion in the press is soonest catch'd.
This makes, that wisely you decline your life
Far from the maze of custom, error, strife,

And keep an even, and unalter'd gait;
Not looking by, or back, like those that wait
Times and occasions, to start forth, and seem.
Which though the turning world may disesteem,
Because that studies spectacles and shows,
And after varied, as fresh objects, goes,
Giddy with change, and therefore cannot see
Right, the right way; yet must your comfort be
Your conscience, and not wonder if none asks
For truth's complexion, where they all wear masks.
Let who will follow fashions and attires,
Maintain their leigers forth for foreign wires,
Melt down their husbands' lands, to pour away
On the close groom and page, on new-year's day,
And almost all days after, while they live;
They find it both so witty, and safe to give.
Let them on powders, oils, and paintings spend,
Till that no usurer, nor his bawds dare lend
Them or their officers; and no man know,
Whether it be a face they wear or no.
Let them waste body and state; and after all,
When their own parasites laugh at their fall,
May they have nothing left, whereof they can
Boast, but how oft they have gone wrong to
    man,
And call it their brave sin: for such there be
That do sin only for the infamy;
And never think, how vice doth every hour
Eat on her clients, and some one devour.
You, madam, young have learn'd to shun these
    shelves,
Whereon the most of mankind wreck themselves,
And keeping a just course, have early put
Into your harbour, and all passage shut
'Gainst storms or pirates, that might charge your
    peace;
For which you worthy are the glad increase

Of your blest womb,[8] made fruitful from above.
To pay your lord the pledges of chaste love;
And raise a noble stem, to give the fame
To Clifton's blood, that is denied their name.
Grow, grow, fair tree! and as thy branches shoot,
Hear what the Muses sing above thy root,
By me, their priest, if they can aught divine:
Before the moons have fill'd their triple trine,
To crown the burden which you go withal,
It shall a ripe and timely issue fall,
T' expect the honours of great Aubigny;
And greater rites, yet writ in mystery,
But which the fates forbid me to reveal.
Only thus much out of a ravish'd zeal
Unto your name, and goodness of your life,
They speak; since you are truly that rare wife,
Other great wives may blush at, when they see
What your tried manners are, what theirs should be;
How you love one, and him you should, how still
You are depending on his word and will;
Not fashion'd for the court, or strangers' eyes;
But to please him, who is the dearer prize
Unto himself, by being so dear to you.
This makes, that your affections still be new,
And that your souls conspire, as they were gone
Each into other, and had now made one.

[8] ———————— *the glad increase*
Of your blest womb, &c.] If this was the first child (as seems probable) the "Epistle" was written in 1608. Lady Aubigny brought her husband four sons and three daughters. Of the sons, three fell nobly in the field in the cause of their sovereign; the fourth, the eldest, lived to perform the last duties to his mangled remains, and died in 1655.

To this nobleman Herrick has a poem in which he alludes to the disastrous fate of his family. *Hesperides*, p. 197.

> "Of all those three brave brothers, faln in war,
>   (Not without glory) noble sir, you are,
>   Despite of all concussions, left the stem
>   To shoot forth generations like to them."

Live that one still ! and as long years do pass,
Madam, be bold to use this truest glass ;
Wherein your form you still the same shall find ;
Because nor it can change, nor such a mind.

.

XIV.

ODE.

To sir WILLIAM SIDNEY, ON HIS BIRTH-DAY.[9]

OW that the hearth is crown'd with smiling
        fire,
      And some do drink, and some do dance,
            Some ring,
            Some sing,
    And all do strive to advance
  The gladness higher;
            Wherefore should I
            Stand silent by,
            Who not the least,
  Both love the cause, and authors of the feast ?

[9] *To sir* William Sidney, *on his birth-day.*] He was the eldest
son of sir Robert Sidney, created earl of Leicester by king James,
and a nephew of sir Philip Sidney. He died unmarried, and was
buried in St. Paul's cathedral. WHAL.

Sir William Sidney appears to have died about the same time
with prince Henry; so that this Ode must be placed among our
author's earlier pieces. G. Wither (the Satyromastix) drew up some
" Mournful Elegies " on the death of the latter, and addressed them
to sir William's father, in which he tells the noble lord that

    " His haplesse loss had more apparent been,
      But darken'd by the Other, 'twas unseen ! "

Furthermore to comfort him he presents him with an anagram on
his son's name, which is about the worst that ever appeared.

        " GULIELMUS SIDNEIUS.
            En vilis gelidus sum.
                But
            Ei' nil luge, sidus sum."

Give me my cup, but from the Thespian well,
  That I may tell to Sidney what
        This day
        Doth say,
  And he may think on that
Which I do tell;
        When all the noise
        Of these forced joys,
          Are fled and gone,
And he with his best Genius left alone.

This day says, then, the number of glad years
  Are justly summ'd, that make you man;
        Your vow
        Must now
  Strive all right ways it can,
T' outstrip your peers:
        Since he doth lack
        Of going back
          Little, whose will
Doth urge him to run wrong, or to stand still.

Nor can a little of the common store
  Of nobles' virtue, shew in you;
        Your blood
        So good
  And great, must seek for new,
And study more:
        Nor weary, rest
        On what's deceas't.
          For they, that swell
With dust of ancestors, in graves but dwell.

And which, lest the consolatory part of it should escape him, is
thus explained at large:
        " Nor do I think it can be rightly said,
        You are unhappy in this *One* that's dead:
        For notwithstanding his first anagram,
        Frights, with *Behold, how cold and vile I am;*
        Yet in his last he seems more cheerful far,
        And joyes with *Soft, mourn not, I am a star.*

'Twill be exacted of your name, whose son,
　Whose nephew, whose grandchild you are;
　　　　And men
　　　　Will then
　Say you have follow'd far,
When well begun:
　　　　Which must be now,
　　　　They teach you how.
　　　　And he that stays
To live until to-morrow', hath lost two days.

So may you live in honour, as in name,
　If with this truth you be inspired;
　　　　So may
　　　　This day
　Be more, and long desired;
And with the flame
　　　　Of love be bright,
　　　　As with the light
　　　　Of bonfires! then
The birth-day shines, when logs not burn, but men.

XV.

TO HEAVEN.

OOD and great God! can I not think of
　　thee,
　　But it must straight my melancholy be?
　　Is it interpreted in me disease,
That, laden with my sins, I seek for ease?
O be thou witness, that the reins dost know
And hearts of all, if I be sad for show;
And judge me after: if I dare pretend
To aught but grace, or aim at other end.
As thou art all, so be thou all to me,
First, midst, and last, converted One, and Three!
My faith, my hope, my love; and in this state,

My judge, my witness, and my advocate.
Where have I been this while exiled from thee,
And whither rapt, now thou but stoop'st to me ?
Dwell, dwell here still ! O, being every where,
How can I doubt to find thee ever here ?
I know my state, both full of shame and scorn,
Conceived in sin, and unto labour born,
Standing with fear, and must with horror fall,
And destined unto judgment, after all.
I feel my griefs too, and there scarce is ground,
Upon my flesh t' inflict another wound :[1]
Yet dare I not complain, or wish for death,
With holy Paul, lest it be thought the breath
Of discontent; or that these prayers be
For weariness of life, not love of thee.[2]

[1] ———————— *and there scarce is found*
Upon my flesh to inflict another wound.] Opposite to this passage, Whalley has written, in the margin of the old folio, " Des Barreaux' Sonnet." What resemblance he found between this lowly expression of a broken spirit, and the daring familiarity of Des Barreaux' defiance, it is not easy to discover. I have nothing to object to the poetry of the Sonnet : its language too is good, but its sentiments are dreadful.

If Jonson had any thing in view besides the Scriptures, in this place, it might be the following verse of Euripides, which is quoted by Longinus, and praised for its nervous conciseness :

Γεμω κακων δη˙ κ᾽ ουκετ᾽ εσθ᾽ ὁπη τεθῃ

[2] This is an admirable prayer : solemn, pious, and scriptural. Jonson's religious impressions were deep and awful. He had, like all of us, his moments of forgetfulness; but whenever he returned to himself, he was humble, contrite, and believing.

U N D E R W O O D S.

CONSISTING OF

D I V E R S   P O E M S.

—— *Cineri, gloria sera venit.*   MART.

Underwoods.] From the second folio, 1641. The poems collected under this head, (with the exception of a small number taken
from published volumes,) were found amongst Jonson's papers.
Whether he designed them all for the press cannot now be known :
it is reasonable to suppose from the imperfect state in which many
of them appear, that he did not.—No selection, however, was
made, though there appears some rude attempt to arrange them,
with a reference to dates ; but the disposition of them, in general,
is very incomplete, and marks of carelessness and ignorance are
visible in every page. Much is misplaced, or mutilated, and more,
perhaps, is lost. It is singular that no notice or memorandum of
any kind should hand down to us the name or condition of the
editor or printer of this unfortunate volume, unless, as there is
some reason to suspect, the whole was put to the press surrep-
titiously.

TO THE READER.

WITH the same leave the ancients called that kind of body Sylva, or Ὕλη, in which there were works of divers nature and matter congested; as the multitude call timber-trees promiscuously growing, a Wood or Forest; so I am bold to entitule these lesser poems of later growth, by this of UNDERWOOD, out of the analogy they hold to the Forest in my former book, and no otherwise.

                                        BEN JONSON.

POEMS OF DEVOTION.

THE SINNER'S SACRIFICE.

I.

To the Holy Trinity.

I.

 HOLY, blessed, glorious Trinity
Of persons, still one God in Unity.
The faithful man's believed mystery,
                    Help, help to lift
Myself up to thee, harrow'd, torn, and
        bruised,
By sin and Satan; and my flesh misused,
As my heart lies in pieces, all confused,
                    O take my gift.

II.

All-gracious God, the sinner's sacrifice,
A broken heart, thou wert not wont despise;
But 'bove the fat of rams, or bulls to prize,
                    An offering meet,
For thy acceptance : O, behold me right,
And take compassion on my grievous plight !
What odour can be, than a heart contrite,
                    To thee more sweet ?

III.

Eternal Father, God, who didst create
This all of nothing, gav'st it form and fate,
And breath'st into it life and light, with state
To worship thee.
Eternal God the Son, who not deniedst
To take our nature ; becam'st man, and diedst,
To pay our debts, upon thy cross, and criedst •
ALL'S DONE IN ME.[1]

IV.

Eternal Spirit, God from both proceeding,
Father and Son; the Comforter, in breeding
Pure thoughts in man : with fiery zeal them feeding
For acts of grace.
Increase those acts, O glorious Trinity
Of persons, still one God in Unity ;
Till I attain the long'd-for mystery
Of seeing your face.

V.

Beholding one in three, and three in one,
A Trinity, to shine in Union ;
The gladdest light dark man can think upon ;
O grant it me !
Father, and Son, and Holy Ghost, you three,
All co-eternal in your majesty,
Distinct in persons, yet in unity
One God to see.

VI.

My Maker, Saviour, and my Sanctifier !
To hear, to mediate, sweeten my desire
With grace, with love, with cherishing entire :
O, then how blest !

---

[1] *All's done in me.*] Alluding to the last words of our blessed
Saviour, upon the Cross. " It is finished."

Among thy saints elected to abide,
And with thy angels placed, side by side,
But in thy presence, truly glorified
                              Shall I there rest !

II.

AN HYMN TO GOD THE FATHER.

HEAR me, O God !
   A broken heart
   Is my best part :
Use still thy rod,
  That I may prove
  Therein, thy love.

If thou hadst not
  Been stern to me,
  But left me free,
I had forgot
  Myself and thee.

For, sin's so sweet,
  As minds ill bent
  Rarely repent,
Until they meet
  Their punishment.

Who more can crave
  Than thou hast done ?
  That gav'st a son
To free a slave :
  First made of nought ;
  With all since bought

Sin, death, and hell
  His glorious name
  Quite overcame ;
Yet I rebel,
  And slight the same.

But, I'll come in,
　　Before my loss,
　　Me farther toss,
As sure to win
　　Under his cross.

III.

An Hymn on the Nativity of my Saviour.

I SING the birth was born to-night,
　The author both of life and light ;
　　　The angels so did sound it.
And like the ravish'd shepherds said,
Who saw the light, and were afraid,
　　　Yet search'd, and true they found it.

The Son of God, the Eternal King,
That did us all salvation bring,
　　　And freed the soul from danger ;
He whom the whole world could not take,[2]
The Word, which heaven and earth did make,
　　　Was now laid in a manger.

The Father's wisdom will'd it so,
The Son's obedience knew no No,
　　　Both wills were in one stature ;
And as that wisdom had decreed,
The Word was now made Flesh indeed,
　　　And took on him our nature.

What comfort by him do we win,
Who made himself the price of sin,
　　　To make us heirs of glory !
To see this Babe, all innocence
A martyr born in our defence ;
　　　Can man forget this story ?

---

[2] *He whom the whole world could not take,*] i. e. contain, a latinism, *Quem non capit.*

A CELEBRATION OF CHARIS.

IN TEN LYRIC PIECES.

A CELEBRATION OF CHARIS.

I.

HIS EXCUSE FOR LOVING.

LET it not your wonder move,
   Less your laughter, that I love.
   Though I now write fifty years,[1]
   I have had, and have my peers ;
   Poets, though divine, are men :
Some have loved as old again.
And it is not always face,
Clothes, or fortune, gives the grace ;

---

[1] *Though I now write fifty years.*]   This fixes the date of this
little collection to 1624, the last year of health, perhaps, which the
poet ever enjoyed.
   There is a considerable degree of ease and elegance in these
effusions ; and, indeed, it may be observed in general, of our poet's
lyrics, that a vein of sprightliness and fancy runs through them
which a reader of his epistles, &c., is scarcely prepared to expect.
In the latter, Jonson, like several other poets of his age, or rather
of his school, who also succeeded in lyrics, sedulously reigns in
the imagination, and contents himself with strength of sentiment
and thought, in simple but vigorous language, and unambitious
rhyme.   His "Charis" has all the vivid colouring of the best ages
of antiquity ; and it is truly delightful to mark the grace and ease
with which this great poet plays with the boundless mass of his
literary acquisitions.

Or the feature, or the youth :
But the language, and the truth,
With the ardour, and the passion,
Gives the lover weight and fashion.
If you then will read the story,
First, prepare you to be sorry,
That you never knew till now,
Either whom to love, or how :
But be glad, as soon with me,
When you know that this is she,
Of whose beauty it was sung,
She shall make the old man young,
Keep the middle age at stay,
And let nothing high decay ;
Till she be the reason, why,
All the world for love may die.

II.

HOW HE SAW HER.

 BEHELD her on a day,
When her look out-flourish'd May :
And her dressing did out-brave
All the pride the fields then have :
Far I was from being stupid,
For I ran and call'd on Cupid ;—
Love, if thou wilt ever see
Mark of glory, come with me ;
Where's thy quiver ? bend thy bow ;
Here's a shaft,—thou art too slow !
And, withal, I did untie
Every cloud about his eye ;
But he had not gain'd his sight
Sooner than he lost his might,
Or his courage ; for away
Straight he ran, and durst not stay,

Letting bow and arrow fall :
Not for any threat, or call,
Could be brought once back to look.
I fool-hardy, there up took
Both the arrow he had quit,
And the bow, with thought to hit
This my object ; but she threw
Such a lightning, as I drew,
At my face, that took my sight,
And my motion from me quite ;
So that there I stood a stone,
Mock'd of all, and call'd of one,
(Which with grief and wrath I heard,)
Cupid's statue with a beard ;
Or else one that play'd his ape,
In a Hercules his shape.

III.

WHAT HE SUFFERED.

AFTER many scorns like these,
Which the prouder beauties please ;
She content was to restore
Eyes and limbs, to hurt me more,
And would, on conditions, be
Reconciled to Love and me.
First, that I must kneeling yield
Both the bow and shaft I held
Unto her ; which Love might take
At her hand, with oaths, to make
Me the scope of his next draft,
Aimed, with that self-same shaft.
He no sooner heard the law,
But the arrow home did draw,
And, to gain her by his art,
Left it sticking in my heart :

Which when she beheld to bleed,
She repented of the deed,
And would fain have chang'd the fate,
But the pity comes too late.
Loser-like, now, all my wreak
Is, that I have leave to speak;
And in either prose, or song,
To revenge me with my tongue;
Which how dexterously I do,
Hear, and make example too.

IV.

HER TRIUMPH.

SEE the chariot at hand here of Love,
     Wherein my Lady rideth !
  Each that draws is a swan or a dove,
     And well the car Love guideth.
As she goes, all hearts do duty
               Unto her beauty;
And enamour'd, do wish, so they might
               But enjoy such a sight,
That they still were to run by her side,
Through swords, through seas, whither she would
     ride.

Do but look on her eyes, they do light
  All that Love's world compriseth !
Do but look on her hair, it is bright
  As Love's star when it riseth !
Do but mark, her forehead's smoother
               Than words that sooth her :
And from her arched brows, such a grace
               Sheds itself through the face,
As alone there triumphs to the life
All the gain, all the good of the elements' strife.

Have you seen but a bright lily grow,
  Before rude hands have touch'd it ?
Have you mark'd but the fall o' the snow
  Before the soil hath smutch'd it ?
Have you felt the wool of the bever ?
              Or swan's down ever ?
Or have smelt o' the bud of the briar ?
              Or the nard in the fire ?
Or have tasted the bag of the bee ?
O so white ! O so soft ! O so sweet is she![2]

v.

HIS DISCOURSE WITH CUPID.

NOBLEST Charis, you that are
  Both my fortune and my star,
  And do govern more my blood,
  Than the various moon the flood,
Hear, what late discourse of you,
Love and I have had ; and true.
Mongst my Muses finding me,
Where he chanced your name to see
Set, and to this softer strain ;
Sure, said he, if I have brain,
This, here sung, can be no other,
By description, but my mother !
So hath Homer praised her hair ;
So Anacreon drawn the air
Of her face, and made to rise
Just about her sparkling eyes,
Both her brows bent like my bow.
By her looks I do her know,

---

[2] The last two stanzas of the " Triumph " are given in the
Devil's an Ass, so that the opening one alone can bear the stamp
of " fifty years."

Which you call my shafts.   And see !
Such my mother's blushes be,
As the bath your verse discloses
In her cheeks, of milk and roses ;
Such as oft I wanton in :
And, above her even chin,
Have you placed the bank of kisses,
Where, you say, men gather blisses,
Ripen'd with a breath more sweet,
Than when flowers and west-winds meet.
Nay, her white and polish'd neck,
With the lace that doth it deck,
Is my mother's : hearts of slain
Lovers, made into a chain !
And between each rising breast,
Lies the valley call'd my nest,
Where I sit and proyne my wings
After flight ; and put new stings
To my shafts : her very name
With my mother's is the same.
I confess all, I replied,
And the glass hangs by her side,
And the girdle 'bout her waist,
All is Venus, save unchaste.
But alas, thou seest the least
Of her good, who is the best
Of her sex : but couldst thou, Love,
Call to mind the forms that strove
For the apple, and those three
Make in one, the same were she.
For this beauty yet doth hide
Something more than thou hast spied.
Outward grace weak love beguiles :
She is Venus when she smiles ;[3]
But she's Juno, when she walks,
And Minerva when she talks.

[3] *She is Venus when she smiles,* &c.]   From Angerianus :

VI.

Claiming a second kiss by desert.

CHARIS, guess, and do not miss,
Since I drew a morning kiss
From your lips, and suck'd an air
Thence, as sweet as you are fair,
What my muse and I have done:
Whether we have lost or won,
If by us the odds were laid,
That the bride, allow'd a maid,
Look'd not half so fresh and fair,
With the advantage of her hair,[4]
And her jewels to the view
Of the assembly, as did you!

Tres quondam nudas vidit Priameius heros
Luce deas; video tres quoque luce deas:
Hoc majus, tres uno in corpore; Cælia ridens
Est Venus, incedens Juno, Minerva loquens.

This quotation (says Dr. Farmer) recalls to my memory a very extraordinary fact. A few years ago, at a great court on the continent, a countryman of ours (sir Charles Hanbury Williams) exhibited, with many other candidates, his complimental epigram on the birth-day, and carried the prize in triumph:

O Regina orbis prima et pulcherrima: ridens
Es Venus, incedens Juno, Minerva loquens.

The compliment has since passed through other hands, and was, not long ago, applied to one who had as little of Venus and Juno in her, as her panegyrist had of originality. Minerva had nothing to do with either.

[4] *With the advantage of her hair.*] Brides, in Jonson's days, were always led to the altar, with their hair hanging down. To this he alludes in several of his masques; and H. Peacham, in describing the marriage of the princess Elizabeth with the Palsgrave, says that " the bride came into the chapell with a coronet of pearle on her head, and her haire disheveled, and hanging down over her shoulders."

Or that did you sit or walk,
You were more the eye and talk
Of the court, to-day, than all
Else that glister'd in Whitehall;
So, as those that had your sight,
Wish'd the bride were chang'd to-night,
And did think such rites were due
To no other Grace but you!
  Or, if you did move to-night
In the dances, with what spite
Of your peers you were beheld,
That at every motion swell'd
So to see a lady tread,
As might all the Graces lead,
And was worthy, being so seen,
To be envied of the queen.
  Or if you would yet have staid,
Whether any would upbraid
To himself his loss of time;
Or have charg'd his sight of crime,
To have left all sight for you.
Guess of these which is the true;
And, if such a verse as this,
May not claim another kiss.

VII.

BEGGING ANOTHER,

ON COLOUR OF MENDING THE FORMER.

OR Love's sake, kiss me once again,
    I long, and should not beg in vain.
        Here's none to spy, or see;
            Why do you doubt or stay?
        I'll taste as lightly as the bee,
That doth but touch his flower, and flies away.

Once more, and, faith, I will be gone,
Can he that loves ask less than one?
    Nay, you may err in this,
      And all your bounty wrong:
    This could be call'd but half a kiss;
What we're but once to do, we should do long.
    I will but mend the last, and tell
    Where, how, it would have relish'd well;
      Join lip to lip, and try:
        Each suck the others breath,
    And whilst our tongues perplexed lie,
Let who will think us dead, or wish our death.

VIII.

Urging her of a promise.

 HARIS one day in discourse
    Had of Love, and of his force,
    Lightly promis'd she would tell
    What a man she could love well:
And that promise set on fire
All that heard her with desire.
With the rest, I long expected
When the work would be effected;
But we find that cold delay,
And excuse spun every day,
As, until she tell her one,
We all fear, she loveth none.
Therefore, Charis, you must do't,
For I will so urge you to't,
You shall neither eat nor sleep,
No, nor forth your window peep,
With your emissary eye,[5]
To fetch in the forms go by,

---

[5] *With your* emissary eye.] *Oculis emissitiis.* Plautus. WHAL.

And pronounce, which band or lace
Better fits him than his face :
Nay, I will not let you sit
'Fore your idol glass a whit,
To say over every purl[6]
There ; or to reform a curl ;
Or with secretary Cis
To consult, if fucus this
Be as good, as was the last :—
All your sweet of life is past,
Make account, unless you can,
And that quickly, speak your Man.

IX.

Her man described by her own dictamen.

F your trouble, Ben, to ease me,
I will tell what Man would please me.
I would have him, if I could,
Noble ; or of greater blood ;
Titles, I confess, do take me,
And a woman God did make me ;
French to boot, at least in fashion,
And his manners of that nation.
   Young I'd have him too, and fair,
Yet a man ; with crisped hair,
Cast in thousand snares and rings,
For love's fingers, and his wings :
Chestnut colour, or more slack,
Gold, upon a ground of black.
Venus and Minerva's eyes,
For he must look wanton-wise.

   [6] *To say over every purl,*] i. e. to try. *Purl,* I believe, is wire
whipt with cotton or silk, for puffing out fringe, lace, hair, &c.   In
some places it seems to mean the fringe itself: the old word is
purrel.

Eyebrows bent, like Cupid's bow,
Front, an ample field of snow;
Even nose, and cheek withal,
Smooth as is the billiard-ball:
Chin as woolly as the peach;
And his lip should kissing teach,
Till he cherish'd too much beard,
And made Love or me afeard.
    He should have a hand as soft
As the down, and shew it oft;
Skin as smooth as any rush,
And so thin to see a blush
Rising through it, ere it came;
All his blood should be a flame,
Quickly fired, as in beginners
In love's school, and yet no sinners.
    'Twere too long to speak of all:
What we harmony do call,
In a body, should be there.
Well he should his clothes, too, wear,
Yet no tailor help to make him;
Drest, you still for man should take him,
And not think he'd eat a stake,
Or were set up in a brake.[1]
    Valiant he should be as fire,
Shewing danger more than ire.
Bounteous as the clouds to earth,
And as honest as his birth;
All his actions to be such,
As to do no thing too much:
Nor o'er praise, nor yet condemn,
Nor out-value, nor contemn;

---

[1] *Or were set up in a* brake.] The inclosure used by black-
smiths and farriers, in which they put vicious and untractable
horses, which they cannot dress or shoe without that assistance, is
commonly called a smith's *brake*. WHAL.
    But see vol. iii. p. 445.

Nor do wrongs, nor wrongs receive,
Nor tie knots, nor knots unweave ;
And from baseness to be free,
As he durst love truth and me.
    Such a man, with every part,
I could give my very heart ;
But of one if short he came,
I can rest me where I am.[8]

X.

ANOTHER LADY'S EXCEPTION,

PRESENT AT THE HEARING.

FOR his mind I do not care,
    That's a toy that I could spare :
    Let his title be but great,
    His clothes rich, and band sit neat,
Himself young, and face be good,
All I wish is understood.
What you please, you parts may call,
'Tis one good part I'd lie withal.

[8] This lively, gallant, and graceful description is above all
praise. Anacreon is not more gay, nor Catullus more elegant, nor
Horace more courtly, than this poet, who is taken on the faith of
the Shakspeare commentators, for a mere compound of dulness and
spleen.

MISCELLANEOUS POEMS.[1]

I.

THE MUSICAL STRIFE.

A PASTORAL DIALOGUE.

She.

COME, with our voices, let us war,
 And challenge all the spheres,
Till each of us be made a star,
 And all the world turn ears.

He. At such a call, what beast or fowl,
 Of reason empty is ?
What tree or stone doth want a soul,
 What man but must lose his ?

She. Mix then your notes, that we may prove
 To stay the running floods ;
To make the mountain quarries move,
 And call the walking woods.

[1] I have little to add to what is already said, (p. 282,) except that many allowances must be made for what follows. Few of these poems are dated, and fewer still bear titles explanatory of their subject. I have availed myself of such collateral helps as I could any where find; but much is necessarily left to the reader's own sagacity. The original text, which is grossly incorrect, has however been revised with great care.

He. What need of me ? do you but sing,
    Sleep, and the grave will wake :
    No tunes are sweet, nor words have sting,
      But what those lips do make.

She. They say, the angels mark each deed,
    And exercise below ;
    And out of inward pleasure feed
      On what they viewing know.

He. O sing not you then, lest the best
    Of angels should be driven
    To fall again, at such a feast,
      Mistaking earth for heaven.

She. Nay, rather both our souls be strain'd
    To meet their high desire ;
    So they in state of grace retain'd,
      May wish us of their quire.

II.

A SONG.

H do not wanton with those eyes,
    Lest I be sick with seeing ;
    Nor cast them down, but let them rise,
      Lest shame destroy their being.

O be not angry with those fires,
    For then their threats will kill me ;
    Nor look too kind, on my desires,
      For then my hopes will spill me.

O do not steep them in thy tears,
    For so will sorrow slay me ;
    Nor spread them as distract with fears ;
      Mine own enough betray me.[2]

---

[2] *Mine own enough betray me.*] How is it that this song is never

III.

IN THE PERSON OF WOMANKIND.

A SONG APOLOGETIC.

MEN, if you love us, play no more
      The fools or tyrants with your friends,
   To make us still sing o'er and o'er,
      Our own false praises, for your ends :
   We have both wits and fancies too,
   And if we must, let's sing of you.

Nor do we doubt, but that we can,
   If we would search with care and pain,
Find some one good, in some one man ;
   So going thorough all your strain,
      We shall at last, of parcels make
      One good enough for a song's sake.

And as a cunning painter takes
   In any curious piece you see,
More pleasure while the thing he makes,
   Than when 'tis made ; why, so will we.
      And having pleas'd our art, we'll try
      To make a new, and hang that by.

mentioned by the critics ? Simply, I believe, because they never
read it. Two or three of Jonson's lyrics are noticed by the earlier
compilers of our Anthologies, and these have been copied and re-
copied a thousand times. Hence the Aikins *et id genus omne* form
their opinion of the poet, and groan over his " tedious effusions."
With respect to the present, if it be not the most beautiful song in
the language, I freely confess, for my own part, that I know not
where it is to be found.

IV.

ANOTHER,

In Defence of their Inconstancy.

HANG up those dull and envious fools
    That talk abroad of woman's change.
We were not bred to sit on stools,
    Our proper virtue is to range :
        Take that away, you take our lives,
        We are no women then, but wives.

Such as in valour would excel,
    Do change, though men, and often fight,
Which we in love must do as well,
    If ever we will love aright :
        The frequent varying of the deed,
        Is that which doth perfection breed.

Nor is't inconstancy to change
    For what is better, or to make,
By searching, what before was strange,
    Familiar, for the uses sake :
        The good from bad is not descried,
        But as 'tis often vext and tried.

And this profession of a store
    In love, doth not alone help forth
Our pleasure ; but preserves us more
    From being forsaken, than doth worth :
        For were the worthiest woman curst
        To love one man, he'd leave her first.

V.

A Nymph's Passion.

LOVE, and he loves me again,
    Yet dare I not tell who ;
For if the nymphs should know my
        swain,
  I fear they'd love him too ;
    Yet if he be not known,
    The pleasure is as good as none,
For that's a narrow joy is but our own.

  I'll tell, that if they be not glad,
    They yet may envy me ;
  But then if I grow jealous mad,
    And of them pitied be,
    It were a plague 'bove scorn :
    And yet it cannot be forborn,
Unless my heart would, as my thought, be torn.

  He is, if they can find him, fair,
    And fresh and fragrant too,
  As summer's sky, or purged air,
    And looks as lilies do
    That are this morning blown ;
    Yet, yet I doubt he is not known,
And fear much more, that more of him be shown.

  But he hath eyes so round, and bright,
    As make away my doubt,
  Where Love may all his torches light
    Though hate had put them out :
    But then, t' increase my fears,
    What nymph soe'er his voice but hears,
Will be my rival, though she have but ears.

I'll tell no more, and yet I love,
    And he loves me; yet no
One unbecoming thought doth move
    From either heart, I know;
        But so exempt from blame,
        As it would be to each a fame,
If love or fear would let me tell his name.

VI.

THE HOUR-GLASS.[3]

CONSIDER this small dust, here, in the glass,
        By atoms mov'd:
    Could you believe, that this the body was
        Of one that lov'd;
And in his mistress' flame, playing like a fly,
Was turn'd to cinders by her eye:

[3] *The* Hour-glass.] In two small editions containing part of our
author's poems, printed in 1640, the title of this epigram is, *On a
Gentlewoman working by an Hour-glass.* The verses are likewise
of a different measure, and I think more agreeable to the ear: I
shall give the whole as it stands in those copies, and afterwards
subjoin the original, of which the English is only a translation.

ON A GENTLEWOMAN

WORKING BY AN HOUR-GLASS.

" Do but consider this small dust,
        Here running in the glass,
            By atoms mov'd;
    Would you believe that it the body was
        Of one that lov'd?

" And in his mistress' flames playing like a flie,
    Was turned into cinders by her eye?
    Yes; as in life, so in their deaths unblest,
    A lover's ashes never can find rest."   WHAL.

    It matters little which we take: the version in Drummond's folio
is the worst, but all are imperfect. I have made a trifling change
or two in the arrangement; for as the lines stood before, some of

Yes; and in death, as life unblest,
    To have 't exprest,
Ev'n ashes of lovers find no rest.

them had no correspondent rhymes. The whole, as Whalley observes, is from the Latin of Jerom Amaltheus, one of the most ingenious and elegant of the modern Italian poets.

Horologium pulvereum, Tumulus Alcippi.

Perspicuo in vitro pulvis qui dividit horas,
    Dum vagus angustum sæpe recurrit iter,
Olim erat Alcippus, qui Gallæ ut vidit ocellos,
    Arsit, et est cæco factus ab igne cinis.
Irrequiete cinis, miseros testabere amantes
    More tuo nulla posse quiete frui.

Iolæ Tumulus.

Horarum in vitro pulvis nunc mensor, Iolæ
    Sunt cineres, urnam condidit acer amor ;
Ut, si quæ extincto remanent in amore favillæ,
    Nec jam tutus eat, nec requietus amet.

It appears that this little translation was made by Jonson, at the
request of his " friend " Drummond, on his auspicious visit to that
mirror of sincerity and hospitality. In Drummond's folio it is prefaced with an address so respectful, so cordial and affectionate, as
to raise a doubt whether the perversity was in the head or the heart
of the man, who could withdraw, upon receiving it, to his closet,
and deliberately commit to his note-book a series of base and
venomous accusations against the moral and religious character of
his unsuspecting guest.

"To the Honouring Respect
Born
To the Friendship contracted with
The Right Virtuous and Learned
Master William Drummond,
And the Perpetuating the same by all Offices of Love
Hereafter,
I Benjamin Jonson,
Whom he hath honoured with the leave to be called his,
Have with my own hand, to satisfy his Request,
Written this imperfect Song,
On a Lover's Dust, made sand for an Hour-glass."

The verses then follow, miserably printed, it must be confessed ;
after which Jonson, with the same warmth of heart subjoins : " Yet
that love, when it is at full, may admit heaping, receive another ;

VII.

My Picture, left in Scotland.

NOW think, Love is rather deaf than blind,
      For else it could not be,
                  That she,
      Whom I adore so much, should so slight me,
And cast my suit behind :
I'm sure my language to her was as sweet,
      And every close did meet
      In sentence of as subtle feet,
      As hath the youngest he,
      That sits in shadow of Apollo's tree.

      Oh ! but my conscious fears,
         That fly my thoughts between,
      Tell me that she hath seen
         My hundreds of gray hairs,
            Told seven and forty years,
      Read so much waste, as she cannot embrace
      My mountain belly, and my rocky face,
And all these, through her eyes, have stopt her ears.

VIII.

Against Jealousy.

WRETCHED and foolish jealousy,
      How cam'st thou thus to enter me ?
            I ne'er was of thy kind ;
      Nor have I yet the narrow mind
         To vent that poor desire,
That others should not warm them at my fire :

and this a Picture of myself." It would seem, from the above,
that Drummond kept a kind of Album, in which he had desired our
author to insert something in his own writing. The second piece
is No. VII.

I wish the sun should shine
On all men's fruits and flowers, as well as mine.

But under the disguise of love,
Thou say'st, thou only cam'st to prove
What my affections were.
Think'st thou that love is help'd by fear?
Go, get thee quickly forth,
Love's sickness, and his noted want of worth,
Seek doubting men to please,
I ne'er will owe my health to a disease.

IX.

THE DREAM.

R scorn, or pity, on me take,
I must the true relation make,
I am undone to-night:
Love in a subtle dream disguised,
Hath both my heart and me surprised,
Whom never yet he durst attempt awake;
Nor will he tell me for whose sake
He did me the delight,
Or spight;
But leaves me to inquire,
In all my wild desire,
Of Sleep again, who was his aid,
And Sleep so guilty and afraid,
As since he dares not come within my sight.

X.

An Epitaph

on master Vincent Corbet.[4]

HAVE my piety too, which, could
It vent itself but as it would,
Would say as much as both have done
Before me here, the friend and son :
For I both lost a friend and father,
Of him whose bones this grave doth gather,
Dear Vincent Corbet, who so long
Had wrestled[5] with diseases strong,
That though they did possess each limb,
Yet he broke them, ere they could him,
With the just canon of his life,
A life that knew nor noise, nor strife ;

---

[4] *An epitaph on Master* Vincent Corbet.] He was the father of bishop Corbet, and lived at Twickenham, where he followed the business of a gardener, and was famous for his nurseries and plantations of trees. We find an allusion both to the genius of his son, and his own eminence in his trade, in the following verses. WHAL.

This beautiful epitaph, as it is justly termed by Mr. Gilchrist, in his late edition of the Bishop's poems, was written in 1619, the year in which this good old man died. It seems intended as a kind of sequel to his son's elegy, which is simple and affecting, though occasionally tinctured with the peculiar humour of the writer, while Ben's poem is solemn, affectionate, and pathetic throughout. Who the " friend" was that preceded our poet in his tribute of regard to the worth of Vincent Corbet, I know not : so excellent a character found many, perhaps, to weep upon his grave.

[5] *Who* so long
Had wrestled, &c.] Thus his son :

> " Years he liv'd well nigh *fourscore*,
> But count his virtues, he liv'd more :
> And number him by doing good,
> He liv'd their age beyond the flood."

But was, by sweetning so his will,
All order and disposure still.
　His mind as pure, and neatly kept,
As were his nurseries, and swept
So of uncleanness, or offence,
That never came ill odour thence !
And add his actions unto these,
They were as specious as his trees.
'Tis true, he could not reprehend—
His very manners taught t' amend,
They were so even, grave and holy ;
No stubbornness so stiff, nor folly
To license ever was so light,
As twice to trespass in his sight :
His looks would so correct it, when
It chid the vice, yet not the men.
Much from him, I profess I won,
And more, and more, I should have done,
But that I understood him scant,
Now I conceive him by my want ;
And pray who shall my sorrows read,
That they for me their tears will shed ;
For truly, since he left to be,
I feel, I'm rather dead than he !

Reader, whose life and name did e'er become
　An Epitaph, deserv'd a Tomb :
Nor wants it here through penury or sloth,
　Who makes the one, so it be first, makes both.

XI.[6]

ON THE PORTRAIT OF SHAKSPEARE.

TO THE READER.

HIS figure that thou here seest put,
It was for gentle Shakspeare cut,
Wherein the graver had a strife
With nature, to out-do the life :
O could he but have drawn his wit
As well in brass, as he has hit
His face ; the print would then surpass
All that was ever writ in brass :
But since he cannot, reader, look
Not on his picture, but his book.[7]

---

[6] I have thought it best to interrupt the arrangement of the old folio, in this place, for the sake of inserting such scattered pieces of Jonson, as have not hitherto found a place in his works, together with such as Whalley had improperly subjoined to his Epigrams, which being published under the author's own care, should naturally terminate where he chose to stop short himself.

[7] These verses are printed with Jonson's name under the portrait of Shakspeare, prefixed as a frontispiece to the first edition of his works in folio, 1623.

"This print (engraved by Martin Droeshout) gives us a truer representation of Shakspeare, than several more pompous memorials of him ; if the testimony of Ben Jonson may be credited, to whom he was personally known. Unless we suppose that poet to have sacrificed his veracity to the turn of thought in his epigram, which is very improbable, as he might have been easily contradicted by several that must have remembered so celebrated a person."

Granger's Biog. Hist. of Eng. 8vo. 1775, vol. ii. p. 6.

XII.

TO THE MEMORY OF MY BELOVED

MASTER WILLIAM SHAKSPEARE,

AND WHAT HE HATH LEFT US.

O draw no envy, Shakspeare, on thy name,
Am I thus ample to thy book and fame;
While I confess thy writings to be such,
As neither man, nor Muse, can praise too
    much.
'Tis true, and all men's suffrage.   But these ways
Were not the paths I meant unto thy praise;
For silliest ignorance on these may light,
Which, when it sounds at best, but echoes right;
Or blind affection, which doth ne'er advance
The truth, but gropes, and urgeth all by chance;
Or crafty malice might pretend this praise,
And think to ruin, where it seem'd to raise.
These are, as some infámous bawd, or whore,
Should praise a matron; what could hurt her more?
But thou art proof against them, and, indeed,
Above the ill fortune of them, or the need.
I therefore will begin: Soul of the age!
The applause! delight! the wonder of our stage!
My Shakspeare rise! I will not lodge thee by
Chaucer, or Spenser, or bid Beaumont lie
A little further off, to make thee room:[8]
Thou art a monument without a tomb,

[8] *My Shakspeare rise! I will not lodge thee by*
    Chaucer, or Spenser, or bid Beaumont lie
    A little further off, to make thee room.]   These verses allude to
an Elegy on Shakspeare, written by W. Basse, which is here subjoined:
        "Renowned Spenser, lie a thought more nigh
            To learned Chaucer; and, rare Beaumont, lie

And art alive still, while thy book doth live
And we have wits to read, and praise to give.
That I not mix thee so, my brain excuses,
I mean with great, but disproportion'd Muses :
For if I thought my judgment were of years,
I should commit thee surely with thy peers,
And tell how far thou didst our Lily outshine,[9]
Or sporting Kyd, or Marlow's mighty line.

A little nearer Spenser, to make room
For Shakespear in your threefold, fourfold tomb.
To lodge all four in one bed make a shift,
For, until doomsday hardly will a fifth,
Betwixt this day and that, by fates be slain,
For whom your curtains need be drawn again.
But if precedency in death doth bar
A fourth place in your sacred sepulchre,
Under this sable marble of thine own,
Sleep, rare tragedian, Shakespeare, sleep alone :
Thy unmolested peace, in an unshared cave,
Possess as lord, not tenant of thy grave.
That unto us, and others, it may be
Honour hereafter to be laid by thee."   Whal.

[9] *And tell how far thou didst our Lily outshine,*
    Or sporting Kyd, or Marlow's mighty line.] These were in
possession of the theatre when Shakspeare first appeared, and
enjoyed a high degree of popularity. Of Kyd little is known,
except that he was the author of the *Spanish Tragedy;* though he
must undoubtedly have had many other pieces on the stage. Lily
was a pedantic and affected writer, with considerable talents, not
indeed for the drama, but for the rude, verbose romance of those
days, and which had a striking influence not only on our colloquial,
but written language.
    Marlow's mighty line is not introduced at random. Marlow has
many lines which have not hitherto been surpassed. His two parts
of *Tamburlaine,* though simple in plot and naked in artifice, have
yet some rude attempts at consistency of character, and many
passages of masculine vigour and lofty poetry. Even the bombast
lines which Shakspeare has put into the mouth of Pistol, are followed by others, in the same scene, and even in the same speech,
which the great poet himself might have fathered without disgrace
to his superior powers.
    Marlow had the sublimity of Milton, without the taste and in-

And though thou hadst small Latin and less Greek,
From thence to honour thee, I will not seek
For names : but call forth thund'ring Eschylus,
Euripides, and Sophocles to us,
Pacuvius, Accius, him of Cordoua dead,
To live again, to hear thy buskin tread,
And shake a stage : or when thy socks were on,
Leave thee alone for the comparison
Of all, that insolent Greece, or haughty Rome
Sent forth, or since did from their ashes come.
Triumph, my Britain, thou hast one to show,
To whom all scenes of Europe homage owe.
He was not of an age, but for all time !
And all the Muses still were in their prime,
When, like Apollo, he came forth to warm
Our ears, or like a Mercury to charm !
Nature herself was proud of his designs,
And joy'd to wear the dressing of his lines !

spiration. It is not just to consign him to ridicule. He and his
contemporary Peele, were produced just as the chaos of ignorance
was breaking up: they were among the earliest to perceive the
glimmering of sense and nature, and struggled to reach the light.

Marlow's end, like his career, was miserable. He fell (see vol. i.
p. 98) in a brothel squabble ; and the doating Aubrey, who im-
plicitly swallows every idle story, and confounds every true one,
tells us that he was killed by Ben Jonson !

Our author's attachment to Marlow was not unknown, nor were
his praises of him singular. He (Cris. Marlow), says a writer of
the last century, wrote besides plays, a poem called *Hero and
Leander*, of whose "mighty lines" master Jonson, a man sensible
enough of his own abilities, was often heard to say, that they were
examples fitter for admiration than parallel." What ! the "envious"
Ben ? Impossible.

Drayton thus characterises him :

> " Next Marlow, bathed in the Thespian springs,
> Had in him those brave translunary things
> That the first poets had : his raptures were
> All air and fire, which made his verses clear ;
> For that fine madness he did still retain,
> Which rightly should possess a poet's brain."

Which were so richly spun, and woven so fit,
As, since, she will vouchsafe no other wit.
The merry Greek, tart Aristophanes,
Neat Terence, witty Plautus, now not please ;
But antiquated and deserted lie,
As they were not of nature's family.
Yet must I not give nature all ; thy art,
My gentle Shakspeare,[10] must enjoy a part.
For though the poet's matter nature be,
His art doth give the fashion : and, that he
Who casts to write a living line, must sweat,
(Such as thine are) and strike the second heat
Upon the Muses anvil ; turn the same,
And himself with it, that he thinks to frame ;
Or for the laurel, he may gain a scorn ;
For a good poet's made, as well as born.
And such wert thou ! Look how the father's face
Lives in his issue, even so the race
Of Shakspeare's mind and manners brightly shines
In his well torned, and true filed lines :
In each of which he seems to shake a lance,
As brandish'd at the eyes of ignorance.
Sweet Swan of Avon ! what a sight it were
To see thee in our water yet appear,
And make those flights upon the banks of Thames,
That so did take Eliza, and our James !
But stay, I see thee in the hemisphere
Advanced, and made a constellation there !
Shine forth, thou Star of poets, and with rage,

[10] *My* gentle *Shakspeare.*]   The uncommon fondness of Jonson
for Shakspeare is visible upon every mention of his name.   This
is the second time that he has applied the epithet of *gentle* to him,
which is now become a part of his name.   Just below, he calls him
the *Sweet Swan of Avon.*   It would *have killed Mr. Malone's heart*
to acknowledge that the two most endearing appellations by which
this great poet has been known and characterised for nearly two
centuries, were first bestowed upon him by " old Ben, who perse-
cuted his memory with clumsy sarcasm, and restless malignity."

Or influence, chide, or cheer the drooping stage,
Which, since thy flight from hence, hath mourn'd like
    night,
And despairs day, but for thy volume's light.[1]

[1] *And despairs day, but for thy volume's light.*] The two greatest
poets of our nation have been divided in their sentiments of the
testimony which Jonson gives in these verses to the merits and the
genius of Shakspeare. Jonson, it must be owned, was not formed
to that facility of praise, which flows indiscriminately where prejudice or humour point the way. His suffrage was never given, but
matured by judgment, and authorised by science. Mr. Dryden
calls it an invidious and sparing, but I incline to Mr. Pope's
opinion in thinking it an ample and honourable panegyrick to the
memory of his friend. WHAL.

I should conceive that every unprejudiced reader must be of
Whalley's mind. But is it possible to be silent and hear the
warmest encomium, the most affectionate tribute of praise, that was
ever offered to the memory of departed worth and genius, taxed
with envy by every scribbler who is profligate enough to belie his
understanding for the sake of indulging his malice? Jonson not
only sets Shakspeare above his contemporaries, but above the
ancients, whose works himself idolized, and of whose genuine merits
he was, perhaps, a more competent judge than any scholar of his
age: yet for this glowing effusion, which does more credit to
the talents and genius of Shakspeare than all that has since
appeared on those subjects, Mr. Malone sneers at him, and Mr.
Steevens adds to the insult. "Now let us compare the present
eulogium of old Ben with such of his other sentiments as have
reached posterity:" and he deliberately proceeds to re-copy the
vile forgery of Macklin, which had been just detected and exposed
in the preceding volume.

With respect to the critical notions of Dryden, I utterly disclaim
them. He saw clearly, and decided justly, where his interest or
his passions did not interpose; but this was so frequently the case,
that no reliance can be securely placed on any one opinion which
he ever advanced. He hated, and what must astonish a reader of
the present day, feared Shadwell; and because Shadwell spoke
with respect of Jonson, and preferred him to all the dramatic writers
of his own times, Dryden laboured to decry and injure him. This
is the true secret of his criticism.

It must mightily console the admirers of Shakspeare to find one
so tremblingly alive to his reputation, as to discover a spirit of detraction in the panegyric of Jonson, thus atoning for the injustice,
in his own name. "Shakspeare writes (Dryden says) in many

8   v

XIII.

ON THE HONOURED POEMS OF HIS HONOURED FRIEND,
SIR JOHN BEAUMONT, BARONET.[2]

HIS book will live ; it hath a Genius ; this
Above his reader, or his praiser, is.
Hence, then, profane ! here needs no words
    expense
In bulwarks, rav'lins, ramparts for defence :
Such as the creeping common pioners use,
When they do sweat to fortify a Muse.
Though I confess it Beaumont's book to be
The bound, and frontier of our poetry ;

places below the dullest writers of ours or any precedent age. He
is the very Janus of poets ; he wears almost every where two faces ;
and you have scarce begun to admire the one ere you despise the
other. His plots are lame, and made up, many of them, of some
ridiculous and incoherent story, which in one play many times took
up the business of an age. Many of his plays, as the *Winter's Tale*,
Love's Labour's Lost, and *Measure for Measure*, are either grounded
on impossibilities, or, at least, so meanly written, that the comedy
neither caused your mirth, nor the serious part your concernment."

   I have yet a word to say of Dryden. Of all the dramatic writers
of Charles's days, who traded in obscenity and profaneness, he is by
far the most inexcusable. Nothing can be so stupid, nothing so
loathsome as his perpetual struggle to be impious and immoral. It
is evident that Nature built up this great poet for the defence of
wisdom and virtue ; and it is truly shocking to see him labori-
ously lashing and spurring his reluctant and jaded powers forward
in the cause of vice. He is wicked by mere effort ; but, happily,
not dangerous :—and it is hard to decide whether his reader or
himself is most obliged to the dulness which renders his mischievous
propensities so innoxious.

   [2] *On the honoured poems of his honoured friend*, sir John Beaumont.] I have taken the following copy from the complimentary
verses, prefixed to the poems which it celebrates. Sir John Beaumont was the elder brother of Francis Beaumont the dramatic
writer, and a man of genius and virtue. His poems were published
after his decease, and dedicated to king Charles, by sir John Beau-

And doth deserve all muniments of praise,
That art, or ingine, on the strength can raise ;
Yet, who dares offer a redoubt to rear,
To cut a dike, or stick a stake up, here,
Before this work ? where envy hath not cast
A trench against it, nor a batt'ry plac't ?
Stay till she make her vain approaches ; then,
If maimed she come off, 'tis not of men,
This fort of so impregnable access ;
But higher power, as spight could not make less,
Nor flattery ; but, secur'd by the author's name,
Defies what's cross to piety, or good fame :
And like a hallowed temple, free from taint
Of ethnicisme, makes his Muse a saint.

mont, his son.   The most esteemed amongst them is the poem of
Bosworth Field.   But the reader will be able to form some idea of
his merit, from the following verses :

AN EPITAPH

UPON MY DEAR BROTHER FRANCIS BEAUMONT.

" On Death thy murd'rer this revenge I take ;
   I slight his terror, and just question make,
   Which of us two the best precedence have,
   Mine to this wretched world, thine to the grave.
   Thou should'st have follow'd me, but Death, to blame,
   Miscounted years, and measur'd age by fame.
   So dearly hast thou bought thy precious lines,
   Their praise grew swiftly, so thy life declines :
   Thy muse, the hearer's queen, the reader's love,
   All ears, all hearts, but Death's, could please and move."
                                             WHAL.

XIV.

To Mr. John Fletcher, upon his Faithful Shepherdess.

THE wise, and many-headed bench, that sits
Upon the life and death of plays and wits,
(Compos'd of gamester, captain, knight,
    knight's man,
Lady or pucelle, that wears mask or fan,
Velvet, or taffata cap, rank'd in the dark
With the shop's foreman, or some such brave spark
That may judge for his sixpence) had, before
They saw it half, damn'd thy whole play, and more :
Their motives were, since it had not to do
With vices, which they look'd for, and came to.
I, that am glad thy innocence was thy guilt,
And wish that all the Muses' blood were spilt
In such a martyrdom, to vex their eyes,
Do crown thy murder'd poem : which shall rise
A glorified work to time, when fire,
Or moths shall eat what all these fools admire.[3]

XV.

EPITAPH

On the Countess of Pembroke.[4]

NDERNEATH this sable herse
Lies the subject of all verse,
Sidney's sister, Pembroke's mother ;
Death ! ere thou hast slain another,

---

[3] This poem, which was taken by Whalley from Seward's edition of Beaumont and Fletcher, must have been written at an early period of Jonson's life, as the *Faithful Shepherdess* was brought out about 1610. See vol. vi. p. 286. Jonson has no reason to be ashamed of his prediction.

[4] *Epitaph on the countess of* Pembroke, *&c.*] This delicate

> Learn'd and fair, and good as she,
> Time shall throw a dart at thee.

epitaph is universally assigned to our author, though it hath never yet been printed with his works : it is therefore with some pleasure, that I have given it a place here. This lady, for whose entertainment sir Philip Sidney wrote the *Arcadia*, lived to a good old age, and died in 1621. She was buried in the cathedral of Salisbury, in the burial-place of the Pembroke family. WHAL.

The exquisite beauty of this little piece (the most perfect of its kind) has drawn a word of approbation from the stern and cynical Osborne. " Lest I should seem (he says) to trespasse upon truth in the praise of this lady, I shall leave the world her epitaph, in which the author doth manifest himself a poet in all things but untruth."

To the lines in the text, Osborne subjoins the following :

> " Marble piles let no man raise
> To her name, for after days.
> Some kind woman, born as she,
> Reading this, like Niobe,
> Shall turn statue, and become
> Both her mourner and her tomb."

On this paltry addition, the editors of the *Secret History of the Court of James I.*, who manifest on all occasions a strange hostility to our author, observe, " It is possible that Jonson cancelled these lines on account of the outrageous wit with which they disgrace the commencement." vol. i. p. 225. It is also possible that Jonson never saw them. Setting aside the absurdity of supposing the poet to say in one line, that such another character would never appear, and to admit in the next that nothing was so likely, the critics ought to have known (for the fact was very accessible) that the verses in question were copied from the poems of the earl of Pembroke, a humble votary of the Muses, to whose pen they are assigned by the prefix of his usual initials. There can, in fact, be no doubt that they proceeded from his lordship, whose singular affection for his venerable parent furnishes a ready apology for their defects.

Whalley has said nothing of the literary merits of the countess of Pembroke, which were of a very distinguished nature. She wrote verse with grace and facility, and she translated the *Tragedie of Antonie* from the French : her chief works, however, were works of piety, and her virtues still went before her talents.

XVI.

A VISION ON THE MUSES OF HIS FRIEND MICHAEL DRAYTON.

T hath been question'd, Michael,[5] if I be
A friend at all ; or, if at all, to thee :
Because, who make the question, have not
    seen
Those ambling visits pass in verse, between
Thy Muse and mine, as they expect : 'tis true,
You have not writ to me, nor I to you.
And though I now begin, 'tis not to rub
Hanch against hanch, or raise a rhyming club
About the town ; this reckoning I will pay,
Without conferring symbols ; this' my day.
   It was no dream ! I was awake, and saw.
Lend me thy voice, O Fame, that I may draw
Wonder to truth, and have my vision hurl'd
Hot from thy trumpet round about the world.
I saw a beauty, from the sea to rise,
That all earth look'd on, and that earth all eyes !
It cast a beam, as when the cheerful sun
Is fair got up, and day some hours begun ;
And fill'd an orb as circular as heaven :
The orb was cut forth into regions seven,
And those so sweet, and well proportion'd parts,
As it had been the circle of the arts :
When, by thy bright Idea standing by,[6]
I found it pure and perfect poesy.

There read I, straight, thy learned Legends three,
Heard the soft airs, between our swains and thee,
Which made me think the old Theocritus,
Or rural Virgil come to pipe to us.
But then thy Epistolar Heroic Songs,
Their loves, their quarrels, jealousies and wrongs,
Did all so strike me, as I cried, who can
With us be call'd the Naso, but this man ?
And looking up, I saw Minerva's fowl,
Perch'd over head, the wise Athenian Owl :[7]
I thought thee then our Orpheus, that wouldst try,
Like him, to make the air one volary.
And I had styled thee Orpheus, but before
My lips cou'd form the voice, I heard that roar,
And rouze, the marching of a mighty force,
Drums against drums, the neighing of the horse,
The fights, the cries, and wond'ring at the jars,
I saw and read it was the Barons Wars.
O how in those dost thou instruct these times,
That rebels actions are but valiant crimes ;
And carried, though with shout and noise, confess
A wild, and an unauthorized wickedness !
Say'st thou so, Lucan ? but thou scorn'st to stay
Under one title : thou hast made thy way
And flight about the isle, well near, by this
In thy admired Periegesis,
Or universal circumduction
Of all that read thy Poly-Olbion ;[8]

pieces. "*Idea*, or the Shepherds' Garland, fashioned in nine
eglogs, 1593." The *Legends* are, I believe, those of "Cromwell,"
"Mortimer," and "Matilda ;" the *Songs* are "England's Heroical
Epistles," published in 1598.
   [7] *The Owl.*] Published in 4to. 1604. The *Barons Wars*, 1598.
   [8] *Thy Poly-Olbion.*] This is Drayton's principal work, and was
once exceedingly popular. It is possessed of considerable merit,
and those who may be inclined to smile at its fantastic chorography,
may yet be pleased to discover many detached passages of high
poetic beauty. Drayton was encouraged to proceed with this

That read it ! that are ravish'd ; such was I,
With every song, I swear, and so would die ;
But that I hear again thy drum to beat
A better cause, and strike the bravest heat
That ever yet did fire the English blood,
Our right in France, if rightly understood.
There thou art Homer ; pray thee, use the style
Thou hast deserv'd, and let me read the while
Thy catalogue of ships, exceeding his,
Thy list of aids and force, for so it is :
The poet's act ; and for his country's sake,
Brave are the musters that the muse will make.
And when he ships them, where to use their arms,
How do his trumpets breathe ! what loud alarms !
Look how we read the Spartans were inflam'd
With bold Tyrtæus' verse ; when thou art nam'd,

poem by prince Henry; and Daniel, who also found, in this
lamented youth, a generous patron, seems to advert to the circumstance with no great complacency.

The poems, to which Jonson alludes in the subsequent lines, are
The Battle of Agincourt, The Miseries of Queen Margaret, the *Quest
of Cynthia,* the *Shepherds' Syrene, The Moon Calf,* and the well-
known *Nymphidia, or the Court of Fairies:* all published in 1627.

The following remarks on Drayton by Granger (bating a little
extravagance in the opening sentence) are not ill drawn up, and
may fitly conclude the notes on the subject of this once celebrated
poet.

" The reputation of Drayton, in the reigns of Elizabeth and James
I., stood on much the same level with that of Cowley, in the reigns
of Charles I. and II., but it has declined considerably since that
period. He frequently wants that elevation of thought which is
essential to poetry ; though in some of the stanzas of his ' Barons
Wars,' he is scarce inferior to Spenser. In his ' England's
Heroical Epistles,' written in the manner of Ovid, he has been, in
general, happier in the choice, than the execution of his subjects ;
yet some of his imitations are more in the spirit of that poet, than
several of the English translations of him. His ' Nymphidia, or
Court of Fayrie,' seems to have been the greatest effort of his
imagination, and is the most generally admired of his works. His
character among his friends was that of a modest and amiable man.
Ob. 1631." *Biog. Hist.* v. i. pp. 10, 11.

So shall our English youth urge on, and cry
An Agincourt! an Agincourt! or die.
This book, it is a catechism to fight,
And will be bought of every lord and knight
That can but read ; who cannot, may in prose
Get broken pieces, and fight well by those.
The miseries of Margaret the queen,
. Of tender eyes will more be wept than seen.
I feel it by mine own, that overflow
And stop my sight in every line I go.
But then, refreshed by thy Fairy Court,
I look on Cynthia, and Syrena's sport,
As on two flow'ry carpets, that did rise,
And with their grassy green restored mine eyes.
Yet give me leave to wonder at the birth
Of thy strange Moon-calf, both thy strain of mirth,
And gossip-got acquaintance, as to us
Thou hadst brought Lapland, or old Cobalus,
Empusa, Lamia, or some monster more,
Than Afric knew, or the full Grecian store.
I gratulate it to thee, and thy ends,
To all thy virtuous and well-chosen friends ;
Only my loss is, that I am not there,
And till I worthy am to wish I were,
I call the world that envies me, to see
If I can be a friend, and friend to thee.

XVII.

EPITAPH

ON MICHAEL DRAYTON.[9]

DO, pious marble, let thy readers know
What they, and what their children owe
To Drayton's name ; whose sacred dust
We recommend unto thy trust.
Protect his memory, and preserve his story,
Remain a lasting monument of his glory.—
And when thy ruins shall disclaim
To be the treasurer of his name ;
His name, that cannot die, shall be,
An everlasting monument to thee.[1]

[9] *On* Michael Drayton.] Tradition hath generally fixed on Jonson as the author of this Epitaph ; nor is it unworthy of his genius, or the friendship between him and Drayton, or unlike the stile and spirit of his smaller poems.   WHAL.

In a MS. in Ashmole's Museum, (38,) this Epitaph is attributed to Randolph ; Aubrey ascribes it to Quarles ; it has also been given to others, and with as little judgment.   I see no reason to dispute the common opinion.

[1] *His name, that cannot die, shall be,*
   An everlasting monument to thee.] This too might *surprize* Mr. Cumberland ; for Jonson seems to have been *poaching* for it among the Greek fragments.   See the epigram of Iön on the tomb of Euripides :

Ου σου μνημα τοδ' εστ', Ευριπιδη, αλλα συ τουδε,
   Τη ση γαρ δοξη μνημα τοδ' αμπεχεται.

XVIII.

To my truly beloved Friend, master Browne:

on his Pastorals.[2]

OME men, of books or friends not speaking
right,
May hurt them more with praise, than foes
with spight.
But I have seen thy work, and I know thee :
And, if thou list thyself, what thou canst be.
For, though but early in these paths thou tread,
I find thee write most worthy to be read.
It must be thine own judgment, yet, that sends
This thy work forth ; that judgment mine commends.
And, where the most read books, on authors' fames,
Or, like our money-brokers, take up names
On credit, and are cozen'd ; see, that thou
By offering not more sureties, than enow,
Hold thine own worth unbroke ; which is so good
Upon the Exchange of Letters, as I wou'd
More of our writers would like thee, not swell
With the how much they set forth, but the how well.

[2] These lines are prefixed to "Britannia's Pastorals, the second
Book," by William Browne, fol. 1616, and 8vo. 1625. They are
now added, for the first time, to these volumes.

Browne was but a young man when he published his pastorals ;
they exhibit, among many pretty passages, some of the character-
istics of youth, a gaudy taste, and an undisciplined judgment.
There was more than enough, however, to justify the expectations
of Jonson, and had he found leisure or inclination to cultivate his
natural talents for poetry, his success could scarcely have been
matter of doubt.

His literary acquirements were considerable, and these, together
with his amiable qualities, powerfully recommended him to our
author's great friend and patron, the earl of Pembroke, under whom
he is said to have acquired considerable property. The "envious"
Ben appears to have felt no jealousy at this ; which I notice as a
phenomenon that calls for grave inquiry.

XIX.

To his much and worthily esteemed Friend, the Author.

HO takes thy volume to his virtuous hand,[3]
Must be intended still to understand :
Who bluntly doth but look upon the same,
May ask, what author would conceal his
    name ?
Who reads may rove, and call the passage dark,
Yet may as blind men sometimes hit the mark.
Who reads, who roves, who hopes to understand,
May take thy volume to his virtuous hand :
Who cannot read, but only doth desire
To understand, he may at length admire.

XX.

To my worthy and honoured Friend, Master George Chapman.[4]

HOSE work, could this be, Chapman, to
    refine
Old Hesiod's ore, and give it thus ! but
    thine,
Who hadst before wrought in rich Homer's mine.

---

[3] *Who takes thy volume, &c.*] This little piece stands with Jonson's name, before "Cynthia's Revenge, or Menander's Extasie," 4to. 1613. This tragedy was written by John Stephens, of whom I only know that he was a learned man, and a member of the honourable Society of Lincoln's Inn. Langbaine, who mentions him, merely tells us that he lived in the reign of James I. "His play (he says) is one of the longest that ever was written, and withal the most tedious." Whether Langbaine, when he made this remark, "read or roved," as I never saw the tragedy, I cannot determine.

[4] These lines are prefixed to the "Translation of Hesiod's Works

What treasure hast thou brought us ! and what store
Still, still, dost thou arrive with at our shore,
To make thy honour, and our wealth the more !

and Days, 4to. 1618." There had always been an extraordinary
degree of friendship between Chapman and our author. They
united their talents in *Eastward Hoe*, and when the former was
thrown into prison for the political reflections in that piece, Jonson
voluntarily accompanied him. He told Drummond in 1619, that
" he loved Chapman ;" and we have just seen how he had com-
plimented him in the preceding year. All this signifies nothing,
and the old calumny of " envy," " jealousy," and I know not what,
is again served up to the nauseated reader. " Jonson," says the
editor of the *Theatrum Poetarum* of Phillips, 8vo. 1800, " being delivered from Shakspeare, (in 1616,) *began unexpectedly to be disturbed
at the rising reputation of a new theatrical rival.*" p. 252. Chapman was born in 1557, (about twenty years before our author,) he
was therefore threescore, at the death of Shakspeare, and the *new*
theatrical rival at whose *rising* reputation Jonson *began* unexpectedly to be disturbed, was one with whom he had lived all his life
in strict intimacy, as appears by their mutual correspondence,
and who had composed almost the whole of his dramatic works,
many years before the period in question.

Can the reader discover any trace of " jealousy " in the heartfelt
and elegant compliment which Jonson here pays his " worthy and
honoured friend ? " Shame on it ! The common decencies of
character are overlooked where this great poet is concerned. To
belie him is all that is thought necessary ; and when ignorance, or
impudence, or both together, have put forth a clumsy falsehood
against him, the slander is greedily hailed by the public as an additional triumph on the side of Shakspeare.

I have yet a word to say to the anonymous Editor of this volume,
(the *Theatrum Poetarum*.) That he is actuated by a spirit of hostility towards Jonson, is manifest ; but even this will scarcely be
admitted as a sufficient apology for quoting a scurrilous attack upon
him from a work where it is *not* to be found. Drummond of Haw-
thornden, he says, has represented the character of Jonson in " no
very unjust light." We are then regaled with the ribaldry of that
splenetic hypocrite, in a tissue of malicious charges, concluding
with this sentence : " In short, Jonson was in his personal character
the very reverse of Shakspeare, as surly, ill-natured, proud and disagreeable, as Shakspeare, with ten times his merit, was gentle, good-
natured, easy and amiable." p. 249.

How has the editor the boldness to father this rancorous language upon Drummond, who has not a syllable of it ! "See Drum-

If all the vulgar tongues that speak this day
Were ask'd of thy discoveries; they must say,
To the Greek coast thine only knew the way.

Such passage hast thou found, such returns made,
As now of all men, it is call'd thy trade,
And who make thither else, rob, or invade.

XXI.

To my chosen Friend,

the learned Translator of Lucan,

Thomas May, esquire.

HEN, Rome, I read thee in thy mighty pair,
And see both climbing up the slippery stair
Of Fortune's wheel, by Lucan driv'n about,
And the world in it, I begin to doubt,
At every line some pin thereof should slack
At least, if not the general engine crack.
But when again I view the parts so pays'd,
And those in number so, and measure rais'd,
As neither Pompey's popularity,
Cæsar's ambition, Cato's liberty,
Calm Brutus' tenor start, but all along
Keep due proportion in the ample song,
It makes me, ravish'd with just wonder, cry
What Muse, or rather God of harmony

mond's Works," he coolly says, at the bottom of page 244: but has
he seen them? The fact is, that the passage in question is a wicked
fabrication, put into Drummond's mouth by Shiels, the Scotchman,
the author of the *Lives of the Poets* which pass under the name of
Theophilus Cibber.
   "Now this is worshipful authority"!—but it does very well in
Jonson's case, and is, indeed, quite as worthy of notice, and quite
as authentic, as most of the matter brought against him.

Taught Lucan these true modes! replies my sense,
What gods but those of arts, and eloquence?
Phœbus, and Hermes? they whose tongue, or pen,
Are still th' interpreters twixt gods and men!
But who hath them interpreted, and brought
Lucan's whole frame unto us, and so wrought,
As not the smallest joint, or gentlest word
In the great mass, or machine there is stirr'd?
The self-same Genius! so the work will say:
The Sun translated, or the son of May.[5]

---

[5] i. e. Hermes. This complimentary poem, which is signed
" Your true friend in judgment and choice, Ben Jonson," is prefixed to May's *Translation of Lucan*, 1627. May, with whom
our author appears to have always lived on terms of the strictest
friendship, is selected by Macklin, with his usual good fortune, to
father one of his scurrilous attacks upon Jonson; much to the
satisfaction of Mr. Steevens, who exults in the clumsy forgery as a
decisive proof of " old Ben's malignity to Shakspeare."

May published a continuation of Lucan in 1630, which was reprinted in Holland, 1640, with this title : *Supplementum Lucani
authore Tho. May, Anglo.* The first edition has never fallen in my
way ; the second is prefaced by the following lines, written, as I
conjecture, by our author, though the foreign press has copied his
name incorrectly.

Dignissimo
Viro
Thomæ Mayo
Amico suo summè honorando.

Terge parentales oculos, post funera mundi
  Roma tui, nondum tota sepulta jaces.
Gloria vivit adhuc radiis evincta coruscis
  Quam tibi perpetuat nobile Vatis opus:
Cujus in historia moreris, pariterque triumphas:
  Exornantque tuas vulnera sæva genas.
Ingenio, Lucane, tuo tua Roma ruinis
  Auctior, et damnis stat veneranda magis
Quam tot terrarum dum sceptra superba tenerēt
  Atque triumphati spargeret orbis opes.
Sed Romæ quodcunque tuæ Lucane dedisti,
  Hoc dedit et Maii subsidialis amor,
Qui tibi succurrit vindex, et divite vena
  Supplevit latices, te moriente, tuos.

XXII.

To my dear Son, and right learned Friend, Master Joseph Rutter.

YOU look, my Joseph, I should something say
Unto the world, in praise of your first play:
And truly, so I would, could I be heard.
You know, I never was of truth afeard,
And less asham'd ; not when I told the crowd
How well I lov'd truth : I was scarce allow'd
By those deep-grounded, understanding men,
That sit to censure Plays, yet know not when,
Or why to like ; they found it all was new,
And newer than could please them, because true.
Such men I met withal, and so have you.
Now, for mine own part, and it is but due,
(You have deserv'd it from me) I have read,
And weigh'd your play : untwisted ev'ry thread,
And know the woof and warp thereof ; can tell
Where it runs round, and even ; where so well,
So soft, and smooth it handles, the whole piece,
As it were spun by nature off the fleece :
This is my censure.   Now there is a new
Office of wit, a mint, and (this is true)
Cried up of late : whereto there must be first
A master-worker call'd, th' old standard burst
Of wit, and a new made ; a warden then,
And a comptroller, two most rigid men
For order, and for governing the pix,
A say-master, hath studied all the tricks
Of fineness, and alloy : follow his hint,
You have all the mysteries of wit's new mint,
The valuations, mixtures, and the same
Concluded from a caract to a dram.[6]

---

[6] These lines are placed before the *Shepherd's Holiday*, a Pas-

XXIII.

EPIGRAM.

In Authorem.[7]

THOU, that wouldst find the habit of true
    passion,
    And see a mind attir'd in perfect strains;
    Not wearing moods, as gallants do a fashion,
In these pied times, only to shew their trains,
Look here on Breton's work, the master print,
    Where such perfections to the life do rise ;
If they seem wry to such as look asquint,
    The fault's not in the object, but their eyes.
For, as one coming with a lateral view,
    Unto a cunning piece wrought perspective,
Wants faculty to make a censure true ;
    So with this author's readers will it thrive ;
Which being eyed directly, I divine,
His proof their praise 'll incite, as in this line.

toral Drama, published in 1635. May joined with Jonson in
commendation of this piece, which is favourably noticed by Langbaine. Rutter, who was probably a man of learning, was tutor to
the son of the earl of Dorset, lord chamberlain, and therefore much
about the court. He is said to have translated the *Cid* of Cor-
neille, at the command of Charles I.

    [7] *In Authorem.*] This Epigram is printed before a poem of
that indefatigable writer, Nicholas Breton, called " *Melancholike
humours,* in verses of diverse natures." 1600.

XXIV.

To the worthy Author,

on the husband.[8]

T fits not only him that makes a book
To see his work be good ; but that he look
Who are his test, and what their judgment is,
Least a false praise do make their dotage his.
I do not feel that ever yet I had
The art of uttering wares, if they were bad ;
Or skill of making matches in my life :
And therefore I commend unto the *Wife*,
That went before—a *Husband*.   She, I'll swear,
Was worthy of a good one, and this, here,
I know for such, as (if my word will weigh)
She need not blush upon the marriage day.

XXV.

To the Author.[9]

N picture, they which truly understand,
Require (besides the likeness of the thing)
Light   posture,   heightening,   shadow,
colouring,
All which are parts commend the cunning hand ;
And all your book, when it is throughly scann'd,

[8] The poem to which these lines are prefixed, is one of the
numerous effusions to which that popular production, *The Wife* of
sir Thomas Overbury, gave rise.   The name of the writer is unknown ; the poem itself is extremely rare : indeed, I am not aware
of the existence of any other copy than that from which the above
transcript was made, in the collection of Mr. Hill.   The title of the
work is " The Husband : a poem expressed in a complete man."
1614, 8vo.
[9] This sonnet stands before a work, by Thomas Wright, called
" The Passions of the Mind in general. 1604, and 1620," 4to.

Will well confess ; presenting, limiting
Each subtlest passion, with her source, and spring,
So bold, as shews your art you can command.
But now your work is done, if they that view
The several figures, languish in suspense,
To judge which passion's false, and which is true,
Between the doubtful sway of reason and sense ;
'Tis not your fault if they shall sense prefer,
Being told there Reason cannot, Sense may err.

XXVI.

To the Author.[1]

TRUTH is the trial of itself,
And needs no other touch ;
And purer than the purest gold,
Refine it ne'er so much.

It is the life and light of love,
The sun that ever shineth,
And spirit of that special grace,
That faith and love defineth.

[1] Taken from the complimentary verses prefixed to *The Touch-stone of Truth*, 12mo. Lond. 1630, by T. Warre.

The last nine little pieces are now, for the first time, added to Jonson's works : I have collected them as I could, and placed them together, without regard to the respective dates of their first appearance, which, indeed, it was not always easy to ascertain. They are not given out of respect to any intrinsic merit which they may be thought to possess, though they are not without their value on another account. Jonson has been held forth to the world as the very soul of envy, jealous of all merit in others, unwilling, and, indeed, unable, to bear a rival candidate for fame. But what is the fact ? that in the long list of English poets, he is decidedly among the most candid and generous : the most free of his advice and assist-ance, the most liberal of his praise. This part of Jonson's character was so well established among his contemporaries, that almost every one who meditated the publication of a book applied to him

It is the warrant of the word,
  That yields a scent so sweet,
As gives a power to faith to tread
  All falsehood under feet.

It is the sword that doth divide
  The marrow from the bone,
And in effect of heavenly love
  Doth shew the Holy One.

for a favourable judgment of it. Whence it has happened that there are far more commendatory verses to be met with by our author than by any other writer of those times. This could not escape Dr. Farmer; and to the utter confusion of Steevens and Malone, he has had the honesty to acknowledge it. He calls the verses on Shakspeare, "sparing and invidious" as they appear to those critics, "the warmest panegyrick that ever was penned; and in truth," adds he, "the received opinion of the pride and malignity of Jonson, at least in the earlier part of his life, is *absolutely groundless;* at this time scarce a play or a poem appeared without Ben's encomium, from the original Shakspeare to the translator of Du Bartas." *Essay,* &c. p. 12. This passage stands at the opening of the second volume of the *Variorum Shakspeare,* which, notwithstanding, is filled with abusive ribaldry on the "early malignity" of our author. Such is the consistency of the wretched confederacy against his reputation!

But even Dr. Farmer might have spared his *"earlier part at least;"* for it is altogether certain that Jonson's *encomiums* were as liberally bestowed in the decline of his life, as at any other period, and that the last productions of his pen were panegyrics on the writings of his contemporaries. In truth, the failings of this poet lay on the side of proneness to commendation, and he was very sensible of it. As early as 1614, he tells the learned Selden, that he had hitherto been too liberal of his applause; but that he would turn a sharper eye upon himself in future, and consider what he wrote,

    —————— "and vex it many days,
Before men got a verse; much less a praise."

Such, however, was the kindly warmth of his disposition, that this resolution was broken as soon as made; and he continued to the close of his life to speak with favour of almost every literary work that appeared. His reward for this is an universal outcry on the peculiar malevolence of his nature!

This, blessed Warre, thy blessed book
Unto the world doth prove ;
A worthy work, and worthy well
Of the most worthy love.

XXVII.

To Edward Filmer,[2]

ON HIS MUSICAL WORK, DEDICATED TO THE QUEEN.

WHAT charming peals are these,
    That, while they bind the senses, do so
            please ?
    They are the marriage-rites
Of two, the choicest pair of man's delights,
        Music and Poesy ;
French air, and English verse, here wedded lie.

    Who did this knot compose,
Again hath brought the lily to the rose ;
    And, with their chained dance,
Re-celebrates the joyful match with France.

    [2] *To Edward Filmer, on his musical work, &c.*] This epigram
first appeared in the folio of 1640, after the death of our poet.
Possibly it might have been prefixed to the work it celebrates, and
from thence transcribed into the edition above mentioned. Though
no date is set to any of the Epigrams, this excepted, yet circumstances will assist us to guess at the time of those addressed to the
greatest persons then living. In general, they were written before
1616, as most of them are contained in the edition of Jonson's
works, which was published in that year. WHAL.
    Here is *much ado about nothing.* What Whalley means by *most
of them,* and *in general,* I know not, since, blunders excepted, the
second edition of the old folio is a mere transcript of the first,
with the reserve of the present lines, which, notwithstanding their
date (1629), are absurdly inserted among the Epigrams printed in
1616.

They are a school to win
The fair French daughter to learn English in ;
    And, graced with her song,
To make the language sweet upon her tongue.[3]

XXVIII.

To RICHARD BROME,

ON HIS COMEDY OF THE NORTHERN LASS.[4]

HAD you for a servant once, Dick Brome,
    And you perform'd a servant's faithful
        parts ;
    Now you are got into a nearer room
Of fellowship, professing my old arts.
And you do do them well, with good applause,
    Which you have justly gained from the stage,
By observation of those comic laws
    Which I, your master, first did teach the age.

---

[3] *To make the language sweet, &c.*] From Chaucer. It is a
pretty compliment to Henrietta, who had probably encouraged the
work, from an attachment to her native tunes.

[4] *The Northern Lass.*] These lines are addressed, " To my faithful
servant, and (by his continued virtue) my loving friend, the author
of this work, master Richard Brome. 1632." I have already
noticed the attempts of Randolph and others to create a feeling of
hostility in our poet towards Brome. That they met with no success is evident ; for Jonson always remained warmly attached to
his old and meritorious servant, and Brome continued no less
grateful and affectionate towards his generous master. Even after
Jonson's death, the kindness of the latter breaks out in a little
poem to the memory of Fletcher :

        " I knew him, (Fletcher)—
        I knew him in his strength ; even then, when HE,
        That was the master of his art, and me,
        Most knowing Jonson, proud to call him son,
        In friendly envy swore he had outdone
        His very self," &c.

You learnt it well, and for it serv'd your time,
   A prenticeship; which few do now a days :
Now each court hobby-horse will wince in rhyme,
   Both learned, and unlearned, all write plays.[5]
It was not so of old : men took up trades
   That knew the crafts they had been bred in right ;
An honest bilboe-smith would make good blades,
   And the physician teach men spew and ——
The cobler kept him to his awl ; but now,
He'll be a poet, scarce can guide a plough.

XXIX.

A Speech[6] at a Tilting.

WO noble knights, whom true desire, and
   zeal,
   Hath arm'd at all points, charge me humbly
   kneel
To thee, O king of men, their noblest parts
To tender thus, their lives, their loves, their hearts.

---

[5] *Both learned, and unlearned, all write plays, &c.*] "Though this," says the watchful Langbaine, "be an imitation of Horace, yet I doubt not but the reader will pardon Ben for his ingenious application :

> *Navem agere ignarus navis timet: abrotonum ægro*
> *Non audet, nisi qui didicit, dare.   Quod medicorum est*
> *Promittunt medici: tractant fabrilia fabri.*
> *Scribimus indocti doctique poemata passim.*

[6] This Speech, which was copied from Ashmole's MSS., and kindly transmitted to me by Mr. Bliss, is said to have been "presented to king James at a tilting, in the behalf of the two noble brothers, sir Robert and sir Henry Rich."

The lines have no date, but were probably produced on one of those festive occasions to which the attachment of prince Henry to martial exercises gave birth.   It was the first appearance, perhaps, of the brothers in arms ; and this address of the knight, who presented them to the sovereign, formed a part of the entertainment : for these little tournaments were usually prefaced with some kind of poetical fable.

The elder of these two[7] rich hopes increase,
Presents a royal altar of fair peace;
And, as an everlasting sacrifice,
His life, his love, his honour which ne'er dies,
He freely brings, and on this altar lays
As true oblations.   His brother's emblem says,
Except your gracious eye, as through a glass,
Made perspective, behold him, he must pass
Still that same little point he was; but when
Your royal eye, which still creates new men,
Shall look, and on him, so,—then art's a liar,
If, from a little spark, he rise not fire.

---

[7] *The elder of these two.*]   These youths were the sons of Robert
Rich, first earl of Warwick, by the too celebrated sister of the earl
of Essex.   Robert, *the elder*, succeeded his father, as earl of Warwick, in 1618.   He *protests much* (like Hamlet's player-queen) in
his speech, and he *kept his word* somewhat in the same manner.
James was scarcely dead, when he deserted his successor, threw
himself into the arms of the parliament, took the command of the
fleet, and carried on a thriving trade, as Lord Clarendon says, "in
the desperate commodity of rebellion."   *His brother*, Henry Rich,
notwithstanding his *emblem*, or impress, trod in Sir Robert's steps.
James loaded him with favours, and not long before his death
created him earl of Holland.   Fresh honours were conferred upon
him by Charles, in return for which he deserted and betrayed him.
He was not long in receiving his reward from his new masters, who,
less scrupulous than his indulgent sovereign, deprived him of his
head for some alleged tergiversation, in 1649.

XXX.

An Epistle to sir Edward Sackvile.

Now earl of Dorset.[8]

F, Sackvile, all that have the power to do
Great and good turns, as well could time
them too,
And knew their how, and where; we should
have then
Less list of proud, hard, or ungrateful men.

---

[8] *An Epistle to sir* Edward Sackvile.]   At that time lord chamberlain; he succeeded his father, Thomas Sackvile, in the title of
earl of Dorset, who died suddenly at the council-table in 1608.
                                                        Whal.
We have here a cluster of mistakes. The father of sir Edward
Sackvile was not Thomas, but Robert, second earl of Dorset, his
son; nor did Edward succeed his father, but his elder brother
Richard, third earl of Dorset, who died in 1624. What Whalley
means by *at that time lord chamberlain*, it is difficult to say.   There
is no allusion to any such office in the poem, nor could there be,
for the earl of Dorset was not made chamberlain till 1642, five
years after the poet's death.
   This sir Edward Sackvile is the person who engaged in that
ferocious and fatal duel with the lord Bruce, of which the interesting account given by himself was copied into the *Guardian*, from
the MS. in the library of Queen's College, Oxford.
   This affair took place in 1613, when he was only three and
twenty. Afterwards, however, he nobly redeemed his extrava-
gancies, and became one of the brightest characters of his day.
Lord Clarendon says that "his person was beautiful, graceful, and
vigorous; his wit pleasant, sparkling, and sublime, and his other
parts of learning and language of that lustre, that he could not
miscarry in the world."
   This "Epistle" was the favourite poem of Horne Tooke. He
had it by heart, and delighted to quote it on all occasions. Its
date may be pretty nearly ascertained by the expression "*now* earl
of Dorset," which seems to imply that sir Edward had not long
enjoyed the title. He returned to England, from Italy, on hearing
of the death of his brother, which took place the 28th of March,

For benefits are ow'd with the same mind
As they are done, and such returns they find :
You then, whose will not only, but desire
To succour my necessities, took fire,
Not at my prayers, but your sense ; which laid
The way to meet what others would upbraid,
And in the act did so my blush prevent,
As I did feel it done, as soon as meant ;
You cannot doubt, but I who freely know
This good from you, as freely will it owe ;
And though my fortune humble me, to take
The smallest courtesies with thanks, I make
Yet choice from whom I take them ; and would shame
To have such do me good, I durst not name.
They are the noblest benefits, and sink
Deepest in man, of which, when he doth think,
The memory delights him more, from whom
Than what, he hath receiv'd.   Gifts stink from some,
They are so long a coming, and so hard ;
Where any deed is forced, the grace is marr'd.
    Can I owe thanks for courtesies received
Against his will that does them ? that hath weaved
Excuses or delays ? or done them scant,
That they have more opprest me than my want ?
Or if he did it not to succour me,
But by mere chance ? for interest ? or to free
Himself of farther trouble, or the weight
Of pressure, like one taken in a strait ?
All this corrupts the thanks : less hath he won,
That puts it in his debt-book ere't be done ;
Or that doth sound a trumpet, and doth call
His grooms to witness : or else lets it fall

1624 : and the poet probably addressed him soon after 1625, when
sickness and want first assailed him.
    There is great vigour of thought, and strength of expression, in
this rough epistle.   The predilection of Horne Tooke for it throws
no discredit on his judgment.

In that proud manner, as a good so gain'd,
Must make me sad for what I have obtain'd.
   No! gifts and thanks should have one cheerful
      face,
So each that's done, and ta'en, becomes a brace.
He neither gives, or does, that doth delay
A benefit, or that doth throw't away;
No more than he doth thank, that will receive
Nought but in corners, and is loth to leave
Least air, or print, but flies it: such men would
Run from the conscience of it, if they could.
   As I have seen some infants of the sword
Well known, and practised borrowers on their word,
Give thanks by stealth, and whispering in the ear,
For what they straight would to the world for-
      swear;
And speaking worst of those, from whom they
      went
But then fist-fill'd, to put me off the scent.
Now, d—n me, sir, if you shall not command
My sword, ('tis but a poor sword, understand,)
As far as any poor sword in the land;
Then turning unto him is next at hand,
Damns whom he damn'd too, is the veriest gull,
Has feathers, and will serve a man to pull.
   Are they not worthy to be answer'd so,
That to such natures let their full hands flow,
And seek no wants to succour; but enquire,
Like money-brokers, after names, and hire
Their bounties forth, to him that last was made,
Or stands to be in commission o' the blade?
Still, still the hunters of false fame apply
Their thoughts and means to making loud the cry,
But one is bitten by the dog he fed,
And hurt, seeks cure; the surgeon bids take bread,
And sponge-like with it dry up the blood quite,
Then give it to the hound that did him bite:

Pardon, says he, that were a way to see
All the town curs take each their snatch at me.[9]
O, is it so ? knows he so much, and will
Feed those at whom the table points at still ?
I not deny it, but to help the need
Of any, is a great and generous deed ;
Yea, of the ingrateful ; and he forth must tell
Many a pound, and piece, will place one well.
But these men ever want : their very trade
Is borrowing ; that but stopt, they do invade
All as their prize, turn pirates here at land,
Have their Bermudas, and their Streights i' the
          Strand :
Man out their boats to the Temple, and not shift
Now, but command ; make tribute what was gift ;
And it is paid them with a trembling zeal,
And superstition, I dare scarce reveal,
If it were clear ; but being so in cloud
Carried and wrapt, I only am allow'd
My wonder, why the taking a clown's purse,
Or robbing the poor market-folks, should nurse
Such a religious horror in the breasts
Of our town-gallantry ! or why there rests
Such worship due to kicking of a punk,
Or swaggering with the watch, or drawer drunk ;
Or feats of darkness acted in mid-sun,
And told of with more license than they're done !
Sure there is mystery in it I not know,
That men such reverence to such actions show,
And almost deify the authors ! make
Loud sacrifice of drink, for their health's sake :
Rear suppers in their names, and spend whole nights
Unto their praise in certain swearing rites !

---

[9] *Pardon, says he, that were a way to see*
   All the town-curs take each their snatch at me.] The allusion is
to a fable of *Phædrus*, who makes Æsop the author of it. WHAL.
   For the *Bermudas*, &c. see vol. iv. p. 407.

Cannot a man be reckoned in the state
Of valour, but at this idolatrous rate ?
I thought that fortitude had been a mean[1]
'Twixt fear and rashness; not a lust obscene,
Or appetite of offending, but a skill,
Or science of discerning good and ill.
And you, sir, know it well, to whom I write,
That with these mixtures we put out her light;
Her ends are honesty, and public good :
And where they want, she is not understood.
No more are these of us; let them then go,
I have the list of mine own faults to know,
Look to, and cure : he's not a man hath none,
But like to be, that every day mends one,
And feels it; else he tarries by the beast.
Can I discern how shadows are decreast,
Or grown, by height or lowness of the sun,
And can I less of substance ? when I run,
Ride, sail, am coach'd, know I how far I have
      gone ;
And my mind's motion not ? or have I none?
No! he must feel and know, that will advance.
Men have been great, but never good by chance,
Or on the sudden.   It were strange that he
Who was this morning such a one, should be
Sydney ere night ! or that did go to bed
Coryat, should rise the most sufficient head
Of Christendom ; and neither of these know,
Were the rack offer'd them, how they came so !

[1] *I thought that fortitude had been a mean, &c.*] This subject
the poet subsequently dilated upon in the *New Inn.* The name
of this unfortunate piece is never mentioned now without a scornful sneer at the dotage which produced it. As a whole, indeed,
much cannot be said in its favour, but it may safely be pronounced
that the observations of Lovel on *true valour* (vol. v. pp. 386-392,) to
which the line just quoted has been referred, will not be easily
paralleled for justness of thought, vigour of sentiment, and beauty
of expression, in this or any other language.

'Tis by degrees that men arrive at glad
Profit in aught ; each day some little add,
In time 'twill be a heap : this is not true
Alone in money, but in manners too.
Yet we must more than move still, or go on,
We must accomplish : 'tis the last key-stone
That makes the arch ; the rest that there were put
Are nothing till that comes to bind and shut.
Then stands it a triumphal mark ! then men
Observe the strength, the height, the why, and when
It was erected : and still walking under,
Meet some new matter to look up and wonder !
Such notes are virtuous men ! they live as fast
As they are high ; are rooted, and will last.
They need no stilts, nor rise upon their toes,
As if they would belie their stature ; those
Are dwarfs of honour, and have neither weight
Nor fashion ; if they chance aspire to height,
'Tis like light canes, that first rise big and brave,
Shoot forth in smooth and comely spaces ; have
But few and fair divisions : but being got
Aloft, grow less and straighten'd ; full of knot,
And last, go out in nothing ! you that see
Their difference, cannot choose which you will be.
You know (without my flattering you) too much
For me to be your indice.   Keep you such,
That I may love your person, as I do,
Without your gift, though I can rate that too,
By thanking thus the courtesy to life,
Which you will bury ; but therein, the strife
May grow so great to be example, when,
As their true rule or lesson, either men,
Donors or donees, to their practice shall
Find you to reckon nothing, me owe all.

XXXI.

An Epistle to Master John Selden.[2]

KNOW to whom I write; here, I am sure,
.Though I be short, I cannot be obscure :[3]
Less shall I for the art or dressing care,
Truth and the Graces best when naked are.
Your book, my Selden, I have read; and much
Was trusted, that you thought my judgment such
To ask it : though, in most of works, it be
A penance where a man may not be free,
Rather than office ; when it doth, or may
Chance, that the friend's affection proves allay
Unto the censure. Your's all need doth fly
Of this so vicious humanity ;
Than which, there is not unto study a more
Pernicious enemy. We see before

---

[2] This Epistle, as the folio calls it, is prefixed to the first edition
of Selden's *Titles of Honour*, 1614, with this address : "Ben Jonson
to his honoured friend, master John Selden."
There was an extraordinary degree of kindness between these
two most learned men, which continued to the end of Jonson's life.
They communicated their works, and mutually assisted each other.
Selden, who was above flattery, affectionately addresses our author
in the work here mentioned, as one that was

> ———— *omnia carmina doctus,*
> *Et callet mythων plasmata, et historiam.*

And he, who was superior to envy, speaks with conscious pride of
the aid which he derived from Selden's unbounded acquaintance
with literary subjects.
Selden's life was useful, and his death instructive. He was
drawn in by the crooked politics of the times in which he lived ;
but he escaped from them to his studies, at every convenient opportunity ; and though he might be sometimes dissatisfied, he was
never factious.
[3] *Though I be short, &c.*]

> ———— *brevis esse laboro,*
> *Obscurus fio.*

A many' of books, even good judgments wound
Themselves, through favouring that is there not
         found ;
But I to your's far otherwise shall do,
Not fly the crime, but the suspicion too :
Though I confess (as every muse hath err'd,
And mine not least) I have too oft preferr'd
Men past their terms, and prais'd some names too
         much ;
But 'twas with purpose to have made them such.
Since, being deceiv'd, I turn a sharper eye
Upon myself, and ask to whom, and why,
And what I write ? and vex it many days
Before men get a verse, much less a praise ;
So that my reader is assured, I now
Mean what I speak, and still will keep that vow.
Stand forth my object, then.   You that have been
Ever at home, yet have all countries seen ;
And like a compass, keeping one foot still
Upon your centre, do your circle fill
Of general knowledge ; watch'd men, manners too,
Heard what times past have said, seen what ours do!
Which grace shall I make love to first ? your skill,
Or faith in things ? or is't your wealth and will
T' inform and teach ? or your unwearied pain
Of gathering ? bounty in pouring out again ?
What fables have you vex'd, what truth redeem'd,
Antiquities search'd, opinions disesteem'd,
Impostures branded, and authorities urg'd !
What blots and errors have you watch'd and purg'd
Records and authors of ! how rectified
Times, manners, customs ! innovations spied !
Sought out the fountains, sources, creeks, paths,
         ways,
And noted the beginnings and decays !
Where is that nominal mark, or real rite,
Form, act, or ensign, that hath scaped your sight ?

How are traditions there examin'd ! how
Conjectures retriev'd ! and a story now
And then of times (besides the bare condúct
Of what it tells us) weav'd in to instruct !
I wonder'd at the richness, but am lost,
To see the workmanship so' exceed the cost !
To mark the excellent seasoning of your style,
And manly elocution ! not one while
With horror rough, then rioting with wit;
But to the subject still the colours fit,
In sharpness of all search, wisdom of choice,
Newness of sense, antiquity of voice !
    I yield, I yield.   The matter of your praise
Flows in upon me, and I cannot raise
A bank against it : nothing but the round
Large clasp of Nature such a wit can bound.
Monarch in letters ! 'mongst the Titles shown
Of others honours, thus enjoy thy own.
I first salute thee so ; and gratulate
With that thy style, thy keeping of thy state ;
In offering this thy work to no great name,
That would, perhaps, have praised and thank'd the
        same,
But nought beyond.   He, thou hast given it to,[4]
Thy learned chamber-fellow, knows to do
It true respects : he will not only love,
Embrace, and cherish ; but he can approve
And estimate thy pains, as having wrought
In the same mines of knowledge ; and thence brought
Humanity enough to be a friend,
And strength to be a champion, and defend
Thy gift 'gainst envy.   O how I do count
Among my comings in, and see it mount,

---

[4]   *He, thou hast given it to,*
    Thy learned chamber-fellow, &c.]   The volume is dedicated by
Selden to " my most beloved friend, and *chamber-fellow*, Edward
Heyward, of Cardeston, in Norfolk, Esq."

8   A A

The gain of two such friendships! Heyward and
Selden! two names that so much understand!
On whom I could take up, and ne'er abuse
The credit, that would furnish a tenth muse!
But here's no time nor place my wealth to tell,
You both are modest. So am I. Farewell.

XXXII.

An Epistle to a Friend,

(MASTER COLBY,)

TO PERSUADE HIM TO THE WARS.

WAKE, friend, from forth thy lethargy! the
            drum
        Beats brave and loud in Europe, and bids
            come
All that dare rouse : or are not loth to quit
Their vicious ease, and be o'erwhelm'd with it.
It is a call to keep the spirits alive
That gasp for action, and would yet revive
Man's buried honour, in his sleepy life :
Quickning dead nature to her noblest strife.
All other acts of worldlings are but toil
In dreams, begun in hope, and end in spoil.
Look on the ambitious man, and see him nurse
His unjust hopes with praises begg'd, or, worse,
Bought flatteries, the issue of his purse,
Till he become both their and his own curse!
Look on the false and cunning man, that loves
No person, nor is loved : what ways he proves
To gain upon his belly ; and at last
Crush'd in the snaky brakes that he had past !
See the grave, sour, and supercilious sir,
In outward face, but inward, light as fur,

Or feathers, lay his fortune out to show,
Till envy wound or maim it at a blow!
See him that's call'd, and thought the happiest man,
Honour'd at once, and envied (if it can
Be honour is so mix'd) by such as would
For all their spite, be like him, if they could :
No part or corner man can look upon,
But there are objects bid him to be gone
As far as he can fly, or follow day,
Rather than here so bogg'd in vices stay.
The whole world here leaven'd with madness
      swells ;
And being a thing blown out of nought, rebels
Against his Maker, high alone with weeds,
And impious rankness of all sects and seeds :
Not to be check'd or frighted now with fate,
But more licentious made and desperate !
Our delicacies are grown capital,
And even our sports are dangers ! what we call
Friendship, is now mask'd hatred ! justice fled,
And shamefac'dness together ! all laws dead
That kept man living ! pleasures only sought !
Honour and honesty, as poor things thought
As they are made ! pride and stiff clownage mix'd
To make up greatness ! and man's whole good fix'd
In bravery, or gluttony, or coin,
All which he makes the servants of the groin !
Thither it flows : how much did Stallion spend
To have his court-bred filly there commend
His lace and starch ; and fall upon her back
In admiration, stretch'd upon the rack
Of lust, to his rich suit, and title, Lord ?
Ay, that's a charm and half ! she must afford
That all respect, she must lie down ; nay, more,
'Tis there civility to be a whore :
He's one of blood and fashion ! and with these
The bravery makes she can no honour leese :

To do't with cloth, or stuffs, lust's name might
    merit,
With velvet, plush, and tissues, it is spirit.
  O these so ignorant monsters, light, as proud !
Who can behold their manners, and not cloud-
Like, on them lighten ?   If that nature could
Not make a verse,[5] anger or laughter would,
To see them aye discoursing with their glass,
How they may make some one that day an ass,
Planting their purls, and curls, spread forth like net,
And every dressing for a pit-fall set
To catch the flesh in, and to pound a ——
Be at their visits, see them squeamish, sick,
Ready to cast at one whose band sits ill,
And then leap mad on a neat picardill,
As if a brize were gotten in their tail ;
And firk, and jerk, and for the coachman rail,
And jealous each of other, yet think long
To be abroad chanting some bawdy song,
And laugh, and measure thighs, then squeak, spring,
    itch,
Do all the tricks of a salt lady bitch !
For t'other pound of sweetmeats, he shall feel
That pays, or what he will : the dame is steel.
For these with her young company she'll enter,
Where Pitts, or Wright, or Modet would not venture ;

---

[5] —————— *If that nature could*
   Not make a verse, &c.]   This epistle, which possesses no
ordinary degree of merit, partakes of the nature of satire.   The
author had his favourite, Horace, in view, when he drew it up,
though the particular allusion in the quotation is to Juvenal :

        Si natura negat, facit indignatio versum.

The couplet just above,
   To do't with cloth, &c. is also from this author, but in a higher
tone :

        —————— *alea turpis*
  Turpe et adulterium mediocribus, hæc eadem illi
  Omnia cum faciant nitidi hilaresque vocantur.   Sat. xi.

And comes by these degrees the style t'inherit
Of woman of fashion, and a lady of spirit.
Nor is the title question'd with our proud,
Great, brave, and fashion'd folk, these are allow'd ;
Adulteries now are not so hid, or strange,
They're grown commodity upon Exchange :
He that will follow but another's wife,
Is loved, though he let out his own for life ;
The husband now's call'd churlish, or a poor
Nature, that will not let his wife be a whore ;
Or use all arts, or haunt all companies
That may corrupt her, even in his eyes.
The brother trades a sister, and the friend
Lives to the lord, but to the lady's end.
Less must not be thought on than mistress ; or
If it be thought, kill'd like her embrions ; for
Whom no great mistress hath as yet infám'd
A fellow of coarse letchery, is nam'd,
The servant of the serving-woman, in scorn,
Ne'er came to taste the plenteous marriage-horn.
    Thus they do talk.   And are these objects fit
For man so spend his money on ? his wit ?
His time, health, soul ?   Will he for these go throw
Those thousands on his back, shall after blow
His body to the Counters, or the Fleet ?
Is it for these that Fine-man meets the street
Coach'd, or on foot-cloth, thrice chang'd every day,
To teach each suit he has, the ready way
From Hyde-park to the stage, where at the last
His dear and borrow'd bravery he must cast ?
When not his combs, his curling-irons, his glass,
Sweet bags, sweet powders, nor sweet words will
        pass
For less security.   O heavens ! for these
Is it that man pulls on himself disease,
Surfeit, and quarrel ? drinks the t'other health ?
Or by damnation voids it, or by stealth ?

What fury of late is crept into our feasts?
What honour given to the drunkenest guests?
What reputation to bear one glass more,
When oft the bearer is born out of door?
This hath our ill-us'd freedom, and soft peace
Brought on us, and will every hour increase.
Our vices do not tarry in a place,
But being in motion still, or rather in race,
Tilt one upon another, and now bear
This way, now that, as if their number were
More than themselves, or than our lives could take,
But both fell prest under the load they make.
 I'll bid thee look no more, but flee, flee, friend,
This precipice, and rocks that have no end,
Or side, but threatens ruin.   The whole day
Is not enough, now, but the nights to play:
And whilst our states, strength, body, and mind we
  waste,
Go make ourselves the usurers at a cast.
He that no more for age, cramps, palsies can
Now use the bones, we see doth hire a man
To take the box up for him; and pursues
The dice with glassen eyes, to the glad views
Of what he throws: like letchers grown content
To be beholders, when their powers are spent.
 Can we not leave this worm? or will we not?
Is that the truer excuse? or have we got
In this, and like, an itch of vanity,
That scratching now's our best felicity?
Well, let it go.   Yet this is better, then
To lose the forms and dignities of men,
To flatter my good lord, and cry his bowl
Runs sweetly, as it had his lordship's soul:
Although, perhaps it has, what's that to me,
That may stand by, and hold my peace? will he,
When I am hoarse with praising his each cast,
Give me but that again, that I must waste

In sugar candied, or in butter'd beer,
For the recovery of my voice?   No, there
Pardon his lordship; flatt'ry's grown so cheap
With him, for he is followed with that heap,
That watch and catch, at what they may applaud,
As a poor single flatterer, without bawd
Is nothing, such scarce meat and drink he'll give
But he that's both, and slave to both, shall live,
And be belov'd, while the whores last.   O times!
Friend, fly from hence, and let these kindled rhymes
Light thee from hell on earth; where flatterers, spies,
Informers, masters both of arts and lies;
Lewd slanderers, soft whisperers, that let blood
The life, and fame-veins, yet not understood
Of the poor sufferers; where the envious, proud,
Ambitious, factious, superstitious, loud
Boasters, and perjur'd, with the infinite more
Prevaricators swarm: of which the store
(Because they're every where amongst mankind
Spread through the world) is easier far to find,
Than once to number, or bring forth to hand,
Though thou wert Muster-master of the land.
   Go, quit them all! And take along with thee,
Thy true friend's wishes, Colby,[6] which shall be,
That thine be just and honest, that thy deeds
Not wound thy conscience, when thy body bleeds;
That thou dost all things more for truth than glory,
And never but for doing wrong be sorry;
That by commanding first thyself, thou mak'st
Thy person fit for any charge thou tak'st:
That fortune never make thee to complain,
But what she gives, thou dar'st give her again;

---

[6] ———— *And take along with thee*
   Thy true friend's wishes, Colby.]   The name of the person to
whom this epistle is addressed; he appears to have been in the
military service, and from the preceding line, was probably muster-
master of the forces. WHAL.

That whatsoever face thy fate puts on,
Thou shrink or start not; but be always one;
That thou think nothing great but what is good;
And from that thought strive to be understood.
So, 'live or dead, thou wilt preserve a fame
Still precious with the odour of thy name.
And last, blaspheme not; we did never hear
Man thought the valianter, 'cause he durst swear;
No more, than we should think a lord had had
More honour in him, 'cause we've known him mad:
These take, and now go seek thy peace in war,
Who falls for love of God, shall rise a star.

XXXIII.

An Epitaph on master Philip Gray.

EADER, stay,
    And if I had no more to say,
    But here doth lie, till the last day,
    All that is left of Philip Gray,
It might thy patience richly pay:
    For if such men as he could die,[7]
    What surety' of life have thou and I?

---

[7] *For if such men, &c.*] The force of this Epitaph is not felt, for want of knowing the character whose fate led to these reflections.

Chetwood has an Epitaph on prince Henry, which he ascribes to Jonson, and which the reader may perhaps expect to find in a collection of his works. I have little confidence in this writer, who seldom mentions his authorities; and, to say the truth, can discover nothing of our author's manner in the composition itself, which appears to be patched up from different poems, and is therefore omitted; though I have thought it right to mention the circumstance.

XXXIV.

EPISTLE TO A FRIEND.

HEY are not, sir, worst owers that do pay
.Debts when they can : good men may break
their day,
And yet the noble nature never grudge ;
'Tis then a crime, when the usurer is judge,
And he is not in friendship : nothing there
Is done for gain ; if't be, 'tis not sincere.
Nor should I at this time protested be,
But that some greater names have broke with me,
And their words too, where I but break my band ;[B]
I add that BUT, because I understand
That as the lesser breach : for he that takes
Simply my band, his trust in me forsakes,
And looks unto the forfeit.   If you be
Now so much friend, as you would trust in me,
Venture a longer time, and willingly :
All is not barren land doth fallow lie ;
Some grounds are made the richer for the rest ;
And I will bring a crop, if not the best.

XXXV.

AN ELEGY.

AN beauty, that did prompt me first to write,
Now threaten, with those means she did
invite ?
Did her perfections call me on to gaze,
Then like, then love ; and now would they amaze !

[B] Where *I but break my band,*] i. e. *whereas,* in the old sense of
the word.   Jonson pleads his cause well ; and probably kept his
word (if it was taken) better than his bond.

Or was she gracious afar off, but near
A terror ? or is all this but my fear ?
That as the water makes things, put in't strait,
Crooked appear ; so that doth my conceit :
I can help that with boldness ; and Love sware,[9]
And Fortune once, t'assist the spirits that dare.
But which shall lead me on ? both these are blind.
Such guides men use not, who their way would
    find,
Except the way be error to those ends ;
And then the best are still the blindest friends.
Oh how a lover may mistake ! to think
Or Love, or Fortune blind, when they but wink
To see men fear ; or else for truth and state,
Because they would free justice imitate,
Vail their own eyes, and would impartially
Be brought by us to meet our destiny.
If it be thus ; come Love, and Fortune go,
I'll lead you on ; or if my fate will so,
That I must send one first, my choice assigns
Love to my heart, and Fortune to my lines.

XXXVI.

An Elegy.

BY those bright eyes, at whose immortal fires
    Love lights his torches to inflame desires ;
    By that fair stand, your forehead, whence
        he bends
His double bow, and round his arrows sends ;
By that tall grove, your hair, whose globy rings
He flying curls, and crispeth with his wings ;

   [9] *And Love* sware.] He alludes to the two proverbs, *Faint
heart, &c.* and *Fortes Fortuna juvat.*

By those pure baths your either cheek discloses,
Where he doth steep himself in milk and roses ;[1]
And lastly, by your lips, the bank of kisses,
Where men at once may plant and gather blisses :
Tell me, my lov'd friend, do you love or no ?
So well as I may tell in verse, 'tis so ?
You blush, but do not :—friends are either none,
Though they may number bodies, or but one.
I'll therefore ask no more, but bid you love,
And so that either may example prove
Unto the other ; and live patterns, how
Others, in time, may love as we do now.
Slip no occasion ; as time stands not still,
I know no beauty, nor no youth that will.
To use the present, then, is not abuse,
You have a husband is the just excuse
Of all that can be done him ; such a one
As would make shift to make himself alone
That which we can ; who both in you, his wife,
His issue, and all circumstance of life,
As in his place, because he would not vary,
Is constant to be extraordinary.

[1] *By those pure baths your either cheek discloses,*
   Where he doth steep himself in milk and roses.] Though no
date is prefixed to this Elegy, it was written before the celebration
of *Charis;* for in the fifth ode there is an allusion to these and the
following verses :

   " ——— ——— And see !
   Such my mother's blushes be
   As the bath your verse discloses
   In her cheeks of milk and roses," &c.   WHAL.

This is a curious mode of settling precedency ; but it shall be as
Whalley pleases. This little piece begins much better than it
ends.

XXXVII.

A Satirical Shrub.[2]

WOMAN'S friendship! God, whom I
    trust in,
Forgive me this one foolish deadly sin,
    Amongst my many other, that I may
No more, I am sorry for so fond cause, say
At fifty years, almost, to value it,
That ne'er was known to last above a fit!
Or have the least of good, but what it must
Put on for fashion, and take up on trust.
Knew I all this afore? had I perceiv'd,
That their whole life was wickedness, though weav'd
Of many colours; outward, fresh from spots,
But their whole inside full of ends, and knots?
Knew I that all their dialogues and discourse
Were such as I will now relate, or worse?

   *   *   *   *   *   *   *[3]
   *   *   *   *   *   *   *

Knew I this woman? yes, and you do see,
How penitent I am, or I should be.
Do not you ask to know her, she is worse
Than all ingredients made into one curse,
And that pour'd out upon mankind, can be:
Think but the sin of all her sex, 'tis she!
I could forgive her being proud! a whore!
Perjur'd! and painted! if she were no more—
But she is such, as she might yet forestall
The devil, and be the damning of us all.

   [2] This is more in the style and manner of Donne than of our
author. It may, however, be his; though I suspect that the loose
scraps found after his death, among his papers, were committed to
the press without much examination. There was undoubtedly an
intercommunity of verse between the two friends; but I do not
wish to carry the argument any further.
   [3] Here (the folio says) something is wanting.

XXXVIII.

A LITTLE SHRUB GROWING BY.

ASK not to know this Man.[4] If fame should speak
His name in any metal, it would break.
   Two letters were enough the plague to tear
Out of his grave, and poison every ear.
A parcel of Court-dirt, a heap, and mass
Of all vice hurl'd together, there he was,
Proud, false, and treacherous, vindictive, all
That thought can add, unthankful, the lay-stall
Of putrid flesh alive! of blood the sink!
·And so I leave to stir him, lest he stink.

XXXIX.

AN ELEGY.

THOUGH beauty be the mark of praise,
   And yours of whom I sing, be such,
   As not the world can praise too much,
Yet 'tis your virtue now I raise.

A virtue, like allay, so gone
   Throughout your form ; as though that move,
   And draw, and conquer all men's love,
This subjects you to love of one,

Wherein you triumph yet ; because
   'Tis of yourself, and that you use
   The noblest freedom, not to choose
Against or faith, or honour's laws.

[4] *Ask not to know this Man, &c.*] This too is in the style of
Donne. It was evidently designed to be a *pendant* of the former ;
whoever wrote that wrote this.

But who could less expect from you,
  In whom alone Love lives agen ?
  By whom he is restor'd to men ;
And kept, and bred, and brought up true ?

His falling temples you have rear'd,
  The wither'd garlands ta'en away ;
  His altars kept from the decay
That envy wish'd, and nature fear'd :

And on them burn so chaste a flame,
  With so much loyalty's expense,
  As Love t' acquit such excellence,
Is gone himself into your name.

And you are he ; the deity
  To whom all lovers are design'd,
  That would their better objects find ;
Among which faithful troop am I.

Who, as an offering at your shrine,[5]
  Have sung this hymn, and here entreat
  One spark of your diviner heat
To light upon a love of mine.

Which, if it kindle not, but scant
  Appear, and that to shortest view,
  Yet give me leave t' adore in you
What I, in her, am grieved to want.

---

[5] *Who, as an* offering, *&c.*] The folio reads *offspring.* Corrected by Whalley.

XL.

An Elegy.[6]

FAIR friend, 'tis true, your beauties move
  My heart to a respect;
Too little to be paid with love,
  Too great for your neglect.

I neither love, nor yet am free,
  For though the flame I find
Be not intense in the degree,
  'Tis of the purest kind.

It little wants of love but pain;
  Your beauty takes my sense,
And lest you should that price disdain,
  My thoughts too feel the influence.

'Tis not a passion's first access
  Ready to multiply;
But like love's calmest state it is
  Possest with victory.

It is like love to truth reduc'd,
  All the false values gone,
Which were created, and induc'd
  By fond imagination.

'Tis either fancy or 'tis fate,
  To love you more than I:
I love you at your beauty's rate,
  Less were an injury.

Like unstampt gold, I weigh each grace,
  So that you may collect
Th' intrinsic value of your face,
  Safely from my respect.

[6] This little piece, which is not without merit, is carelessly thrown in towards the conclusion of the old folio, where it is united to " A New-year's Gift to king Charles ! "

And this respect would merit love,
        Were not so fair a sight
Payment enough ; for who dares move
        Reward for his delight ?

                    XLI.

                AN ODE.

                To HIMSELF.

WHERE dost Thou careless lie
        Buried in ease and sloth ?
    Knowledge, that sleeps, doth die ;
        And this security,
    It is the common moth,
That eats on wits and arts, and [so] destroys them
        both :[7]

Are all the Aonian springs
    Dried up ? lies Thespia waste ?
Doth Clarius' harp want strings,
That not a nymph now sings ;
    Or droop they as disgrac'd,
To see their seats and bowers by chattering pies
    defac'd ?

If hence thy silence be,
    As 'tis too just a cause ;
Let this thought quicken thee :
Minds that are great and free
    Should not on fortune pause,
'Tis crown enough to virtue still, her own applause.

    [7] *That eats on wits and arts, and destroys them both.*]   A syllable
is evidently lost, necessary to complete the measure; I have inserted a monosyllable that helps it out,
                    Versus fultura cadentis.   WHAL.
    Whalley's choice fell on *quite;* I prefer *so :* the reader, perhaps,
may stumble upon a better substitute than either.

What though the greedy fry
  Be taken with false baits
Of worded balladry,
And think it poesy ?
  They die with their conceits,
And only piteous scorn upon their folly waits.

Then take in hand thy lyre,
  Strike in thy proper strain,
With Japhet's line, aspire
Sol's chariot for new fire,[8]
  To give the world again :
Who aided him, will thee, the issue of Jove's brain.

And since our dainty age
  Cannot indure reproof,
Make not thyself a page,
  To that strumpet the stage,
But sing high and aloof,
Safe from the wolf's black jaw, and the dull ass's hoof.

[8] *With* Japhet's *line aspire*
  Sol's chariot for new fire.] He means *Prometheus*, the son of
Japetus, who, as the poets say, was assisted by *Minerva*, in the for-
mation of his man, whom he animated with fire taken from the
chariot of the Sun. WHAL.

'This spirited Ode was probably among our author's early performances. A part of the concluding stanza we have already had
in the "Apologetical Dialogue" at the conclusion of the *Poetaster ;*
and the whole might be written about the period of the appearance
of that drama. Jonson's dislike to the stage here breaks out :—
but, in truth, this is not the only passage from which we are
authorized to collect that necessity alone led him to write for the
theatres.

XLII.

THE MIND OF THE FRONTISPIECE TO A BOOK.[9]

ROM death and dark oblivion (near the same)
    The mistress of man's life, grave History,
    Raising the world to good and evil fame
    Doth vindicate it to eternity.
Wise Providence would so : that nor the good
    Might be defrauded, nor the great secured,
But both might know their ways were understood,
    When vice alike in time with virtue dured :
Which makes that, lighted by the beamy hand
    Of Truth, that searcheth the most hidden springs,
And guided by Experience, whose straight wand
    Doth mete, whose line doth sound the depth of
        things ;
She cheerfully supporteth what she rears,
    Assisted by no strengths but are her own,
Some note of which each varied pillar bears,
    By which, as proper titles, she is known
Time's witness, herald of Antiquity,
The light of Truth, and life of Memory.

---

[9] These lines are prefixed to sir Walter Raleigh's *History of the World*, fol. 1614: they are descriptive of the ornamental figures in the serious frontispiece to that volume, and can scarcely be understood without a reference to the plate itself. Jonson assisted Raleigh in this great work ; and, indeed, there were not many literary undertakings of importance, in his days, to which " the envious Ben " did not liberally afford his aid.

The folio has been corrected from Raleigh's copy. It seems that Whalley was not acquainted with the purport of this little piece, or with its appearance in any volume previously to that of 1641.

XLIII.

AN ODE

To James earl of Desmond.[1]

WHERE art thou, Genius ? I should use
    Thy present aid : arise Invention,
    Wake, and put on the wings of Pindar's
        Muse,
    To tower with my intention
High as his mind, that doth advance
Her upright head, above the reach of chance,
        Or the times envý.
        Cynthius, I apply
My bolder numbers to thy golden lyre :
        O then inspire
Thy priest in this strange rapture ! heat my brain
        With Delphic fire,
That I may sing my thoughts in some unvulgar strain.

[1] One of our author's earliest pieces. " It was written," (the
folio says,) "in queen Elizabeth's time, since lost, and recovered."
    This earl was, I believe, the son of Gerald, sixteenth earl of Des-
mond, a most powerful nobleman, and a formidable rebel, who
gave Elizabeth a world of uneasiness. He was, however, mastered
at length, and his vast possessions, which extended over several
counties, were in 1582 forfeited to the crown. His son James, the
person, I presume, to whom this ode was addressed, was restored
in blood and honour in 1600. From the allusions to his state of
disfavour, and the call upon him to continue in his loyalty, and
wait the reward of his virtue, the poem must have been written
before that period. There is something prophetic in the last
stanza :

                " If I auspiciously divine,
        As my hope tells—then our fair Phœbe's shine
                Shall light those places
                With lustrous graces
        Where darkness, with her gloomy-scepter'd hand,
                Doth now command."

Rich beam of honour, shed your light
   On these dark rhymes, that my affection
May shine, through every chink, to every sight,
         Graced by your reflection !
   Then shall my verses, like strong charms,
Break the knit circle of her stony arms,
            That holds your spirit,
            And keeps your merit
Lock'd in her cold embraces, from the view
            Of eyes more true,
Who would with judgment search, searching con-
   clude,
            As prov'd in you,
True noblêsse.   Palm grows straight, though handled
   ne'er so rude.

         Nor think yourself unfortunate ;
         If subject to the jealous errors
Of politic pretext, that wries a state,
         Sink not beneath these terrors :
         But whisper, O glad innocence,
Where only a man's birth is his offence ;
            Or the disfavour
            Of such as savour
Nothing, but practise upon honour's thrall.
         O virtue's fall !
When her dead essence, like the anatomy
            In Surgeons' hall,
Is but a statist's theme to read phlebotomy.

      Let Brontes, and black Steropes,
         Sweat at the forge, their hammers beating ;
Pyracmon's hour will come to give them ease,
         Though but while the metal's heating :
         And, after all the Ætnæan ire,
Gold, that is perfect, will outlive the fire.
            For fury wasteth,
            As patience lasteth.

No armour to the mind ! he is shot-free
      From injury,
That is not hurt ; not he, that is not hit ;
      So fools, we see,
Oft scape an imputation, more through luck than wit.

    But to yourself, most loyal lord,
    (Whose heart in that bright sphere flames
      clearest,
Though many gems be in your bosom stor'd,
      Unknown which is the dearest.)
      If I auspiciously divine,
As my hope tells, that our fair Phœbe's shine,[2]
      Shall light those places
      With lustrous graces,
Where darkness, with her gloomy scepter'd hand,
      Doth now command ;
O then, my best-best lov'd let me importune,
      That you will stand,
As far from all revolt, as you are now from fortune.

XLIV.

AN ODE.

HIGH-SPIRITED friend,
    I send nor balms, nor corsives to your
      wound ;
      Your faith hath found
A gentler, and more agile hand, to tend
The cure of that which is but corporal,
And doubtful days, which were nam'd critical,

---

[2] *Our fair* Phœbe's *shine.*] Whalley corrupted this into fair
Phœbus' shine. *Fair* is not the best epithet for the god ; but he
did not see the author's meaning, nor that the allusion was to " the
beautified " Elizabeth, who loved to be flattered with the appella
tion of *Phœbe* or *Diana.*

Have made their fairest flight,
  And now are out of sight.
Yet doth some wholsome physic for the mind,
  Wrapt in this paper lie,
Which in the taking if you misapply,
                You are unkind.

  Your covetous hand,
Happy in that fair honour it hath gain'd,
  Must now be rein'd.
True valour doth her own renown command
In one full action ; nor have you now more
To do, than be a husband of that store.
  Think but how dear you bought
  This same which you have caught,
Such thoughts will make you more in love with
    truth :
  'Tis wisdom, and that high,
For men to use their fortune reverently,
                Even in youth.

XLV.

AN ODE.

HELEN, did Homer never see
  Thy beauties, yet could write of thee ?
  Did Sappho, on her seven-tongued lute,
  So speak, as yet it is not mute,[3]
Of Phaon's form ? or doth the boy,
In whom Anacreon once did joy,

---

[3] —— *as yet it is not mute, &c.*] From Horace :
—————— *Spirat adhuc amor,*
  Vivuntque commissi calores
    Æoliæ fidibus puellæ.
  Nec si quid olim lusit Anacreon,
  Delevit ætas, &c.

Lie drawn to life in his soft verse,
As he whom Maro did rehearse ?
Was Lesbia sung by learn'd Catullus,
Or Delia's graces by Tibullus ?
Doth Cynthia, in Propertius' song,
Shine more than she the stars among ?
Is Horace his each love so high
Rapt from the earth, as not to die ;
With bright Lycoris, Gallus' choice,
Whose fame hath an eternal voice ?
Or hath Corinna, by the name
Her Ovid gave her, dimm'd the fame
Of Cæsar's daughter, and the line
Which all the world then styled divine ?
Hath Petrarch since his Laura raised
Equal with her ? or Ronsart praised
His new Cassandra 'bove the old,
Which all the fate of Troy foretold ?
Hath our great Sidney, Stella set
Where never star shone brighter yet ?
Or Constable's ambrosiac muse
Made Dian not his notes refuse ?[4]

[4] *Or* Constable's *ambrosiac muse*
Made Dian *not his notes refuse ?*] This author, though honour'd
with so ample a testimony from Jonson, is almost unknown in this
age. "*Henry Constable,*" in the words of Antony Wood, "was a
great master of the English tongue ; and there was no gentleman
of our nation who had a more pure, quick, and higher delivery of
conceit than he : witness, among all others, that sonnet of his before the poetical translation called the *Furies,* made by king James
the first of England, while he was king of the Scots. He hath also
several sonnets extant, written to sir Philip Sidney ; some of which
are set before the *Apology for Poetry,* written by the said knight."
This author flourished in the reign of queen Elizabeth. WHAL.
    Antony's taste in poetry was not very refined, and he did not
therefore discover that his author (Edmund Bolton) had unluckily
fixed upon one of Constable's worst sonnets. The *Diana* of which
Jonson speaks, was published in 1594. Constable seems to have
been the most voluminous sonnet-writer of those sonneteering times ;
and to have acquired a reputation rather more than equal to his

Have all these done—and yet I miss
The swan so relish'd Pancharis—[5]
And shall not I my Celia bring,
Where men may see whom I do sing ?
Though I, in working of my song,
Come short of all this learned throng,
Yet sure my tunes will be the best,
So much my subject drowns the rest.

XLVI.

A SONNET,

To the noble lady, the lady Mary Wroth.

THAT have been a lover, and could shew it,
Though not in these, in rhymes not wholly
    dumb,   .
    Since I exscribe your sonnets,[6] am become
A better lover, and much better poet.

merits : since, besides Jonson, he is mentioned with praise by
others of his contemporaries, and placed immediately after Spenser
by Judicio, in the *Return from Parnassus :*
> "Sweet Constable doth take the wondering ear,
>   And lays it up in willing prisonment."

  [5] *And yet I miss*
    The swan so relish'd Pancharis.] This was the French poet
Bonefons or *Bonefonius;* who, in imitation of Secundus, wrote *Basia,*
in the praise of his mistress Pancharis. He has a character for
tenderness and delicacy. Whal.

    [6] *Since I exscribe your sonnets, &c.*] The allusion is probably to
lady Wroth's *Urania,* a pastoral romance published in 1621. This,
in imitation of her uncle's (sir Philip Sidney's) *Arcadia,* is inter-
spersed with songs, sonnets, and other little pieces of poetry, which
our author, who seems to have been favoured with the MS., was
permitted to copy. The *Urania* has long been forgotten, and no
revolution in taste or manners can ever revive its memory ; yet it
was once in considerable vogue ; it did not, perhaps, like Tetra-
chordon, *number good intellects,* yet it certainly counted many bright

Nor is my Muse or I asham'd to owe it
To those true numerous graces, whereof some
But charm the senses, others overcome
Both brains and hearts; and mine now best do know it:
For in your verse all Cupid's armory,
   His flames, his shafts, his quiver, and his bow,
   His very eyes are yours to overthrow.
But then his mother's sweets you so apply,

eyes, among its admirers. The poetical part of *Urania* is rather above than below the usual standard of ladies' rhymes, and though the *chariest maid* of these times may read it without the smallest peril, (except of her patience) it was looked upon as inflammatory by the combustible damsels of James's days:

> " The lady Wroth's *Urania* is complete
> With elegancies; but *too full of heat*,"

sir Aston Cokayne says; and he was not singular in his opinion. The following sonnet may serve as a specimen of the poetry which our author *exscribed:* it is neither the best nor the worst of the collection:

SONNET.

" Late in the forest I did Cupid see,
   Cold, wet, and crying, he had lost his way;
   And being blind was farther like to stray:
Which sight a kind compassion bred in me.
I gently took and dried him, while that he,
   Poor child, complain'd he starved was with stay,
   And pined for want of his accustom'd prey;
For none in that wild place his host would be.
I glad was of his finding, thinking sure
This service should my freedom still procure;
   And to my breast I took him then unharm'd,
Carr'ing him safe unto a myrtle bower:
But in the way he made me feel his power,
   Burning my heart, who had him kindly warm'd."

Sir Robert Wroth, the husband of this celebrated lady, was also a poet: fortunately his genius was turned to wit, as hers to love; so that the respective pursuits of this tuneful pair did not clash, and the domestic harmony continued unbroken to the end:

> *Felices ter et amplius*
> *Quos irrupta tenet copula, nec malis*
>   *Divulsus querimoniis*
> *Suprema citius solvet amor die!*

Her joys, her smiles, her loves, as readers take
For Venus' ceston every line you make.

XLVII.

A FIT OF RHYME AGAINST RHYME.

RHYME, the rack of finest wits,
  That expresseth but by fits
      True conceit,
  Spoiling senses of their treasure,
Cozening judgment with a measure,
      But false weight;
Wresting words from their true calling;
Propping verse for fear of falling
      To the ground;
Jointing syllabes, drowning letters,
Fastening vowels, as with fetters
      They were bound!
Soon as lazy thou wert known,
All good poetry hence was flown,
      And art banish'd:
For a thousand years together,
All Parnassus' green did wither,
      And wit vanish'd!
Pegasus did fly away,
At the wells no Muse did stay,
      But bewailed,
So to see the fountain dry,
And Apollo's music die,
      All light failed!
Starveling rhymes did fill the stage,
Not a poet in an age
      Worthy crowning.
Not a work deserving bays,
Nor a line deserving praise,
      Pallas frowning:

Greek was free from rhyme's infection,
Happy Greek, by this protection,
       Was not spoiled.
Whilst the Latin, queen of tongues,
Is not yet free from rhyme's wrongs,
       But rests foiled.
Scarce the hill again doth flourish,
Scarce the world a wit doth nourish,
       To restore
Phœbus to his crown again ;
And the Muses to their brain ;
       As before.
Vulgar languages that want
Words, and sweetness, and be scant
       Of true measure,
Tyrant rhyme hath so abused,
That they long since have refused,
       Other cesure.
He that first invented thee,
May his joints tormented be,
       Cramp'd for ever ;
Still may syllabes[7] jar with time,
Still may reason war with rhyme,
       Resting never !
May his sense when it would meet
The cold tumour in his feet,
       Grow unsounder ;
And his title be long fool,
That in rearing such a school
       Was the founder !

---

[7] *Still may* syllabes.] Whalley reads syllables here and in the
preceding page, but injuriously in both places. Jonson uses *syllabe*
almost invariably ; for which he is commended by Horne Tooke.

XLVIII.

AN EPIGRAM

ON WILLIAM LORD BURLEIGH, LORD HIGH TREASURER OF ENGLAND.[8]

F thou wouldst know the virtues of mankind,
    Read here in one, what thou in all canst
        find,
    And go no further : let this circle be
Thy universe, though his epitome.
Cecil, the grave, the wise, the great, the good,
What is there more that can ennoble blood ?
The orphan's pillar, the true subject's shield,
The poor's full store-house, and just servant's field.
The only faithful watchman for the realm,
That in all tempests never quit the helm,
But stood unshaken in his deeds and name,
And labour'd in the work ; not with the fame :
That still was good for goodness' sake, nor thought
Upon reward, till the reward him sought.
Whose offices and honours did surprise,
Rather than meet him : and before his eyes
Clos'd to their peace, he saw his branches shoot,
And in the noblest families took root,
Of all the land : Who now at such a rate,
Of divine blessing, would not serve a state ?

[8] *An Epigram, &c.*] " Presented (the fol. says) upon a plate of gold to his son Robert earl of Salisbury, when he was also Treasurer." Lord Burleigh died in August, 1598. There are no means of ascertaining the date of this epigram : if it was written on the same occasion as that noble one, p. 177, it was produced in 1608. But whatever might be the period of its appearance, it was equally worthy of the poet, and the patron, who must have been highly gratified with the judicious and characteristic applause bestowed on the great statesman to whose honours he succeeded.

AN EPIGRAM

To Thomas lord Elesmere,[9]

THE LAST TERM HE SAT CHANCELLOR.

O, justest lord, may all your judgments be
Laws; and no change e'er come to one
    decree :
    So may the king proclaim your conscience is
Law to his law ; and think your enemies his :
So, from all sickness, may you rise to health,
The care and wish still of the public wealth :
So may the gentler muses, and good fame,
Still fly about the odour of your name ;
As, with the safety' and honour of the laws,
You favour truth, and me, in this man's cause !

L.

ANOTHER TO THE SAME.[*]

HE judge his favour timely then extends,
When a good cause is destitute of friends,
Without the pomp' of counsel ; or more aid,
Than to make falsehood blush, and fraud
    afraid :

[9] For this excellent person see p. 184. He held the seals, in compliance with the reiterated intreaties of James, till the 3rd of March, 1617, when, as Camden tells us, the king received them from him with tears of gratitude.

This Epigram (Jonson says) was written *for a poor man*, who had a suit depending before lord Elesmere. Its date may be referred to Michaelmas Term, 1616.

[*] For the same poor man.

When those good few, that her defenders be,
Are there for charity, and not for fee.
Such shall you hear to-day, and find great foes
Both arm'd with wealth and slander to oppose,
Who thus long safe, would gain upon the times
A right by the prosperity of their crimes ;
Who, though their guilt and 'perjury they know,
Think, yea, and boast, that they have done it so,
As, though the court pursues them on the scent,
They will come off, and 'scape the punishment.
When this appears, just lord, to your sharp sight,
He does you wrong, that craves you to do right.

LI.

AN EPIGRAM

TO THE COUNSELLOR THAT PLEADED,

AND CARRIED THE CAUSE.

HAT I hereafter do not think the bar,
The seat made of a more than civil war,[1]
Or the great hall at Westminster, the field
Where mutual frauds are fought, and no side
    yield,
That henceforth I believe nor books, nor men,
Who 'gainst the law weave calumnies, my Benn ;[2]
But when I read or hear the names so rife,
Of hirelings, wranglers, stitchers-to of strife,

---

[1] *A more than civil war.*]
—————— *plusquam civilia bella.* LUCAN.

[2] *Who 'gainst the law weave calumnies, my* ——.] This blank, I
imagine, was to have been filled with the name of the counsellor
who pleaded in the cause : it must be a word of one syllable, and
answer in rhyme to *men*, the close of the preceding verse. From
these particulars, it is probable, the person here meant was *Anthony
Benn*, who succeeded the solicitor Coventry in the recordership of
London. WHAL.

Hook-handed harpies, gowned vultures, put
Upon the reverend pleaders; do now shut
All mouths that dare entitle them, from hence,
To the wolf's study, or dog's eloquence;
Thou art my cause: whose manners since I knew,
Have made me to conceive a lawyer new.
So dost thou study matter, men, and times,
Mak'st it religion to grow rich by crimes;
Dar'st not abuse thy wisdom in the laws,
Or skill to carry out an evil cause:
But first dost vex, and search it! if not sound,
Thou prov'st the gentler ways to cleanse the wound,
And make the scar fair; if that will not be,
Thou hast the brave scorn to put back the fee!
But in a business that will bide the touch,
What use, what strength of reason, and how much
Of books, of precedents hast thou at hand!
As if the general store thou didst command
Of argument, still drawing forth the best,
And not being borrow'd by thee, but possest.
So com'st thou like a chief into the court
Arm'd at all pieces, as to keep a fort
Against a multitude; and, with thy style
So brightly brandish'd, wound'st, defend'st! the while
Thy adversaries fall, as not a word
They had, but were a reed unto thy sword.
Then com'st thou off with victory and palm,
Thy hearer's nectar, and thy client's balm,
The court's just honour, and thy judge's love.
And (which doth all achievements get above)
Thy sincere practice breeds not thee a fame
Alone, but all thy rank a reverend name.

LII.

An Epigram to the Small-pox.

ENVIOUS and foul Disease, could there not be
    One beauty in an age, and free from thee?
What did she worth thy spite? were there not store
Of those that set by their false faces more
Than this did by her true? she never sought
Quarrel with nature, or in balance brought
Art her false servant; nor, for sir Hugh Plat,[3]
Was drawn to practise other hue, than that
Her own blood gave her: she ne'er had, nor hath
Any belief in madam Bawdbee's bath,
Or Turner's oil of talc: nor ever got
Spanish receipt to make her teeth to rot.
What was the cause then? thought'st thou, in disgrace
Of beauty, so to nullify a face,
That heaven should make no more; or should amiss
Make all hereafter, hadst thou ruin'd this?
Ay, that thy aim was; but her fate prevail'd:
And, scorn'd, thou'st shown thy malice, but hast fail'd!

---

[3] *Sir Hugh Plat.*] He was a compiler of recipes for making cosmetics, oils, ointments, &c. &c.; one of his books is entitled, "Delights for ladies to adorne their persons, &c. 1628."

LIII.

An Epitaph.

HAT beauty would have lovely styled,
What manners pretty, nature mild,
What wonder perfect, all were filed
Upon record, in this blest child.
And till the coming of the soul
To fetch the flesh, we keep the roll.

LIV.

A SONG.

Lover.

OME, let us here enjoy the shade,
For love in shadow best is made.
Though Envy oft his shadow be,
None brooks the sun-light worse than he.

Mistress.

Where love doth shine, there needs no sun,
All lights into his one do run ;
Without which all the world were dark ;
Yet he himself is but a spark.

Arbiter.

A spark to set whole world a-fire,
Who, more they burn, they more desire,
And have their being, their waste to see ;
And waste still, that they still might be.

Chorus.

Such are his powers, whom time hath styled,
Now swift, now slow, now tame, now wild ;
Now hot, now cold, now fierce, now mild ;
The eldest god, yet still a child.

LV.

AN EPISTLE TO A FRIEND.

IR, I am thankful, first to heaven for you ;
Next to yourself, for making your love true :
Then to your love and gift.   And all's but
       due.

You have unto my store added a book,
On which with profit I shall never look,
But must confess from whom that gift I took.

Not like your country neighbours that commit
Their vice of loving for a Christmas-fit ;
Which is indeed but friendship of the spit :

But, as a friend, which name yourself receive,
And which you (being the worthier) gave me leave
In letters, that mix spirits, thus to weave.

Which, how most sacred I will ever keep,
So may the fruitful vine my temples steep,
And fame wake for me when I yield to sleep !

Though you sometimes proclaim me too severe,
Rigid, and harsh, which is a drug austere
In friendship, I confess : but, dear friend, hear.

Little know they, that profess amity,
And seek to scant her comely liberty,
How much they lame her in her property.

And less they know, who being free to use
That friendship which no chance but love did choose,
Will unto license that fair leave abuse.

It is an act of tyranny, not love,
In practis'd friendship wholly to reprove,
As flattery, with friends' humours still to move.

From each of which I labour to be free,
Yet if with either's vice I tainted be,
Forgive it, as my frailty, and not me.

For no man lives so out of passion's sway,
But shall sometimes be tempted to obey
Her fury, yet no friendship to betray.

.

LVI.

AN ELEGY.

IS true, I'm broke ! vows, oaths, and all I had[4]
Of credit lost.   And I am now run mad ;
Or do upon myself some desperate ill :
This sadness makes no approaches, but to kill.
It is a darkness hath block'd up my sense,
And drives it in to eat on my offence,
Or there to starve it.   Help, O you that may
Alone lend succours, and this fury stay.
Offended mistress, you are yet so fair,
As light breaks from you that affrights despair,
And fills my powers with persuading joy,
That you should be too noble to destroy.
There may some face or menace of a storm
Look forth, but cannot last in such a form.
If there be nothing worthy you can see
Of graces, or your mercy here in me,
Spare your own goodness yet ; and be not great
In will and power, only to defeat.
God and the good know to forgive and save ;
The ignorant and fools no pity have.

---

[4] *'Tis true, I'm broke, &c.*]   This, and the next three Elegies,
are all addressed to the same person.   The lady, whoever she was,
appears to have had a love affair with the poet, who, in a moment
of intoxication, had betrayed her confidence, and disclosed the
secret of their connection.

I will not stand to justify my fault,
Or lay th' excuse upon the vintner's vault ;
Or in confessing of the crime be nice,
Or go about to countenance the vice,
By naming in what company 'twas in,
As I would urge authority for sin ;
No, I will stand arraign'd and cast, to be
The subject of your grace in pardoning me,
And (styled your mercy's creature) will live more,
Your honour now, than your disgrace before.
　　Think it was frailty, mistress, think me man,
Think that yourself, like heaven, forgive me can :
Where weakness doth offend, and virtue grieve,
There greatness takes a glory to relieve.
Think that I once was yours, or may be now ;
Nothing is vile, that is a part of you.
Error and folly in me may have crost
Your just commands ; yet those, not I, be lost.
I am regenerate now, become the child
Of your compassion ; parents should be mild :
There is no father that for one demerit, ·
Or two, or three, a son will disinherit ;
That is the last of punishments is meant ;
No man inflicts that pain, till hope be spent :
An ill-affected limb, whate'er it ail,
We cut not off, till all cures else do fail ;
· And then with pause ; for sever'd once, that's gone,
Would live his glory, that could keep it on.
Do not despair my mending ; to distrust
Before you prove a medicine, is unjust :
You may so place me, and in such an air,
As not alone the cure, but scar be fair.
That is, if still your favours you apply,
And not the bounties you have done, deny.
Could you demand the gifts you gave, again !
Why was't ? did e'er the clouds ask back their
　　　rain ?

The sun his heat and light? the air his dew?
Or winds the spirit by which the flower so grew?
That were to wither all, and make a grave
Of that wise nature would a cradle have.
Her order is to cherish and preserve;
Consumption's, nature to destroy and sterve.
But to exact again what once is given,
Is nature's mere obliquity; as heaven
Should ask the blood and spirits he hath infus'd
In man, because man hath the flesh abus'd.
   O may your wisdom take example hence,
God lightens not at man's each frail offence:
He pardons slips, goes by a world of ills,
And then his thunder frights more than it kills.
He cannot angry be, but all must quake;
It shakes e'en him that all things else doth shake,
And how more fair and lovely looks the world
In a calm sky, than when the heaven is hurl'd
About in clouds, and wrapt in raging weather,
As all with storm and tempest ran together!
   O imitate that sweet serenity
That makes us live, not that which calls to die.
In dark and sullen morns do we not say,
This looketh like an execution-day?
And with the vulgar doth it not obtain
The name of cruel weather, storm and rain?
Be not affected with these marks too much
Of cruelty, lest they do make you such;
But view the mildness of your Maker's state,
As I the penitent's here emulate.
He, when he sees a sorrow, such as this,
Straight puts off all his anger, and doth kiss
The contrite soul, who hath no thought to win
Upon the hope to have another sin
Forgiven him: and in that line stand I,
Rather than once displease you more, to die,
To suffer tortures, scorn, and infamy,

What fools, and all their parasites can apply;
The wit of ale, and genius of the malt
Can pump for, or a libel without salt
Produce; though threat'ning with a coal or chalk,
On every wall, and sung where-e'er I walk.
I number these, as being of the chore
Of contumely, and urge a good man more
Than sword, or fire, or what is of the race
To carry noble danger in the face:
There is not any punishment or pain,
A man should fly from, as he would disdain.
Then, mistress, here, here let your rigour end,
And let your mercy make me asham'd t' offend;
I will no more abuse my vows to you,
Than I will study falsehood, to be true.
   O that you could but by dissection see
How much you are the better part of me;
How all my fibres by your spirit do move,
And that there is no life in me, but love!
You would be then most confident, that though
Public affairs command me now to go
Out of your eyes, and be awhile away;
Absence or distance shall not breed decay.
Your form shines here, here, fixed in my heart:
I may dilate myself, but not depart.
Others by common stars their courses run,
When I see you, then I do see my sun:
Till then 'tis all but darkness that I have;
Rather than want your light, I wish a grave.

LVII.

An Elegy.

TO make the doubt clear, that no woman's true,
Was it my fate to prove it full in you ?[5]
Thought I but one had breath'd the purer air,
And must she needs be false, because she's
fair ?
Is it your beauty's mark, or of your youth,
Or your perfection, not to study truth ?
Or think you heaven is deaf, or hath no eyes,
Or those it hath wink at your perjuries ?
Are vows so cheap with women ? or the matter
Whereof they are made, that they are writ in water,

[5] *To make the doubt clear, that no woman's true,*
Was it my fate to prove it full *in you ?*] There is a collection
of Dr. Donne's poems in 8vo. 1669, amongst which is this elegy :
how it came there I know not, for there is no doubt but it is Jonson's. WHAL.
Whalley appears not to have known that the elegy was printed
in a 4to. edition of Donne's Poems, which came out in 1633. I
have already observed that there was a mutual communication of
MSS. between the two poets, and the verses before us might be
found among the doctor's papers (for he was now dead), and published by his son, or by those who collected them, as his own.
The preceding poem, in which the poet so ingenuously confessed
his fault, and so earnestly sued for pardon, appears to have had its
effect, and reconciled the lovers. They were still, however, im-
prudent : the lady in her turn trusted a false friend, who abused
her confidence, and traduced the parties to each other, till he had
stirred up a mutual jealousy, and finally separated them. On the
discovery of this treachery, Jonson writes the second elegy, which,
like the first, led to a reconciliation.
I have no knowledge of the person to whom these Elegies were
addressed. I once thought them to be scholastic exercises like the
desperate love verses of Donne and Cowley ; but they now strike
me as too earnest for any thing but a real intrigue.
The text of the folio (the blunders of which I am weary of
noticing) has been much improved by a collation with the copy in
Donne's works.

And blown away with wind ? or doth their breath,
Both hot and cold at once, threat life and death ?
Who could have thought so many accents sweet
Tuned to our words, so many sighs should meet
Blown from our hearts, so many oaths and tears
Sprinkled among, all sweeter by our fears,
And the divine impression of stol'n kisses,
That seal'd the rest, could now prove empty blisses ?
Did you draw bonds to forfeit ? sign to break ?
Or must we read you quite from what you speak,
And find the truth out the wrong way ? or must
He first desire you false, would wish you just ?
O, I profane ! though most of women be
The common monster, thought shall except thee,
My dearest love, though froward jealousy
With circumstance might urge the contrary.
Sooner I'll think the sun would cease to cheer
The teeming earth, and that forget to bear ;
Sooner that rivers would run back, or Thames
With ribs of ice in June would bind his streams ;
Or Nature, by whose strength the world endures,
Would change her course, before you alter yours.
     But, O, that treacherous breast ! to whom weak
          you
Did trust our counsels, and we both may rue,
Having his falsehood found too late ! 'twas he
That made me cast you guilty, and you me ;
Whilst he, black wretch, betray'd each simple word
We spake, unto the cunning of a third !
Curst may he be, that so our love hath slain,
And wander wretched on the earth, as Cain ;
Wretched as he, and not deserve least pity !
In plaguing him, let misery be witty.
Let all eyes shun him, and he shun each eye,
Till he be noisome as his infamy ;
May he without remorse deny God thrice,
And not be trusted more on his soul's price ;

And after all self-torment, when he dies,
May wolves tear out his heart, vultures his eyes,
Swine eat his bowels, and his falser tongue,
That utter'd all, be to some raven flung;
And let his carrion corse be a longer feast
To the king's dogs, than any other beast!
  Now I have curst, let us our love revive;
In me the flame was never more alive.
I could begin again to court and praise,
And in that pleasure lengthen the short days
Of my life's lease; like painters that do take
Delight, not in made works, but whilst they make.
I could renew those times when first I saw
Love in your eyes, that gave my tongue the law
To like what you liked, and at masques or plays,
Commend the self-same actors the same ways;
Ask how you did, and often with intent
Of being officious, grow impertinent;
All which were such soft pastimes, as in these
Love was as subtly catch'd as a disease.
But, being got, it is a treasure sweet,
Which to defend, is harder than to get;
And ought not be profaned on either part,
For though 'tis got by chance, 'tis kept by art.

LVIII.

An Elegy.

HAT love's a bitter sweet, I ne'er conceive,
  Till the sour minute comes of taking leave,
  And then I taste it: but as men drink up
  In haste the bottom of a med'cined cup,
And take some sirup after; so do I,
To put all relish from my memory
Of parting, drown it, in the hope to meet
Shortly again, and make our absence sweet.

This makes me, mistress, that sometimes by stealth,
Under another name, I take your health,
And turn the ceremonies of those nights
I give, or owe my friends, unto your rites ;
But ever without blazon, or least shade
Of vows so sacred, and in silence made :
For though love thrive, and may grow up with cheer,
And free society, he's born elsewhere,
And must be bred, so to conceal his birth,
As neither wine do rack it out, or mirth.
Yet should the lover still be airy' and light,
In all his actions, rarified to sprite :
Not like a Midas, shut up in himself,
And turning all he toucheth into pelf,
Keep in reserv'd in his dark-lantern face,
As if that excellent dulness were love's grace :
    No, mistress, no, the open, merry, man
Moves like a sprightly river, and yet can
Keep secret in his channels what he breeds,
'Bove all your standing waters, choak'd with weeds.
They look at best like cream-bowls, and you soon
Shall find their depth ; they are sounded with a
            spoon.
They may say grace, and for Love's chaplains pass,
But the grave lover ever was an ass ;
Is fix'd upon one leg,[6] and dares not come
Out with the other, for he's still at home :
Like the dull wearied crane, that, come on land,
Doth while he keeps his watch, betray his stand ;

----

[6] *Is fix'd upon one leg, &c.*] Jonson, like Donne, seems fond of
drawing illustrations from this familiar implement. In his verses
to Selden, p. 352, he has done it very gracefully :

> ———————— "You that have been
> Ever at home, yet have all countries seen ;
> And, like a compass, keeping one foot still
> Upon your center, do your circle fill
> Of general knowledge."———

Where he that knows will like a lapwing fly
Far from the nest, and so himself belie
To others, as he will deserve the trust
Due to that one that doth believe him just.
And such your servant is, who vows to keep
The jewel of your name, as close as sleep
Can lock the sense up, or the heart a thought,
And never be by time or folly brought,
Weakness of brain, or any charm of wine,
The sin of boast, or other countermine,
Made to blow up love's secrets, to discover
That article may not become your lover :
Which in assurance to your breast I tell,
If I had writ no word, but, Dear, farewell !

LIX.

An Elegy.

SINCE you must go, and I must bid farewell,
Hear, mistress, your departing servant tell
What it is like : and do not think they can
Be idle words, though of a parting man.
It is as if a night should shade noon-day,
Or that the sun was here, but forced away ;
And we were left under that hemisphere,
Where we must feel it dark for half a year.
What fate is this, to change men's days and hours,
To shift their seasons, and destroy their powers !

Donne is yet more fanciful and ingenious. He says to a wife
who remains at home while her husband is abroad :

" Thy soul, the fix'd foot, makes no show
To move, but doth if th' other do :
And though it in the center sit,
    Yet, when the other far doth roam,
It leans, and hearkens after it,
    And grows erect as that comes home."

Alas! I have lost my heat, my blood, my prime,
Winter is come a quarter ere his time.
My health will leave me; and when you depart,
How shall I do, sweet mistress, for my heart?
You would restore it! no; that's worth a fear,
As if it were not worthy to be there:
O keep it still; for it had rather be
Your sacrifice, than here remain with me.
And so I spare it: come what can become
Of me, I'll softly tread unto my tomb;
Or, like a ghost, walk silent amongst men,
Till I may see both it and you agen.

LX.

An Elegy.

ET me be what I am: as Virgil cold,
As Horace fat, or as Anacreon old;
No poet's verses yet did ever move,
    Whose readers did not think he was in
        love.
Who shall forbid me then in rhyme to be
As light, and active as the youngest he
That from the Muses fountains doth endorse
His lines, and hourly sits the poet's horse?
Put on my ivy garland, let me see
Who frowns, who jealous is, who taxeth me.
Fathers and husbands, I do claim a right
In all that is call'd lovely; take my sight,
Sooner than my affection from the fair.
No face, no hand, proportion, line or air
Of beauty, but the muse hath interest in:
There is not worn that lace, purl, knot, or pin,
But is the poet's matter; and he must,
When he is furious, love, although not lust.

Be then content, your daughters and your wives,
If they be fair and worth it, have their lives
Made longer by our praises ; or, if not,
Wish you had foul ones, and deformed got,
Curst in their cradles, or there chang'd by elves,
So to be sure you do enjoy, yourselves.
Yet keep those up in sackcloth too, or leather,
For silk will draw some sneaking songster thither.
It is a rhyming age, and verses swarm
At every stall ; the city cap's a charm.
    But I who live, and have lived twenty year,
Where I may handle silk as free, and near,
As any mercer, or the whale-bone man,
That quilts those bodies I have leave to span ;
Have eaten with the beauties, and the wits,
And braveries of court, and felt their fits
Of love and hate ; and came so nigh to know
Whether their faces were their own or no :
It is not likely I should now look down
Upon a velvet petticoat, or a gown,
Whose like I have known the tailor's wife put on,[7]
To do her husband's rites in, ere 'twere gone
Home to the customer : his letchery
Being the best clothes still to preoccupy.
Put a coach-mare in tissue, must I horse
Her presently ? or leap thy wife, of force,
When by thy sordid bounty she hath on
A gown of that was the caparison ?
So I might doat upon thy chairs and stools,
That are like cloth'd : must I be of those fools

---

[7] *Whose like I have known the tailor's wife put on, &c.*] Whether
this be the original sketch of the countess Pinnacia Stuffe in the
New Inn, or be itself taken from that unfortunate play, as the lines
are not dated, cannot be told ; the resemblance, however, is perfect :

            ———— " Master Stuffe,
    When he makes any fine garment that will suit me,
    Or any rich thing that he thinks of price,
    Then must I put it on," &c.

Of race accounted, that no passion have,
But when thy wife, as thou conceiv'st, is brave?
Then ope thy wardrobe, think me that poor groom
That, from the footman, when he was become
An officer there, did make most solemn love
To every petticoat he brush'd, and glove
He did lay up; and would adore the shoe
Or slipper was left off, and kiss it too;
Court every hanging gown, and after that
Lift up some one, and do—I tell not what.
Thou didst tell me, and wert o'erjoyed to peep
In at a hole, and see those actions creep
From the poor wretch, which though he plaid in prose,
He would have done in verse, with any of those
Wrung on the withers by lord Love's despite,
Had he the faculty to read and write!
    Such songsters there are store of; witness he
That chanc'd the lace, laid on a smock, to see,
And straightway spent a sonnet; with that other
That, in pure madrigal, unto his mother
Commended the French hood and scarlet gown
The lady may'ress pass'd in through the town,
Unto the Spittle sermon.[8] O what strange
Variety of silks were on the Exchange!
Or in Moor-fields, this other night, sings one!
Another answers, 'las! those silks are none,
In smiling l'envoy,[9] as he would deride
Any comparison had with his Cheapside;
And vouches both the pageant and the day,
When not the shops, but windows do display
The stuffs, the velvets, plushes, fringes, lace,
And all the original riots of the place.

[8] *Unto the Spittle sermon.*] The Spittle sermons were preached
at that time, in a pulpit erected for the purpose, in what is now
called Spittle Square. They lasted through the Easter week.
[9] *In smiling* l'envoy,] i. e. in a kind of supercilious *close.* For
l'envoy, see vol. iii. p. 460.

Let the poor fools enjoy their follies, love
A goat in velvet; or some block could move
Under that cover, an old midwife's hat!
Or a close-stool so cased; or any fat
Bawd, in a velvet scabbard! I envý
None of their pleasures; nor will ask thee why
Thou art jealous of thy wife's or daughter's case;
More than of either's manners, wit, or face!

LXI.

AN EXECRATION UPON VULCAN.

ND why to me this? thou lame Lord of
Fire![1]
What had I done that might call on thine
ire?
Or urge thy greedy flames thus to devour
So many my years' labours in an hour?
I ne'er attempted aught against thy life;
Nor made least line of love to thy loose wife;
Or in remembrance of thy affront and scorn,
With clowns and tradesmen, kept thee clos'd in
horn.[2]——

[1] *And why to me, &c.*] This poem has no date affixed to it: it
was printed in 4to. and 12mo. 1640, and again in the folio of that
year; the present text has been formed from a careful collation of
all the copies.

There is a degree of wit and vivacity in these verses which does
no little credit to the equanimity of the poet, who speaks of a loss
so irreparable to him, not only with forbearance, but with pleasantry and good humour. The *lame lord* is from Catullus:

> *Scripta tardipedi deo daturum*
> *Infelicibus ustulanda flammis.*

[2] *With clowns and tradesmen kept thee clos'd in horn.*] This is a
joke of very ancient standing: *Heus tu, qui Vulcanum conclusum
in cornu geris!* Plaut. *Amphytr.* WHAL.

'Twas Jupiter that hurl'd thee headlong down,
And Mars that gave thee a lantern for a crown.
Was it because thou wert of old denied,
By Jove, to have Minerva for thy bride ;
That since, thou tak'st all envious care and pain
To ruin every issue of the brain ?
   Had I wrote treason here, or heresy,
Imposture, witchcraft, charms, or blasphemy ;
I had deserv'd then thy consuming looks,
Perhaps to have been burned with my books.
But, on thy malice, tell me, Didst thou spy
Any least loose or scurril paper lie
Conceal'd, or kept there, that was fit to be,
By thy own vote, a sacrifice to thee ?
Did I there wound the honour of the crown,
Or tax the glory of the church, or gown ?
Itch to defame the state, or brand the times,
And myself most, in lewd self-boasting rhymes ?
If none of these, then why this fire ? Or find
A cause before, or leave me one behind.
   Had I compiled from Amadis de Gaul,
The Esplandians, Arthurs, Palmerins, and all
The learned library of Don Quixóte,
And so some goodlier monster had begot ;
Or spun out riddles, or weav'd fifty tomes
Of Logographes, or curious Palindromes,
Or pump'd for those hard trifles, Anagrams,
Or Eteostics, or your finer flams
Of eggs, and halberds, cradles, and a herse,
A pair of scissars, and a comb in verse ;
Acrostichs, and telestichs on jump names,[3]
Thou then hadst had some colour for thy flames,

---

   [3] *Acrostichs, and telestichs, &c.*] All these fooleries in verse were
practised ages ago, by writers who atoned for want of genius by
the labour of their compositions.   This is Whalley's remark, and it
was undoubtedly so ; but the folly was again become epidemic, in
consequence of the publication of Puttenham's *Arte of English*

On such my serious follies : but, thou'lt say,
There were some pieces of as base allay,
And as false stamp there ; parcels of a play,
Fitter to see the fire-light, than the day ;
Adulterate monies, such as would not go :—
Thou shouldst have staid, till public Fame said so ;
She is the judge, thou executioner :
Or, if thou needs would'st trench upon her power,
Thou might'st have yet enjoy'd thy cruelty
With some more thrift, and more variety :
Thou might'st have had me perish piece by piece,
To light tobacco, or save roasted geese,
Singe capons, or crisp pigs, dropping their eyes ;
Condemn'd me to the ovens with the pies ;[4]
And so have kept me dying a whole age,
Not ravish'd all hence in a minute's rage.—
But that's a mark whereof thy rites do boast,
To make consumption ever where thou go'st.

Had I foreknown of this thy least desire
To have held a triumph, or a feast of fire,
Especially in paper ; that that steam
Had tickled thy large nostrils ; many a ream,
To redeem mine, I had sent in : Enough!
Thou shouldst have cried, and all been proper stuff
The Talmud and the Alcoran had come,
With pieces of the Legend ;[5] the whole sum
Of errant knighthood, with the dames and dwarfs ;
The charmed boats, and the inchanted wharfs,

Poetrie, in which "these prettie conceits, eggs, altars, wings, lozenges, rondels, and piramids" are recommended to the poet's imitation. "At the beginning" (he says) "they will seeme nothing pleasant to the English eare ; but time and usage will make them acceptable inough."

   [4] The MS. of this piece in the British Museum reads, with more variety,

      "Clothe spices, or guard sweet-meats from the flies."

   [5] *With pieces of the Legend.*] The Lives of the Saints : these are well coupled with the Jewish and Mahomedan dreams.

8   D D

The Tristrams, Lancelots, Turpins, and the Peers,
All the mad Rolands, and sweet Olivers ;
To Merlin's marvels, and his Cabal's loss,
With the chimera of the Rosie-cross,
Their seals, their characters, hermetic rings,
Their jem of riches, and bright stone that brings
Invisibility, and strength, and tongues ;
The art of kindling the true coal by Lungs ;
With Nicolas' Pasquils, Meddle with your match,
And the strong lines that do the times so catch ;[6]
Or captain Pamphlet's horse and foot, that sally
Upon the Exchange still, out of Pope's-head alley ;
The weekly courants, with Paul's seal ;[7] and all
The admired discourses of the prophet Ball.

These, hadst thou pleas'd either to dine or sup,
Had made a meal for Vulcan to lick up.[8]
But, in my desk, what was there to accite
So ravenous and vast an appetite ?
I dare not say a body, but some parts
There were of search, and mastery in the arts.

---

[6] *The art of kindling the true coal by* Lungs ;
With Nicolas' Pasquils, Meddle with your match,
And the strong lines *that do the times so catch.*]　*Lungs* (see vol.
iv. p. 45) were the unhappy drudges kept by the alchemists to blow
their *true* (i. e. their beechen) coal ; for bellows were not used by
them.

Nicolas is probably Nic. Breton, a voluminous publisher, who
has many little pieces under the name of *Pasquil :* such as Pasquil's
Passion, Pasquil's Mad-cap, &c.　In the pointing this line, the MS.
in the British Museum has been followed.　The *strong lines,* &c.,
are the political satires which were now dispersed in great numbers,
and *caught the times* but too successfully.

[7] *The weekly courants, with Paul's seal, &c.*]　A sarcastical allusion to the stories fabricated by the idle walkers in St. Paul's,
and weekly detailed by Butter and others as authentic intelligence.
For the prophet Ball, see vol. v. p. 227.

[8] ———— *a meal for Vulcan to* lick up.]　Thus Pope :

" From shelf to shelf see greedy Vulcan roll,
　And *lick up* all the physic of the soul."

All the old Venusine, in poetry,
And lighted by the Stagerite, could spy,
Was there made English ; with a grammar too,
To teach some that their nurses could not do,[9]
The purity of Language ; and, among
The rest, my journey into Scotland sung,
With all the adventures : three books, not afraid
To speak the fate of the Sicilian maid,
To our own ladies ; and in story there
Of our fifth Henry, eight of his nine year ;
Wherein was oil, beside the succours spent,
Which noble Carew, Cotton, Selden lent :
And twice twelve years stored up humanity,
With humble gleanings in divinity ; .
After the fathers, and those wiser guides,
Whom faction had not drawn to study sides.

   How in these ruins, Vulcan, dost thou lurk,
All soot and embers ! odious as thy work !
I now begin to doubt if ever Grace,
Or goddess, could be patient of thy face.

  [9] *All the old Venusine, &c.*] He alludes to his translation of
Horace's *Art of Poetry*, illustrated with notes from Aristotle's
Poetics. The translation is preserved ; and much of what seemed
to have been intended for the notes is likewise to be met with in
the *Discoveries:* the *Grammar* is also preserved, and printed.
WHAL.
  Literature sustained no little loss by the destruction of the *Art
of Poetry*, illustrated, as it appears to have been, by a perpetual
commentary from Aristotle. If any part of the *Discoveries* were
appended as notes, to the translation, it could not be very considerable. What we have now, forms, I believe, but a small part
of the original matter ; consisting of occasional recollections only,
set down, as they occurred, and several of them evidently of a late
date. The translation itself, perhaps, is not what it was at first ;
for the two copies of it which have reached us, and which may be
only transcripts of transcripts, differ from each other in numberless
instances. Whalley is evidently wrong also in what he says of the
Grammar. The perfect copy was destroyed ; and all that is come
down to us are mere fragments ; parts, indeed, of the original
materials, but dislocated, and imperfect.

Thou woo Minerva! or to wit aspire!
'Cause thou canst halt with us in arts and fire!
Son of the Wind! for so thy mother, gone
With lust, conceiv'd thee; father thou hadst none.
When thou wert born, and that thou look'dst at
        best,
She durst not kiss, but flung thee from her breast;
And so did Jove, who ne'er meant thee his cup.
No marle the clowns of Lemnos took thee up!
For none but smiths would have made thee a god.
Some alchemist there may be yet, or odd
'Squire of the squibs, against the pageant day,
May to thy name a Vulcanale say;
And for it lose his eyes with gun-powder,
As th' other may his brains with quicksilver.—
    Well fare the wise men yet, on the Bank-side,
My friends, the watermen! they could provide
Against thy fury, when to serve their needs,
They made a Vulcan of a sheaf of reeds,
Whom they durst handle in their holiday coats,
And safely trust to dress, not burn their boats.
But, O those reeds! thy mere disdain of them,
Made thee beget that cruel stratagem,
Which some are pleased to style but thy mad prank,
Against the Globe, the glory of the Bank :[1]

[1] *Against the* Globe, *the glory of the* Bank.]   The *Globe play-house,* situate on the *Bank-side,* burnt down about this time.
                                    WHAL.
    About what time?   The only notice which we have of this poem is found in a letter by Howell "to his father, master Ben Jonson," dated 27th June, 1629.   "Desiring you to look better hereafter to your charcole fire and chimney, which I am glad to be one that preserved from burning, this being the *second time* that Vulcan hath threatened you;—it may be because you have spoken ill of his wife, and been too busy with his horns; I rest your son," &c. Here the allusion is evidently to the first ten lines of the "Execra-tion:" but this decides nothing with respect to the period of its first appearance.
    The date of the fire at the Globe can be distinctly ascertained

Which, though it were the fort of the whole parish,
Flank'd with a ditch, and forced out of a marish,

from a letter of Mr. Chamberlaine to sir Ralph Winwood, among
the State papers.

"The burning of *the Globe*, or Playhouse on the Bankside, on
St. Peter's day cannot escape you; which fell out by a peale of
chambers, that I know not upon what occasion were to be used in
the play:—the tompin or stopple of one of them lighting in the
thatch that covered the house, burned it down to the ground in
less than two hours, with a dwelling house adjoining; and it was
a great marvaile and fair grace of God that the people had so
little harm, having but two narrow doors to get out." July 8th,
1613.

It is useless to inquire why Jonson, whose memory, though less
retentive than formerly, was yet perhaps sufficiently strong, remained inactive; but with the exception of the two fragments just
mentioned, he apparently made no effort to repair his loss.

The *Journey into Scotland* was the ever memorable visit to
Drummond, "that false friend," as Chetwood calls him, "who
treats the memory of Ben as if he were an idle madman." Drummond could not appear more base than he now does—but, such
was the honest warmth and affection of Jonson—had this poem
survived, his admirers would not have dared to insult the common
sense and feeling of mankind by terming the splenetic hypocrite
the *friend* of Jonson.

The *Rape of Proserpine* may not perhaps be much regretted:
but the destruction of the *History of Henry fifth*, which was so
nearly completed, must ever be considered as a serious misfortune.
The vigor and masculine elegance of Jonson's style, the clearness
of his judgment, the precision of his intelligence, aided by the intimate knowledge of domestic and general history possessed by
Carew (George, lord Carew,) Cotton, and Selden, three of the most
learned men of that or any other age, could not have been exerted
without producing a work, of which, if spared to us, we might be
justly proud.

Of the value of the *philological collections of twenty-four years*,
some idea may be formed from what remains of the *Discoveries* or
notes on the *Poetics* of Aristotle and Horace; and the *gleanings* in
Divinity, if they had not answered a nobler and better purpose,
would at least serve to bring additional shame on those who, in
defiance of so many proofs to the contrary, spitefully persist in
accusing the poet of a marked indifference to religion, or, yet
worse, of a restless tendency to ridicule and profane it.

I saw with two poor chambers taken in,
And razed ; ere thought could urge this might have
     been !
See the World's ruins ! nothing but the piles
Left, and wit since to cover it with tiles.
The brethren they straight nosed it out for news,
'Twas verily some relict of the stews ;
And this a sparkle of that fire let loose,
That was raked up in the Winchestrian goose,
Bred on the Bank in time of Popery,
When Venus there maintain'd the mystery.[3]
But others fell, with that conceit, by the ears,
And cried it was a threatning to the bears,
And that accursed ground, the Paris-garden :
Nay, sigh'd a sister, Venus' nun, Kate Arden,
Kindled the fire !—but then, did one return,
No fool would his own harvest spoil or burn !—
If that were so, thou rather wouldst advance
The place that was thy wife's inheritance.
O no, cried all, Fortune, for being a whore,
Scap'd not his justice any jot the more :[4]
He burnt that idol of the Revels too.
Nay, let Whitehall with revels have to do,

----

[2] *I saw with two poor* chambers taken in,] i. e. destroyed with
two small pieces of ordnance.

[3] *And this a sparkle of that fire let loose,*
   That was raked up in the Winchestrian goose,
   Bred on the Bank *in time of Popery,*
   When Venus there maintain'd the mystery.] Anciently the
Bank-side was a continued row of brothels, which were put down
by proclamation in the time of Henry VIII. As this place was
within the limits of the bishop of Winchester's jurisdiction, a person
who had suffered in venereal combats, was opprobriously called
a *Winchester goose.* WHAL.

[4] ———— Fortune, *for being a whore,*
   'Scap'd not his justice any jot the more.] There was in the city
a theatre called the *Fortune play-house,* which likewise suffered by
fire about this time. WHAL.

    Again ! *about this time.* This is a very convenient mode of

Though but in dances, it shall know his power;
There was a judgment shewn too in an hour.
He is right Vulcan still! he did not spare
Troy, though it were so much his Venus' care.
Fool, wilt thou let that in example come?
Did not she save from thence to build a Rome?
And what hast thou done in these petty spites,
More than advanced the houses and their rites?
I will not argue thee, from those, of guilt,
For they were burnt but to be better built:
'Tis true, that in thy wish they were destroy'd,
Which thou hast only vented, not enjoy'd.
So would'st thou've run upon the rolls by stealth,[5]
And didst invade part of the common-wealth,

fixing events. But the *Fortune* was not burnt down till more than eight years after the *Globe*, that is, not till 1621.

It appears from Heywood's *English Travellers*, that this theatre took its name from a figure of Fortune.

"*Old Lio.* Sirrah, come down.

Reig. Not till my pardon's seal'd: I'll rather stand here,
    Like a statue, in the full front of your house
    For ever; like the picture of dame Fortune,
    Before the Fortune play-house."

In the preface to this comedy, Heywood says, "that modesty prevents him from exposing his plays to the public view in numerous sheets, and a large volume, under the title of works, as others." Here, says the *Biographia Dramatica*, a stroke was probably aimed at Ben Jonson, who gave his *plays* the pompous title of "Works." This stupid falsehood has been repeated a thousand times. Jonson no more gave his plays the title of "Works," than Shakspeare, Fletcher, Shirley, or any other writer; nor is there a single instance of such a fact in existence. The whole matter is, that, when he collected his various pieces, consisting of Comedies, Tragedies, Masques, Entertainments, Epigrams, and a selection of Poetry, under the name of *Forest*, with equal taste and judgment, and with a classical contempt of the mountebank titles of his time, he called the multifarious assemblage simply "The Works of Ben Jonson." For this proof of his good sense, he was slandered even in his own time; and the charge of arrogance and vanity is, in our's, still repeated from fool to fool.

[5] *So would'st thou've run upon the rolls, &c.*] This alludes to a

In those records, which, were all chronicles gone,
Would be remembered by Six Clerks to one.
But say all six, good men, what answer ye ?
Lies there no writ out of the Chancery
Against this Vulcan ? no injunction,
No order, no decree ?—though we be gone
At common-law ; methinks, in his despite,
A court of equity should do us right.
But to confine him to the brew-houses,
The glass-house, dye-fats, and their furnaces ;
To live in sea-coal, and go forth in smoke ;
Or, lest that vapour might the city choak,
Condemn him to the brick-kilns, or some hill-
Foot, (out in Sussex,) to an iron mill ;
Or in small faggots have him blaze about
Vile taverns, and the drunkards piss him out ;
Or in the Bellman's lanthorn, like a spy,
Burn to a snuff, and then stink out and die :
I could invent a sentence, yet were worse ;
But I'll conclude all in a civil curse.
Pox on your flameship, Vulcan ! if it be
To all as fatal as't hath been to me,
And to Paul's steeple ; which was unto us
'Bove all your fire-works had at Ephesus,
Or Alexandria ;[6] and, though a divine
Loss, remains yet as unrepair'd as mine.
    Would you had kept your forge at Ætna still !
And there made swords, bills, glaves, and arms
                your fill :
Maintain'd the trade at Bilboa, or elsewhere,
Struck in at Milan with the cutlers there ;

fire which took place in the Six Clerks' Office ; but I cannot specify
the date of it : nor of that at Whitehall, mentioned in the preceding
page.
    [6] *'Bove all your fire-works had at* Ephesus
    And Alexandria.] The burning of the temple of Diana at
Ephesus, and the library at *Alexandria*. WHAL.

Or staid but where the friar and you first met,
Who from the devil's arse did guns beget;
Or fixt in the Low Countries, where you might
On both sides do your mischief with delight:
Blow up and ruin, mine and countermine,
Make your petards and granades, all your fine
Engines of murder, and enjoy the praise
Of massácring mankind so many ways!
We ask your absence here, we all love peace,
And pray the fruits thereof and the encrease;
So doth the king, and most of the king's men
That have good places: therefore once agen,
Pox on thee, Vulcan! thy Pandora's pox,
And all the ills that flew out of her box
Light on thee! or, if those plagues will not do,
Thy wife's pox on thee, and Bess Broughton's too!

LXII.

A SPEECH, ACCORDING TO HORACE.

HY yet, my noble hearts, they cannot say,
But we have powder still for the king's day,
And ordnance too: so much as from the
Tower,
T' have wak'd, if sleeping, Spain's ambassadour,
Old Æsop Gundomar:[7] the French can tell,
For they did see it the last tilting well,
That we have trumpets, armour, and great horse,
Lances and men, and some a breaking force.

[7] *Old Æsop Gundomar.*] Gundomar appears not to have owed
many obligations to nature: he was however a shrewd politician,
and a bold and able negotiator. He was dreaded by the court,
and disliked by the people, of which we have sufficient proof in the
repeated attacks made upon him by the dramatic poets, the true
mirrors of their times.

They saw too store of feathers, and more may,
If they stay here but till St. George's day.
All ensigns of a war are not yet dead,
Nor marks of wealth so from a nation fled,
But they may see gold chains and pearl worn then,
Lent by the London dames to the Lords' men:
Withal, the dirty pains those citizens take,
To see the pride at Court, their wives do make;
And the return those thankful courtiers yield,
To have their husbands drawn forth to the field,
And coming home to tell what acts were done
Under the auspice of young Swinnerton.[8]
What a strong fort old Pimlico had been!
How it held out! how, last, 'twas taken in!—
Well, I say, thrive, thrive, brave Artillery-yard,
Thou seed-plot of the war! that hast not spar'd
Powder or paper to bring up the youth
Of London, in the military truth,
These ten years day; as all may swear that look
But on thy practice, and the posture book.

   He that but saw thy curious captain's drill,
Would think no more of Flushing or the Brill,
But give them over to the common ear,
For that unnecessary charge they were.
Well did thy crafty clerk and knight, Sir Hugh,
Supplant bold Panton, and brought there to view
Translated Ælian's tactics to be read,
And the Greek discipline, with the modern, shed
So in that ground, as soon it grew to be
The city-question, whether Tilly or he
Were now the greater captain? for they saw
The Berghen siege, and taking in Bredau,
So acted to the life, as Maurice might,
And Spinola have blushed at the sight.

   [8] *Young Swinnerton.*] Sir John Swinnerton was mayor of London
in 1612. This aspiring and heroic youth was probably his son. The
father had endeared himself to the citizens by many benefactions.

O happy art ! and wise epitome
Of bearing arms ! most civil soldiery !
Thou canst draw forth thy forces, and fight dry
The battles of thy aldermanity ;
Without the hazard of a drop of blood ;
More than the surfeits in thee that day stood.
Go on, increas'd in virtue and in fame,
And keep the glory of the English name
Up among nations.   In the stead of bold
Beauchamps and Nevills, Cliffords, Audleys old,
Insert thy Hodges, and those newer men,
As Stiles, Dike, Ditchfield, Millar, Crips, and Fen :
That keep the war, though now 't be grown more
          tame,
Alive yet in the noise, and still the same,
And could, if our great men would let their sons
Come to their schools, shew them the use of guns ;
And there instruct the noble English heirs
In politic and military affairs.
But he that should persuade to have this done
For education of our lordlings, soon
Should he [not] hear of billow, wind, and storm
From the tempestuous grandlings, who'll inform
Us, in our bearing, that are thus and thus,
Born, bred, allied ? what's he dare tutor us ?
Are we by book-worms to be aw'd ? must we
Live by their scale, that dare do nothing free ?
Why are we rich or great, except to show
All license in our lives ? what need we know
More than to praise a dog, or horse ? or speak
The hawking language ? or our day to break
With citizens ? let clowns and tradesmen breed
Their sons to study arts, the laws, the creed :
We will believe like men of our own rank,
In so much land a year, or such a bank,
That turns us so much monies, at which rate
Our ancestors imposed on prince and state.

Let poor nobility be virtuous : we,
Descended in a rope of titles, be
From Guy, or Bevis, Arthur, or from whom
The herald will : our blood is now become
Past any need of virtue.   Let them care,
That in the cradle of their gentry are,
To serve the state by councils and by arms :
We neither love the troubles nor the harms.
What love you then? your whore ; what study? gait,
Carriage, and dressing.   There is up of late
The Academy, where the gallants meet——
What! to make legs? yes, and to smell most sweet:
All that they do at plays.   O but first here
They learn and study ; and then practise there.
But why are all these irons in the fire,
Of several makings ?   Helps, helps, to attire
His lordship ; that is for his band, his hair
This, and that box his beauty to repair ;
This other for his eye-brows : hence, away,
I may no longer on these pictures stay,
These carcases of honour ; tailors' blocks
Cover'd with tissue, whose prosperity mocks
The fate of things ; whilst tatter'd virtue holds
Her broken arms up to their empty moulds !

LXIII.

An Epistle

TO MASTER ARTHUR SQUIB.

WHAT I am not, and what I fain would be,
Whilst I inform myself, I would teach thee,
My gentle Arthur, that it might be said
One lesson we have both learn'd, and well
    read.
I neither am, nor art thou one of those
That hearkens to a jack's pulse, when it goes

Nor ever trusted to that friendship yet,
Was issue of the tavern or the spit :
Much less a name would we bring up, or nurse,
That could but claim a kindred from the purse.
Those are poor ties depend on those false ends,
'Tis virtue alone, or nothing, that knits friends.
And as within your office[9] you do take
No piece of money, but you know, or make
Inquiry of the worth ; so must we do,
First weigh a friend, then touch and try him too :
For there are many slips and counterfeits.[1]
Deceit is fruitful : Men have masks and nets ;
But these with wearing will themselves unfold,
They cannot last.   No lie grew ever old.
Turn him, and see his threads ; look if he be
Friend to himself that would be friend to thee.
For that is first required, a man be his own :
But he that's too much that, is friend of none.
Then rest, and a friend's value understand,
It is a richer purchase than of land.

[9] *And as within your office, &c.*] It appears that this gentleman
was one of the principal clerks in the Exchequer.   I find several
of his name, in succession, in the books of that office.
   [1] *For there are many* slips *and* counterfeits.] For these terms,
see vol. vi. p. 71.

LXIV.

AN EPIGRAM ON SIR EDWARD COKE,[2]

WHEN HE WAS LORD CHIEF JUSTICE OF ENGLAND.

E that should search all glories of the gown,
And steps of all raised servants of the crown,
He could not find than thee, of all that store,
Whom fortune aided less, or virtue more.
Such, Coke, were thy beginnings, when thy good
In others evil best was understood :
When, being the stranger's help, the poor man's aid,
Thy just defences made th' oppressor afraid.
Such was thy process, when integrity,
And skill in thee now grew authority,

---

[2] *An epigram on sir* Edward Coke.] Addressed to him, probably when he was created lord chief justice, in the year 1606. WHAL.

Whalley assigns too early a date to this Epigram : Coke was, as he says, created lord chief justice in 1606; but it was of the Common Pleas : he did not take the style of *lord chief justice of England*, till he was advanced to the King's-bench in 1613, when he was in his sixty-fifth year. Jonson follows the style of sir Edward in giving him this title, which he appears to have affected, and which James objected to his assuming—"He calls himself in his books," the king says, "lord chief justice of England, whereas he can challenge no more but lord chief justice of the King's-bench."

This great lawyer did not *bear his faculties meekly*. His proud and overbearing spirit involved him in various prosecutions; his office was taken from him in 1616, and the residue of his life was spent in a strange and rapid alternation of favour and disgrace, of turbulence and submission. He died in 1634 at the age of eighty-six : had it been his good fortune to follow his royal mistress to the grave, he would have come down to us not only as one of the most eminent lawyers this country ever produced, but as one of the most dignified and respectable characters of his age.

As a composition, this Epigram boasts considerable merit. It is vigorous and manly; has truth for its basis, and characterizes both the author and his works with discrimination and judgment. I suppose it to be written in 1613.

That clients strove in question of the laws,
More for thy patronage, than for their cause,
And that thy strong and manly eloquence
Stood up thy nation's fame, her crown's defence ;
And now such is thy stand, while thou dost deal
Desired justice to the public weal,
Like Solon's self, explat'st the knotty laws
With endless labours,[3] whilst thy learning draws
No less of praise, than readers, in all kinds
Of worthiest knowledge, that can take men's minds.
Such is thy all, that, as I sung before,
None Fortune aided less, or virtue more.
Or if chance must to each man that doth rise,
Needs lend an aid, to thine she had her eyes.

[3] *Like Solon's self,* explat'st *the knotty laws*
With endless labours, &c.] I never yet met with the word
explat'st, but do not take upon me to pronounce it a corruption.
When I consider the license which Jonson sometimes allowed himself of coining an expressive word, I am tempted to think this proceeded from the same poetic mint. WHAL.

Whalley is wrong. Jonson sometimes uses a Latin word, but
then he prints it in a different character: his latinisms are those
of his contemporaries. All our old writers use pleat, plight, for
wreath, curl, fold, &c., from *plico*: expleat is as correctly formed
from *explico*, to open, smooth, display, &c. *Explation*, a kindred
word, is in Cole, and displeat and unpleat are sufficiently common
in our old poets. *Explica frontem* is rendered by Jo. Davies, in
his eclogue, 1620, "Unpleat thy brow."

LXV.

An Epistle,

ANSWERING TO ONE THAT ASKED TO BE SEALED OF
THE TRIBE OF BEN.[4]

EN that are safe and sure in all they do,
Care not what trials they are put unto :
They meet the fire, the test, as martyrs
    would,
And though opinion stamp them not, are gold.
I could say more of such, but that I fly
To speak myself out too ambitiously,
And shewing so weak an act to vulgar eyes,
Put conscience and my right to compromise.
Let those that merely talk, and never think,
That live in the wild anarchy of drink,
Subject to quarrel only ; or else such
As make it their proficiency, how much
They've glutted in, and letcher'd out that week,
That never yet did friend or friendship seek,

---

[4] *An Epistle, &c.*] This appears, from internal evidence, to
have been written not long before the death of James. It was the
practice of the older poets, upon request, to adopt young men of
talents in whose reputation, or success in life, by a species of
patronage or filiation, they became warmly interested. Jonson
had many sons of this kind, and to an aspirant for the honour of
becoming such (probably, to Randolph or Cleveland) he addresses
the above Epistle. The number of his adopted progeny is alluded
to in the foolish expression of one " that asked," &c.
    There is a spirit and vigour in this Epistle which do the poet
great credit. The sentiments are manly, and some of them drawn
from the higher philosophy. It wants the smoothness and the
artificial rhythm of these times; but what poem of equal length,
of these times, possesses such depth of thought and force of expression ?

But for a sealing :⁵ let these men protest.
Or th' other on their borders, that will jest
On all souls that are absent ; even the dead,
Like flies or worms, which man's corrupt parts fed :
That to speak well, think it above all sin,
Of any company but that they are in,
Call'd every night to supper in these fits,
And are received for the Covey of Wits ;
That censure all the town, and all the affairs,
And know whose ignorance is more than theirs :
Let these men have their ways, and take their
       times
To vent their libels, and to issue rhymes,
I have no portion in them, nor their deal
Of news they get, to strew out the long meal ;⁶
I study other friendships, and more one,
Than these can ever be, or else wish none.
    What is't to me, whether the French design
Be, or be not, to get the Valteline ?
Or the States' ships sent forth be like to meet
Some hopes of Spain in their West Indian fleet ?
Whether the dispensation yet be sent,
Or that the match from Spain was ever meant ?
I wish all well, and pray high heaven conspire
My prince's safety, and my king's desire ;
But if for honour we must draw the sword,
And force back that which will not be restor'd,
I have a body yet that spirit draws,
To live, or fall a carcase, in the cause.
So far without enquiry what the States,
Brunsfield, and Mansfield, do this year, my fates

---

⁵ *But for a* sealing,] i. e. becoming sureties for them, joining them in their bonds.

⁶ ——————— *nor their deal*

    Of news they get, to strew out the long meal.] This is the *town's honest man*, described with such scorn and indignation in a former page. See Epig. cxv.

8   E E

Shall carry me at call; and I'll be well,
Though I do neither hear these news, nor tell
Of Spain or France; or were not prick'd down one,
Of the late mystery of reception;
Although my fame to his not under-hears,
That guides the motions, and directs the bears.
But that's a blow, by which in time I may
Lose all my credit with my Christmas clay,
And animated porcelaine of the court;
Ay, and for this neglect, the coarser sort
Of earthern jars there, may molest me too:
Well, with mine own frail pitcher, what to do
I have decreed; keep it from waves and press,
Lest it be justled, crack'd, made nought, or less.
Live to that point I will, for which I am man,
And dwell as in my centre, as I can,
Still looking to, and ever loving heaven;
With reverence using all the gifts thence given:
'Mongst which, if I have any friendships sent,
Such as are square, well-tagg'd, and permanent,
Not built with canvas, paper, and false lights,
As are the glorious scenes at the great sights:
And that there be no fevery heats nor colds,
Oily expansions, or shrunk dirty folds,
But all so clear, and led by reason's flame,
As but to stumble in her sight were shame;
These I will honour, love, embrace, and serve,
And free it from all question to preserve.
So short you read my character, and theirs
I would call mine, to which not many stairs
Are ask'd to climb.   First give me faith, who know
Myself a little; I will take you so,
As you have writ yourself: now stand, and then,
Sir, you are Sealed of the tribe of Ben.

LXVI.

THE DEDICATION OF THE KING'S NEW CELLAR TO BACCHUS.

Accessit fervor capiti, numerusque lucernis.

SINCE, Bacchus, thou art father
Of wines, to thee the rather
We dedicate this Cellar,
Where now thou art made dweller,
And seal thee thy commission :
But 'tis with a condition,
That thou remain here taster
Of all to the great master ;
And look unto their faces,
Their qualities and races,
That both their odour take him,
And relish merry make him.
For, Bacchus, thou art freër
Of cares, and overseër
Of feast and merry meeting,
And still begin'st the greeting :
See then thou dost attend him,
Lyæus, and defend him,
By all the arts of gladness,
From any thought like sadness.
So may'st thou still be younger
Than Phœbus, and much stronger,
To give mankind their eases,
And cure the world's diseases !
So may the Muses follow
Thee still, and leave Apollo,
And think thy stream more quicker
Than Hippocrene's liquor :
And thou make many a poet,
Before his brain do know it !

So may there never quarrel
Have issue from the barrel,
But Venus and the Graces
Pursue thee in all places,
And not a song be other
Than Cupid and his mother!
That when king James above here
Shall feast it, thou may'st love there
The causes and the guests too,
And have thy tales and jests too,
Thy circuits and thy rounds free,
As shall the feast's fair grounds be.
Be it he holds communion
In great St. George's union ;
Or gratulates the passage
Of some well wrought embassage,
Whereby he may knit sure up
The wished peace of Europe :
Or else a health advances,
To put his court in dances,
And set us all on skipping,
When with his royal shipping,
The narrow seas are shady,
And Charles brings home the lady.[7]

LXVII.

AN EPIGRAM ON THE COURT PUCELLE.

DOES the Court Pucelle then so censure me,
    And thinks I dare not her? let the world
      see.
    What though her chamber be the very pit,
Where fight the prime cocks of the game, for wit ;

---

[7] *And Charles brings home the* lady.] This was written when the

And that as any are struck, her breath creates
New in their stead, out of the candidates!
What though with tribade lust she force a muse,
And in an epicœne fury can write news
Equal with that which for the best news goes,
As airy, light, and as like wit as those!
What though she talk, and can at once with them
Make state, religion, bawdry, all a theme;
And as lip-thirsty, in each word's expense,
Doth labour with the phrase more than the sense!
What though she ride two mile on holydays
To church, as others do to feasts and plays,
To shew their tires, to view, and to be view'd!
What though she be with velvet gowns endued,
And spangled petticoats brought forth to th' eye,
As new rewards of her old secrecy!
What though she hath won on trust, as many do,
And that her truster fears her! must I too?
I never stood for any place: my wit
Thinks itself nought, though she should value it.
I am no statesman, and much less divine;
For bawd'ry, 'tis her language, and not mine.
Farthest I am from the idolatry
To stuffs and laces; those my man can buy.
And trust her I would least, that hath forswore
In contract twice; what can she perjure more?
Indeed her dressing some man might delight,
Her face there's none can like by candle-light:
Not he, that should the body have, for case
To his poor instrument, now out of grace.

match with the *Infanta* of *Spain* was in agitation, and the prince
was at the Spanish court. WHAL.

    This cellar was built by Inigo Jones. The circumstance is
worth mentioning, as it serves to corroborate what has been more
than once asserted, that till the period of the appearance of *Chloridia*, no breach of friendship had taken place between him and
our author.

Shall I advise thee, Pucelle ? steal away
From court, while yet thy fame hath some small day;
The wits will leave you if they once perceive
You cling to lords ; and lords, if them you leave
For sermoneers : of which now one, now other,
They say you weekly invite with fits o' th' mother,
And practise for a miracle ; take heed,
This age will lend no faith to Darrel's deed ;[8]
Or if it would, the court is the worst place,
Both for the mothers, and the babes of grace ;
For there the wicked in the chair of scorn,
Will call't a bastard, when a prophet's born.

LXVIII.

AN EPIGRAM

TO THE HONOURED COUNTESS OF * * *.

THE wisdom, madam, of your private life,
   Wherewith this while you live a widow'd
       wife,
   And the right ways you take unto the right,
To conquer rumour, and triúmph on spite ;

[8] *This age will lend no faith to* Darrel's *deed.*] Many impostures
of possession by evil spirits were practised about this time by
Roman Catholics to delude and make converts of the vulgar. The
boy of *Bilson* is a famous instance. Several others, amongst whom
is this of *Darrel*, are mentioned in the *Devil is an Ass. Darrel*
was the author of a book printed in 4to. 1600, intituled, *A true
narration of the strange and grievous vexation by the devil, of seven
persons in Lancashire, and William Sommers of Nottingham:* as
perhaps he was equally concerned in carrying on the imposture.
This book was answered by Dr. Harsnet, afterwards archbishop of
York, in a piece intituled, *A discovery of the fraudulent practices of*
John Darrel *minister*. WHAL.
   See the *Devil is an Ass*, for a fuller account of these impostures.
The last couplet of this poem has a singular bearing on the juggle
of Joanna Southcote.

Not only shunning by your act to do
Aught that is ill, but the suspicion too,
Is of so brave example, as he were
No friend to virtue, could be silent here;
The rather when the vices of the time
Are grown so fruitful, and false pleasures climb,
By all oblique degrees, that killing height
From whence they fall, cast down with their own
      weight.
And though all praise bring nothing to your name,
Who (herein studying conscience, and not fame)
Are in yourself rewarded; yet 'twill be
A cheerful work to all good eyes, to see
Among the daily ruins that fall foul
Of state, of fame, of body, and of soul,
So great a virtue stand upright to view,
As makes Penelope's old fable true,
Whilst your Ulysses hath ta'en leave to go.
Countries and climes, manners and men to know,
Only your time you better entertain,
Than the great Homer's wit for her could feign;
For you admit no company but good,
And when you want those friends, or near in blood,
Or your allies, you make your books your friends,
And study them unto the noblest ends,
Searching for knowledge, and to keep your mind
The same it was inspired, rich and refined.
   These graces, when the rest of ladies view,
Not boasted in your life, but practis'd true,
As they are hard for them to make their own,
So are they profitable to be known:
For when they find so many meet in one,
It will be shame for them, if they have none.[9]

[9] This is an excellent little poem. There seems to have been
no occasion for suppressing the lady's name. It would not be
difficult to suggest a person whom the lines would fit; but the
safer way, perhaps, is to follow the poet's executors.

LXIX.

On lord Bacon's birth-day.

HAIL, happy Genius of this ancient pile!
How comes it all things so about thee smile?[1]
The fire, the wine, the men! and in the midst
Thou stand'st as if some mystery thou didst!
Pardon, I read it in thy face, the day
For whose returns, and many, all these pray;

[1] *Hail, happy genius of this ancient pile!*
How comes it all things so about thee smile?] When lord Bacon was high chancellor of England, he procured from the king York-house for the place of his residence, for which he seems to have had an affection, as being the place of his birth, and where his father had lived all the time he possessed the high office of lord keeper of the great seal. Here, in the beginning of the year 1620, he kept his birth-day with great splendor and magnificence, which gave occasion to the compliment expressed in the short poem above. The verse indeed, like most of Jonson's, is somewhat harsh, but there is much good sense, and a vein of poetry to recommend it to our notice. The reader will observe the poem implies a very beautiful fiction; the poet starting, as it were, on his entering York-house, at the sight of the *Genius* of the place performing some mystery, which he discovers from the gaiety of his look, and takes occasion from thence to form the congratulatory compliment.
WHAL.

Nothing is more remarkable in Jonson's character than the steadiness of his friendship. It is for this reason (for I can discover no other,) that Steevens and Malone insist particularly on the *fickleness* of his attachments! When Jonson wrote this poem, lord Bacon was in the full tide of prosperity; the year after, misfortune overtook him; and he continued in poverty, neglect, and disgrace till his death, which took place in 1627. Yet the poet did not change his language; nor allow himself to be checked by the unpopularity of the Ex-chancellor's name, or the dread of displeasing his sovereign and patron, from bearing that generous testimony to his talents and virtues which is inserted in his *Discoveries*, and which concludes with these words. "My conceit of lord Verulam's person was never increased by his place or honour: but I have, and do reverence him for the greatness that was only proper to himself, in that he seemed to me ever by his work one of

And so do I. This is the sixtieth year,
Since Bacon, and thy lord was born, and here ;
Son to the grave wise Keeper of the Seal,
Fame and foundation of the English weal.
What then his father was, that since is he,
Now with a title more to the degree ;
England's high Chancellor : the destin'd heir,
In his soft cradle, to his father's chair :
Whose even thread the fates spin round and full,
Out of their choicest and their whitest wool.
  'Tis a brave cause of joy, let it be known,
For 'twere a narrow gladness, kept thine own.
Give me a deep-crown'd bowl, that I may sing,
In raising him, the wisdom of my king.

LXX.

THE POET TO THE PAINTER.[2]

AN ANSWER.

WHY, though I seem of a prodigious waist,
    I am not so voluminous and vast,
    But there are lines, wherewith I might be'
      embrac'd.
'Tis true, as my womb swells, so my back stoops,
And the whole lump grows round, deform'd, and
    droops ;
But yet the Tun at Heidelberg had hoops.

the greatest men, and most worthy of admiration, that had been in
many ages. In his adversity I ever prayed that God would give
him strength, for *greatness* he could not want. Neither could I
condole, in a word or syllable for him ; as knowing no accident
could do harm to virtue ; but rather help to make it manifest."
This, with the commentators' leave, is a very pretty specimen of
" old Ben's flattery of kings," and " hatred of all merit but his
own ! "

  [2] *The Poet to the Painter.*] This is an " answer," as Jonson

You were not tied by any painter's law
To square my circle, I confess, but draw
My superficies : that was all you saw.

Which if in compass of no art it came
To be described by a monogram,
With one great blot you had form'd me as I am.

But whilst you curious were to have it be
An archetype, for all the world to see,
You made it a brave piece, but not like me.

O, had I now your manner, mastery, might,
Your power of handling, shadow, air, and spright,
How I would draw, and take hold and delight!

But you are he can paint, I can but write :
A poet hath no more but black and white,
Ne knows he flattering colours, or false light.

calls it, to the following miserable attempt at verse, by sir William
Burlase :—

"THE PAINTER TO THE POET.

To paint thy worth, if rightly I did know it,
And were but painter half like thee, a poet ;
          Ben, I would shew it :

But in this skill my unskilful pen will tire,
Thou, and thy worth will still be found far higher ;
          And I a liar.

Then, what a painter's here ? or what an eater
Of great attempts ! when as his skill's no greater,
          And he a cheater ?

Then, what a poet's here ! whom, by confession
Of all with me, to paint without digression
          There's no expression."

I cannot be confident that I understand this : It would seem as if
sir W. Burlase had made a drawing or a painting of the poet, to
which this doggrel served as an accompaniment.

There is an Edmund Burlase who has a copy of verses on the
death of sir Horace Vere (1642), but whether related to this sir
William, I cannot tell. If he was his son, the family vein of poetry
had much improved, for he writes well.

Yet when of friendship I would draw the face,
A letter'd mind, and a large heart would place
To all posterity; I will write Burlase.

LXXI.

AN EPIGRAM

to William Earl of Newcastle. [3]

WHEN first, my lord, I saw you back your
horse,
Provoke his mettle, and command his force
To all the uses of the field and race,
Methought I read the ancient art of Thrace,

[3] Of this distinguished nobleman, the pride and ornament of the British Peerage, a most interesting account is given by lord Clarendon, with whom he stood deservedly high. "Nobody but lord Orford (says sir E. Bridges), who could decry sir Philip Sidney" (and lord Falkland), "would have traduced a man possessed of so many qualities to engage the esteem of mankind as the duke of Newcastle : but lord Orford had a tendency to depreciate the loyalists." He had a tendency to depreciate whatever was great and good. Dead to every generous feeling, selfish, greedy, and sneakingly ostentatious, Walpole, in the midst of a baby-house, surrounded with a collection of childish trumpery, had the audacity to speak in this manner of a man, who, after strenuously fulfilling every duty of life, as a patriot, a soldier, and a statist, retired to his paternal seat, where he lived in the practice of a magnificent hospitality, the friend of genius, the liberal patron of worth, employing the close of an active and honourable life in innocent and elegant pursuits which might benefit many, and could injure none.

"What a picture of *foolish* nobility was this stately poetic couple (the duke and duchess) retired to their own little domain" (it was at least as extensive as Strawberry-hill) "and intoxicating one another with circumstantial flattery on what was *of consequence to no mortal but themselves*." Surely the demon of Vengeance must have been at Walpole's elbow, when he penned this sentence. *Royal and Noble Authors.*

And saw a centaur,[4] past those tales of Greece,
So seem'd your horse and you both of a piece!
You shew'd like Perseus upon Pegasus,
Or Castor mounted on his Cyllarus;
Or what we hear our home-born legend tell,
Of bold Sir Bevis, and his Arundel;
Nay, so your seat his beauties did endorse,
As I began to wish myself a horse:[5]
And surely, had I but your stable seen
Before, I think my wish absolv'd had been.
For never saw I yet the Muses dwell,
Nor any of their household, half so well.
So well! as when I saw the floor and room,
I look'd for Hercules to be the groom;
And cried, Away with the Cæsarian bread!
At these immortal mangers Virgil fed.[6]

[4] *Methought I read the ancient art of Thrace,*
And saw a centaur, &c.]   The earl of Newcastle was the most
accomplished horseman of his time: his celebrated work on the
method of managing horses, of which a magnificent edition in folio
appeared some years ago, was not published during the poet's life.

[5] *As I began to wish myself a horse.*] This is probably an allusion
to the very pretty incident with which sir Philip Sidney so aptly
opens his *Defence of Poesy.*   Pietro Pugliana, he says, discoursed
with such fertileness and spirit on the various merits of the animal,
"that if I had not been a piece of a logician before I came to
him, I think he would have persuaded me *to have wished myself a
horse.*"

[6] *Away with the* Cæsarian bread!
At these immortal mangers Virgil *fed.*]   Alluding to that circumstance in the life of Virgil, of his being employed in the stables
of Augustus, and having his customary allowance of *bread* doubled,
for the judgment he gave of a colt the emperor had just bought.

WHAL.

LXXII.

EPISTLE

TO MASTER ARTHUR SQUIB.

AM to dine, friend, where I must be weigh'd
For a just wager, and that wager paid
If I do lose it; and, without a tale,
A merchant's wife is regent of the scale.
Who when she heard the match, concluded straight,
An ill commodity! it must make good weight.[7]
So that, upon the point, my corporal fear
Is, she will play dame justice too severe;
And hold me to it close; to stand upright
Within the balance, and not want a mite;
But rather with advantage to be found
Full twenty stone, of which I lack two pound;
That's six in silver:[8] now within the socket
Stinketh my credit, if, into the pocket
It do not come: one piece I have in store,
Lend me, dear Arthur, for a week, five more,
And you shall make me good in weight and fashion,
And then to be return'd; or protestation

---

[7] *An* ill *commodity, &c.*] The lady alludes, I presume, to the *decisive depression* of the scale, exacted in the weighing of *coarse* merchandize.

[8] *But, rather with advantage to be found*
   Full twenty stone; of which I lack two pound:
   That's six in silver.] The wager, it seems, was that the poet weighed full twenty stone, but he found that he wanted two pounds of that weight. This he artfully turns to a reason for borrowing five pounds in money of his friend Mr. Squib, which added to the pound he had of his own, would make up the deficiency in his weight. Six pounds in silver, he says, will weigh two pounds in weight: it may be so; we will take his word. WHAL.
   I doubt whether we understand the nature of this wager, which was probably a mere jest. If the sense be as Whalley states it, there is as little of *art* as of honesty in it.

To go out after :——till when take this letter
For your security.   I can no better.

LXXIII.

TO MASTER JOHN BURGES.[9]

WOULD God, my Burges, I could think
    Thoughts worthy of thy gift, this ink,
    Then would I promise here to give
    Verse that should thee and me outlive.
But since the wine hath steep'd my brain,
I only can the paper stain ;
Yet with a dye that fears no moth,
But scarlet-like, out-lasts the cloth.

[9] *To master John Burges.*] Burges was probably the deputy
paymaster of the household. He had made Jonson a present of
some ink, and this little production, which wants neither spirit
nor a proper self-confidence, inclosed, perhaps, the return for it.
Master Burges might have sent the wine at the same time.

Jonson, who lived much about the court while his health permitted him to come abroad, seems to have made friends of most of
those who held official situations there, and to have been supplied
with stationery, and, perhaps, many other petty articles. The
following is transcribed from the blank leaf of a volume of miscellaneous poetry, formerly in the possession of Dr. John Hoadley,
son of the bishop of Winchester. He has written over it, " A Re-
lique of Ben Jonson."

> " To my worthy and deserving Brother
>   M[r]. Alexander Glover,
>   as the Token of my Love,
>   And the perpetuating of our Friendship,
>   I send this small, but hearty Testimony ;
>   And with Charge, that it remayne wth Him,
> Till I at much expense of time and taper,
> With 'Chequer-Ink, upon his gift, my paper,
> Shall pour forth many a line, drop many a letter
> To make these good, and what comes after, better.
>   BEN JONSON."

LXXV.

EPISTLE

TO MY LADY COVELL.

YOU won not verses, madam, you won me,
When you would play so nobly, and so free,
A book to a few lines! but it was fit
You won them too, your odds did merit it.
So have you gained a Servant and a Muse:
The first of which I fear you will refuse,
And you may justly; being a tardy, cold,
Unprofitable chattel, fat and old,
Laden with belly, and doth hardly approach
His friends, but to break chairs, or crack a coach.
His weight is twenty stone within two pound;
And that's made up, as doth the purse abound.[1]
Marry, the Muse is one can tread the air,
And stroke the water, nimble, chaste and fair;
Sleep in a virgin's bosom without fear,
Run all the rounds in a soft lady's ear,
Widow or wife, without the jealousy
Of either suitor, or a servant by.
Such, if her manners like you, I do send:
And can for other graces her commend,
To make you merry on the dressing-stool
A mornings, and at afternoons to fool
Away ill company, and help in rhyme
Your Joan to pass her melancholy time.
By this, although you fancy not the man,
Accept his muse; and tell, I know you can,
How many verses, madam, are your due!
I can lose none in tendering these to you.

---

[1] *And that's made up, &c.*]   Is this too a hint?—If so, it must
have sorely puzzled the lady, unless she had previously seen the
Epistle to master Squib.

I gain in having leave to keep my day,
And should grow rich, had I much more to pay,

LXXV.

TO MASTER JOHN BURGES.

FATHER John Burges,
  Necessity urges
  My woeful cry
  To Sir Robert Pie :[2]
And that he will venture
To send my debenture.
Tell him his Ben
Knew the time, when
He loved the Muses ;
Though now he refuses,
To take apprehension
Of a year's pension,
And more is behind :
Put him in mind
Christmas is near ;
And neither good cheer,
Mirth, fooling, nor wit,
Nor any least fit
Of gambol or sport
Will come at the court ;
If there be no money,
No plover or coney

---

[2] *My woeful cry*
To sir Robert Pie.] Sir Robert Pie was appointed to the Exchequer about 1618, upon the resignation of sir John Bingley, who was implicated in a charge of peculation with the lord treasurer, the earl of Suffolk. Sir Robert was a retainer of Buckingham's, to whose interest he owed his promotion. He was the ancestor of the late laureat, under whose hands the family estate vanished. Mr. Pye had probably raised his *woeful cry* to the treasurer of the day as loudly as Jonson, for he was equally clamorous and necessitous. Such are the mutations of time !

Will come to the table,
Or wine to enable
The muse, or the poet,
The parish will know it.
Nor any quick warming-pan help him to bed;
If the 'Chequer be empty, so will be his head.

LXXVI.

EPIGRAM

TO MY BOOKSELLER.

HOU, friend, wilt hear all censures; unto
thee
All mouths are open, and all stomachs free:
Be thou my book's intelligencer, note
What each man says of it, and of what coat
His judgment is; if he be wise, and praise,
Thank him; if other, he can give no bays.
If his wit reach no higher, but to spring
Thy wife a fit of laughter; a cramp-ring
Will be reward enough; to wear like those,
That hang their richest jewels in their nose:
Like a rung bear or swine; grunting out wit
As if that part lay for a ——[3] most fit!
If they go on, and that thou lov'st a-life
Their perfumed judgments, let them kiss thy wife.

[3] A word has been dropt in the folio, and I cannot re-instate it.

8 F F

LXXVII.

AN EPITAPH

ON HENRY LORD LA-WARE.[4]

IF, Passenger, thou canst but read,
Stay, drop a tear for him that's dead :
Henry, the brave young lord La-ware,
Minerva's and the Muses' care !
What could their care do 'gainst the spite
Of a disease, that lov'd no light
Of honour, nor no air of good ;
But crept like darkness through his blood,
Offended with the dazzling flame
Of virtue, got above his name ?
No noble furniture of parts,
No love of action and high arts ;
No aim at glory, or in war,
Ambition to become a star,
Could stop the malice of this ill,
That spread his body o'er to kill :
And only his great soul envièd,
Because it durst have noblier died.

[4] The son of Thomas, lord De-la-ware, the first settler of the colony of Virginia, of which he was appointed captain-general by James I. in 1609. Henry succeeded him as fourth lord De-la-ware, in 1618, and died in 1628, the date of this Epitaph, at the early age of 25. He was a young man of great promise.

LXXVIII.

AN EPIGRAM[5]

TO THE LORD - KEEPER.

THAT you have seen the pride, beheld the sport,
And all the games of fortune, play'd at Court,
View'd there the market, read the wretched rate,
At which there are would sell the prince and state :
That scarce you hear a public voice alive,
But whisper'd counsels, and those only thrive ;
Yet are got off thence, with clear mind and hands
To lift to heaven, who is't not understands
Your happiness, and doth not speak you blest,
To see you set apart thus from the rest,
T'obtain of God what all the land should ask ?
A nation's sin got pardon'd ! 'twere a task
Fit for a bishop's knees ! O bow them oft,
My lord, till felt grief make our stone hearts soft,
And we do weep to water for our sin.—
He, that in such a flood as we are in,
Of riot and consumption, knows the way,
To teach the people how to fast and pray,
And do their penance to avert the rod,
He is the Man, and favourite, of God.

[5] This is not inscribed to any one in the folio ; but was evidently addressed to the lord-keeper Williams, bishop of Lincoln. It was probably written in 1625, when the chancellorship was transferred from him to sir Thomas Coventry.

LXXIX.

AN EPIGRAM

TO KING CHARLES, FOR AN HUNDRED POUNDS HE
SENT ME IN MY SICKNESS.

MDCXXIX.[6]

GREAT Charles, among the holy gifts of grace,
    Annexed to thy person and thy place,
    'Tis not enough (thy piety is such)
        To cure the call'd *king's-evil* with thy touch ;
But thou wilt yet a kinglier mastery try,
To cure the *poet's-evil*, poverty :

[6] Jonson has given the date of this Epigram, 1629. In that wretched tissue of ignorance and malice called in Cibber's Collection, "the Life of Ben Jonson," it is stated that "in the year 1629, Ben fell sick, and was then poor, and lodged in an obscure alley ; his Majesty was supplicated in his favour, who sent him ten guineas. When the messenger delivered the sum, Ben took it in his hand, and said, ' His Majesty sent me ten guineas because I am poor and live in an alley ; go and tell him that his soul lives in an alley.' " Vol. i. p. 238. Here is a fair specimen of the injustice with which the character of Jonson is universally treated. The writer of his "Life" had before him not only the poet's own acknowledgment that the sum sent to him by the king was one hundred pounds, but three poems in succession full of gratitude, thankfulness, and respectful duty, all written at the very period selected by his enemies for charging him with a rude and ungrateful message to his benefactor.

    This fabrication was too valuable to be neglected ; it has therefore been disseminated in a variety of forms by most of the Shakspeare commentators. Mr. Malone, indeed, rejects the falsehood, as well he might : he goes farther, and "wonders," why Smollett should insert this contemptible lie in his " History of England," and above all, "where he found it." Mr. Malone's surprise is gratuitous. He could not be ignorant of Cibber's publication, for he has borrowed from it ; and he must have been equally aware that it was the polluted source from which Smollett, who was probably acquainted with the writer, (Shiels, a Scotchman) derived his ridiculous anecdote. Smollett knew less of Jonson than even Mr. Malone ; he

And in these cures dost so thyself enlarge,
As thou dost cure our evil at thy charge.
Nay, and in this, thou show'st to value more
One poet, than of other folks ten score.[7]
O piety, so to weigh the poors' estates !
O bounty, so to difference the rates !
What can the poet wish his king may do,
But that he cure the people's evil too ?

LXXX.

To king Charles and queen Mary, for the loss

OF THEIR FIRST-BORN.

An Epigram consolatory,

MDCXXIX.

WHO dares deny, that all first-fruits are due
To God, denies the Godhead to be true :
Who doubts those fruits God can with gain
restore,
Doth by his doubt distrust his promise more.
He can, he will, and with large interest, pay
What, at his liking, he will take away.

knew enough, however, of the public to be convinced that in calumniating him, he was on the right side.

Is it too much to hope that this palpable perversion of a recorded fact will be less current hereafter? Or is the calumniation of Jonson so indispensable to the interests of sound literature, that a falsehood once charged upon him must immediately assume a sacred character, and in despite of shame, be promulgated, as a duty, from book to book, and from age to age?

[7] *——— to value more*
     One *poet, than of other folks* ten score.] This alludes to the *angel*, or ten shilling piece which was given to all who presented themselves to be touched for the king's-evil, and which undoubtedly presents the true key both of the numerous applications and the cures. Ten-score angels make an hundred pounds.

Then, royal Charles and Mary, do not grutch
That the Almighty's will to you is such :
But thank his greatness and his goodness too ;
And think all still the best that he will do.
That thought shall make, he will this loss supply
With a long, large, and blest posterity :
For God, whose essence is so infinite,
Cannot but heap that grace he will requite.

LXXXI.

AN EPIGRAM

TO OUR GREAT AND GOOD KING CHARLES,[8]

ON HIS ANNIVERSARY DAY,

MDCXXIX.

OW happy were the subject if he knew,
  Most pious king, but his own good in you !
  How many times, Live long, Charles ! would
    he say,
If he but weigh'd the blessings of this day,

---

 [8] *To our great and good king Charles.*] In taking leave of the
Epigrams of this year, let me pluck one solitary sprig to adorn the
head of this "good king," (who has been stripped of all his honours
by the insatiable rancour of the heirs of the ancient puritanism,)
from the garland woven for him by Dr. Burney.

 "This prince, (Charles I.) however his judgment, or that of his
counsellors, may have misled him in the more momentous con-
cerns of government, appears to have been possessed of an in-
variable good taste in all the fine arts ; a quality which, in less
morose and fanatical times, would have endeared him to the most
enlightened part of the nation : but now his patronage of poetry,
painting, architecture, and music, was ranked among the deadly
sins, and his passion for the works of the best artists in the nation,
profane, pagan, popish, idolatrous, dark, and damnable. As to
the expenses of his government, for the levying which he was
driven to illegal and violent expedients, if compared with what has

And as it turns our joyful year about,
For safety of such majesty cry out ?
Indeed, when had Great Britain greater cause
Than now, to love the sovereign and the laws ;
When you that reign are her example grown,
And what are bounds to her, you make your own ?
When your assiduous practice doth secure
That faith which she professeth to be pure ?
When all your life's a precedent of days,
And murmur cannot quarrel at your ways ?
How is she barren grown of love, or broke,
That nothing can her gratitude provoke !
O times ! O manners ! surfeit bred of ease,
The truly epidemical disease !
'Tis not alone the merchant, but the clown,
Is bankrupt turn'd ; the cassock, cloke and gown,
Are lost upon account, and none will know,
How much to heaven for thee, great Charles, they
    owe !

been since peaceably and cheerfully granted to his successors, his extravagance in supporting the public splendour and amusements of his court, will be found more moderate, and perhaps more innocent, than that of secret service in later times ; and however gloomy state-reformers may execrate this prince, it would be ungrateful, in professors of any of the fine arts, to lose all reverence for the patron of Ben Jonson, Vandyke, Inigo Jones, and Dr. Child." *History of Musick*, vol. iii.

This Epigram is addressed, in the Newcastle MS. "To the great and good king Charles, by his Majesty's most humble and *thankful* servant, Ben Jonson." Another proof of the poet's "insolence and ingratitude " !

LXXXII.

AN EPIGRAM

ON THE PRINCE'S BIRTH,

MDCXXX.

AND art thou born, brave babe? blest be thy
       birth,
   That so hath crown'd our hopes, our spring,
      and earth,
The bed of the chaste Lily and the Rose!
What month than May was fitter to disclose
This prince of flow'rs? Soon shoot thou up, and grow
The same that thou art promised, but be slow,
And long in changing. Let our nephews see
Thee quickly come the garden's eye to be,
And still to stand so. Haste now, envious moon,
And interpose thyself,[9] (care not how soon)

---

[9] —————— *Haste now, envious moon,*
  And interpose thyself, &c.] The prince (Charles II.) was born
this year, on the 29th of May, on which day there was an eclipse
of the moon. This day was also memorable for the appearance of
a star. "On the 29th of May (sir Richard Baker says) the queen
was brought to bed of a son which was baptized at St. James's, on
the 27th of June, and named Charles. It is observed that at his
nativity, at London, was seen a star about noon-time: what it por-
tended, good or ill, we leave to the astrologers."

Bishop Corbet has a congratulatory poem,—"To the new-borne
prince, upon the opposition of a star and the following eclipse."
It abounds in all that extravagance of conceit, which characterizes
the poetry of his school. Of the moon, he says,

   "And was't this news that made pale Cynthia run
     In so great haste to intercept the sun!"

And he questions the infant very significantly, on the appearance
of the star:

   "Was heaven afraid to be out-done on earth
     When thou wert born, great prince, that it brought forth

And threat the great eclipse; two hours but run,
Sol will re-shine : if not, Charles hath a son.

    ——*Non displicuisse meretur*
Festinat Cæsar qui placuisse tibi.[1]

LXXXIII.

AN EPIGRAM

TO THE QUEEN, THEN LYING IN,

MDCXXX.

HAIL, Mary, full of grace ! it once was said,
    And by an angel, to the blessed'st maid,
    The Mother of our Lord : why may not I,
    Without profaneness, as a poet, cry,
Hail, Mary, full of honours ! to my queen,
The mother of our prince ? when was there seen,
Except the joy that the first Mary brought,
Whereby the safety of mankind was wrought,
So general a gladness to an isle,
To make the hearts of a whole nation smile,
As in this prince ? let it be lawful, so
To compare small with great, as still we owe
Glory to God.   Then, hail to Mary ! spring
Of so much safety to the realm and king !

    Another light to help the aged sun,
    Lest by thy lustre he might be outshone ?
    Or, were the obsequious stars so joy'd to view
    Thee, that they thought their countless eyes too few
    For such an object ? " &c.

[1] After this Epigram the 12mo. edition, 1640, inserts two others on the same subject. The first, *on the Birth of the Prince,* bears, perhaps, some remote resemblance of Jonson's style, at least as much of it as is here subjoined ; but the concluding part is of a different character, and could only have proceeded from some wretched imitator of Donne. The second piece called a *Parallel*

LXXXIV.

AN ODE or SONG,

BY ALL THE MUSES,

IN CELEBRATION OF HER MAJESTY'S BIRTH-DAY,

MDCXXX.

1. *Clio.*

U P, public joy, remember
　　This sixteenth of November,
　　　　Some brave uncommon way :
　　And though the parish-steeple
　　Be silent to the people
　　　　Ring thou it holy-day.

2. *Mel.* What though the thrifty Tower,
　　And guns there spare to pour
　　　　Their noises forth in thunder :
　　As fearful to awake　　　　.
　　This city, or to shake
　　　　Their guarded gates asunder ?

of the Prince to the King, is utterly unworthy of notice.　I cannot
descend to vindicate the poet from either of them.

"　On the Birth of the Prince.

"Another Phœnix, though the first is dead,
　A second's flown from his immortal bed,
　To make this our Arabia to be
　The nest of an eternal progeny.
　Choice nature fram'd the former, but to find,
　What error might be mended in mankind :
　Like some industrious workmen, which affect
　Their first endeavours only to correct :
　So this the building, that the model was,
　The type of all that now is come to pass :
　That but the shadow, this the substance is
　All that was but the prophecy of this :
　And when it did this after birth forerun,
　'Twas but the morning star unto this sun
　The dawning of this day," &c.

3. *Thal.* Yet let our trumpets sound,
 And cleave both air and ground,
  With beating of our drums :
 Let every lyre be strung,
 Harp, lute, theorbo sprung,
  With touch of learned thumbs.

4. *Eut.* That when the quire is full,
 The harmony may pull
  The angels from their spheres :
 And each intelligence
 May wish itself a sense,
  Whilst it the ditty hears.

5. *Terp.* Behold the royal Mary,
 The daughter of great Harry !
  And sister to just Lewis !
 Comes in the pomp and glory
 Of all her brother's story,
  And of her father's prowess !²

6. *Erat.* She shows so far above
 The feigned queen of love,
  This sea girt isle upon :
 As here no Venus were ;
 But that she reigning here,
  Had put the ceston on !

² *Comes in the pomp and glory*
Of all her brother's *story,*
And of her father's *prowess.*] So the folio : in the 4to. and
12mo. 1640, the words *brother* and *father* stand in each other's
places. I think the present reading is most consonant to the truth
of history. WHAL.

 As I have carefully collated all the editions, and formed the text
according to the best of my judgment, I do not think it necessary
to encumber the page with a list of minute variations, most of
which, probably, originated at the press.

7. *Call.* See, see our active king,
          Hath taken twice the ring,[3]
             Upon his pointed lance:
          Whilst all the ravish'd rout
          Do mingle in a shout,
             Hey for the flower of France!

8. *Ura.* This day the court doth measure
          Her joy in state and pleasure;
             And with a reverend fear,
          The revels and the play,
          Sum up this crowned day,
             Her two and twentieth year.

9. *Poly.* Sweet, happy Mary, all
          The people her do call,
             And this the womb divine!
          So fruitful, and so fair,
          Hath brought the land an heir,
      ·   And Charles a Caroline!

---

[3] *See, see our active king,*
     Hath taken twice the ring.]   This amusement generally made
a part of the court entertainments in those active days. A ring of
small diameter was suspended by a riband from a kind of traverse
beam of which the horizontal beam moved on a swivel. At this
the competitors rode, with their spear couched, at full speed. The
object was to carry off the ring on the point of the spear, which
was a matter of some nicety: the usual reward of the victor was an
ornamented wreath from the lady of the day.

LXXXV.

AN EPIGRAM

TO THE HOUSEHOLD, MDCXXX.[4]

WHAT can the cause be, when the king hath
  . given
  His poet sack, the Household will not pay?
  Are they so scanted in their store? or driven
For want of knowing the poet, to say him nay?

Well, they should know him, would the king but grant
  His poet leave to sing his Household true;
He'd frame such ditties of their store and want,
  Would make the very Green-cloth to look blue:

And rather wish in their expense of sack,
  So the allowance from the king to use,
As the old bard should no canary lack;
  'Twere better spare a butt, than spill his muse.
For in the genius of a poet's verse,
The king's fame lives. Go now, deny his tierce![5]

[4] It is said by the anonymous author of a little collection of
"Poems, by Nobody must know whom," (and who nevertheless
every body may know to be John Eliot) that this Epigram was
thought too severe by the board of green-cloth, and that Ben therefore wrote a second, in a smoother style, and with better success.

 "You swore, dear Ben, you'd turn 'the green-cloth blue'
 If your dry muse might not be bath'd in sack;
 This with those fearless lords nothing prevailing,
 The scene you alter'd," &c. p. 26.

This poor man, who seems to be a kind of counterpart of Fenner
(vol. vii. p. 414), affects to be familiar with Jonson, and styles himself his *friend*, a title to which he proves his claim somewhat after
the manner of Jonson's other "friend," Drummond of Hawthorn-
den, by yelping at him.

[5] *Go now, deny his* tierce.] Of wine; part of his salary as poet
laureat. WHAL.

This was the second to which the poet was entitled. The Household quickly fell into arrears in those days.

LXXXVI.

AN EPIGRAM

SON, and my friend, I had not call'd you so
To me; or been the same to you, if show,
Profit, or chance had made us: but I know,
What, by that name, we each to other owe,
Freedom and truth; with love from those begot:
Wise-crafts, on which the flatterer ventures not.
His is more safe commodity or none:
Nor dares he come in the comparison.
But as the wretched painter, who so ill
Painted a dog, that now his subtler skill
Was, t' have a boy stand with a club, and fright
All live dogs from the lane, and his shop's sight,
Till he had sold his piece, drawn so unlike:
So doth the flatterer with fair cunning strike
At a friend's freedom, proves all circling means
To keep him off; and howsoe'er he gleans
Some of his forms, he lets him not come near
Where he would fix, for the distinction's fear;
For as at distance few have faculty
To judge; so all men coming near, can spy;
Though now of flattery, as of picture, are
More subtle works, and finer pieces far,
Than knew the former ages; yet to life
All is but web and painting; be the strife
Never so great to get them: and the ends,
Rather to boast rich hangings, than rare friends.

ADDITIONAL NOTES.

NOTES TO TIME VINDICATED.

Page 2.

IME Vindicated, &c.] Chamberlain writes to Carleton, January 25, 1622(3): "More feasting and dancing this Christmas than ever. The masque scenes were devised by Inigo Jones, and the masque written by Ben Jonson, but he runs a risk by impersonating George Withers, the poet, as a Whipper of the Times [Chronomastix], which is a dangerous jest."

P. 6. *Pardon me, madam, more than most accurst.*] This ancient joke had now done duty for so many years that it must have appeared rather out of date in 1623.

P. 6. *T' have given the stoop, and to salute the skirts, &c.*] This use of the word *stoop* settles the question of its meaning in *The Alchemist*, vol. iv. p. 130.

P. 7. *My glorious front, and word at large,*
      Triumphs in print at my admirers' charge.] Jonson refers to the portrait of Wither, engraved by Hole. It is indeed a "glorious front," in the true sense of the word *glorious*. The clothes are as glorious as Queen Elizabeth's. The inscription is:

" Loe this is he whose infant muse begann
 To brave the World before yeares stil'd him Man.
 Though praise he sleight, and scornes to make his Rymes
 Begg favors or opinion of the Tymes,
 Yet few, by good men, have bine more approv'd,
 None so unseene so generally loved."

Sr. T. I.

And then follows an independent couplet:

8   G G

"Non pictoris opus fuit hoc, sed pectoris, unde
   Divinæ in tabulam mentis imago fluit."

J. M.

So that I think Jonson's second line should be printed *admirer's*, in the singular, rather than *admirers'*.

P. 7. *The* sempster *hath sat still as I pass'd by,*
   And dropt her needle.] Minsheu explains *sempster* to be a *needle-woman*, as Jonson uses it ; but it also meant a male sewer.

P. 8. *The unctuous Bounty is the boss of Billingsgate.*] It is true that there was a famous spring at Billingsgate called The Boss, but Jonson is here playing on the other meaning of the word, with which we are made acquainted by Cotgrave, "A Fat Bosse, *Femme bien grasse et grosse; une coche.*" So Marlowe in *Tamburlaine* makes *Zenocrate* call *Zabina*,

"Disdainful Turkess, and unreverend Boss ! "

and Lyly in *Euphues* (Arber, p. 115), "Wrest all parts of her body to the worst, be she never so worthy. If shee be well sett, then call hir a Bosse," &c. Our word *bosom* is plainly of the same origin, and this may explain how the secondary meaning grew up.

P. 10. *The other zealous* rag *is the compositor.*] So in *Richard the Third*, Act v. Sc. 3 :

"Lash hence these overweening *rags* of France."

P. 10. *Time whipt, for terror to the* infantry.] This pleasant way of talking of the *children* as *infantry*, originated with Jonson. Mr. Thackeray was partial to it.

P. 12. *His dog piping* Lachrymæ.] In Dyce's *Beaumont and Fletcher* (vol. x. p. 398) we find—

"Arion, on a dolphin, playing Lachrymæ."

Nares says, " It is the first word of the title of a musical work, composed by John Dowland, in the reign of James I." The full title was " Lachrimæ, or seven Teares figured in seven passionate Pavans, with divers other Pavans, Galiards and Almands, as set forth to the Lute, Viols or Violins in five parts." The popularity of the work is apparent from the constant allusions to it. In *No Wit like a Woman's*, Middleton expressly mentions it as Dowland's : "Now thou plaiest Dowland's Lachrymæ to thy master."

Page 22.

EPTUNE'S Triumph, &c.] A great deal of writing has been wasted about the date of the performance of this masque. One long argument will be found in Dyce's *Beaumont and Fletcher* (vol. x. p. 398), and Mr. Collier too has had his own views on the subject. Gifford would seem to have had some exclusive information : " *Neptune's Triumph* appears to have been celebrated with uncommon magnificence. All hearts and hands were in it; and the Spanish influence then received a check, from which it has not recovered to this day." I am sorry to be obliged to tell a tale less redounding to Jonson's fame, but the fact is, *Neptune's Triumph* was never performed at all ! It was rehearsed more than once in the first week of January, 1623-4, but the jealousies between the Spanish and French ambassadors were then at such a height, that it was thought prudent to have no performance, and the king's health was made an excuse for its indefinite postponement. Jonson thought himself at liberty after this to work the materials into his other pieces. See in particular *The Fortunate Isles*, and a passage in *The Staple of News*.

P. 24. *No, but one that has a good title.*] This should be as in the folio, " one that has *as* good title."

P. 24. *You are to know the palates of the times.*] This is not improved by being changed from "*palate* of the times."

P. 26. *What ranks, what files, to put the dishes in.*] The folio has properly, " put *his* dishes in."

P. 28. *And Neptune's guard hath drunk all that they meant.*] Nichols says this is aimed at " the King's Guard, in a hit at whom Jonson delights."

P. 29. *In a brave broth, &c.*] These same lines occur in *The Staple of News*, vol. v. p. 241 :

> " Send in an Arion
> In a brave broth, and of a watery green,
> Just the sea-colour, mounted on the back
> Of a grown conger, but in such a posture,
> As all the world would take him for a dolphin."

The Staple of News was first acted in 1625. With regard to Fletcher's assumed imitation in the *Bloody Brother* (Dyce's *Beau-*

mont and Fletcher, vol. x. p. 398), of which I am by no means certainly convinced, it is possible that Fletcher, or the writer of that portion of the play, may have been present at one of the rehearsals of this masque, and carried away a general impression of the passage.

P. 31. *The clouds, the* cortines, *and the mysteries.*] I at first thought that the retention of the spelling *cortines* in this place was capricious on Gifford's part, but I now believe it was to indicate its meaning, as in Latin, the screen from behind which an oracle was delivered.

P. 31. *What* correspondencies *are held.*] This should unquestionably be *correspondences*, as in the folio.

P. 31. *The way of your* gallimaufry.] Nares describes it as "a confused heterogeneous jumble, from *gallimafrie.*" The word is used by Shakspeare, and we have Taylor's *Water-Worke; or the Sculler's Travels from Tyber to Thames ; with his Boat laden with a Hotch-Potch, or Gallimawfrey of Sonnets, Satyres and Epigrams.*

P. 36. *Where Proteus' herds, and Neptune's* orcs *do keep.*] *Orks*, as the folio spells the name, were marine animals of some sort. Drayton (*Polyolb.* ii. p. 687) speaks of them as—

> " The ugly orks that for their lord the ocean woo ; "

and Phineas Fletcher elevates them into monsters of the deep,

> " So Neptune bids that who shall touch the tree
> With hands profane, shall by Malorcha die ;
> Malorcha bred in seas, yet seas so dread him,
> As much more monstrous than the seas that bred him."
> > *Grosart* ed. (vol. i. p. 20).

In a fine passage in *The Roman Actor*, vol. ii. p. 218, Massinger speaks of

> " the sea spouted into the air
> By the angry Orc, endangering tall ships
> But sailing near it ; "

and Gifford here explains it to be a " fabulous sea monster, depicted on most of the marine charts of Massinger's time—the Whale of our old romances."

P. 37. *Relish like anchovies or* caveare.] *Caveare* was twice mentioned in *Cynthia's Revels*, vol. ii. p. 249 and p. 257.

NOTES TO PAN'S ANNIVERSARY.

Page 40.

THERE is a great difficulty both about the date and the whereabouts of the performance of this masque. Mr. Nichols, who bestowed both thought and research upon the question, feels convinced that its *position* among the other pieces in the folio of 1641 is correct, and that there is no reason to doubt its having been performed before King James, though a year earlier than the date assigned to it. On the whole he thinks it most likely that it was commissioned by Buckingham for the entertainment he gave James at Barley-on-the-Hill in August, 1624. There is an obstacle in the way in the fact of our knowing that a masque by young. Maynard was acted on that particular occasion, but Mr. Nichols sees less difficulty in believing that Buckingham had provided two masques than in any other theory. See his *Progresses*, vol. iii. p. 986.

P. 41. *Bright day's-eyes, and the* lips of cows.] Southey remarks (*Common Place Book*, Fourth Series, p. 327) that he had seen "this odd inversion in some very sweet verses."

P. 42. *Blue hare-bells*, pagles, *pansies*, calaminth.] *Pagles* were *cowslips*, and *calaminth* was *mint*.

P. 44. *The looking to* all of *their lungs*.] The folio expresses this much more naturally, " the looking to *of* all their lungs."

P. 46. *And on the pipe more airs than Phœbus* can.] This word *can*, which recurs in every stanza of this hymn, should surely have a note to explain that "it is not the *potential* of some verb, but the present of the Saxon term for *know* or *comprehend*, used by our old writers in all the inflections." See vol. vi. p. 15.

P. 48.   *It will be good*
        To see them *wave it like a wood,*
              And others *wind it like a flood.*] For some incomprehensible reason the second line has been made nonsense of by altering it from
              " *To see some* wave it like a wood,"
as it stands in the folio.

P. 49. *So may the first of all our* fells *be thine.*] For this word *fell* see vol. vi. p. 244, and vol. ix. p. 176.

P. 49. *And both the* beestning *of our goats and kine.*] *Beestning* is the first milk given by a cow, ewe, or she-goat.

NOTES TO THE MASQUE OF OWLS.

Page 52.

HE Masque of Owls, &c.] "In all the editions of Jonson, from the folio of 1641, in which it was first printed, this masque has been erroneously dated 1626. That however it was performed before Prince Charles, previously to his accession to the throne, is proved by his being addressed in it as *Your Highness*, and by a previous allusion to the Prince of Wales' three feathers; but Mr. Chamberlain's letter to Sir Dudley Carleton of August 21, 1624, puts the matter beyond doubt by mentioning it as having been performed two days since" (*i.e.* August 19, 1624). Nichol's *Progresses*, vol. iii. p. 997.

P. 55. From thence *the story was ta'en.*] *From thence* is very unlike the scholarly Jonson's mode of expressing himself. The folio has

(*For* thence the story was ta'en).

P. 58. *Coventry blue.*] This celebrated dye was mentioned in the *Gipsies Metamorphosed*, vol. vii. p. 388.

NOTES TO THE FORTUNATE ISLES.

Page 62.

HE Fortunate Isles, &c.] The position of this masque in the 1641 folio appears quite correct, but the date should have been Twelfth Night, 1624-25, instead of 1626(7), which has so misled Gifford. In Chalmers' *Second Apology*, p. 219, I find that the following entry had been made :—"29th December, 1624.—For the Palsgrave's company a new play called *The Masque*. The Masque's book was allowed of for the Press, and was brought me by Mr. Jon[son] the 29th December, 1624." This had not been noticed by Gifford, and it was altogether unknown to him that there were sundry copies in existence of a quarto of thirteen leaves, with the title, "The Fortunate Isles and their Union, celebrated in a Masque designed for the Court, on the Twelfth Night, 1624." Sir Henry Herbert says: "Upon twelve night, the masque being put off, and the Prince only there, *Tu Quoque*, by the Queen of Bohemia's servants at Whitehall," and "Upon Sunday night following, being the 9th of January (1624-5), the masque was performed." The king's mortal illness had evidently shown itself, for Chamberlain, writing on January 8, 1624-5, says : " The King kept his chamber all Christmas, only going out in his litter in fair weather, to see some flights at the brook " (*Cal. Jac.* p. 431). In the Inigo Jones volume of the old Shakspeare Society publications, there is a fac-simile of the great architect's sketches for the costume of four figures in this masque, from the originals in the possession of the Duke of Devonshire. There are also valuable descriptions by Mr. J. R. Planché. Plate iii. p. 58. Jonson will be found to have turned to the unused pages of *Neptune's Triumph.*

P. 64. *With* bombing *sighs.*] I cannot remember to have met this word elsewhere. If it did not speak its own meaning, it would be sufficiently explained by the following passage from Bacon's *Natural History*, fol. p. 151 : " It would make a little flat noise in the room where it was struck, but it would make a great *bombe* in the chamber beneath."

P. 69. *And risse again like cork.*] This *risse* was a favoured form of Jonson's which Gifford by some lucky chance took under his special patronage. See *Poetaster*, vol. ii. p. 370, and *English Grammar*, vol. ix. p. 284 (chapter xix.)

P. 72. *Enter* Skogan *and* Skelton, *in like habits as they lived.*] These are two of the characters whose costume, as sketched by Inigo Jones, is facsimiled in the Shakspeare Society volume.

P. 73. *Except the four* knaves *entertain'd for the guards*
 Of the kings and the queens that triumph *in the cards.*] A *triumph* at cards we now call a *trump.* Cotgrave explains " *Tri-omphe*, the card-game called *Ruffe* or *Trump*, also the *Ruffe* or *Trump* at it." Perhaps Jonson was alluding to the duty of the *Knaves* in this game.

P. 74. *But she is not* grill.] Nares is of no assistance here, but in Peter Levins' *Rhyming Vocabulary*, A.D. 1570, I find, " *Gril*, cold, *algidus*," and Mr. Wheatley, the excellent editor, quotes *Rom. de la Rose*:
 " While they han suffred cold full strong
 In wethers grille, and derke to light."

P. 75. *Mary Ambree.*] This famous lady has been already noticed in *The Silent Woman*, vol. iii. p. 418, and in *A Tale of a Tub*, vol. vi. p. 133.

P. 75. *Or* Westminster Meg.] Some of the notices of this Amazon are amusing; and crop up in unexpected places. For instance, in Vaughan's *Golden Grove*, 1608, we find that "Long

Meg of Westminster kept alwaies twenty courtezans in her house, whom by their pictures she sold to all commers." And in *Holland's Leaguer*, 1632, "It was out of the citie, yet in the view of the citie, only divided by a delicate river . . . it was renowned for nothing so much as for the memory of that famous Amazon *Longa Margarita*, who had there for manie yeares kept a famous infamous house of open hospitality."

P. 75. *Doctor Rat.*] It is strange that Nares should be in doubt whether this was the name of anybody. Doctor Rat is one of the leading characters in that genuine old English piece of fun, *Gammer Gurton's Needle*.

P. 80. *Where Proteus' herds, and Neptune's orcs do keep.*] See *ante*, p. 36, and my note thereon.

NOTE TO CHLORIDIA.

Page 99.

 GAME call'd nine-pins, or keils.] *Keils* from the French "Quille," defined by Cotgrave to be "a big peg, or pin of wood, used at nine-pins."

NOTES TO AN EXPOSTULATION WITH INIGO JONES.

Page 106.

N Expostulation, &c.] It is idle to assert that there was no ill feeling between Jonson and Inigo before 1633. As early as 1619 he told Drummond that "Jones having accused him for naming him behind his back, A foole ; he denied it, but, says he, I said He was ane arrant knave, and I avouch it." Vol. ix. p. 403. And again, "He said to Prince Charles of Inigo Jones, that when he wanted words to express the greatest villaine in the world he would call him *ane Inigo.*" Vol. ix. p. 403.

The question of authenticity has long ago been settled by Mr. Collier, who discovered among the Bridgewater MSS. a copy of the Expostulation in Jonson's autograph.

P. 109. *Both him and Archimede; damn* Archytas.] It is rather bold of Gifford to say that the fifth verse could not have been written by Jonson. How does he know that Archimede was intended to be only a trisyllable? Remember too what Macaulay says, "Ben's heroic couplets resemble blocks [for sails] rudely hewn out by an unpractised hand with a blunt hatchet," and then goes on to describe them as "jagged mis-shapen distiches." Archytas was a philosopher, mathematician and practical mechanic, whose wooden flying dove was the wonder of antiquity. He was a Greek of Tarentum, and lived about 400 B.C.

P. 109. *Control Ctesibius.*] Ctesibius, a native of Alexandria, lived about 250 B.C. He is said to have invented a water-clock, a hydraulic organ, &c.

P. 110. *You'd be an* Assinigo *by your ears.*] Some versions print *years* for *ears*. *Assinigo* is a Portuguese word meaning a young donkey. Jonson uses it in *The Staple of News*, vol. v. p. 287, without any reference to the Architect; and R. Brome too has it in his *Mad Couple*, vol. i. p. 13.

P. 112.   *His feat*
          Of lantern-lerry, with fuliginous heat.] This phrase, as Nares observes, seems to give some colour to the notion of Lanthorn Leatherhead being intended for Inigo. See note, vol. iv. p. 383.

P. 114. *A cave for wine or ale.*] See *post* p. 419, *The Dedication of the King's new cellar to Bacchus*.

NOTES TO LOVE'S WELCOME AT WELBECK.

Page 120.

HEN was old Sherwood's head more quaintly curl'd?] Thomas Warton, p. 100, notes Milton's imitation:
    "To nurse the saplings tall, and curl the grove
    With ringlets quaint, and wanton windings wove."
But Jonson himself remembered Drayton's line:
    "Where Sherwood her curl'd front into the cold doth shove."—
                    Polyolb. st. xxxiii.

P. 120. *When did the air so smile, the* wind *so chime.*] The editors have changed *winds* into *wind* to the injury of the sense.

P. 121. Out-cept, *sir, you can read with the left-hand.*] This is the other instance in which Jonson brings in the quaint word which so tickled Horne Tooke. See vol. vi. pp. 131, 155.

P. 121. *Derbyshire.*] Jonson wrote and his friends printed Darbyshire—the pronunciation which the head of the Stanleys has still the good sense to retain.

P. 121. *By his* thewes *he may*.] Spenser uses this word as Jonson does:

"And straight delivered to a fairy knight,
    To be upbrought in *gentle thews* and martial might."

P. 121. *A poor neighbour of your honour's in the* country.] The editors have injuriously altered this from the *county* of the folio.

P. 122. *The* surety *of his girdle*.] Why is Jonson robbed of his little joke, "the sure-tie of his girdle," as the folio has it?

P. 125. *All reckon'd o' the* country *skirts*.] Here again something like nonsense is made by the change from the "*county* skirts" of the folio.

P. 127. [*Safe from the ground*.] This line is quite unnecessarily interpolated. The word "found," which he considers to be without a corresponding rhyme, had already two, as anybody can satisfy himself who reads the two lines preceding it.

NOTES TO LOVE'S WELCOME AT BOLSOVER.

Page 139.

HE Fates spinning them round and even threads, and of their whitest wool, without brack *or* purl.] This must remind every one of the couplet in the lines on Lord Bacon's birthday, *post*, p. 425:

"Whose even thread the Fates spin round and full,
    Out of their choicest and their whitest wool."

Brack is a *crack* or *break*. For *purl* see vol. ii. p. 146.

P. 140. *Both your pious and just progenitors*.] In this same year was published a noble engraving by Van Voerst, after Vandyck, in which the queen (in a most interesting condition) is presenting an olive wreath to the king. The couplet beneath it may have been supplied by Jonson:

"Filius hic Magni est Jacobi, hæc filia Magni
    Henrici: soboles dic mihi qualis erit?"

NOTES TO EPIGRAMS.

Page 146.

O my Bookseller.] Up to 1616 Jonson's publishers appear to have been Nicholas Linge, William Holme, Walter Burre, M. L., Thomas Thorpe, Nicholas Oky.

P. 146. *How, best of poets, dost thou laurel wear!*] King James was a very tolerable versifier, and did no discredit to George Buchanan's tuition. Besides *The Essayes of a Prentise in the Divine Art of Poesie*, which was published in Edinburgh eighteen years before he came to England, he was also the author of *Some Reulis and Cautelis to be observit and eschewit in Scotts Poesie.* Bishop Hurd before he reprehended Jonson for adulation of the new king, should have remembered the dedication of the Bible to the "Sun in his Strength."

P. 148. *On the new Hot-house.*] See *Every Man out of his Humour*, vol. ii. pp. 47 and 132. It seems to have been a kind of Turkish bath.

P. 150. *Shift, here in town, not meanest* amongst *squires.*] Jonson wrote and printed *among*, and, with a hissing word before and after it (mean*e*st among *s*quires), who will say he was not right?

P. 151. *And for his letchery, scores, god pays.*] I think there can be no doubt that *scores* is here a *verb*, and that the commas before and after it should be expunged.

P. 154. *Sir Cod the perfumed.*] *Cod* was a name commonly given to perfumers. So in Shirley's *Wedding:* "As thou goest call upon *Cod the Perfumer*, tell him he uses us sweetly, has not brought home the gloves yet." *Works*, vol. i. p. 382. In Gifford's note (3) on this Epigram, he quotes *The Woman's Prize*, and gives a mysterious line about

"Counterfeit cods, or musty English *crocus.*"

P. 155. *On my first daughter.*] Peter Cunningham found in the Register of St. Martin's-in-the-Fields: "1593, *Nov.* 17. *Seplta. fuit Maria Johnson, peste.*" If this was Jonson's daughter he must have been married at least as early as August, 1592, when he was about 20, and this I suspect to be the true state of the case.

P. 156. *Donne, the delight of Phœbus and each Muse.*] Jonson told Drummond that he esteemed Donne "the first poet in the world in some things." He had "written his best pieces ere he was twenty-five years old." See vol. ix. p. 373, 374.

P. 157. *And now her hourly her own* cucquean *makes.*] Nares says this is "a familiar word, fabricated by taking the first syllable of *cuckold*, and adding *quean* to it." *Cotquean* is quite a different word. See *The Poetaster*, vol. ii. p. 456.

P. 158. *On sir John Roe.*] Jonson said emphatically to Drummond that "Sir John Roe loved him." "He died in his arms of the pest."

P. 159. *He has* tympanies *of business in his face.*] Samuel Johnson defines *tympany* to be "a kind of obstructed flatulence that swells the body like a drum."

P. 159. *For thy late* sharp device.] It is plain from several passages that Jonson was in the habit of attending at the tiltings, and of supplying devices to his friends among the tilters. See post, pp. 183 and 343.

P. 160. *On* Banks *the Usurer.*] In the folio this man's name is *Banck*, not *Banks*, and I think it worth preserving, as in all probability it was a nick-name given to him from his profession.

P. 160. *Note* (1). *Why Whalley chose to give us vile English instead of copying the elegant Latin of the original, I cannot tell.*] After this Gifford ought not to have left it to me to give the elegant Latin:

D. JOANNI ROWE,
Amico
Probatissimo,
Hunc Amorem et delicias
Suas, Satiricorum doctissimum
Persium, cum
Doctissimo commentario
Sacravit
Ben : Jonsonius
et
L. M. D. D.
Nec prior est incipi parens amico.

Having thus given one of Jonson's Latin inscriptions, I may as well insert another which I believe to be hitherto unpublished. It was transcribed by Mr. Dyce from the fly-leaf of a copy of *Camdeni Annales*, 1615, fol.:

In ædibus D. Margaretæ in Lothbury.

Quid divinare magnos invides, Parca ?
Heu
Robertus
Jerminorum a Rushbrooke nobili germine
Hic situs est.
Flos juvenum sub ævi flore raptus,
Qui virtutum utriusque ætatis apicibus potitus,
Ingenio et indole juventutis
Nec non senili pietate ac prudentia
Infra se turbam coetaneam reliquit,
Impubes senex :
Et quod negavit seculo, cælo dedit.
Sic sapere ante annos nocuit, nam maxima virtus
Persuasit morti ut crederet esse senem.
P. P. P.   Ben. Jonson.

P. 161. *The cold of Mosco, and fat Irish air,*
His often change of clime, though not of mind,
All could not work.] That "*All* could not work" is

substituted most tastelessly for the "*What* could not work" of Jonson, which is absolutely necessary for the symmetry of a most carefully studied piece.   If these words are placed in front of the two lines which precede them, the construction ;will be self-evident :

> "What could not work
>   The cold of Mosco, and fat Irish air,
>   His often change of clime (though not of mind) ;
>   At home, in his repair, was his blest fate."

The parenthesis is in the original.

P. 161.   *Thou art but gone before,*
         Whither the world must follow : and I, now,
         Breathe to expect my When, and make my How.] Southey was greatly struck with these lines, and notes, "His own anticipation of death.   A fine manly strain."   .

P. 163. *On* Cheveril *the lawyer.*]   A cheveril-conscience was a conscience that would stretch like kid-skin.   See *The Poetaster,* vol. ii. p. 382.   See also *post,* p. 172, which shows that the present epigram had hit hard.

P. 164. *On Margaret Ratcliffe.*]   I have been more fortunate than Gifford in tracing the history of the object of these exquisite lines.   She was a great beauty and wit, and a favourite Maid of Honour of Queen Elizabeth.   She died in November, 1599, aged 24, and was buried in Westminster Abbey.   See *Prefatory Notice,* vol. i. p. 10.

P. 166. *Note* (8). *Robert, Earl of Salisbury.*]   This note is well worth reading, as exhibiting Gifford in one of his most rabid moods : "When the time shall come for Walpole himself to be added to the number of Noble Authors, by a sterner biographer than Mr. Parke, he will, if fairly represented, be found to be one of the most odious and contemptible of the whole *Catalogue.*" There must have been some private cause of dislike to account for this extreme virulence of abuse, and it may, perhaps, have been connected with some grievance of his friend Hoppner, the painter, who was more likely to have come in contact with Walpole, and who also disliked him heartily, as may be seen in his excellent article in the first number of the *Quarterly Review*.   With reference to the estimate of Walpole's talents, it must be remarked in justice to Gifford, that his marvellous powers as a letter writer were unknown in 1816.   Even the letters to Montagu were then unpublished, and none indeed known, except such as were selected by himself for the quarto edition of his works.   More abuse of Walpole will be found further on, vol. ix. p. 6.

P. 167. *On my first son.*] The abuse of Drummond contained in note (9) is best answered by asking the reader to turn to vol. ix. p. 390, and read what the "vile calumniator" really did "report."

P. 169. *I have no salt, no bawdry he doth mean.*] In spite of Gifford, the word *sallets* still holds its own in *Hamlet*, and is likely to do so. "*Sawte bytche* of my lorde Bonner," is one article in the Table of Contents of "Yet a course at the Romyshe Fox."

P. 172. *Note. To Francis Beaumont.*] Beaumont's famous letter, which Gifford strangely omitted to print, will be found at vol. i. p. 172, of the present edition. It is not to be forgotten, however, that Jonson told Drummond that "Francis Beaumont loved too much himself and his own verses." Vol. ix. p. 378.

P. 173. *On Poet-Ape.*] I have no doubt there is some connection between this epigram and a remarkable passage in *Poetaster*, vol. ii. p. 371 :

"Are there no players here? no poet-apes,
    That come with basilisk's eyes, whose forked tongues
    Are steep'd in venom, as their hearts in gall?"

P. 175. *Note. To William lord Mounteagle.*] The poem mentioned at the end of this note should of course be *Castara*, not *Castora*. It was published in 1634.

P. 176. *To Fool, or Knave.*] Gifford remarks that Jonson frequently used the word *to stroke* for *to flatter*. See vol. vi. p. 78, where "my lady's *stroker*" is used for "my lady's she-parasite."

P. 180. *To Thomas earl of Suffolk.*] This is the Lord Suffolk who "ushered" Jonson and Sir John Roe from a masque, see vol. ix. p. 378. He was the father of the infamous Countess of Essex.

P. 182. *To Courtling.*] In this little piece there are two small, but quite unnecessary departures from the genuine text. In the second line, "*doth* dine" should be "*dost* dine;" and in the fifth, "*thy* prejudice" should be "*the* prejudice."

P. 183. *In solemn cyprus, th' other cobweb lawn.*] Cotgrave has "*Crespe*, Cipres, also cobweb-lawn," so there would seem to have been little difference between them. Most probably *Cypres* (so Jonson speaks it, as well as Cotgrave), was black, and *cobweb-lawn* white.

P. 183. *Item, a gulling imprese for you, at tilt.*] See *ante*, p. 159, and *post*, p. 343.

P. 188. *To Lucy countess of Bedford.*] Drummond notes that the epigram on "my lady Bedford's bucke" was among the "most common places of his repetition." Vol. ix. p. 372.

P. 188. *To sir Henry Goodyere.*] This Sir Henry Goodyere must not be confounded with his uncle, whose daughter he married, and whose estate of Polesworth he inherited. The tetrastich quoted by Camden must have been addressed to the uncle.

P. 190. *On captain Hazard, the cheater.*] Whalley says that Cheater and Gamester were "synonymous terms in Jonson's age." *Here* Cheater certainly means one who plays falsely, and I have no doubt it has always done so.

P. 191. *And* shoe, and tye.] These were introduced from France, and hence *shoe-tye* became a name for a traveller. So Shakspeare, "Master Forthright, the tilter, and brave Master Shoetye, the great traveller." *Measure for Measure*, A. iv. S. 3.

P. 191. *Or hung some Monsieur's picture on the wall.*] In the hope, I suppose, that it would have the effect of the peeled sticks in Scripture.

P. 194. *And the Gazetti, or Gallo-Belgicus.*] For a note on Gazettes, see *The Fox*, vol. iii. p. 211; and for the *Gallo-Belgicus* see *Poetaster*, vol. ii. p. 502.

P. 195. *At Bill's.*] This noble old printer and publisher is still represented by two opulent families descended from him. The one settled at Storthes Hall, in Yorkshire, the other at Farleigh, in Staffordshire.

P. 195. *To sir John Radcliffe.*] I have not been able to discover any particulars of the death of the first brother, or whether he was older than the sir Alexander Radcliffe, who was killed with sir Conyers Clifford in the Curlew Mountains near Sligo, in August, 1699. On this occasion Essex wrote to the queen : "Too much of the unhappy province of Connaught, I have written to my L.L. : to your maj. only this, that if your maj. be not gracious to *poor Jack Radclyffe*, in bestowing his wardship on him, he that is heir of a brave race, and has lost his two older brothers in your maj. service, is utterly undone ; his last worthy brother who did as much honour to his name by his death as ever any young gentleman did, hath so impaired the estate, as without your maj. goodness it is irrecoverable." This fight at the Curlews was not honourable to the English arms, but the rout at Rhé, in which "poor Jack Radcliffe" was destined to be slain, was infinitely more disgraceful. As Holles wrote to Strafford, "No man can tell what was done, nor no account can be given how any man was lost, not the Lieutenant-Colonel how his Colonel, or Lieutenant how his Captain, or any one man knows how another was lost. This only every one knows, that, since England was England, it received not so dishonourable a blow." *Strafford Letters*, vol. ii. p. 42.

P. 197. *With Master Donne's Satires.*] As this epigram was published in 1616, and no earlier edition of Donne's Satires is known than that of 1633, it may be presumed that the volume sent to the Countess of Bedford must have been a manuscript transcript such as is now in the British Museum with the date of 1593. There is, however, a letter from Donne to Sir H. G., dated "Vigilia Sti. Tho. 1614," in which he mentions his resolution to print his poems, "not so much for public view, but at mine own cost, a *few copies;*" and there can be little doubt that Mr. Collier is right in his conjecture that a "now lost edition of his Satires was once in circulation."

P. 198. *To sir Henry Savile.*] In the *Discoveries* (vol. ix. p. 164), Jonson speaks of Sir Henry Savile, as "grave and truly lettered." When he told Drummond that "the first foure bookes of Tacitus were ignorantly done in English," he was speaking of the *Annals,* which were translated by a totally different person.

P. 200. *To John Donne.*] Gifford's assertion in the note that Jonson's vocabulary "has no peculiarities," is very amusing. I began a list of them, but soon desisted. In the third line of this epigram for instance:
"That so alone canst judge, so alone dost make,"
the word *make* is so often used by him in this sense of "compose poetry" as to amount to a "peculiarity." In the last line but one there are no fewer than three unnecessary commas. By placing one after "burst," the sense (!) becomes "their backs are to be loaded till they burst," whereas it really means "they load them until they burst (i.e. *break*) their backs.

P. 201. *By his each glorious* parcel *to be known.*] Each *parcel* is here used for each *part* or *particular.*

P. 203. *On Playwright.*] In the note Gifford calls those wretched victims Henry Weber and Stephen Jones a "case of asses." As he had only found out the meaning of the word at p. 189, he deserves some credit for bringing it so speedily into use.

P. 204. Knat, *rail, and ruff too.*] A *knat,* or knot, is a bird of the snipe kind.

P. 206. *To Mary lady Wroth.*] It ought to have been mentioned that Jonson dedicated the *Alchemist* to this lady. See vol. iv. p. 5. It is pleasant to find that when it became known to her father's old captains of the Flushing garrison, that his eldest daughter was about to be married, they sent £200 to London "to buy her a chayn of Perle, or otherwise to employ as she pleases. We humbly desyre that it may be accepted as a Remembrance of the love of her poore Servants hear." *Sidney Papers*, vol. ii. p. 305.

P. 209. *To sir Edward Herbert.*] Jonson's great critical work on the Art of Poetry was to have been introduced by an epigram of Sir Edward Herbert, the future Lord Herbert of Cherbury, see vol. ix. p. 371. The loss of that portion of the work need not cause much regret.

P. 209. *To captain Hungry.*] This is a vigorous denunciation of a class of men, of which specimens must have been continually cropping up as they returned from serving out their time with the English, Scotch, and Irish mercenaries, who during James's peaceful reign had been playing such a conspicuous part in the German wars—Dugald Dalgettys, with all his effrontery, and habits of laying in *provant*, but without his manly and soldierly qualities. They must have been particularly offensive to Jonson, who knew what soldiering was, and with his keen perception of *humours* must have been doubly able to see through them.

P. 210. *Than can a flea at twice skip in the map.*] This passage would be much more easily understood if the line preceding this were printed as a parenthesis :

(If but to be believed you have the hap).

P. 210. *Nay, now you puff, tusk, and draw up your chin.*] Richardson takes for granted that this is the verb, from the common word *tusk*, and means to *show the teeth*. But there is another *tuske*, or "tuske of heyres," which Peter Levins (A.D. 1570) translates by *crinetum*, and I feel sure that Jonson intended his *tuske* in this place for pulling out the moustachios, and giving them the appearance of tusks, à la Wild Boar of Ardennes. Mr. Wheatley also quotes, "Tuske of heer, *monceau de cheveulx*" (*Palsgrave*). But see *Bartholomew Fair* (vol. iv. p. 392), "Vapours ! never tusk or twirl your dibble."

P. 213. *To make thy* lent *life good against the fates.*] I suppose the editors have taken for granted that "*lent* life" refers to the temporary tenure on which we hold it. I think, however, that *lent* in this place means *mild* and *gentle*, and is the *positive* of the *comparative* "lenter"—"all those *lenter* heats"—which Jonson uses in the *Alchemist*, vol. iv. p. 94. The word in either form is, I suppose, peculiar to Jonson, "who has no peculiarities."

P. 214. *Clement Edmonds on his* Cæsar's Commentaries.] This work, according to Lowndes, was published in three parts from

8   H H

1600 to 1609. My copy (which belonged to the Library so ruthlessly cast to the winds by the Royal Society in 1873) is of the three volumes bound in one, without separate title pages, but with a general engraved title without date. At the top of it is an excellent portrait of Prince Henry, by whose command the translator had "supplied such parts as were wanting to make up the Totall of these Commentaries." Camden, Sam. Danyell, and Joshua Sylvester, keep Jonson company as commendators.

P. 217. *To mistress Philip Sidney.*] It is perfectly preposterous for Gifford to suppose that these lines could be addressed to the widow of the hero and poet, who had become Countess of Essex as early at least as the spring of 1590, when Jonson, according to Gifford's reckoning, was in his sixteenth year. The exact date of her marriage to Essex has never been ascertained, but their son the Parliamentary General was christened 22nd January, 1591, in Lady Walsingham's house in Seething Lane. But under no circumstances, as I understand the custom of the time, could "the daughter of that great statesman Sir Francis Walsingham" have been addressed by Jonson as *mistress Philip Sidney.*

I had written this note many months ago, and was about to send it to the press as it is, when it occurred to me that as Jonson had told Drummond that one of Lord Lisle's sons was the express image of his uncle Sir Philip, so perhaps one of the daughters might for the same reason have been called "Mistress Philip" as an affectionate family nick-name. On searching in the right quarter I was delighted to find that on the 18th August, 1594, a daughter was born to Sir Robert Sidney, who was christened *F.iilip.* "So wrote in the Register of Penshurst," says Collins quite grumblingly, "who married Sir John Hobart," &c. &c. &c. Who can doubt that this lady, "so wrote in the Register," is the mistress Philip Sidney of Jonson's verses, and one of that family so beautifully described, post, p. 248? She married Sir John Hobart, son and heir of the Lord Chief-Justice Hobart, who wrote a most touching letter to her father on her death in September, 1620. In after years it was docketed by her brother, the second Earl of Leicester. "From my Lord Chief-Justice, after the death of my deare sister, for whom he sheweth much sorrow."

P. 220. *On Groine.*] The whole point of this turns on the then fashionable meaning of the word *occupy.* Jonson says in the *Discoveries* (vol. ix. p. 185), "Many, out of their own obscene apprehensions, refuse proper and fit words, as *occupy, nature and the like;*" and that high authority Doll Tearsheet exclaims: "A captain! God's light, these villains will make the word as odious as the word *occupy,* which was an excellent good word before it was ill-sorted."

I am half sorry to find that the next epigram, clever as it is, was among the "most common-places of his repetition" (vol. ix. p. 372).

P. 223. *To Benjamin Rudyerd.*] Sir Benjamin Rudyerd's Poems and Speeches have been collected, and his Memoirs written (after a sort) by James Alexander Manning of the Inner Temple. The best notion of his character and talents and position will be gathered from the numerous mentions of him in Mr. Forster's *Life of Sir John Eliot.* The penultimate line of the epigram is not a little impaired by the unauthorized substitution of "*can* be thought unfit*" for the "to be thought unfit" of the original.

P. 225. *Underneath this stone doth lie, &c.*] Gifford winds up his note by reprehending the *Spectator* for misquoting Jonson, and commences the sentence by misquoting the *Spectator.* "I cannot close this moral" is converted into "I cannot close this essay."

P. 226. *Sir William Uvedale.*] "July 1st, 1609," I find a "grant to William Uvedale, jun., in reversion after Sir Francis Bacon, of the office of Clerk of the Council of the Star Chamber;" and on July 1st, 1615, another grant to "succeed Sir Thomas Overbury, in his reversion of the Treasurership of the Chamber." On January 13, 1618, he obtained the actual office of Treasurer, and on May 11, a "warrant for allowance of diet of three dishes of meat as Treasurer."

P. 229. *To Alphonso Ferrabosco.*] The third line affords another instance of the extraordinary carelessness of Gifford : "Speak her *own* effects!" What is the meaning of it? Jonson wrote and printed "Speak her *known* effects." In the fifth line "Declineth anger," means "turns aside anger."

P. 234. *And with both bombast style and phrase, rehearse.*] Why Gifford should have substituted *bombast* for the far more expressive *bombard* of the original is more than I can pretend to explain.

P. 236. *And bade her farewell* sough *unto the* lurden.] *Sough* is a long sigh, as of the wind, and is still in use in Scotland. *Lurden,* says Nares, is "any great lumpish body," and is here applied to the *lighter.*

P. 237. *For, yet, no* nare *was tainted.*] *Nare* was *nose*—or rather *nostril.* The learned Archdeacon who gives the former interpretation remarks, "It is fortunate for me that the word was never common, as it would have exposed my name to many bad puns."

P. 239. *My Muse had plough'd with his that sung A-JAX.*] From the grave Camden downwards everybody seemed to think this

joke was never to grow old. Pope was one of the last to make
use of the word:

> " Here all his suffering brotherhood retire,
> And scape the martyrdom of jakes and fire :
> A Gothic Library of Greece and Rome
> Well purged, and worthy Settle, Banks and *Broome.*"

To the last name, which I have no doubt was in reality intended
for William Broome, who translated sundry books of his Odyssey,
he adds a note which is not out of place in an edition of Ben Jonson :
" Broome was a serving-man of Ben Jonson's, who once picked up
a comedy from his letters, or from some cast scenes of his master,
not entirely contemptible." The fact being that Brome was the
author of fifteen original plays, the worst of which is considerably
better than a certain *Three Hours After Marriage*, in the making of
which some great wits are said to have aided. But the truth is
that Pope knew nothing about Richard Brome but the name, and
only wished to make use of him as a screen against William
Broome.

NOTES TO THE FOREST.

Page 243.

F touch *or marble.*] *Touch* seems never to have been admitted to be marble. In Lord Bacon's will I find that
he provides specially for the disposal of the " armour, and
also tables of marble and touch."

P. 244. *Thy mount, to which* thy *Dryads do resort.*] Jonson's
line is :

> " Thy mount to which *the* Dryads do resort."

P. 248. *Sir Robert Wroth.*] Sir Robert, it is understood, was
not in every way worthy of the race into which he married, and
did not long survive the occasion on which these verses were
written. On March 17, 1614, I find Chamberlain writing to
Carleton, "Sir Robert Wroth dead, leaving a young wife with
£1,200 jointure, a son a month old, and his estate £23,000 in
debt."

P. 250. *They think not then, which side the cause shall* leese.] See
Every Man out of His Humour, vol. ii. p. 163. It is found in

Nicolas Udall's admirable comedy of *Ralph Roister Doister*, Act i.
Sc. 1.

> " But such sporte have I with him, as I would not leese,
> Though I should be bounde to lyve with bread and cheese."

Bacon too uses it in his *Natural History* (1639), p. 5.

P. 256. *Women are but men's shadows.*] In the *Conversations*,
vol. ix. p. 397, Drummond says, " Pembrok and his lady discoursing, the earl said, The woemen were but men's shadowes, and
she maintained them. Both appealing to Johnson he affirmed it
true ; for which my lady gave a pennance to prove it in verse :
hence his epigrame."

This seems circumstantial enough ; but a writer in *Notes and
Queries*, 3rd S., viii. 187, gives some Latin lines, which if really
written by Barthol. Anulus (who died *circ.* 1565) would tend to
impugn the truth of the story :

> " Umbra suum corpus radianti in lumine solis
> Cum sequitur refugit ; cum fugit insequitur.
> Talis naturæ quoque sint muliebres amores :
> Optet amans, nolunt : non velit, ultro volunt.
> Phœbum virgo fugit Daphne inviolata sequentem ;
> Echo Narcissum, dum fugit, insequitur.
> Ergo voluntati plerumque adversa repugnans
> Fœmina, jure sui dicitur umbra viri."

P. 261. *Pallas, nor thee I call on*, mankind *maid.*] This word,
which simply means masculine, is used very ludicrously by *Morose*,
in *The Silent Woman*, vol. iii. p. 470.

P. 265. *Peace*, Luxury,] Stevens no doubt, as Gifford says, was
not averse to " pour out pages of the grossest indecency." It would
have been sufficient if he had quoted Florio and Cotgrave for the
meaning attached to the word at that period in Italy and France.
" *Lussuria*, lechery, lust, riot, rankness." " *Luxure*, sensuality,
excess in carnal delights." This was departing from the Latin
meaning. Seneca simply says, " Pestis blanda luxuria."

P. 267. *Elizabeth countess of Rutland.*] See *ante*, p. 186. She
died in August, 1612, and was privately buried in St. Paul's, by the
side of her father. Chamberlain (August 11, 1612), tells Carleton
that " Sir Walter Raleigh is said to have sent her pills that dis-
patched her." She is mentioned particularly in the *Conversations.*

P. 267. *And some one* apteth *to be trusted then.*] This word is
used twice by Jonson in *The Poetaster*, vol. ii. pp. 381, 520.

P. 269. *You, and that* other star.] For more about Jonson and
Daniel, see Gifford's note, vol. i. p. 146.

P. 275. *Maintain their leigers forth for foreign wires,*
    Melt down their husbands' lands,] *i.e.* retain persons as permanent emissaries to communicate foreign fashions. *Lands* is *land* in the folio.

P. 276. *Hear what the Muses sing* above *thy root.*] I cannot see why "*above* thy root" should have been substituted for the "*about* thy root," which Jonson wrote and printed.

P. 277. *Sir William Sidney.*] The eldest son of this noble family was a young man of high promise, and must have completed his twenty-first year very shortly before his death, as Jonson mentions that the birthday was in winter, and he died on December 3rd, 1612. The last mention of him in the Sidney Papers is on the 28th December, 1602, "The Queen kissed Mr. William Sidney in the presence as he came from the chappell; my Lady Warwick presented him" (vol. ii. p. 262). When Gifford speaks of "G. Wither, the *Satyromastix,*" it is of course a slip of the pen for *Chronomastix.*

NOTES TO THE UNDERWOODS.

Page 288.

HE gladdest light dark man can think upon.] This was a favourite line of Southey's.

P. 296. *Her triumph.*] Hazlitt says of this: "One of his most airy effusions is *The Triumph of his Mistress;* yet there are some lines in it that seem inserted almost by way of burlesque. It is however well worth repeating. . . . His *Discourse with Cupid* that follows is infinitely delicate and piquant, and without one single blemish. It is a perfect nest of spicery." *Lit. of Eliz.* p. 183·4.

P. 300. *Begging another, on colour of mending the former.*] Jonson often repeated to Drummond a different version of this first stanza, or perhaps the lines got changed in Drummond's memory (see vol. ix. p. 372):

> "But kisse me once and faith I will be gone;
>   And I will touch as harmelesse as the bee
>   That doth but taste the flower and flee away."

P. 312. *My Picture, left in Scotland.*] For another version of this, see vol. ix. p. 415, where we have it as recorded by Drummond. I certainly think it more likely that Jonson wrote "*hundred* of grey hairs" than *hundreds,* as we may suppose him to have been getting very bald about this period. *Waste* too, I think, ought to be *waist*. Both words were spelt alike *waste*. In the English version he makes the years forty-*seven*, which deducted from 1619 leaves 1572 clearly as the year of his birth, and shows that he perfectly understood the difference between the English and Scotch calendars.

P. 316. *Note. These verses are printed with Jonson's name under the portrait of Shakspeare, prefixed as a frontispiece to the first edition of his works in folio,* 1623.] The writer of this could never have seen a copy of the Shakspeare folio. The portrait is impressed upon the title page, and the verses are printed with Jonson's name, on a separate leaf opposite to it.

Gifford here missed an excellent opportunity for a hit at George Stevens. That "nefarious man," as Johnson called him, patronized a spurious portrait of Shakspeare, which had not a leg to stand upon if the Droeshout engraving was a good likeness, and the difficulty was to get over Jonson's testimony. Stevens was equal to the occasion : "It is probable that Ben Jonson had no intimate acquaintance with the graphick art, and *might not have been over solicitous about the style in which Shakspeare's lineaments were transmitted to posterity.*" In other words, Jonson lied about the likeness in order that posterity might think Shakspeare an ugly fellow ! Gifford has no case so ludicrous as this.

P. 319. *From thence to honour thee, I* will *not seek.*] The folio has, " From thence to honour thee, I *would* not seek."

P. 319. *To* live *again, to hear thy buskin tread.*] The folio has, " To *life* again, to hear thy buskin tread."

P. 320. *In his well torned, and true filed lines.*] Here, as Upton observes (*Crit. Obs. Shak.* p. 82, note), Jonson had the expression of the ancients in view, "*bene tornatos et limatos versus.*" See also the *Discoveries*, vol. ix. p. 202.

P. 323. *Upon my dear brother Francis Beaumont.*] Charles Lamb transcribed this Epitaph in that copy of the Beaumont and Fletcher folio, which he made so interesting by a notice in one of his Elia's Essays.

P. 324. *Lady* or pucelle, *that wears mask or fan.*] The folio has *pusill,* which had better have been left. Richard Brome, whose vocabulary everywhere carries traces of his up-bringing, has *depusilated.*

" *Cur.* The virgin says she is depusilated by your son. *Touch.* Depusilated ! Ha, ha, ha !"
The Sparagus Garden, vol. iii. p. 182.

P. 324. *The Countess of Pembroke.*] Spenser addressed a very beautiful sonnet to this lady, which is not so well known as it ought to be. It will be found in vol. i. p. 169, of Collier's edition. She is celebrated by Drayton as Pandora:

> "Pandora thou, our Phœbus was thy brother."

P. 331. *My truly beloved friend, master Browne.*] The following lines by Browne should find a place in every edition of Jonson:

> "Johnson, whose full of merit to reherse
> Too copious is to be confinde to verse;
> Yet therein only fittest to be knowne,
> Could any write a line which he might owne:
> One so judicious: so well knowinge: and
> A man whose least worth is to understand:
> One so exact in all he doth preferre
> To able censure; for the Theater,
> Not Seneca transcends his worth of praise;
> Who writes him well shall well deserve the Bayes."
> *Britannia's Pastorals*, Book ii. Song 2, Hazlitt's ed.
> vol. ii. p. 10.

It is interesting to know that Milton, in the margin of his copy of the *Pastorals*, wrote the name of *Johnson* against this passage.

P. 332. *Who hadst before wrought in rich Homer's mine.*] In the British Museum is a copy of Chapman's *Seaven Bookes of the Iliades*, and *Achilles Shield*, with the autograph inscription, SUM BEN. JONSONII.

P. 337. *Note* (7). *In Authorem.*] Gifford may well call Nicholas Breton an indefatigable writer. In the *Scornful Lady*, Beaumont says:

> "And undertook with labour and expense,
> The re-collection of those thousand pieces,
> Consumed in cellars and tobacco shops,
> Of that our honoured Englishman, Nich. Breton."
> Dyce's *Beaumont and Fletcher*, vol. iii. p. 28.

Lowndes gives the titles of fifty-four publications by him, extending from 1575 to 1618. Hazlitt gives fifty-one titles.

In 1601, Breton was, jointly with Jonson and Marston, made the object of attempted ridicule in a publication called *Whipping of the Satire*. See Collier's *Bib. Cat.* ii. 516. Collier (ib. i. 88) says, "He began his career of authorship in 1575, and he did not conclude it until 1636, at least that is the date of the *Figure of Foure*, his latest known work."

P. 338. *Light posture, heightening, shadow, colouring.*] What exquisite nonsense is made of this passage by leaving out the comma after the first word:

"Light, posture, heightening, shadow, colouring."

P. 342. *To Richard Brome.*] Jonson was proud, as he well might be, of the attainments of Richard Brome. He had taken uncommon pains with him, and he was rewarded in every way. In Epigram ci. *ante*, p. 204, he says:

> "My man
> Shall read a piece of Virgil, Tacitus,
> Livy or some better book to us,
> On which we'll speak our minds, amidst our meats."

See also the opening of the Induction to *Bartholomew Fair*, vol. iv. p. 341. It is not known when Brome died, but he must have survived his master at least ten years. He was certainly dead in 1653.

In the original edition of *The Northern Lass*, Jonson's two last lines stand as follows:

> "The Cobbler kept him to his *nall*, but now
> He'll be a *Pilot*, scarce can guide a plough."

Where the question is one of guidance, Pilot versus Poet speaks for itself. The word *nall*, too, was very commonly used for *awl*. I find it in a preface of Bacon's, 1561: "The Smith giveth over his hammer and stithy; the tailor his shears and mateward; the shoemaker his *nalle* and thread," &c. In the same way *ale* was often written *nale:* e. g.—

> "Their hearts then at rest with perfect security
> With a pot of good nale, they stuck up their plaudity."
> Prologue to *Gammer Gurton's Needle.*

P. 343. *A Speech at a Tilting.*] Nicholls says that this must have been written for the tilting at the anniversary of the king's accession in 1612-13, that being the only occasion of the kind at which the names of "these two noble brothers" appear together.

P. 345. *An Epistle to sir Edward Sackvile.*] There were two passages specially dear to Horne Tooke. The first is at the top of p. 349, and it will be noticed that he altered two of the lines and omitted two others:

> "I thought that fortitude had been a mean
> 'Twixt fear and rashness; not a lust obscene,
> Or appetite of offending, but a skill
> *And nice discernment between* good and ill.
> Her ends are honesty and public good
> And *without these* she is not understood."

The other passage commences in the middle of the sixth line of p. 350: "'Tis the last key-stone," &c. He quotes the lines in his Reply to Junius of July 13, 1771, and calls them "the words of his ancient monitor."

P. 351. *An Epistle to Master John Selden.*] The version given by Selden himself, in his quarto of 1614, presents a few variations. Line 4, for instance, which now stands:

"Truth and the Graces best when naked are,"
was originally,

"Since naked, best, Truth and the Graces are."
Line 17 is now,

"But I to yours far otherwise shall do,"
but it stood originally,

"But I to yours, far from this fault, shall doo."
And in line 8 of p. 353, "*manly* elocution" was in the first instance "masculine elocution." The image in p. 352, of "like a compass, keeping one foot still," was often present to Jonson's mind. See more particularly the use made of it in *The Sad Shepherd*, vol. vi. p. 282.

P. 356. *Who can behold their manners, and not cloud-Like, on them lighten.*] Let any reader turn to this passage, and, after being told that the folio has, "*upon* them lighten," ask himself which is the true reading. Some one of Gifford's predecessors had counted upon his fingers, and found that *upon* made eleven syllables, so out it went.

P. 356. *Planting their* purls, *and curls, set forth like net.*] This word is frequently used by Jonson, but I have not been able to arrive at any precise understanding of its meaning. See vol. ii. p. 146 and note.

P. 356. *And then leap mad on a neat* picardill, *As if a* brize *were gotten in their tail; And* firk, *and jerk, and for the coachman* rail.] For *picardill*, see vol. v. p. 52, and vol. vii. p. 217. It is always a word of great interest. A *brize* is a *gadfly*. Cotgrave has "*Tahon*, a Brizze, Brimsee, Gadbee, Dunflie, Oxeflie." For *firk*, see vol. iv. p. 75, p. 99. I would rather not say what I believe to be the meaning of *rail*.

P. 357. *For man so* spend *his money on.*] The folio reads, "*to* spend his money on."

P. 357. *For less security. O* heavens! *for these.*] The word *heavens* is an insertion of Gifford's. The folio leaves the space a dead blank there,

> " For less security.   O   for these."

Mr. Dyce mentions in a note to Middleton's *Works*, vol. ii. p. 122, that he possesses several pieces by Marston, in which objection-able words are thus left out, the printer being afraid to insert them.   There will soon be another instance, *post*, p. 433.

P. 358. *Well, let it go.   Yet this is better*, then

To lose the forms and dignities of men.]   In the first line the last word merely represents the old way of spelling *than*, to which no doubt Gifford ought to have changed it, and have con-verted *men* into *man*, in the next line, if he so pleased it.

P. 365. *An Elegy.*]   Mr. Tennyson would, I am sure, be proud to acknowledge that he was well acquainted with this noble Elegy before he commenced his *In Memoriam.*

P. 376. *To the lady Mary Wroth.*]   The word *exscribe* in the third line is drawn direct from the Latin *exscribo.*   Let us be thankful that it did not take root in our language.

P. 379. *Still may* syllabes *jar with time.*]   Gifford's note here is very amusing.   See, for instance, the bottom line of vol. v. p. 278, and the examples might be multiplied to any extent.

P. 400. *Had I wrote treason* here, *or heresy.*]   The folio reads *there* for *here*, and I think rightly.

P. 400. *Had I compiled from Amadis de Gaul.*]   Southey calls attention to this renewed expression of Jonson's contempt for romances.

P. 401. *Condemn'd me to the* ovens with the pies.]   This seems prophetic of the doings of Mr. Warburton and his cookmaid in the next century.

P. 402. *All the mad Rolands, and* sweet *Olivers.*]   Why was this epithet of *sweet* always applied to Olivers?   Young *Knowell* even uses it to *Oliver Cob*, the tankard bearer.

P. 409. *Old Æsop Gundomar.*]   My friend Don Pascual de Gayangos informs me that some few years ago he had an oppor-tunity of examining the library of Count Gondomar.   There were several English books, and among them a well-preserved copy of the First Folio of Shakspeare, full of MS. corrections in a contem-porary English hand.   In some instances, passages of many lines were scored out, and others substituted.   This library has since been scattered to the winds, and this unique First Folio in all probability sold for waste paper.

P. 410. *Nor marks of wealth so from a nation fled.*] The folio has, "from *our* nation fled." The unwarranted change is meaningless.

P. 410. *What a strong fort old Pimlico had been !*

How it held out! how, last, 'twas taken in.] The "taking in" of Pimlico has been already proposed in *The Devil is an Ass*, vol. v. p. 82. The "powder corns shot at the Artillery Yard" are celebrated in *The Alchemist*, vol. iv. p. 13; and the couplet about training "the youth of London in the military truth," is also to be found in vol. v. p. 75.

P. 415. *Like Solon's self*, explat'st *the knotty laws.*] Gifford says that the word *explation* is in Coles, but Nares sought for it there in vain. The adjective *explete* is in the *Manipulus Vocabulorum* of Peter Levins, a curious old Rhyming Dictionary of 1570, which has been reprinted for the Camden Society, and most carefully edited by Mr. H. B. Whestley.

P. 419. *Dedication of the King's new cellar to Bacchus.*] This is the same building of which Jonson speaks so contemptuously as a "cave for wine" in his *Expostulation with Inigo Jones, ante,* p. 114.

P. 420. *And Charles brings home the lady.*] Charles embarked February 14, 1623, Valentine's day.

P. 420. *On the Court Pucelle.*] This word *Pucelle* was more commonly used in Jonson's day than ours, when it seems to be confined to Joan of Arc, and to fortresses that have never been captured. The French (see Cotgrave) had also the verb *puceler,* to deflower, which I don't find in modern dictionaries, but Bacon used it in writing to Queen Elizabeth (Spedding, *Letters,* ii. 165), "the best of your possessions useth to be pucelled and deflowered." Richard Brome also made another verb out of it, see *ante,* p. 324, note.

This set of verses was a source of trouble to Jonson. Drummond reports, in the *Conversations,* "That piece of the Pucelle of the Court was stolen out of his pocket by a gentleman who drank him drousie, and given Mrs. Boulstraid; which brought him great displeasure. Donne, in his Elegy on the death of this lady, speaks of her as young, beautiful, and witty, and proof against the sins of youth."

P. 421. *What though with* tribade *lust she force a muse.*] From the Greek τριβάς, "an immodest woman of a most abandoned kind."

P. 422. *To the honoured countess of * * **] The phrase "widowed wife" leaves little doubt that this is addressed to the Countess of Rutland, the only child of Sir Philip Sidney. See vol. ix. p. 385.

P. 424. *On lord Bacon's birth-day.*] Although the poet expressly says,

"This is the *sixtieth* year
Since Bacon, and thy lord, was born and here,"

he means us to understand that it was written on the Chancellor's *fifty-ninth* birthday; *i.e.* on what we should now call the 22nd January, 1620. For some reason this particular anniversary of the birthday was kept with special care, as Camden thought it worthy of note in his *Annalium Apparatus*, 1620, January 12 :— *Franciscus Baconus, Cancellarius Angliæ, natalem diem LIX. ætatis celebrat.*"

P. 425. *Out of their choicest and their whitest wool.*] See the same expressions in *Love's Welcome at Bolsover, ante*, p. 139.

P. 427. *To William Earl of Newcastle.*] This affords an opening for another attack upon Horace Walpole, about the importance, historical, literary and artistic, of whose collections people have altered their opinions a good deal since 1816.

"Bold Sir Bevis and his horse Arundel" were celebrated in *Every Man in his Humour*, vol. i. p. 79.

P. 429. *To master Arthur Squib.*] I can find nothing regarding Arthur Squib, except that on September 21, 1616, he received a grant of a Tellership in the Exchequer for life; and that on December 27, 1623, the surrender of this Tellership was brought into the Enrolment Office.

P. 430. *To master John Burges.*] The Mr. Alexander Glover, mentioned in the note, was most probably the same who on April 18, 1616, was appointed "keeper of the game," in Lambeth, and throughout the county of Surrey, for life. He was still in the office in 1620.

P. 432. *My woeful cry
To Sir Robert Pie.*] Sir Robert Pye was not appointed to the Auditorship of the Exchequer so early as Gifford supposes. Chamberlain writes to Carleton, January 22, 1620, " Lady Bingley gone to Newmarket to solicit against her husband's loss of his place, but she will fail, the place being given to Sir Robert Pye, a creature of Buckingham's." Though a *creature* of the favourite's, he appears to have been an honest and an out-spoken one, warning him against his personal extravagance, as well as the impolicy

of his public conduct. In 1627 he lost his seat for Westminster, "the feeble cry of his for a Pye ! a Pye ! being overwhelmed with derisive shouts for a Pudding ! a Pudding !" Forster's *Life of Eliot*, vol. ii. p. 100. According to Clarendon he was holding Leicester for the king in 1645.

P. 433. *As if that part lay for a —— most fit.*] Here in the folio there is no dash ——, but simply a blank space. See *ante*, p. 357.

P. 440. *On the Prince's birth,* 1630.] According to the note on this epigram, the moon on this occasion had the singular power of being able to eclipse itself. The king was on his way to St. Paul's to return thanks for the birth of his son, when the star made its appearance.

P. 443. *With touch of* learned thumbs.] The folio has "*dainty* thumbs," which is surely preferable ; and in the last line of the page, instead of "*put* the ceston on," the folio reads, "*got* the ceston on," which I also like better.

END OF VOLUME VIII.

CHISWICK PRESS :—PRINTED BY WHITTINGHAM AND WILKINS,
TOOKS COURT, CHANCERY LANE.

6

www.ingramcontent.com/pod-product-compliance
Lightning Source LLC
Chambersburg PA
CBHW032008110726
47901CB00004B/1015